SURVIVORS

Also by G X Todd

Defender
Hunted

SURVIVORS

GX TODD

HEADLINE

First published in Great Britain in 2019 by
HEADLINE PUBLISHING GROUP

1

Cataloguing in Publication Data is available from the British Library

Hardback ISBN 978 1 4722 3316 5

Typeset in Bembo by Avon DataSet Ltd, Bidford-on-Avon, Warwickshire

Printed and bound in Great Britain by Clays Ltd, Elcograf S.p.A.

Headline's policy is to use papers that are natural, renewable and recyclable
products and made from wood grown in well-managed forests and other
controlled sources. The logging and manufacturing processes are expected to
conform to the environmental regulations of the country of origin.

HEADLINE PUBLISHING GROUP
An Hachette UK Company
Carmelite House
50 Victoria Embankment
London EC4Y 0DZ

www.headline.co.uk
www.hachette.co.uk

Dedicated to all UK Public Libraries (past and present).

An essential, invaluable and irreplaceable service that is being
whittled away year after year by short-sighted bureaucrats.
Without libraries, and their trained and professional staff,
I would never have become a writer.

Thank you for everything you do.

THE PART BEFORE ALL OTHERS

When the Voices Came

CHAPTER 1

The Unit

Monday, 11.31 a.m. (49 hours to go)

The Unit's day room was a too-bright suntrap. The yellows of the walls and floor glowed. The air was tepid and still. Only one window opened and the seats nearest to it were all taken. There was a hodgepodge of other seating options, some chairs boasting arms and cushions, others made of plastic with hard seats, and daily arguments raged over who got to sit where, mainly due to there being too many patients and not enough chairs. There weren't enough beds, either.

The Unit was past capacity. It was a twenty-four-bedder ward but cots had been brought in over the last few days. They lined the corridors, pushed up against the walls. At breakfast, Jackson had counted thirty-six heads, and that didn't include the patients in isolation.

He'd have liked to watch the news, but the single flat-screen TV attached high on the wall played only sitcoms, PG-13 rated movies and daytime TV. Currently *Adventure Time* was on. It was a kids' show, but everyone seemed to either like it or tolerate it. Three sofas hemmed the TV in and Jackson sat on the one furthest right. It was angled so he could see the nurses' station and the corridors that branched off from it. He could see the whole room without turning his head.

Sol passed in front of him, walking his rounds. He was on his second circuit, each wall touched, each table-top and chair patted, the open-faced cupboards that housed board games and decks of cards tapped on each shelf, the stereo system stroked. He was on his way to count the magazines and books, paperbacks and hardbacks alike. They were an area he was especially fastidious over. At one time, Sol would have even touched the potted plants, but a new patient had arrived and the flowerheads had begun to disappear, the leaves found with chunks bitten from them. No more potted plants. One less thing for Sol to worry about.

In hospital bathrobe and boots (Jackson often wondered why the guy was happy to wear a robe but refused hospital slippers), Sol cut a strange figure. He was tall although not big, the robe hitting him at knee-level and leaving his legs bare to his boots. Jackson was grateful the guy wore boxer shorts.

Sol was harmless enough. As long as you didn't interrupt him or get in his way.

A short buzz sounded and the Unit's main automatic doors unlocked, yawning their slow, creaky way open.

Abernathy nudged Jackson with her elbow and leaned closer. 'They're bringing more in.'

Jackson could have closed his eyes and still known it was Gibbs walking across the foyer; the cadence to the jangle of his keys was unmistakeable. One of two ward managers, Gibbs hadn't worked on the Unit the last time Jackson had been admitted, and Jackson didn't like or dislike him. He was just a guy who covered the day shift and inhabited part of Jackson's life here. Gibbs believed there was an innate goodness in everybody, that everyone wanted to help each other, and that humans were an amazing species – no, they were *the best*. Abernathy said that kind of talk usually meant the person hadn't had much shit to deal with in their life.

Gibbs paused at the nurses' station, a kid on either side of him. He said something to the woman behind the partition window, tapped the glass to punctuate the end of the conversation, and walked into the day room. The kids trailed behind him as if pulled along by invisible leashes. Raw, acned faces and gangly-armed awkwardness marked them as teenagers. Their feet dragged and their too-large clothes draped their angular bodies. Teenager No.1 projected a nonchalance that screamed of bravado. Jackson remembered being that age; outwardly indifferent to the world yet angry at everything in it. Teenager No. 2 wasn't angry; he was timid and fragile, as if a single touch might shatter him. This kid knew how scary the world could be. He nervously tugged the cuffs of his hoodie's sleeves over his hands until only the curled tips of his fingers peeked out.

'Weird,' Abernathy said. 'Why're we getting minors in here?'

Gibbs caught Jackson's eye and made a beeline for him. Jackson's stomach sank, a tugboat slowly taking on water.

Gibbs looked exhausted. His eyes were the bloodshot eyes of a gambler three days into a week-long bender in Vegas. His thinning hair was messy, as if fingers had been repeatedly run through it. He blinked too many times as he stopped in front of them.

'Newbies.' Gibbs had to speak over the din of the room: the murmurs of patients, the arguing over someone cheating at cards, the TV. 'I'm trusting you to give them the tour. Lunch is in thirty minutes. Make sure they get fed, okay?'

The argument was escalating, one moment mutters, the next a deck of playing cards erupting in the air in an explosion of confetti. Gibbs closed his eyes. A flash of something crossed his face.

Impatience? Despair?

No. Defeat.

It surprised Jackson. Much like the day room, Gibbs was a human suntrap, catching unwilling victims in his sunny disposition wherever he went. This sallow-faced, weary-eyed man was a stranger. Gibbs said nothing more and headed over to the poker players, two of whom were on their feet, their chairs pushed back. Sol had almost reached them on his circuit. Jackson counted the steps as the tall man headed their way. One, two, three, four, I declare a thumb war. Above their heads, trapped in its domed metal cage, the black eye of a security camera stared blankly. Its red light blinked. A lot of damage could be done in the time it took whoever was monitoring the feed to get in here.

'Hey there.'

Teenager No. 1 smiled at Abernathy. It was a lewd, crooked smile, full of arrogance.

Jackson felt Abernathy sigh, the couch sighing along with her.

'What?' she said.

The kid's grin widened, as if they were playing a game. 'How's it going, girl?'

'Don't "girl" me, you fucking retard. There're three people sitting here. Say hello to all of us.'

Teenager No. 2 quickly said hello. The guy at the end of their couch didn't look away from the yellow cartoon dog frolicking on the TV's screen.

Teenager No. 1's smile had vanished. A slow flush mottled the base of his throat.

The sinking tugboat of Jackson's stomach hit the bottom. He got up from his seat, not waiting for the teenager's embarrassment to turn sour. Fights on the ward were handled swiftly and severely. A new kid didn't need that kind of hassle, not on his first day.

'There's no room for you on the juvenile ward?' Jackson asked him.

The kid's face rearranged itself into confusion. 'Huh?'

Abernathy got up, too, and Jackson watched the teenagers' eyes follow her. Her hair was unwashed and unbrushed and her clothes were an unflattering baggy schlump, but she still could have turned these kids to mush with one smile if she'd wanted to. Which she didn't. Jackson rarely saw her smile in a nice way at anyone.

'You're in the *adult* psych ward, Junior,' she told him. 'We don't take kids.'

'I'm not a *kid*. They said they had nowhere else to put us.'

'It's getting to be a squeeze in here, too,' Jackson said. 'We're running out of space for cots. You know what's going on?'

Junior switched his attention from him to Abernathy and back again. 'Maybe. What's it to you?'

Teenager No. 2 shot Junior a look, worried by his hostility.

'Aw, did we hurt your feelings, baby?' Abernathy cooed, and Jackson had to hold back from rolling his eyes. 'Should I have flashed my tits at you instead? Would that have been better?'

'It wouldn't have hurt.'

Gibbs had calmed the poker players down, had even collected all the playing cards off the floor and dealt them another hand. Jackson was starting to think he shouldn't have rushed over there, not now tensions were gaining traction on this side of the room.

He can't be in all places at once.

'Know what I think?' Abernathy propped her hands on her hips, eyes narrowing on Junior even as the kid's gaze dropped to leer at her pelvis. 'I think you're trying too hard.'

Jackson sighed. Here it comes.

'I think you're here because you've been sucking on Daddy's cock too long and got to like it too much.' Her smile was slow and taunting.

Jackson wanted to take a step back from this scene, extricate himself from it, but Abernathy was already moving on to the universal mime of fist pumping to her mouth and tongue prodding into her cheek.

'Got it in one, didn't I?' she said.

Junior's reaction was immediate and unavoidable. He spat out a '*Bitch!*' and launched himself at her.

Any sane person would have ducked out of his way but, of course, this place wasn't exactly full of sane people. Abernathy swung a punch and hit Junior in the head, cracking him above his ear. The kid fell into her and they tumbled on to the couch. The guy at the end, who'd been minding his own business, got kicked and elbowed as the two laid into each other. Abernathy was laughing breathlessly. Jackson heard the exhilaration in it.

'Hey! Break it up!'

Junior landed a solid punch to Abernathy's side – Jackson heard the hollowed-out *thud* – and her laughter cut off.

Gibbs pushed past and grabbed Junior by the collar, worming his arm around the kid's shoulders, about to heave him backwards when the kid let out a high, bleating squeal. He practically leapt into Gibbs's arms, and they both fell, Gibbs collapsing under the teenager's weight.

Abernathy spat and a gob of red meat sprayed out. She grinned and Jackson winced at the red stain on her teeth, the dribble of blood rolling down her chin. She lay half sprawled over the guy who'd been sharing their couch. He was curled in a ball against the couch's arm, hands locked over his head. A long monotonous droning came from him.

'What?' she asked, seeing Jackson's expression.

He shook his head at her.

'Blood!' a woman shrilled. 'Blood! They're *killing* each other!'

'No one's killing anyone!' Gibbs called, struggling to his feet. He bent down to inspect Junior's head. The kid was rocking back and forth, his hand clamped over his ear. 'Jesus, Abernathy,' Gibbs muttered.

Jackson caught a glimpse of the ragged tear in the kid's ear, a piece of it missing. Well, not missing – the glob of flesh was stuck to the parquet flooring where Abernathy had spat it.

'He attacked me first,' Abernathy said, sitting up and wiping the back of her wrist over her bloody mouth. She straightened her sweater. 'I was defending myself.'

She frowned at the guy huddled in his ball beside her. He was still emitting his one-note drone. 'Jesus. You sound like a cow getting fucked up the ass.' She poked him in the arm.

His moan cut off and his head came up. Seeing he was no longer in danger of catching an elbow to the face, he threw Abernathy an affronted look, snatching his arm away from her and uncurling from his ball. He left her on the couch alone, her legs splayed, arms limp and hands resting palm up.

Footsteps pounded into the day room. Three orderlies came with them, Peter Bird being one. His black hair, normally slicked neatly back, had worked its way loose and stringed in his eyes. On seeing him, Jackson almost felt sorry for Abernathy.

Birdy wasn't a big man, but he didn't need to be. He had plenty of ways to get patients to do what he wanted, few of which relied on force. He was exactly the kind of person you didn't want working in a place like this. Abernathy was one of only a select number of patients he sometimes resorted to getting physical with, and Jackson had a few theories as to why that was, not least of which was that Abernathy was a far better manipulator than he was. Birdy's techniques didn't often work on her.

Orderlies two and three veered off to go calm down the other patients. Violence always seemed to unlock a primitive wildness in some of them, a call to chaos that was difficult to tame once it broke out. One woman had started to wail and yank at her hair. An older, frailer man had fallen to his knees, his bloodied fingernails scratching at the parquet, as industrious as a dog digging for a buried bone. Sol had pinned a man against the wall with his forearm but had dropped it when he'd seen the orderlies enter and backed up a full five steps, his eyes tracking Birdy.

9

A clinking noise brought Jackson's eyes back to Birdy, too. A set of leather wrist restraints dangled from his hand. Jackson frowned.

'Oh, come on, Birdy,' Abernathy said, eyeing the cuffs as he advanced on her, and Jackson saw a flash of unease in her, even if no one else did. 'There's no need to get all bondage-happy. I'm docile as a lamb.'

'Katherine,' Gibbs said, still bent over Junior, who continued to rock and snivel on the floor. 'You bit off his ear.'

Abernathy pinned the ward manager with a dangerous look. 'That's not my name.'

Birdy didn't say a word. Didn't even pause. He went past the injured teen and grabbed Abernathy's arm. From the clenched look on her face, Jackson knew he wasn't being gentle about it, either. In a neat economy of movement – a quick twist and a shove – Birdy had her face down on the couch with her arm pinned behind her back with his knee. She immediately began to struggle, her cries muffled as he pushed her head into the cushion. He leaned in to speak in her ear.

'The more you struggle, the more you'll hurt yourself.'

She bucked at his words, hips rising under him, the buried fury at being made to look so powerless in front of others eating her up, Jackson had no doubt. But he didn't move to intercede, didn't speak up in her defence, because Birdy had wrongfooted him by coming in here and manhandling her from the outset. That wasn't his usual modus operandi. It had left Jackson hesitant, uncertain.

He hadn't heard Sol approach but suddenly he was there, crouching next to Abernathy, one hand coming to rest on her shoulder near to Birdy's mouth. The man jerked back as if afraid he'd catch something.

'Enough,' Sol said to her, and Jackson could imagine the angry heat of her burning into Sol's palm, feel the tautness of her trembling muscles. 'Stop.'

As if Sol had spoken a magic incantation, all the tension drained from Abernathy and she lay still.

'Take your hand off her.'

A white build-up of saliva had gathered at the corners of Birdy's mouth, bits of it threading gossamer strands between his lips. He stared at Sol, his eyes black holes dug into hard-packed dirt. Nothing moved in them. No bugs or worms. They were as cold and indifferent as the earth. 'Take. It. Off.'

Birdy's words weren't so much a warning as a line drawn in the sand. And Jackson knew Birdy wanted Sol to cross it. One tiny step over, that was all it would take.

Sol returned his stare, and it wasn't confrontational, only considering. The kind you gave a kid after he'd stomped on a caterpillar for no good reason, when you were trying to figure out why he'd do such a thing when the kid himself didn't even know why.

'Sol,' Gibbs said quietly, his gaze flicking nervously from him to Birdy. 'Come on, now. That's enough.'

Jackson didn't know if Gibbs's gentle tone was what tipped the balance, but Sol was the first to break eye contact. He stood, taking his hand from Abernathy's shoulder, and stepped back. No lines were crossed and no missteps taken. He turned his back on them and retreated to the other side of the room, to the corner he always occupied when he wasn't walking his rounds.

Birdy finished buckling Abernathy's wrists in the restraints. Jackson saw the extra cinch he gave the cuffs so that her skin pinched tight, the flesh whitening above the leather. Birdy glanced across the room at Sol, but he wasn't watching them; he was gazing out the window, seemingly lost to everyone but himself. Birdy's expression didn't change, but he used more force than necessary when he gripped Abernathy under her arm and jerked her upright. She didn't cry out and she didn't fight back. She'd stopped mouthing off altogether. A wave of hair obscured one eye, but Jackson spied no amusement lurking in the eye he could see, no sense of fun. She gave him a faint smile then winced when Birdy wrenched her around and frogmarched her from the room.

Lunch was meatloaf and gravy. Jackson hated meatloaf. Teenager No. 2 sat across from him and didn't seem to like it much, either. The kid pushed bits of it around his plate with a plastic fork.

'You don't like meatloaf?' Jackson asked him.

The kid glanced up but quickly dropped his eyes to his food again. 'It's okay, I guess. I'm not very hungry.'

His hoodie's sleeves had been shoved up while he ate, baring his fingers. Jackson could see the sore, cracked skin around the kid's fingernails, as if he'd gnawed on them like sticks of celery. His wrists were as slim-boned as a girl's. Jackson studied the delicate line of the kid's jaw, the pronounced angle of his cheekbones. The blade of his nose was thin enough to cut. He'd say he looked anorexic, but that wasn't a guy thing.

It's not a gender-specific condition.

Jackson forked a bite of mashed potato into his mouth. 'They watch you more closely if you don't eat,' he said around the food.

'Oh. Right.' It was mumbled but the kid bent back to his food. A minute later, he laid his fork down and cleared his throat. 'I didn't do anything wrong. I don't need watching. I shouldn't even be in here.'

'Okay,' Jackson said, looking down at his tray and spearing a baby carrot. He didn't want to have this conversation.

'What're you in here for anyway? You seem pretty normal.'

Jackson took his time chewing, his insides knotted into the size of fists. His appetite had suffered over the past few days and he suspected it would only get worse. He wished Abernathy hadn't gotten herself locked in her room and left him on babysitting duties.

'You don't ask questions like that,' Sol said, not looking up from his tray (his meatloaf was almost gone). He sat at the far end of their table, away from everybody, and no one had sat near him. Jackson didn't think he'd be in a talkative mood after the incident in the day room.

'It's bad etiquette,' Jackson explained when Sol didn't elaborate. He shrugged. 'People share when they want to, or they don't. Either way, it's no one's business but theirs.'

The kid leaned forward, his face moving into Jackson's orbit, too close. It made him want to lean back.

'I'm here because I want to kill myself.' The teen didn't blink as he said it.

If he was expecting a response, Jackson didn't know what to give him. When neither he nor Sol replied, the kid picked his fork up and went back to pushing his food around.

Jackson glanced at the kid's hand. The fork trembled in his grip.

Bet he ate a bunch of pills.

'I tried to hang myself,' the kid murmured at his tray. 'With a dishcloth.'

A dishcloth? How is that even possible?

'My mom found me and called 911. I was assessed, got admitted, got dumped in here, but it doesn't matter. Not really. I'll try again when I can. I have to. I can barely bring myself to swallow any more.' He looked up, the brightness in his eyes fevered and intense. 'The thought of my own saliva sliding down my throat is like . . . it's like . . . *ugh.*' He heaved, his Adam's apple bobbing, a floating fisherman's lure with a bite snagged on its hook. Bob, bob, bob. 'I can't do this any more. It says I don't have to do this any more.'

Jackson didn't know what to say. He wasn't a therapist. He had no fairy-tale words to make it all better. He looked over at Sol but the man was sat gazing at his near-empty plate, his hands and cutlery held still.

Jackson hissed in pain. The kid had gripped his forearm, his fingernails digging in.

'It's not just me,' the teenager whispered. 'Loads are doing it. That's why we're here – there's no room in the juvenile psych ward. There's too many of us. Everyone is realising we don't need to deal with this shit any more. It's okay to let go, you know? You don't need to be scared or feel like you're alone, because we're not alone, are we? No one's really alone. And your parents will be happy deep down, right? They say they love you but you can see the pain in their eyes. They hide it just like we do, but this'll all be for the best, you'll see. You'll understand when you get out of here.'

Jackson pried his arm out from the kid's grip. Fingers clung for a moment, nails scratching. The teenager slammed his fork down and for a split second Jackson thought he'd impaled his own forearm with it, but the tines were stabbed upright in his uneaten meatloaf. He tore at the ground beef, shredding it to bits. The kid gagged again, louder than before. A stream of saliva drooled from his mouth. He hacked, his bony shoulders hitching with the effort.

Jackson glanced at Sol and this time found the man watching, dark-eyed and grim.

A huge volume of spit had pooled on to the kid's lunch tray now. He spat and heaved and more saliva strung from his mouth. It drowned what remained of his destroyed meatloaf.

The teenager started laughing, his wet lips stretching wide and drool spilling out of his dumb, grinning mouth. But it didn't sound like laughter to Jackson, it sounded like the kid was drowning.

CHAPTER 2

Isolation

Jackson drifted towards the women's corridor. There were twelve women's rooms in total, six on either side of the hall. Between each room, and hugging the walls, a further six cots had been set up. Three were currently occupied. A woman was stretched out on her back, feet flat, knees raised. She held her heavily bandaged hands aloft, staring at them as if she couldn't fathom whether they belonged to her or not. She didn't acknowledge him, and that suited him just fine.

The two other cots' occupants didn't move. They appeared to be sleeping.

He sat with his back to her door and crossed his ankles. Couldn't get comfortable and had to shift his hip to slip a slim paperback from his rear pocket. He smoothed it straight on his thigh. He'd taken the copy from the day room's bookshelf after asking permission from Sol (he didn't want to be responsible for causing a meltdown if Sol was one book short on his next count).

Jackson heard the squeak of bare feet but knew better than to look up, even when Abernathy's roommate stopped at the end of his outstretched legs. The lazy hem of a gypsy skirt brushed the tops of her naked feet, the stitches loose and frayed.

'When can I go in?' Pip said. 'I need my stuff.'

Jackson flicked through the pages of *Slaughterhouse-Five* under the pretence of searching for his place. 'When they unlock it again,' he said. None of the doors was supposed to be locked. People weren't supposed to be kept in isolation or held in restraints, either, but that happened a lot, too.

'I didn't *do* anything.' Pip's bare foot stomped down, making a soft, ineffective thump on the floor. 'I shouldn't be the one being punished.'

'Quit whining.' Abernathy's voice came from the other side of the door. 'I promise to resist using your contraband tweezers to manicure my pubes.'

Pip audibly gasped. It brought Jackson's eyes up.

It was uncomfortable looking at Pip directly. Her smooth and unblemished face, with its absence of eyebrows and eyelashes, always made him feel like he was meeting a new species. She had painfully removed all evidence of eyebrows and eyelashes, each hair meticulously plucked out, one by one. Recently, she had started plucking the hair at the top of her forehead, giving herself a prematurely receding hairline. The staff routinely spot-checked rooms, but they'd never been able to find where Pip hid her treasured tweezers. Seemed Abernathy was the only other person to be let in on the secret.

She'll look like an egg by the time she's through with them.

Pip shuffled past his legs and smacked her palm against the door. 'I swear, Abbie, you touch them and I'll make you sorry.' Panic laced her voice.

'Sorry how? You'll break a couple more teeth off my comb? How about refusing to sit next to me in group therapy? You're not fooling anyone, Pip-Pip. We all know you won't do shit.'

Pip's breathing had become short and choppy, and Jackson worried she might burst into tears. The hand flat against the door rubbed at the wood, as if trying to placate.

'She won't touch your tweezers,' Jackson said, returning Pip's gaze when she looked down at him. She appeared even stranger with her eyes wide and no eyebrows to add expression to them. He raised his voice. 'Will you, Abernathy? You'll leave them alone.'

'Fuck, man, you're such a party pooper. I'm only winding her up. I won't touch her precious hair pluckers, okay? Cross my heart and hope my hair drops out.'

'You swear?' Pip asked her, and there was such a plaintive, childlike pleading on her face that Jackson had to look away.

'I said so, didn't I?' Abernathy said. 'Now get lost.'

Pip retreated a few steps, glanced back at Jackson, then wandered further down the hallway, heading for the faint sounds of a quiz show coming from the day room. She shot a few more glances back up the corridor at him before she disappeared.

'I can feel your disapproval right through the door, you know.'

'You're mean,' Jackson said. 'Even when you don't need to be.'

'We're all mean. I just don't hide it like the rest of you do.'

'Maybe. But some people deserve it more than others.'

He heard her laugh. 'Pip is the meanest little shit in here. You should hear what she says when I'm stuck in here alone at night with her. She's vicious.' The position of her voice had slid lower, as if she'd moved to sit on the other side of the door to him. 'You wouldn't believe what she says about *you*.'

Part of him wanted to ask, but he knew Abernathy was baiting him and it would bring her great pleasure if he bit. He heard a tiny thump and a small grunt come from her. Something bumped against his back. 'Did Birdy take your restraints off?'

'What do you think?'

He frowned down at his book and quietly closed it. 'How're your hands holding up?'

'What hands? I stopped feeling them an hour ago.'

'Want me to go kick up a fuss about it?'

'Nah. What's the point? Maybe I deserve a little discomfort. It won't kill me.'

They were quiet for a while.

Jackson checked the cots' occupants. No one had moved. The corridor was getting dim but the ward's fluorescent lights hadn't turned on. Long shadows crept along the gleaming floor. The tall window at the far end gave the illusion of freedom, the outside world just beyond that single sheet of opaque, chicken-wired glass. Normality. Life. The world turning and people going about their business, and here he sat, surrounded by mad people.

Yeah, but Twin Peaks *is starting soon.*

He didn't mention it to Abernathy. She'd be pissed if she missed it.

'Two more days,' she said through the door.

He'd been having this countdown from her for the past week. 'I know.'

'Scared?'

'No.' His gut twisted on the lie.

'If you are, we could make a daring break for freedom.'

He couldn't tell if she was joking or not.

'I'm *more* than happy to get out of here,' she said. 'Did you see how Birdy came at me? No sweet-talking, no nothing. Something's up with him. He's never done that before.'

'He's never seen you eat someone's ear before.'

'Har har.'

He decided to change the subject. 'I talked to that other kid at lunch,' he told her. 'You know, the one you didn't try to chew on? He had some weird things to say.'

'What kinds of things?'

He filled her in on everything. Even mentioned the hacking-up-of-saliva part, stopping before he described how it had run over the lip of the kid's tray by the time an orderly intervened.

'That's disgusting.'

'Yeah. I never knew a person could make so much spit.'

'What did he mean by "loads are doing it"?'

'No idea.'

'*I* know.' The woman who was lying across from Jackson, her hands bandaged into bulky white mitts, had turned her head towards him. She was middle-aged, maybe in her mid-forties, attractive in a clean-cut sort of way. Her greying hair curled under her cheek, her parting crisp down the centre. Her eyes were clear and intelligent.

'You know what the opposite of "not being alone" is?' she asked him. 'It's having company. And I have all the company I'll ever need. Right here.' She smiled and touched a bandaged hand to her temple.

A crawling sensation skittered up the back of Jackson's neck.

'I'd be worried if I thought I was crazy,' she continued. 'But I'm not crazy. For the first time in my life, I'm seeing everything so very, very clearly. Like a switch has been flicked on.' She rolled on to her side to face him and he saw she was wearing a smart silk blouse and dark tapered trousers. As if she had dropped by on her way home from the office.

'Lawyer. I work in a law firm. That's what you're wondering, isn't it?'

He was. He couldn't lie. Jobs could say a lot about a person.

She tucked one bandaged hand under her head, cushioning her cheek. She looked comfy. 'I should be locked up in a holding cell somewhere, not in here. But the police are very busy. They have their hands and their heads full.'

Jackson could feel the stillness behind the door at his back. He imagined Abernathy with her ear pressed to the wood, listening.

'Want to know what I did to land myself in here?'

He took in her bandaged hands again. Looking closer, he noticed the black smears on the sleeves of her blouse, the singed cuffs, a missing button beneath her breasts. The frilly peek of a lace camisole.

'You have to say it if you want to know.'

Did he?

Yes. Tell her you want to know.

He rubbed at a cold spot at the back of his head and heard himself say, 'I want to know.'

Another smile passed over her lips. 'Well, first, I deactivated the sprinkler system. Which is a lot easier than you'd think. Then I blocked the fire exits to my office floor so no one could get out, and pushed a coffee table to block the elevator doors from closing and being called to their floor, and then I went to the copier room and doused it and every entrance with lighter fluid and set it all alight on my way out. It was all very simple.' She lifted the bandaged hand that wasn't being used as a cushion, showing it to him. A single, silver-tracked tear slid over the bridge of her nose. 'Got my war wounds to prove it.'

'Did they die?'

'I think so. I hope so.'

'Why?'

'Because it explained *everything* to me. It told me what had to happen.'

Jackson shook his head. Wet his lips. 'What told you?'

More tears followed, slipping from the corners of her eye to soak into the bandages beneath her cheek. 'The voice in my head, of course.'

The overhead strip lighting still hadn't come on. The gloom cast an ominous quality over the motionless women in their cots. The lawyer, who'd burned her colleagues to death, had silently turned her back on him after her admission.

Jackson got to his feet and stretched, hearing his spine crack. He didn't take his eyes from the dark, slumbering shape of the lawyer. A bandaged hand was tucked over her waist as if she were hugging herself in her sleep.

'Jack?' Abernathy whispered. 'You there?'

'Yeah.' He slipped *Slaughterhouse-Five* into his rear pocket.

'I think I'm about done in here. Get me out?'

'Sure. Hang tight.'

He had to pass the day room on his way to the nurses' station. The only illumination in there came from the TV. It flickered in static flashes as a car chase ran in frenetic motion on the screen. The room was half full. No one talked. Everyone sat, stood or lay silent. It was eerie. Jackson did a quick scan for Birdy, but he wasn't in attendance.

Sol had diverted from his usual corner to stand next to the nurses' station, his arms folded. From this vantage point he could see the length of the women's corridor as well as the day room's occupants. Jackson had to wonder if the man had moved so he could keep a watchful eye over Abernathy's room. He nodded to Sol as he passed, but Sol didn't respond. The whites of his eyes flashed with the TV.

The nurses' station was empty. Jackson lifted up on to his toes to check the area at the bases of the three swivel chairs. They often left handbags down there, totes containing snacks, a piece of fruit maybe, a Kindle or a magazine.

The space was free of clutter.

He checked the large clock hanging on the back wall. 5.46 p.m. Fourteen minutes to dinner. He sidestepped to peer up the backbone of the ward – the central corridor that led to the dining room, a bank of telephones, the crafts room and the men's bedrooms. There was no rattle of food trolleys. No hum of activity. Two of the phones were in use, but the speakers' conversations were hushed, secretive, buried behind hunched shoulders.

'What do you want?'

It was all Jackson could do not to flinch. He turned to find Birdy standing five feet away, watching him, eyes dulled to an anaemic shine in the dimness.

'Where are the nurses?' The nurses were the only ones who

could dispense medication, and meds were doled out before and after dinner.

'Running late. Off sick.' A shrug. 'You have me.' And Birdy smiled, slow and pleasant. He reached under his smock and pulled out a set of keys. A furry brown rabbit paw dangled from its chain. The keys bristled as he searched through them and Jackson took an instinctive step back. Birdy glanced up. The keys, with their jagged edges, were spread out, sharp tips pointing at him.

Something hung in the air, hot and alive.

Be careful of him.

Birdy moved and Jackson tensed, but all he did was brush by him and insert the key into the door's lock. A white dot had been stuck to the lock plate, as small and round as a tab of Risperdal. Jackson was supposed to take his meds before food. A nurse needed to be back for then.

Birdy let himself into the nurses' station and went to the control panel on the far wall. The fluorescent strip lighting came to life section by section – at the far end of the main corridor, outside the dining room, over the bank of telephones, outside the crafts room, blinking on over Jackson's head. The day room flooded with artificial light and a tidal wave of fluorescence swept up the women's corridor, dead-ending at the tall chicken-wired window. It was dark beyond the glass. Full evening had arrived.

The light banished some of Jackson's unease, the soft buzz emanating from the overhead tubes throwing a calming blanket over his nerves.

'Better?' Birdy asked as he came out of the office. He tugged at the door to make sure it had locked. Birdy was average in all regards – height, weight, age – but there was hidden nuance in everything he said. When he said 'Better?' what he meant was 'Scared of the dark, pussy?'

'Abernathy needs out,' Jackson said.

'Does she now?'

'It's been over five hours.'

'You're right, it has.'

'It's against protocol to keep someone in restraints past when they're needed.'

A long beat of silence. Birdy tilted his head to the side. 'You telling me you know more about my job than I do?'

Jackson thought it best he didn't answer that.

'Don't worry, I'm sure Abernathy likes it. Has a real taste for it, if you get my meaning.'

Jackson didn't get his meaning. Not one bit. 'Look, she's calm. It's past time she was let out.'

Birdy's tone didn't change, but something in his face did. 'Maybe it's past time you minded your own business.'

This isn't going well.

'I'm not trying to step on your toes here—'

'No. That would be a stupid thing to do.'

A few patients wandered out of the day room, dopey-eyed and listless, roused from whatever stupor they had fallen into by the switching-on of the lights. Sol hadn't moved and Jackson got the distinct feeling he was silently watching him and Birdy. Maybe he was counting invisible things, like the seconds in which neither of them spoke.

As the moment stretched out, Jackson's frustration grew. He didn't want to wage a war with this guy. He was in here because he'd been getting worse. All he wanted was to take his meds, get his shit together and get sprung. Birdy meant nothing to him. All he was trying to do was help Abernathy out.

An electronic *beep* sounded and the access-controlled doors to the ward opened. The sight of Rosie, in all her overweight frump, banished the last of Jackson's unease. She was Gibbs's counterpart, the second ward manager. Old-school. A stickler for the rules. Jackson heard tell she'd reported an orderly a few years back for squirting shaving foam down a patient's throat when they'd refused to stop screaming. The staff on duty covered for over a week before Rosie prised the truth out of them. She wasn't having any of that shit on her ward.

'What're you boys standing around like lumps for? It's almost chow time. Dinner trays are on their way up.' When neither of them moved, she glanced from Jackson to Birdy. 'It's up to us to maintain a semblance of normality here, Mr Bird. Now, I believe the water jugs will need filling.'

'I'll do it,' Jackson said. 'You were in the middle of your rounds, right, Birdy? You said you still had the women's corridor to do.' Jackson's inference was clear: go let Abernathy out.

Birdy smiled and bobbed his head. 'Sure did.' One of his front teeth was darker than the rest. A bluish-grey. It was what happened when the root died. Jackson couldn't help but wonder what it felt like to have something dead sitting inside you like that.

'Teamwork, that's what I like to see. Now, shoo.' Rosie clapped her hands to get them going. 'There's lots to do.'

Birdy was still smiling as he turned away to head up the women's corridor. His smiles held nuance, too.

CHAPTER 3

Group

Tuesday, 10.17 a.m. (26 hours to go)

'It's like this,' Abernathy said to her trapped audience. 'Every woman who has a kid becomes a milk-producing, shit-cleaning, dribble-wiping automaton.'

There were seven of them in group therapy this morning, their chairs organised into an informal circle, the crafts room's tables pushed back to the edges. It had taken a while for everyone to settle: their usual group leader was absent and Gibbs was filling in.

Pip gazed at Abernathy, captivated, her mouth partway open and fingers absently stroking the place where one eyebrow used to be.

'A new mother's sense of self sloughs off at the same moment her placenta slops out of her.' Abernathy spread her thighs and mimed catching something that plopped out from between her legs. Jackson stopped listening.

Gibbs was staring down at his notes. If the guy had looked exhausted the last time Jackson saw him, he now looked as though the concept of sleep was some vague, ungraspable activity he'd enjoyed back in his college days. A silver twinkle sparkled under his left eye, a herpes-like glitter contaminant from one of the craft boxes they had moved to clear space.

A humming started up in the back of Jackson's head, a verse of 'Moonage Daydream' drifting through, all electric eyes and space faces. Gibbs looked up, an artificial haze of attentiveness dampening his tired eyes. They got taught how to feign interest, desks in rows, a projector beaming suitable facial expressions on to a screen matched with its accompanying emotion. EMPATHY. COMPASSION. UNDERSTANDING.

Condescension.

Yes. That, too. Although Gibbs was much better at hiding it than most of the staff here.

Abernathy was slinging the invisible afterbirth over her shoulder when Jackson brought his attention back to her. '*Et voilà.* Her old self dies, discarded with the offal, murdered by the very baby she wanted so desperately to have in the first place.'

'That's so gross.' Junior's nose had wrinkled as if it had caught the heavy copper scent of the imaginary placenta. He was draped slovenly in his seat, his ear bandaged in a dressing so white it hurt to look at. In comparison, his salivating buddy next to him hadn't glanced up since entering the room; he sat in silence, a sleeved hand pressed tight over his mouth as if he were muzzling himself.

Probably working up a whole gutful of saliva to share later.

'No,' Abernathy corrected. 'What's gross is how unfair it is that *you* get to rut to your heart's content with no consequences to worry about. Unless you count dick-rot from sticking it in one too many rank holes.'

'Oh, I've stuck my dick in *plenty* of holes.' He grabbed his crotch at her.

'Enough,' Gibbs told them. 'You're both on thin ice, especially after yesterday.'

Abernathy held up her hands, contrite, although the teeth in her smile said she didn't give one shit about any ice, thin or otherwise. 'You're right. I'm sorry. I'll try not to talk about such adult topics in front of the kiddiewinks.'

Junior's face shut down. 'What're you even so butt-hurt about? Does your mom hate you for being a crazy bitch and ruining her life?'

'Hey now, let's tone down the language.' But there was no real conviction in how Gibbs said it.

Abernathy twisted in her seat to face Junior. She was smiling but her lips were thin, her jaw tight. Jackson felt the muscles in his back tense.

'It's funny you mention being butt-hurt, Junior, because I wanted to apologise for outing you yesterday. I shouldn't have done that. I know how you queers like to come out on your own terms.'

Pip burst out giggling. She smothered the sound with her hands.

Junior's chair went clattering.

Here we go again.

Jackson scraped his own chair back a safe distance, and Pip, hiccupping laughs, hiked her bare feet up on to her seat, not wanting them to get trampled. Her gleeful eyes darted from Junior to Abernathy to Gibbs, who'd shot out of his seat along with Junior. He slotted himself between the teenager and Abernathy, using himself as a buffer as the kid tossed obscenity after obscenity, a crass roll call of expletives that was pretty inventive in parts. Abernathy didn't bother to retaliate; she leaned back in her seat, looking bored and inspecting her fingernails.

Junior shoved Gibbs in the chest and he staggered away. The ward manager bumped into a table, his folder of notes dropping to the floor. Sheets of A4 slid across the laminate. Jackson trapped a few pages under his foot, spying paragraphs written in blocks of red, green, blue and purple ink. Pages of text in a rainbow of colour-codes.

Sol stood up. He'd been there the whole time, of course, but he never talked in group. No one expected him to. He was there as a box-ticking exercise.

Pip's giggles choked to a stop and Junior's tirade wound down as fast as it had begun. The room fell silent.

Jackson found himself gripping the edges of his chair.

The kid with the bandaged ear eyed Sol warily.

'No,' Sol said. One word. That was all. The most he'd ever said in here. There was displeasure in the utterance. An offence dealt. Jackson wasn't sure if it was the push to Gibbs or the messy scattering of papers that had done it.

Abernathy rose from her chair, hand held out, a placating gesture that said, *Take it easy*.

Gibbs had straightened himself on the table. He ran a hand over his thinning hair and met Jackson's eyes for an instant. 'It's all right,' he said to the room. 'Everyone calm down. It was just an accident.'

Still, nobody moved.

Drawn-out seconds passed while Sol stared at the kid. Everyone in that crafts room felt it, that long stretch of time; it was almost painful, the stillness of it. Jackson's forearms burned from holding on to his chair. He didn't want to have to throw it. Didn't want to have to get into a brawl. Abernathy had a soft spot for Sol, and Jackson had moments when he understood why. There was more to him than his circuits and his counting. Sometimes you caught unexpected glimpses of it, like flashes of sunlight behind the swaying, green-leafed branches of a tree.

At last, Sol broke eye contact and bent to the floor. He began gathering Gibbs's spilled notes together.

Jackson unclamped his fingers from his chair and took a slow, deep breath. He leaned over and collected the paper he'd trapped under his foot. Sol accepted the sheets from him without comment and slid everything inside their folder. He sat down with it.

Jackson didn't miss the tension uncoil from Junior's arms and fists. He seemed to slump where he stood. An almost imperceptible twitch caught at the corner of the kid's eye when Abernathy stepped up to him. She was taller, besting the teenager by a good three inches.

'You need to stop being such a sensitive little flower,' she told him quietly. 'You react like that to everything you don't like, you'll end up with no appendages left. Not even your favourite one.' She shot a meaningful glance south to his crotch.

She leaned in, mouth moving towards his unbandaged ear. The kid froze but didn't shrink back. He was too proud for that. She whispered something, too low for Jackson to hear, and Junior's face smoothed out, softened.

He calmed down pretty quickly after that. Even righted his chair and apologised to Gibbs for pushing him. It turned out to be the most civilised group therapy session Jackson had ever attended.

'Jackson, can I have a word?'

Jackson considered opening the door and leaving the crafts room anyway. He didn't want a word with Gibbs. He wanted to grab a cigarette, bum a light from one of the orderlies and stand outside in the sunshine for five minutes, inhaling smoke into his lungs until the singeing burn eased the tightness that lived in his chest.

'It'll only take a minute.'

Gibbs waited for him to release the handle. As soon as he did, Gibbs moved in to rest his hand flat to the door, physically preventing Jackson from leaving. The guy's fingernails were bitten and chewed painfully short. The third fingernail was broken and ragged.

'I need to ask – what's it been saying to you?'

Jackson frowned. He didn't know what he was talking about.

'The voice. I know you still hear it.'

Busted, said that dark, hidden voice that sounded so like him.

Gibbs glanced over at the Perspex windows into the corridor, checking that no one was peering in at them. Abernathy was out there but she was deep in conversation with Junior, of all people.

When Gibbs's eyes returned to him, they were earnest, but an underlying urgency ate away at the tiredness in them. 'You get this look on your face. Your head cocks, just slightly. Only small tells, but they're there. The drugs aren't working, are they?'

He's cleverer than he looks. Need to be more careful.

'Unless you're honest with us – with me – we can't help you.'

You can trust me more than you can trust him. I mean, look at him. He writes in purple pen and wears glitter like David Bowie. He's a flake.

Jackson closed his eyes. 'I know,' he said, unsure who he was answering.

'I'm not asking you this because it's my job.' Gibbs's eyes flicked to the windows again. Abernathy was still out there but Junior had disappeared. She saw them looking and tapped her bare wrist as if to say *Tick-fucking-tock*. Like they had anything more pressing to do than play Connect Four and watch *Maury* on TV.

'My partner . . .' Gibbs stopped, a ghost of uncertainty passing over his face.

Jackson glanced at the man's hand, at his ring finger. Bare. That made sense. It was best to keep your personal business separate from this place.

Gibbs tried again. 'Not just my partner, but generally. People are acting . . . odd. There've been incidents. This morning a pilot flew a commercial A330 into Mount Elbert in Colorado. They don't think any of the two hundred and sixty-two passengers could have survived. Even one of our new admissions here – she works for Brooks & Heinemann downtown; a high-end law practice – she burned up her entire office. Twenty-two people dead.'

As successful at setting fires as she is at practising law.

'People snap,' Jackson said. 'Stresses at home. Debt. Lots of reasons.'

'I agree. But not like this. Not so many. There have been multiple road accidents. Cars, motorbikes, *buses*. Statistically speaking, buses hardly ever crash. Four have been involved in collisions resulting in fatalities since last weekend. *Four*. And that's just in St Louis. On Friday evening a bomb was disarmed at Union Station. Right next to the Ferris wheel. Listen to me.' Gibbs placed a hand on Jackson's shoulder, drawing him away from the door and towards a chair, and in that one action Jackson realised how rattled Gibbs was. He never touched patients, not unless he had to restrain one or to stop someone from hurting themselves.

Jackson found himself sitting without fully knowing how he'd got there. Gibbs pulled a chair out and sat opposite him. The skin of his neck was flushed, his bloodshot eyes darted, and it wasn't just fatigue that had rimmed them red. This guy was scared.

'I'm not coming to you with this lightly. You must understand I would never normally talk about these things with a patient. Not ever. But I've already discussed this with colleagues, with doctors, with professionals, and no one wants to face up to the facts.'

Jackson tried to not look at Abernathy, who had pushed her face up against the window so that her mouth and nose squashed grotesquely against the Perspex. 'I'm listening,' he said.

Gibbs fixed him with a look. 'My partner hasn't *done* anything. Not yet. But he says . . . he says he hears someone. A voice. Talking to him. He has no history of mental illness. He's had no fevers, not on any medication. He's been sleeping fine. Way better than me. But he says it's been telling him to . . . to *do* things.'

'What things?'

Gibbs bit his bottom lip. 'Hurt me. Hurt himself.'

Jackson stared hard at him. 'This isn't some whacked-out therapy role play I don't know about, is it?'

'*No.* I swear to you. This isn't a game.'

'All right,' Jackson said slowly, studying him carefully, that tiny bit of glitter stuck to his cheek twinkling at him, a sparkle of cheer in all this macabre talk of death and violence. 'Let me get this straight. You're telling me he's hearing voices.'

'Yes. No. *A* voice. Singular.'

'You think what's happening to him is happening to others?'

'You don't see what's going on out there. The news channels are full of this stuff.'

Tell him what Light 'em Up Lawyer and Spit McGee said.

'Have you read the admission notes for those two new teenagers yet?' Jackson asked.

'Yes. I've had one-to-ones with them both after everything that happened yesterday.'

'That one kid – the nervy one – is there any previous history of audial hallucinations with him?'

'No. None. Until now.'

They stared at each other.

'At lunch yesterday, he told me he'd tried to kill himself. He has some kind of eating problem.'

Gibbs nodded. 'Anorexia nervosa, yes.'

I told you *it wasn't gender-specific.*

'He ever try to kill himself before?'

'No. He's had suicidal ideations in the past, but it's never manifested in more than thoughts. He said he's had low points but never considered following through on them before. He said he was coerced. That it picked at him. Told him he was a burden to his parents. That it would solve everyone's problems. That everything would be better for everyone if he were gone. We sometimes call it the "bullying voice".'

'And what about the lawyer?'

'God, I'd get into so much trouble for telling you this. It's confidential.'

'The lawyer?' Jackson repeated.

'Same thing but targeted differently. Outwardly, on to others. She's been overlooked for promotions twice this year while some young male hotshot waltzed into senior positions. Whatever she was listening to worked on her until she broke. It made her resent her co-workers. Hate them. Especially her bosses. She's repentant for what she did – horrified, even – but there's more to it than that. I think there's a part of her that's proud of it.'

We saw the proud part. She didn't seem very sorry, though.

Jackson stared past Gibbs, his thoughts turning. He barely saw Abernathy mime putting a noose around her neck and stringing herself up, her patience all but run dry. 'You need to get your partner help,' he said finally.

'You think I haven't thought of that?' The ward manager was wringing his hands. There was a wet shine to his eyes as if he was holding back tears. He spoke fast, words tumbling over one another. 'You haven't wondered at all the new admissions in here? Why we're running on a skeleton staff? All the psychiatric services are overrun. You should see the emergency room downstairs. It's utter chaos. There is no quick help. There's too many of them and nothing seems to be working. *Your* drugs aren't working, are they?'

Jackson hesitated but only for a second. 'Not entirely,' he admitted. 'But apart from the occasional breaks when it completely fucks me over—'

I'm looking out for you, it defended. *I'm the only one who does.*

'—it generally doesn't try to hurt me.'

'I need to know if it's said anything to you. Anything different. Anything . . . destructive.'

'Not any more destructive than normal. The drugs have quietened it a little, which helps.'

It's not that easy getting rid of me, Gibbs.

'It's not tried to get you to *do* anything?' Gibbs asked, watching him.

'Not since being admitted, no. It's good for me . . . being in here.' It was a hard admission to make but he felt that, for this, honesty was needed.

'Okay. Okay.' Gibbs seemed to deflate, leaning back in his chair, digging his fingers into his hair. He studied him for a long, protracted moment and Jackson began to wonder if he should get up and leave. But then Gibbs let out a heavy sigh and dropped his hands to his lap. 'I read in your notes you've been scheduled for ECT. Did you know that?'

ECT. Those three letters were like taking punches to the chest. It left him a little breathless. 'Abernathy's not likely to let me forget. She's been enjoying counting down the days.'

'Dr Tanner discussed it with you?'

'Yeah. It's scheduled for Wednesday.'

'You think it'll work?' Gibbs asked.

Jackson laughed, which surprised them both. 'Zapping electricity into my head? What do you think? You're supposed to be the expert.'

'I'm just a ward manager, Jackson. Honestly, at this point, I'd say it couldn't hurt.'

'So what were you two jabbering about?'

He and Abernathy were standing in the birdcage. That's what everyone called the smoking area, accessed by a single fire door off the women's corridor. It must have contravened a slew of fire regulations: a narrow, slabbed patio, entirely caged in from ground to roof, the grated walkway overhead making up part of the fire escape for the floors above. There was a gate at the south end of the birdcage but it was chained and padlocked. Jackson had never seen it open. The padlock had been rusted back on his first visit here three years ago and it hadn't been changed since.

He had bummed a cigarette from Abernathy. She had somehow got a whole packet from somewhere. She drew in a long,
hazy inhalation of nicotine and held it. Her voice sizzled as she
breathed out, one eye squinting, muddied by smoke. 'It looked
pretty intense,' she said.

Sol came over and she wordlessly handed him a cigarette. Lit
it for him. He went to sit in a patio chair a few feet away from
them. Abernathy smiled after him; a small, fond smile that
Jackson couldn't square with the Abernathy everyone else knew
in here.

'He's worried about his partner,' Jackson replied, watching
her watch Sol.

'Can't get his pecker up to satisfy her?'

Jackson blew out a stream of his own smoke. It gave him
time to swallow his annoyance. 'Why is it always about dicks
and peckers with you?'

Her attention came back to him. She seemed amused.
'Because I'm sex-obsessed?'

'You aren't, though.'

She arched an eyebrow and silently drew on her cigarette.

'He said his partner's been hearing voices,' he told her. 'He's
worried. About him. About what's going on.'

Her eyes widened. 'Holy shit, Gibbs is *gay*?'

'That isn't the point.'

'I know. But God. He doesn't come across as gay, like, at all.
Does he? It's not just me, is it?'

'Abernathy.'

She shrugged, flicked ash off her cigarette and took another
drag. 'It was bound to happen at some point, I guess – his work
following him home. These things always end up bleeding into
each other.' She squinted an eye at him. 'What does *your* little
voice say about all this?'

Jackson sent a quick glance around the birdcage. Luckily,
only Sol was close enough to hear and he was hunched over in

his chair, elbows on thighs, cigarette burning forgotten between his fingers. The other smokers had congregated around the two patio tables a staff member had carted in during the first week of summer. Jackson and Abernathy tended to shirk the comfort of a patio chair in favour of staying close to the gate. It was the last part of the birdcage to be warmed by the sun. It was also the spot Jenks came to when he was out on the prowl.

'You know better,' was all he said, the constriction in his chest tightening another inch.

'Yeah, I do.' Abernathy stubbed her cigarette out on the hospital's red-brick wall, not looking at him. 'But my question still stands.'

'It has nothing to say. Why would it?'

She shrugged again. 'I don't know. But it's all kind of freakily connected, don't you think? Something weird's going on. Even I can see that and I'm amazingly self-involved. I'm starting to think breaking out of this place is the best idea I've had all week.'

She's right when she's right.

'Until she's not.'

'Say what?' Abernathy said, frowning at him.

'Nothing. Thinking out loud.'

'Sure you are. But I'm being serious. All that padlock needs is a solid whack and it'd pop right off.' She tilted her chin, indicating the chained gate.

'A whack with what? There's nothing out here but plastic garden furniture.'

'I could find something.'

He stared at the crusted padlock, at the red flakes of rust fusing it solid, and his limbs began their own oxidising process, his joints stiffening and seizing up. It felt a lot like panic. 'Nothing short of bolt-cutters are getting that thing open,' he said.

Abernathy was watching him closely. 'Did you know Sol's

been having ECT, on and off, since he got here? He was probably just like you when they started on him.'

Jackson looked over at him. Smoke from Sol's cigarette, pinched between two fingers, drifted upward, curling into his eyes, but Sol didn't move and he didn't blink. A cascade of ash disintegrated from the end, landing in glowing flakes on the slabs.

Abernathy turned her back to the gate, leaned a shoulder against the railings. 'How long would you say we've known each other?' she asked.

This was the third time she and Jackson had crossed paths in here; the first time was on his fourth visit and her on her first. In total, their time together probably amounted to little more than nine months.

'A few years, on and off,' he answered.

'And yet I don't know a single thing about you. Your family, what jobs you've worked, whether you had a dog called Spot when you were a kid or how old you were when you popped your cherry. Nothing.'

'I know you're from Milwaukee,' he said, and that was the sum total of his knowledge. They didn't generally talk about their personal lives.

'Sure, a city of six hundred thousand people. Big deal. Do you know why we don't know any of that stuff?'

He knew she had the answer ready, she just wanted him to ask for it. 'Why?'

'Because it *doesn't matter*. Not to us. Not even to crazy Sol there. These dick-holes in here, they're obsessed with learning who we were to understand who we *are*. But us? We don't need that stuff, because we're not trying to fix each other.'

She turned away to gaze out across the lawn to the hospital's back lot. Even from here the orange staff parking permits were clearly visible on the windshields. The cars didn't move for most of the day. The hoods and fenders gleamed in the sun, a rainbow of hot metallic paint, like children's toys newly unboxed and lined up. There was something charged in them, the latent kinetic energy in their wheels, the resting gasoline in their tanks. All it would need was a crisp turn of a key and the engine would spark to life, rumbling, growling, vibrating with intent. An escape from this place.

Further out, on the far side of the interstate, winks of sunshine glittered on the surface of the Mississippi. It brought with it an even greater sense of ungraspable freedom. Such a huge stretch of water, winding its course far away from here. From them.

Abernathy had wrapped her slim fingers around the birdcage's rails, a prisoner gazing out at the type of freedom neither of them could ever truly have, but now she glanced at him from the corner of her eye. It was an assessing glance, gauging his reaction. She smiled one of her sneaky smiles. 'Wanna know what Junior said to me while I was waiting for you to finish your gay conversation with Gibbs?'

He didn't comment on her change of subject. 'Sure?'

Her smile became more genuine. 'You don't sound very sure.'

'Oh, I am. The anticipation is killing me.'

'Of course it is, but you'll like this, I promise. He said, and I'm quoting, "The world is crashing."'

'"Crashing"? Is that videogame speak?'

'"Videogame speak". What are you? Fifty? Who knows what it means. But it's like *Bam!* More cryptic shit to add to the heap. He didn't say what it meant.' She waved a dismissive hand, as if it didn't really matter. 'He's a drama-queen teen who's got himself admitted after throwing his little brother down the stairs.' She leaned in and added in a stage whisper, 'That's a secret. Don't repeat it. He's telling everyone it was an accident.'

'Fit of pique?' Jackson asked.

'That, or the voices told him to do it. I meant what I said, you know – about getting out of here. Your time's running out. Hey! Jenks!' Forgetting their conversation entirely, she dropped to a crouch and made a shushing *ch-ch-ch* sound that always made Jackson think of sashaying belly dancers and their tiny finger-cymbals. It worked. The big ginger tom sauntered over, tail high, its tip flicking.

Abernathy slid her arm through the fence, her sleeve snagging. It pushed it up to reveal a colourful tattoo winding around her lower arm. If they hadn't been in direct sunlight, Jackson doubted he'd have seen the white scarring running up the inside of her forearm. Dozens upon dozens of healed cuts expertly camouflaged by inked ocean waves, an old-fashioned timepiece and a matching set of swallows. No, not swallows. *Swifts*, she'd told him, seemingly disappointed that he'd been so predictable in his guess. Sometimes things weren't what they appeared, she'd said.

The cat preened against her hand, rubbing himself along the fencing, turning around and rubbing his other side on the railings as Abernathy stroked an arching back.

'Sorry, buddy. I had porridge for breakfast.'

A scrape of a chair leg and Sol was out of his seat. He slipped one hand inside his bathrobe's pocket and pulled out a folded green napkin.

Abernathy accepted the napkin from him and opened it, beaming a smile at its contents. 'Want to do the honours?' she asked him.

Sol frowned as if she'd suggested he stick pins in his eyeballs. He returned to his seat and his rumination of the slabs.

'I guess that's a "No".'

'Who's ever heard of a cat who likes toast?' Jackson asked as Abernathy poked a bread crust through the fence. The tom sniffed at the offering before delicately taking it between his teeth. He dropped the crust to the grass, sniffed some more, then started gnawing on it.

'He's a stray. He'll eat whatever's going.'

'A stray? Look at the size of him. He's fat.'

'Shhh. You'll give him a complex.'

There was a notch in the tom's ear and a bald patch on the top of his head; a perfectly round circle the size of a dime. Jackson leaned against the railing and watched Abernathy play with the cat's tail, winding it through her fingers.

A clanging boot shook the fence and Jackson jerked away, his heart clanging with it.

'Smoke break's over,' Birdy said. He gave the fence another kick but the cat was already a good twenty yards away, staring back at them and licking his chops. 'This isn't a petting zoo. Stop feeding the wildlife.'

Abernathy stood and, not once taking her eyes from Birdy, emptied her napkin, the remaining bits of toast tumbling to the grass.

Jackson smiled at her act of rebellion.

Birdy bent and picked up a pebble. Smooth and rounded. He idly tossed it up and down, speaking to Jackson without breaking Abernathy's stare. 'Nurse wants to speak to you, Jackson. At the nurses' station. Now.'

The rest of the smokers had filtered back inside, leaving the birdcage empty but for the three of them and Sol (who continued to sit and stare at the ground as if it held all the secrets to the universe).

Birdy caught the pebble he'd been tossing and threw it, hard and fast. It passed easily through the birdcage's railings, hitting the grass a foot away from Jenks. The cat streaked off.

'Hey!' Abernathy snapped.

Birdy tracked Jenks right up until the cat disappeared behind a row of parked cars. 'Next time,' he told her, 'I won't use something so small as a stone.'

Jackson didn't move. He looked a question at Abernathy. He didn't want to leave her out here with him.

She was frowning but she nodded at him to go. 'It's fine. I'm fine. No big deal.'

'Go on,' Birdy ordered when he still didn't move. 'Or do you need me to escort you?'

There was that unspoken nuance again.

Jackson started walking away, noticing how Birdy leaned casually against the fence, having already forgotten him. It was the same way a guy in a bar would lean as he sweet-talked a girl, the dull beat of music and alcohol thumping a stupid confidence into him. Abernathy's face stayed locked up, eyes tight against the sun, right up until Jackson pulled open the fire door and he caught sight of Sol.

The man's head had turned. Their eyes met and an understanding seemed to pass between them. The edge of worry that had been nibbling away at Jackson withdrew and he stepped inside.

A muted patter of running shower water reached his ears as he wandered up the corridor, but it wasn't the noise that made his steps falter. A spreading cloud of steam had leaked into the hallway. Each of the three single-occupant shower stalls had its own ventilation fan that did a pretty good job of dispelling mist, and yet the steam from under the middle door had turned the floor slippery with condensation. He stopped in front of it. The hot steam broiled his legs from the shins down, his socks turning soggy in his slippers.

The colour marker on the door was slid to green. (There were no locking mechanisms on the showers, only a simple colour-coded system: green for available, red for occupied.) He looked over his shoulder at the only other person in the corridor with him, an older woman lounging on her side on her cot like Cleopatra waiting to be served a bowl of grapes.

'Did someone go in here?' he asked.

Cleopatra lifted a hand and held it, palm out, offering a high-five. She said nothing and it dawned on him that she wasn't offering a salutation but blocking him from her view, as if the sight of him offended her.

'Great.' He turned back to the door and knocked. 'Hello?'

No answer.

'Anyone in there?'

He should get a nurse. It wouldn't go down well if he walked in on a woman while she was showering. But something stopped him, an invisible hand on his back, holding him in place. His feet were boiling but a cold clamminess closed over the nape of his neck. He peered at the green marker on the door, and what did green mean again?

Green means go, that voice whispered in his head.

'Green means go,' he whispered.

A fissure of energy zapped through his hand and he pushed open the door.

A wall of muggy heat hit him. Sweat broke out on his brow. Steam swirled around him as the cool outside air stormed an attack. He wiped a palm down his damp face as the mist cleared.

The lawyer was slumped in the bottom of the shower tray, her wet, greying hair stuck to the side of her face. He hissed at her boiled skin, a red so bright it brought to mind lobster shells, clown's noses, fire hydrants. The skin had peeled away in sheets from her shoulders, her breasts, the tops of her thighs. Fluid-filled blisters as large as his palm covered her arms and chest. The bandages were missing from her hands and his eyes flinched away from what was left of them.

Jackson lurched inside and a glove of ice encased him, instantly followed by a thousand puncturing bee stings. He gasped and slipped, his shoe squeaking as it jolted against the shower tray's lip, almost dumping him on top of her. He instinctively turned his face away as acid ate into his cheek and neck, streamed down his chest, plastering the scalding material of his shirt to his skin. He groped blindly for the shower controls, a scream burbling in his throat as his burning fingers fumbled for the dial.

The water shut off.

It was hard to breathe. All the oxygen had been sucked from the room, leaving him in the vacuum of space: no gravity, no time, everything spinning in a vortex of whirling steam. The thundering pound of water continued to drum in his ears, to blear his eyes, but the lawyer didn't move. Didn't wince or cry or scream. All he could see was the scalded red line of her scalp in the perfect parting of her hair. And what was red again?

Red means stop.

'Red means stop.' And his voice was the hiss of water as it panted out of him.

He grabbed her arm, called her name, shook her. Her flesh separated from her arm, peeling away in a sleeve; it was like stripping the skin from an overripe peach. He stared in horror at her degloved flesh hanging from his fingers. He realised he was murmuring, 'Oh my God, oh my God, oh my God.'

'Overcooked.'

He looked over his shoulder. Cleopatra filled the doorway, her white bedsheet draped over one shoulder like a Grecian robe.

'They overcooked her,' she said. 'Meat's too tender.'

'Get help.'

She didn't react.

'*Get help!*' he roared, and she blinked, her face creasing in a frown, more scandalised by his tone than by the scalded woman slumped dead at his feet.

All the patients had been relegated to their rooms until the lawyer was wheeled away under a sheet. The rattle of her gurney's castors had been the only sound in the hallways as it rolled by. It had taken a long time for anyone to come and collect her. Longer than it should have. Jackson was reminded of

Gibbs's words about other parts of the hospital falling into chaos.

The removal of her body lifted the pall of silence on the ward and, long into the evening, panicked shouts, bangs, thuds and animalistic howls echoed through the corridors. Restlessness ran like a fever, crawling under skin and scratching at brains with fingernails that, for many, had been sharpened by years of anxiety and paranoia. At one point, Gibbs poked his head into Jackson's room, checking on him, coming in only to hand Jackson a book.

'I've seen you reading,' he whispered, so as to not disturb Jackson's sleeping roommate. 'I wanted you to have this.' Gibbs laid his palm flat on the book Jackson held. 'My gift to you.'

Beautiful Chaos. A book of poetry. It weighed heavier in Jackson's hand than it should have. He thanked him.

The ward manager's presence was ghostlike and brief, his eyes unwilling to meet Jackson's again after he'd lifted his hand from the book's cover. The jangle of his keys as they faded down the corridor was an ethereal sound, like an old, half-forgotten memory. Jackson put the book on his nightstand, unread.

While his roommate snored, Jackson lay above the covers in a pair of shorts, the chill night air crawling over his hot skin. The thought of the covers rubbing against him was unbearable; his shoulders and chest stung from his brief dousing under the scalding shower.

He stared at the red light of the CCTV camera, its eye watching, and wondered if Birdy was sitting on the other side of it, staring back.

Sirens warbled out in the real world, emergency vehicles speeding to some unknown catastrophe where hot, jagged metal scorched into the road and oily smoke belched from twisted wreckages. From the other bed, his roommate yipped in his sleep like a pup that had been stolen from his litter and yearned to be back among his warm, wriggling siblings.

Outside his room, nothing stirred. No regular *pit-pat* of footsteps as an orderly made their rounds, no ticking of the big wall clock hanging behind the nurses' station (which Jackson often convinced himself he could hear in the dead of night). No soft murmur of voices as staff talked about what they'd had for dinner, how the latest episode of a popular TV show had ended, what the chances were of this sports team winning over that in the next game of the season.

The door cracked open and a bar of tepid, greyish light painted the wall, growing as the gap widened and blacking over as someone slipped inside.

Silence.

Stillness.

Breathing.

A shadow detached from the wall and Jackson's heart thudded in his chest, a sluggish beat as if he'd been drugged, as if this were all a dream and soon he would wake in his bed to the smell of pancakes, his mother pottering in his childhood kitchen. He felt fingers smooth over the bedcovers near his arm, move down and brush the back of his hand. They curled around his fingers and gripped. Tugged at him to get up.

He rose stiffly to his feet, breath hissing through his teeth, and was led from the room. No one was in the nurses' station to ask them why they weren't in bed. In the unlit day room, a silhouette stood in front of the only window that unlatched. The blinds were cracked open, strips of moonlight slashing the front of the man's body, slicing him vertically as if cut by the precision of a surgeon's scalpel. His bare skin was alabaster-white where the light laid it bare, and even if Sol didn't speak at first, even if he was missing his bathrobe and was dressed only in boxers, he still wore his boots.

'It's happening,' Sol murmured, gazing out the window. 'Burning. So much madness and death.'

Abernathy clasped Jackson's hand tighter, and her fingers

were cold, the moonlight having somehow slipped inside with them so that she carried it within her cells. She pulled him to the window and reached for Sol's hand with her other, standing between them, shored up on both sides.

Out in the night, lights flared. Not the oxidised glare of streetlights, although the hospital grounds were flooded with those. These were further out. Wavering. Hot. A long line of fires. Burning in the darkness.

'What is that?' Jackson asked.

'Interstate 55,' Abernathy said.

Another flash lit up the night, a mini detonation, a billow of orange, starkly bright and somehow more real against the murky artificial haze of the city. It was like a brief-burning bulb filament branding itself on his retina, the explosion compacting back down in size to add another blaze to the line of vehicle fires. They perfectly delineated the I-55 for a number of miles. Car wrecks. Scores of them.

Through the open window, over the faint scent of mud and cold Mississippi River water, the city burned.

'Junior was right,' Abernathy said, her cold fingers painfully clenched around Jackson's. 'The world, it's crashing.'

CHAPTER 4

Sparks

Wednesday, 10.43 a.m. (2 hours to go)

Jackson stared at his Scrabble tiles.

ZCOSSHK

The universe was laughing at him.

Quiet clicks came from Abernathy's tiles as she half-heartedly rearranged them. She didn't like playing Scrabble. It was a waste of time, according to her. Only assholes made up nonsense words to make themselves feel clever.

They were sitting opposite each other at the games table in the day room. Abernathy had one leg drawn up. Her knee jigged up and down. She was more agitated than Jackson had seen her in weeks.

'We need to get out of here.'

There was no doubt as to whether or not she was joking this time.

'As soon as Rosie shows up,' she continued, 'I'm going to ask her what the hell's going on. Seriously. This is bullshit.'

Jackson didn't reply. They'd already been over this.

'Gibbs! Hey, *Gibbs!*'

Jackson turned to look, but Gibbs wasn't standing at the back of the room where he would usually be. He wasn't passing by

47

on his way to one of the other corridors, either. He was nowhere to be seen. Jackson cocked his head to listen but there was no tell-tale rhythmic jangling of his keys.

'He just *ignored* me.' Abernathy's eyes were wide with outrage. 'Christ, this place is going down the shitter, and fast.'

All sense of normalcy on the ward had disappeared. The atmosphere was brittle and ready to snap. Breakfast had been cold muesli, slopped on to trays. Staff were terse and didn't interact, though Jackson had caught a couple in hushed conversation that had ceased as soon as they'd noticed his eyes on them. The dirty cutlery and trays remained in the dining room. No one had cleared up.

There were only two staff on duty when usually there would be at least five. Eight more patients had been admitted over the last day alone; they milled in the corridors, they lay on the floor, they wandered in and out of rooms, and Sol walked his route, working his way around the increased number of obstacles. Sol was remaining calm for the time being, any frustration he felt mollified by the fact that Jackson, in his wisdom, had put Bob Dylan on the stereo. Sol liked music. Sometimes Jackson caught him mouthing the lyrics.

'They can't just keep us in the dark like this,' Abernathy muttered.

'They can.' Jackson played his move, placing SHOCKS through the star tile in the middle of the board. A score of forty.

'It's Wednesday,' Abernathy told him, her knee jiggling away. 'Shock day,' she added, in case he was unaware what 'Wednesday' meant. 'Clock's ticking.'

'I know,' he said, picking out his new tiles, ignoring the fine tremble in his fingers.

On their smoke break after breakfast, he had noticed the significant fall in staff cars in the parking lot. He'd expected the hospital to be teeming with activity after the explosions and crashes they'd witnessed along the Interstate. Emergency sirens had become the soundtrack to the city. Yet it was all strangely quiet on this side of the hospital. Through the open window in the day room, the smell of burning was constant.

Sol went past, the tread of his boots heavy. He was muttering to himself, his brow tucked low, mouth dipped at the corners. He now seemed as agitated as Abernathy. He was on his fifth circuit – two more than usual.

A young, skinny guy with needle scabs running up his arms lay sleeping in front of the shelves where the magazines, books and board games were stacked. His mouth gaped open. Jackson could see the small, blackish nubs of his teeth, the white fur coating his tongue. He seemed to be rotting from the inside.

Starting at the top, Sol tapped each of the shelves, his finger hitting a soft beat in time with Bob Dylan's singing. His tapping stopped when he reached Scabby's prone body.

Sol gazed down at the guy.

He'll have to poke him awake if he wants to count that bottom shelf.

But Sol had other ideas. He lifted a booted foot and stomped the sleeping guy in the hip, a downward stamp that seemed to compress him into the floor.

'Da'*fuck*?' Scabby jerked upward, grabbing on to the shelves and dragging himself up as if scaling a climbing frame. His face screwed up in a semblance of anger and alarm, the emotions confused by sleep.

'Move,' Sol told him.

Scabby wasn't in here because he was coached in polite discourse and civilised behaviour. He attacked Sol, leaping on him and attaching himself to his front like a limpet. He whooped and hollered, a cowboy riding a bronco as Sol swung him round, bathrobe billowing. Sol shoved, dislodging Scabby in a powerful heave.

The stereo's song had ended and 'A Hard Rain's a-Gonna Fall' was playing. Someone hooted a laugh as Scabby crashed into the games table and the whole thing upended, Scrabble tiles flying in the air, gaming board catapulting into the wall. Jackson was too shocked to move, but Abernathy lurched out of her chair and bumped into a cupboard. A cascade of magazines dislodged themselves from a shelf and slid to the floor.

Sol immediately moved to tidy them up and his boot skated across the glossy Photoshopped face of Beyoncé. He went down, wiping out so spectacularly Jackson felt the shudder of his fall shiver through the bones of his feet.

Abernathy burst out laughing, hands clutching her stomach, as if the hilarity of it might split her open. Sol sat up, rubbing his shoulder, disgruntled but unhurt.

'Oh man, that was *awesome*.' She grinned down at him, chuckling. 'Are you okay?' She reached for him but Sol scooted away. 'Aw, don't be like that. You know, for such a tall guy, you're surprisingly elegant when you go ass over tit.' She choked on her laughter again, slapping at her thigh.

On the other side of the overturned table, Scabby rose unsteadily to his feet. His glare danced between the *ow-you-hurt-me* variety to the irrational hatred murderers held for their victims.

'Hey,' Jackson said, standing up. 'What're you looking at?'

The tightrope-walk in Scabby's eyes collapsed. He backed away, muttering to himself, throwing them baleful looks as he hurried over to drop into the couch in front of the TV.

'What the high heck is going on over here?'

Jackson didn't know when Rosie had come on shift, but there she stood, hands on ample hips, surveying her charges with the stern air of a headmistress. At her shoulder was Birdy. Of course. Always Birdy.

Sol was gathering himself up, moving stiffly. He bent to scoop up the fallen magazines, stacking them neatly in the crook of one arm. Jackson saw him touch a single fingertip to the bottom shelf as he did. Inventory complete.

A cellphone trilled, modern technology's version of an old-fashioned turn-dial telephone. Jackson saw Rosie start. She looked over to the empty nurses' station.

She looked back at Birdy. 'You got this?' she asked.

Birdy was running a palm back over his hair, brow to crown, smoothing the gel-slicked strands into order. 'I got it,' he said.

'Make sure you do, Mr Bird,' Rosie said over her shoulder as she headed briskly back to the nurses' station. The cellphone trilled some more. 'We can't have any more undue upset today.'

Birdy watched her go. Jackson didn't detect any emotion in the man's expression, but Birdy stared after her for too long, his eyes too watchful. He turned back to them.

'Pick it up.' He nodded at the table.

'What's the magic word?' Abernathy asked. Her smile had stayed to kick around for a while, have some fun. Seeing Sol tumble on his ass had cheered her up immensely.

Birdy said nothing, as if waiting her out would get her to do what he wanted. When she didn't move, he shunted Jackson's chair out of his way and closed in on her.

'If you make me ask again,' he said, stopping a foot away so they were eye to eye; he wanted to make sure she could see it when he sent looks to Sol, then to Jackson. 'I'm going to stop being so nice to everyone.'

Sometimes Jackson believed Birdy should be a patient in here along with the rest of them, watching daytime TV and dining with plastic cutlery while dribbling into his meatloaf.

Abernathy's gaze flicked past Birdy to Jackson, her smile gone, and Birdy didn't like the ease with which they silently communicated with each other. Didn't like it, at all. He stepped back and ran his hand over his hair again, neatening it, taking his time as he moved over to the open-faced cupboard where Sol had neatly stacked the fallen magazines on to their shelf. He chose a paperback book, opened it. Idly fanned through its pages.

'You like these, don't you, Sol?' He held up the book he was flicking through. 'Do you have a favourite? Hmm? Is it this one?'

Sol stood by the window, his face impassive. His eyes didn't leave Birdy, though, didn't leave the book he was riffling through.

'No? Not your thing?' Birdy tore the book in half with a single clean *shrrrrpt* and dropped the pieces to the floor.

'Hey, come on. Don't do that,' Jackson said.

Birdy ignored him. 'What about this one?' He picked up a second book, holding it up for Sol to see. 'Is this any good?'

Sol's hands curled into fists.

Birdy's mouth curved up. He opened the book and perused its contents. 'Going by your silence, I guess you don't think much of this one, either.'

A swift yank. A tearing sound. Pages fluttered loose.

'Maybe it got better by the end,' Birdy said. He shredded a page free, stripping the book, chapter by chapter, the paper peeling free as easily as petals plucked from a flower. 'But I guess we'll never know.'

Abernathy snatched what remained of the book out of his hands. 'You're a limp-dicked asshole, do you know that?'

Birdy hit her, a powerful backhand that happened so fast Jackson had no time to react. Abernathy's head jerked to the side and, when she turned back around, she was bleeding from her lip.

Strands of hair hung in Birdy's eyes but he didn't push them away. The hand he lifted pointed a slow, deliberate finger at Abernathy's face, and Jackson was sure he would say something viciously callous to her, something designed to rip through all her defences, but instead he swung his hand to the side, pointed at the upturned gaming table and said, 'Pick that *fucking* table up.' White gobs of spit caked the corners of his mouth. He licked his lips.

Dark eyes passed over Jackson but didn't stick. A hand

checked his hair. 'There's your magic word,' he said, and turned on his heel and walked away. Scrabble tiles clacked and skittered under his feet.

Jackson and Abernathy stood and stared after him. They exchanged looks but didn't speak a word as they went to the table, righted it and placed it back in its spot.

'Fuck this place. I'm getting out.'

Abernathy had accompanied Jackson to his room after they'd cleared up. Sol had returned to his own room, carrying what remained of the torn and damaged books. Abernathy had snagged a few pages for herself. She was twisting them into a roll, wringing them between her hands and pacing back and forth. She paused at the bedroom window.

'I'd rather take my chances outside than be stuck in here with *him* and his baby Bird fucking tantrums.' Done looking outside, she restlessly paced back to where Jackson leaned against the wall next to the open door (shutting bedroom doors wasn't allowed during the day and he didn't want to attract any more unwanted attention).

'I'm not sure it's any safer out there,' he said.

She gave him a look. Her bottom lip was swollen and crusted over with blood. 'I said I'll take my chances.'

His chest was tightening again. He needed a smoke.

'Did you see Rosie?' she asked. 'She didn't even look up when we went past. Her eyes were glued to her cellphone. I'd have bet a thousand bucks that bitch didn't own a cell.'

Cellphones weren't allowed on the ward, staff included. Jackson hadn't ever seen Rosie in possession of one and she was always pulling up staff on having theirs out instead of locked away.

'I'm going,' Abernathy said. 'I've thought about it, and you were right about the padlock in the birdcage. The only way out is through the main doors.'

Jackson applied the brakes on her rashness as best he could. 'The door release is in the nurses' station. And the panel activation for the doors is on the outside of the main entrance.'

'I *know* that. I'm not stupid.'

'You'll be waiting forever for someone to open it – I don't think any more staff are coming in today.'

There was an intensity in the way Abernathy was looking at him. An untamed twitchiness, like an animal who'd been backed not only into a corner but had a sleeping rattlesnake spooled up next to her. It made him nervous.

'You're not coming with me?' she asked.

'What?'

'You said, "You'll be waiting forever." As in me. Alone.'

She's got you there.

'I'm just not sure leaving is the best option. Not when we don't have any real idea of what's going on out there.'

'But we have an idea what's going on in *here*. We're on a ward full of psychotic, violent people, Jack. What do you think will happen when the meds stop being handed out?'

She's got you there, too.

'Shut up,' he grated, and he saw indignation flare in Abernathy's eyes. 'Not you,' he said.

'I'll set a fire,' Abernathy said. 'I already have kindling.' She waved the rolled-up paper she'd twisted into a stick. 'If I make it big enough, the fire alarm will trigger the main doors and they'll automatically open.'

He shook his head. 'They won't even let us use scissors unsupervised. How're you going to start a—' But he stopped, because he already knew.

Abernathy's smile was hard and triumphant. 'We have lit cigarettes every day. All I have to do is bring one in after our next smoke break.' She spoke fast, eager to convince him. 'I have mine and Pip's bathrobes. Add yours and Sol's and we're set. They're super flammable. Says so on the label.' Her eyes dropped to his bed. She ran her fingers along its edge, no doubt searching for the sheet's warning label. 'Maybe these are flammable, too . . .'

She wants to start a bonfire. It sounded excited.

'And what if the fire gets out of control?' Jackson asked. 'What if the main doors don't open?' He didn't remember straightening away from the wall and approaching her, but she didn't seem to notice him. 'There're still people dosed up on opioids, Abernathy. They can't run.' He didn't mention the patients locked up in isolation; he knew she was aware of them.

'The main doors will be open.' Her voice held more than a hint of obstinacy. 'If the others know what's good for them, they'll get out, too.'

She gripped the bedcovers and yanked them off, having decided they were flammable enough for her needs. She screwed them up and dropped them to the floor. 'Where's your bathrobe?' she asked, brushing past him and heading for his closet.

Everything was careening out of control. Sweat pricked at his temples. His head felt ready to combust.

'Abernathy, I'm not saying you're wrong, but just listen to me for a sec—'

She pushed open the closet's concertina doors and the noise that came out of her was somewhere between a whine and a gasp.

There were no hooks or railings in the closets on the Unit, nothing that could be used to tie things to or hang things from. But a railing had been rigged up from a mop's handle and jammed horizontally into the space above the doorjamb. Patients weren't allowed anything that could be used as a ligature. Only members of staff had access to janitor's equipment and were allowed to wear belts with their uniforms.

Gibbs didn't look tired any more. His belt dug an obscene crevasse into his neck, his face purple-red and bulging above its leather strap. His eyes were no longer bloodshot but swam red, their whites swallowed entirely by the blood of burst capillaries.

Jackson looked quickly away, his stomach caving in. A whistling washed through his ears, a high-pitched ringing that nearly masked the rustle of paper. Abernathy hadn't scrunched up her kindling in a reflex of revulsion or shock, she had plucked a note from Gibbs's shirt pocket and was unfolding it.

When she spoke, her voice was whisper-quiet through the hissing in Jackson's head.

'"No man means evil but the Devil, and we shall know him by his horns."'

Gibbs's handwriting sloped steeply down to the bottom-right corner, as if he hadn't been able to control his pen. Abernathy flipped the note over and on the reverse Gibbs had scribbled two final words.

Beautiful Chaos.

Jackson stared at them until the words blurred. Acid burned up his throat and he swallowed, the caustic sting bringing tears to his eyes.

'What does that mean?' Abernathy asked.

Gibbs wasn't a patient. He didn't suffer from mental illness or undiagnosed behavioural conditions. He was a seemingly sane man who'd strung himself up in Jackson's closet to escape everything that was happening on the outside of it.

'I don't know what will happen if I leave here,' Jackson murmured, trying to ignore the squirming sensation behind his ear. The tickle was almost unbearable. He needed his meds. 'I'll get worse again, Abernathy. What if I get even worse? I'm scared of what I might do.' The hissing in his head grew louder. The tears that swam in his eyes had little to do with the lingering burn in his throat.

He felt a hand push at him, backing him up from the closet so that neither of them could see Gibbs hanging there, a macabre skin-suit waiting for a Halloween party.

The intensity of Abernathy's stare demanded he look at her.

'We stick together,' she said. 'Even when we're out of here, we stick together. Me, you, Sol. We'll look out for each other, okay? You won't be alone.'

He broke her gaze to look over at his bedside table.

Her hand scrunched up his shirt, the heat of her palm urgent and insistent. '*Jack*,' she hissed. 'Please. Let's *go*.'

The poetry book Gibbs had given him sat beside a plastic cup half filled with tepid water. 'I know a way,' he murmured, and the hissing stopped dead in his ears. His words came so clear it was as though someone else were speaking them for him. 'I'll need a distraction, but, Abernathy, no fires.'

He felt her eyes searching his face, probing for a way in. 'How do y—'

'No fires,' he repeated.

She gave in and nodded.

Chaos really is beautiful, isn't it? the voice whispered in his ear.

CHAPTER 5

Escape

Jackson stood at the bank of telephones in the main corridor, plastic receiver pressed to his ear, pretending to listen to someone on the other end. There wasn't even a dial tone, no *beep*s encouraging him to replace the receiver on its cradle. The phone's earpiece was dead, the lines cut. He tried not to think about what that meant. Instead he kept an eye on the nurses' station door, waiting for Rosie to appear.

You're going to get caught.

'And what? They'll lock us up? We're already locked up.'

It's bad out there.

Jackson was quiet for a moment. 'You don't know that.'

You don't know anything. You're always doing what she wants. You can't think for yourself.

Jackson didn't reply. He didn't need a lecture, especially not from it. 'We can't stay here,' he said, speaking into the phone's mouthpiece. 'We can't hide from this.'

You hide from me. But you know that won't help you, right? No one can make me leave – not all the useless doctors in this hospital or all the pills in the world.

The plastic of the receiver creaked in his hand. Jackson became very aware of his racing heart; it galloped in his chest and thumped in his ears, pounding for attention, but he was saved from further discussion by a piercing scream. It shrilled through the Unit like an endless, high-pitched alarm, the kind that could make your ears bleed if you were too close to it.

Rosie burst out of the nurses' station. She didn't even glance up the corridor where Jackson stood but yanked the door shut and hurried in the opposite direction, heading for the women's corridor, where the screams were coming from.

If you're really doing this, do it.

Jackson replaced the receiver and jogged up the hall. He didn't look into any of the rooms he passed, though he glimpsed movement in many of them. He kept one hand clamped in a tight, sweaty grip, fastened around a single key. He had found it tucked inside the pages of the poetry book. Stuck to the key's head, and secured by a piece of see-through tape, was a small white stickered dot the same size as a tab of Risperdal. Gibbs had always been organised. He colour-coded everything.

As Jackson reached the nurses' station, Abernathy was arriving to meet him, sidling out of the day room, eyes sweeping the area about her as she did. She looked suspicious as hell.

'Where's Birdy?' he asked, keeping his voice low.

'I haven't seen him. And I couldn't get Sol to leave his fucking books, the stubborn bastard.'

He glanced at her, pausing. 'You want me to try?'

She wasn't looking at him, her attention fixed on the women's corridor, keeping watch. 'There's no time,' she said shortly. 'Just hurry it up.' He could hear the hurt in her voice, but he didn't push it. The cut on the inside of his bottom lip was still sore and he didn't want it reopened.

('That's what you get for lying to me,' Abernathy had said. Gibbs's key was laid flat in the middle of Jackson's palm; his other covered his mouth where she'd struck him. 'Now we have matching bust lips,' she'd said, and smiled, not in a particularly nice way.)

The piercing screams had fallen into wails. Inconsolable,

grief-stricken wails that didn't give any indication of letting up.

'What did you *do*?' Jackson muttered, bending to the door's lock.

He'd talked Abernathy out of setting a blazing conflagration made up of their bathrobes but had left the means of distraction up to her.

'Snapped Pip's tweezers in two and left them on her pillow,' she replied.

The key he'd been gripping all this time could have easily slipped through his fingers, as sweaty as his hand was, but it didn't. He was careful. The surprise came when a voice spoke up from directly behind them.

'What's going on?'

Jackson cursed as the key clinked to the tiles at his feet.

The bandage over Junior's ear hadn't been changed. It was grimy but still bulked out the side of his head, making him look misshapen and odd.

'Christ,' Jackson snapped, bending down to chase after the dropped key. Abernathy beat him to it and pressed it into his hot, damp hand.

'Take it easy,' she murmured, giving his fingers a squeeze. She looked over at Junior. 'We're getting out of here. Now shut your mouth.'

'Can I come?'

'If you go away so we don't all look like we're crowding around the fucking door, yes.'

The little white circle stuck to the office door's keyplate matched Gibbs's key's spot perfectly. Jackson inserted the key and twisted. The door unlocked with a quiet *click*.

He turned to Abernathy. 'Go wait by the main entrance. Take the kid. Block them open if they start to close.'

'What about you?' she asked.

'I'll hit the release button and be right out.'

She stared at him, not moving.

'Can you just do something without arguing for once in your goddamned life? Please? It'll take two minutes.'

She frowned and would have given him some serious lip if the situation had been different, but she let it go. She moved off without another word, Junior trailing after her.

Jackson entered the nerve centre of the Unit. There was something powerful looking out on the ward from this side of the nurses' station. A large computer monitor was set up on a desk, its screen segmented into camera angles, six in total, offering views of the day room, the dining hall, the crafts room, the men's and women's corridors and, of course, the area directly outside the main doors to the Unit. In the corner of the screen, a tiny version of Pip walked out of Abernathy's room. The image was black and white and grainy, but Jackson could see the large, dark stain on the front of her shirt.

Blood.

'Shit.'

He couldn't see what was left of the tweezers Abernathy had broken, but by the way Pip held her arm stiffly at her side he suspected she was gripping them. She wandered up the corridor in her bare feet, heading his way.

'*Shit.*'

Hurry up.

He checked the desktop for the door release, the space beside the keyboard, in front of the monitor. No button.

Where *was* it? He *knew* it was here. Whenever the intercom buzzed outside, whoever was on duty always responded with 'Pull the handle when you hear the buzzer.' It *had* to be here. Why hadn't he paid better attention?

Abernathy and the kid weren't the only ones hanging out by the main ward doors any more. Intuition, or herd mentality, had prompted a few patients to gravitate towards the entrance, aware that something hinky was going down.

A smacking thud from behind spun him around. Pip, with

her perfectly smooth face and lashless eyelids, stared at Jackson through the partition window and he suddenly didn't feel so powerful any more. He felt trapped and alone, a fish in his fishbowl. She'd slapped her palms flat to the pane. Red palms that left bloody smears on the glass.

This close, and in full Technicolor, Jackson could see the splash of fresh blood covering the side of her face and dripping down her neck. The collar of her shirt was wet with it. But more than that, he could see the unravelling of her sanity in the nervous swipe of her tongue across her lips, in the whites of her too-large eyes. Past her shoulder, a low, hulking creature heaved itself out of Abernathy's room. It half crawled, half dragged itself into the corridor and collapsed, one arm outstretched. A dark pool of blood expanded around Rosie's head and shoulders. She didn't move again.

'What're you doing in there, Jackson?' Pip's voice was cracked. Probably from all the screaming.

'Trying to find the door-release button,' he answered truthfully.

She pointed with one bloodied finger. 'It's under the desk.'

And there it was. The green button was recessed in a small bracket attached to the underside of the desktop.

'Jack!'

Abernathy's voice came not only from outside but from the tinny speakers at desk level. At the same time a tremendous bang shuddered through the nurses' station as though a giant hand had swatted it.

Pip's face was crushed against the partitioned glass and for a split second Jackson flashed back to Abernathy doing the same while she waited for him and Gibbs to finish their conversation after group therapy. Her face had been grotesquely pushed out of all recognition, but no blood or gore had accompanied her show like Pip's did.

Behind Pip, Birdy swung the chair a second time, slamming

it into the back of her head. Jackson heard the crunch as something in Pip's face broke. Her nose maybe, or her cheekbones.

A third shuddering crash shook the nurses' station and blood
splattered the glass, and Pip wasn't Pip any more – she was just a
mush of bone and flesh.

Through the window, Birdy's eyes found him. He dropped
the chair and pointed at Jackson.

'Don't touch that door release.'

Jackson wasn't getting out of this box. He knew that now.

Birdy had stepped over Pip's body (which had slumped out
of view), and was skirting the nurses' station, his eyes never
leaving Jackson. Jackson didn't look away from him, either, as
he pushed the green button.

A low, continuous buzz sounded from the console.

Birdy broke into a run.

Jackson's eyes darted to the entrance, searching, wanting one
last glimpse of Abernathy before she was gone. A crowd had
gathered around the doors now, but her head craned above
them, looking for him as a tide of patients, as many as twenty,
surged forward and carried her and Junior through the doors
and out of the Unit. He thought he heard her call his name.

Birdy was at the nurses' station door, all semblance of calm
gone, eyes crazy, teeth bared. His key scraped in the lock and
the door swung inward.

On the surveillance monitor, a sea of heads swept under the
camera as patients flooded out. Two people fell in the scrum –
one looked like Junior's buddy, the saliva-making factory – but
no one stopped to help pick him up. The images grew large and
blurred so fast that Jackson didn't know what was happening
until his face smashed the screen.

He didn't bother fighting it, he even found himself laughing, blood spattering the screen as a stinging wrench on his hair
drew his head back and Birdy smashed his face into the monitor
again. And again. And again.

And then it stopped.

No more blows came. Jackson was on his knees, hanging on to the desk, dizzy, sick, blood pouring from his nose. Why wasn't he being hit? Blankly, he watched as Sol grabbed Birdy by the scruff of his neck and yanked him away from Jackson, and there was no instinctive robotic behaviour in Sol here – not like when he'd planted that stomp on top of Scabby to encourage the man away from the cabinet. There was only a cold, animal viciousness in how he hit Birdy, his arm a piston, driving punch after punch into Birdy's head and face, the man's greasy hair in disarray.

He would have killed Birdy, Jackson was sure of it, if Birdy hadn't materialised a syringe out of nowhere and jabbed the needle deep into Sol's thigh. Within seconds Sol's punches lost their steam, became sloppy, glancing off his target and then missing altogether. He staggered. He looked at Jackson and there was regret in his eyes. Confusion. And then Sol dropped to one knee and collapsed, wiping out the security monitor as he did.

'Sol!' Jackson reared up, but his legs wouldn't hold, dizziness tilting the world to the left. He expected to see items slide off their desks, the office chairs to go skidding past.

He didn't see what hit him next, but if he had to guess from the clacking sound he'd say Birdy had grabbed the keyboard that went with the monitor and swung it at his head. It was the last sound Jackson heard as he followed Sol down, down, down into a dizzying, dark hole.

Chapter 6

ECT

Wednesday, 12.50 p.m. (0 hours to go)

Jackson lay on a hospital gurney. The safety railings were raised on both sides and soft material restraints held him down at wrist and ankle. A strap crossed his chest. His right nostril – the only one not blocked – hooted as he inhaled. His whole head throbbed, his face bones swollen and tender. He was fairly sure his nose was broken. The room was cool but not cold. He wore his civilian clothes and, under him, a rubber mackintosh sheet squeaked when he moved. Which wasn't right. There should be hospital linens on the mattress. Under his rump, he could feel the copy of *Slaughterhouse-Five* in his back pocket.

The room was a double-occupant room, with enough space for two hospital beds and for medical staff to move around them. A counter with a sink, sterilising dispensers, countertop plastic drawers and a rack of folded scrubs, latex gloves, masks, tubing – you name it – all of it organised and labelled. There were also three machines – giving off the occasional beep or click – stacked on to rolling trolleys.

Sol was stretched out on the adjacent bed, similarly secured with restraints. He lay motionless, his chest rising and falling with his breathing. Jackson called his name but got no response.

He strained at the wrists, kicked at the foot restraints, but nothing budged.

A stampede of running feet thundered along the corridor outside the room and Jackson froze, lifting his head off the pillow, body shaking and tensed as more footsteps rushed past the door. Fraught voices accompanied them, fading as they continued on their way, discernible words lost in the confusion.

Distantly, he heard cries of pain and panic.

Are we in the Emergency Department?

He didn't know, but none of this felt right.

Of course it doesn't. You're strapped to a bed.

The door to the corridor opened and the noises grew louder, less like hospital sounds and more like a prison cellblock in the middle of a riot. Birdy slipped in and closed the door behind him.

'You definitely know everything's gone to crap when the psych ward turns out to be the least crazy part of the hospital.'

Birdy was a mess, his hair hanging in oily strands, blood staining the smock of his uniform. Both eyes were swollen and an unsightly ink spill discoloured his thickened nose and darkened his eye sockets.

First, he went to the man who was responsible for his injuries and checked the straps holding Sol down. He slapped Sol across the face, a hard smack that jerked Sol's head. It elicited no response. He was completely out of it.

'What's going on out there?' Jackson asked.

Birdy stepped across to Jackson's bed. 'Everyone's lost their minds, that's what.' His stiff smile pushed his swollen face into new and interesting shapes. He moved up the gurney, tugging at Jackson's ankles and arms, ensuring his restraints were tight. 'Well, *some* have lost their minds. The rest of us are just getting dragged down with them.'

'I don't understand.'

'"I don't understand,"' Birdy mocked, and yanked hard on

the strap over Jackson's chest, jolting the bed. He leaned in and Jackson smelled cigarettes and spearmint gum on his breath, caught the chemical whiff of hair gel. 'Of course you don't understand. You and your friends have been living in the land of Monopoly and Checkers, dribbling down your fronts and *duh-duh*ing at each other. You don't know *anything* about what's been going on.'

Birdy wasn't giving him enough credit.

'Are you hearing one, too?' Jackson asked quietly. 'Is a voice telling you to do this?'

Birdy let go of the chest strap and straightened. He smoothed Jackson's shirt down for him. 'It's funny how fast it's all happened. How quickly people have given up. Makes you wonder, doesn't it? Whether we've been waiting for an excuse like this to turn on each other. *Two* weeks. That's it. Barely any time at all. Goes to show you never really know anyone. Not deep down. Not where it counts. Every day, we put on our masks. We go to work, we go home, we open our mouths and plaster smiles on our faces, when all we want to do is scream and giggle. Do you have any idea *how much* I wanted to pound my keys into your face that day outside the nurses' station? Just pound and pound until there was nothing left but ground beef. Of course you didn't. Because I wore my mask, like everybody else. The only people who don't are you and the rest of your kind on that piss-stained ward. Throwing your hissy fits. Bawling and spitting. Never knew how good you had it, even as you wallowed in your own shit.

'Well, you're not alone now. Everyone's masks have slipped and you can see all the nasty stuff that's been hiding underneath. It's terrifying, too. Believe me.' Birdy's eyes burned. With fear and a wild liberation. It didn't matter whether Birdy heard a voice or not – he'd taken his mask off.

He's going to kill us.

'I can help you,' Jackson said, biting down on the panic

slowly cramming its way into his throat. 'Whatever's going on, I can help.'

Birdy patted him on the chest and smiled again. Jackson had never seen him smile so much. 'No one needs another crazy bastard on the loose.'

Birdy turned to one of the machines and picked up a sprouting of white cabling with electrodes dangling from their ends. 'We wouldn't usually restrain you for this,' Birdy explained, as if Jackson were a normal patient on any normal day. 'We'd have shot you full of muscle relaxants by now.' Castors clattered as he busied himself with wheeling the trolley closer. 'You'd have heart-monitor electrodes, blood-pressure cuffs, oxygen levels going – the whole shebang. But we'll leave all that stuff for today. Today, we're going to be pioneers, you and me.'

'Where's Abernathy?' Jackson asked, not because he expected the guy to have an answer but because distraction might be his only option.

'Gone.' The delivery was flat. 'Same as the rest of your friends. Apart from good old Sol here. Swarmed out like rats from a flooded tunnel. Rosie would've been *so* mad. If she hadn't already bled out on the floor, that is.' Birdy laughed and placed an electrode on each of Jackson's temples. 'They'd normally measure placements for these, too, but you don't mind if we miss that step, do you?' A warm gust of air bathed the top of Jackson's head when Birdy chuckled, and a cheerful, smiling Birdy was not a Birdy that Jackson liked. Not even a little.

He tried again. 'Look, you don't have to do this. Just let Sol go, okay? He didn't know what he was doing. Abernathy will—'

'Saying her name won't bring her rushing in here to save you. You need to accept the fact that she abandoned you, like she does everybody. She doesn't care about you or me or anyone else.'

There's something there. Keep talking.

Jackson felt it, too. 'I'm sure she—'

'She's another one, with her mask and her plastered-on smiles. Don't think you know her – no one knows her. She plays people. Tells you what you want to hear so you'll give her what she wants. Cigarettes. Chocolate. Books for *him*.' His lip curled as he nodded towards Sol. 'She whispers in your ear, slides you a touch, makes out she likes you. But it's all on *her* terms. She never *gives* you anything. She's crazy, just like the rest of you, but the difference with her is she's clever with it.'

He was right. Abernathy *was* clever. She had an uncanny ability to know what buttons to push to get a reaction.

Exactly like she does to Mr Bird.

One time, when Pip had become hysterical over discovering her pet goldfish dead and floating in its bowl, Abernathy had pinned the woman down and held a pillow over her face until she'd stopped screaming. Abernathy didn't understand why Pip was so upset, nor did she care. All she cared about was the amount of noise she was making.

She bites people's ears off. She's a psychopath.

He didn't agree with that. Abernathy cared about what happened to him, to Sol.

We're not her friends.

Maybe not, but she placed some value on them.

Because it suits her needs.

Two more electrodes were placed on the crown of Jackson's head. He pulled on his restraints again, pulled until the bed groaned and the rubber sheet squeaked, but it did no good.

'You were scheduled for treatment today,' Birdy said. A flick of a switch and an electronic alert sounded. 'And as I'm still technically employed by St Louis Hospital, it's only fair and right I fulfil my contractual obligations.'

But Jackson wasn't listening. Something danced at the edges of his thoughts, something tantalisingly out of reach.

'I want you to know,' Birdy continued, looking down at

him, 'that even when playing her games, and poking her fun, I enjoyed her. She was a challenge and I appreciated that. But now she's gone and all I have left is you. So, are you ready?'

Button-pushing. *That* was it. For Birdy, he had a big red button with Abernathy's name written all over it, and that was something Jackson could use.

'It's not only that she doesn't care about you,' Jackson said, staring back up at him. 'You're nothing to her. Not even a smear of bug guts on her windshield. I bet she's already forgotten you exist.'

The bruising on Birdy's face darkened his eyes, turned them into obsidian.

'We don't call you Birdy because of your name, you know. We call you it because you're this sad, puffed-up little bird that spends its time strutting around, not realising its wings have withered down to stumps. You were never going to leave this place. You were never going to mean anything to anyone, least of all her.'

There was truth in Jackson's words and Birdy knew it. Even as Jackson came and went, came and went, Birdy remained. An orderly forever walking his rounds, going nowhere.

Jackson lifted his head off the gurney, moving into Birdy's personal space. 'Even with all the dribblers and bed-wetters, you've always been the most pathetic person on that ward, and everyone knows it.'

Jackson expected fists and blows to rain down on him – a chance to maybe snap at Birdy's face with his teeth or bite off a finger – but instead Jackson got his head shoved back into the mattress and a gum guard mashed into his mouth. Thumbs dug into the hinges of his jaw as Birdy prised his teeth apart to receive it.

'No more words out of you,' he grunted, working the mouthpiece into place.

Jackson gagged. It tasted of latex.

'We don't want you biting your tongue off now, do we? Even if it would be fun to see you drown in your own blood. We don't want it to be so quick.' Teeth gritted, gelled hair in his eyes, Birdy finished and backed away to a machine that whirred above Jackson's head.

Jackson bucked and yelled, mouth stoppered by the gumshield. The gurney clanked. The handrails shook. He'd never been able to confess to Abernathy that he'd been the one to ask for ECT, that he'd *wanted* to be treated. She'd mocked and teased him, counting down the days, not knowing he'd been counting the days with her, full of trepidation, yes, but also full of hope. He'd wanted to get better, but this wasn't what he—

His yell cut off as a seizure strangled him, a grip that tightened every cord in his body. His hands balled into fists. His toes curled inward. All the muscles in his body contracted and pulled tight. He strummed like a guitar string.

It came in pulses that drubbed him against the bed. He wasn't aware of his head arching back, his chest and hips rising off the mattress, the ligaments in his neck standing clear of his skin. His mouth pulled wide around the gum guard and his eyes scrunched closed so tightly his face creased into someone his own mother wouldn't recognise.

The current ceased and he dropped to the bed, panting through his sobs. Tears rolled down his temples, trickled into his ears. His heart palpitated so fast all he could hear was the humming of his blood, feel it throb through his eyes and pulse in his head.

'Wow.' Birdy breathed a laugh.

Do something! For God's sake, do anything!

The voice sounded weaker, fainter, the loudness of his own body drowning it out.

Stop him or he'll kill us!

Jackson tried to speak but nothing came out.

'What?' Birdy cupped a hand around his ear. 'I didn't catch that.'

He mumbled something, not a single syllable of it decipherable.

'You want another blast? Is that what you said?'

'*Please* . . .' Jackson tried to struggle but all his strength was gone. His bones felt hollowed out. His gut was emptied of organs. His fingertips and toes tingled with numbness; they were disappearing, fading from the edges of him.

No!

All pleas were cut off with an instantaneous, agonising clench of muscles. The world crackled white-hot and the gum shield creaked between his teeth, synapses firing so fast his lids fluttered and his eyes wrenched up into his head. And with a final electric *SNAP*, something broke inside him and he was gone, he was gone, he was gone.

LETTER #116

September 22, Friday

My new friend,

Do you remember when I wrote this? We are in a thrift store – you, me, Albus – and a mama bear paid us a visit. She stared at us through the window for so long I thought she would come inside and eat us. Do you remember? I didn't know your real name then, and I doubt I know it now, as you read this, but I hope that someday you'll share it with me. But until that day comes, I will tell you one of my secrets in return.

I know another name for you.

We all have more than one, don't we? I am Ruby, but I am also Red. I was Gummy Bear to my dad and Bee to my brother when he was little, because that's all he could say. We wear different names for different people. We swap and change depending on who we're with and where we are. You're now this person because it fits the world we find ourselves in, because you have suffered. And not suffered like the rest of us, watching our loved ones die, discovering we are not alone with our thoughts any longer. No, you had something ripped from you long before the world came crashing down around us. And in losing it, you lost parts of yourself, too. Parts you've let fall away like empty water-bags on a long, arduous trek through the desert. So, let me say another name to you, to see if it will help you discover a new part of yourself.

Agur.

It won't mean anything to you yet, I know. Agur is a funny name, isn't it? But it's an important one. You see, we were meant to meet, here in this place, at this moment. We were meant to touch each other's lives and, in so doing, alter the paths we walk. Already our meeting has changed our destinies. You have changed my destiny. All it takes is a small divot in the earth to alter the course of trickling water. A rivulet can widen and become a stream, and a stream can run all the way to join the ocean.

I'm getting carried away with my analogies, so let me tell you two things. First, those moments when you see a colour that dances brightly, or a number that sings in perfect pitch — heed them. They mean something to you, if to no one else. And that makes them important. Don't be afraid to trust your instincts.

Second, there is an Inn on the East Coast. It will welcome you when you're ready. Not now, of course. Not yet. You won't need it yet. But if you are ever lost and don't know which way to turn, it will be there, waiting. Albus and I will be waiting. It's beautiful, you'll see. Even when the storms roll in and the thunder shivers through your bones — and the waves crash and beat the sand black — there is a peace that I've never experienced anywhere else. There are warm beds and fresh mussels hand-picked from the beach. We have a vegetable garden and lemon trees. Lemons! Can you believe it? It's funny, but I think I miss lemons almost as much as I miss anything else.

Come see us there. Come visit if you're ever lost.
Your friend, always,
Ruby

PART ONE

The Man Who Buried Himself

CHAPTER 1

Lightning

The world shivered.

No, that was wrong. *He* was the one who shivered, and the grass and the sky and the earth shivered with him.

He was caked in mud from boots to hair, as if he'd been born of the earth, a ready-made golem. He didn't remember falling into the long grass, but he did remember the ear-ripping *snap* as the sky lit up in a detonation of electricity, the power of it running hot through the ground beneath him, through *him*. He hummed with static. He hadn't seen where the lightning struck but it must have been near; he fought to breathe the heavy, soupy air that carried the scent of scorched ozone and fire-lit wood. A burning river seared down his windpipe to his tenderised lungs.

Rain had soaked through his shirt, his pants. They weighted him down, water and mud making a cast of him where he lay on his back. The heat of discharged electricity was gone. The grass was cold. Everywhere was cold. The world shivered.

His throat. Jesus, his throat.

He opened his mouth and rainwater hit his greedy tongue. He lapped at the moisture around his mouth. It wasn't enough.

A whisper brushed by his ear and his head jerked around, fear skittering inside him, rattling his bones.

A house. There. Across the lawn. A single Gothic-style turret jutting skyward. Black arachnid-eyed windows watched him. The rain made a monotonous thrumming on the roof's shingles, water flooding along the guttering and spilling down pipes with phlegm-choked gurgles.

Water. Shelter.

How did he get outside?

He didn't know.

Angry thunder rumbled over him, building to a roar so terrible he clapped his hands over his ears. A muscle ticked in his thigh. A prod. *Get up*, it said. He dragged his feet free from their muddy graves, his stomach muscles weak, straining. His cold fingers snatched at the long, toughened grass, gripped on, pulled himself on to his side. Pain exploded and the world stopped shivering and lit up in a second apocalyptic flash. He screwed his eyes shut, everything burning red behind his eyelids, and with the lightning came words that crackled and snapped, running over each other so that it all became one terrible sound.

BURNING MADNESS DEATH.

He was on his stomach, sobbing into the earth, grass shredded in his fists, the words eating into him. Rabid jaws clamped tight to the back of his head. He groaned in agony as his skull cracked open, bone creaking apart to reveal the glistening mass beneath. And then the writhing pain switched off. A flash as swift as the lightning itself.

His mouth gaped open as he collected his breaths, gathered them close and wiped snot from his lip. Shaking fingers touched the place behind his ear. The spot was spongy-soft, painful, but mercifully whole.

He began to mindlessly crawl, elbows digging, his belly slithering. Hands gripped grass and released, gripped and released. After hours of this, solid foundations met his groping searches.

Hooking fingers into windowsills and doorframes, he fought his way higher, sliding up the wall to the second floor, a giant growing taller as his eyes moved past the upper-storey windows. His legs jittered so much he locked his knees and threw his arms around the turret.

A colossus, he looked down at the yard from his lofty height, eyes dropping to the child's playhouse he clung to. It was a perfect replica, in every scaled-down detail, of the owner's house, which hulked like a mountain a thousand miles away across the backyard.

He may have laughed, then.

A thousand miles later, he reached the back corner of the full-sized house and didn't recall a single step of the journey. He dropped to his knees beside the gushing rain-pipe and stuck his mouth under the spout and drank and drank and drank.

Another scuttle of a whisper.

His head came up, a nocturnal animal caught in the trash cans. The world's shivering came in waves. He could make out a trail of mud leading back to a mound of earth and a half-canted cross, its short beam resting on the ground. It looked like an X.

X marks the spot.

Something tapped on a locked door inside his head – *rap rap rap* – wanting to be let in.

Keeping watch on that mound of dirt, he felt something peel away from his chest, a shifting weight that slid down his belly to his waist, trapped in his shirt. He stuck a hand inside and pulled out a dirt-streaked book. On its black-and-green cover was a man in a tall hat (more raps knocked in his head).

He flung the book away as if it burned.

He woke up, curled on his side in a kitchen. He was dry. The shivers had passed. His head on the tiles, a forest of chair and table legs sprouted from the floor in front of him. When he moved, his clothes cracked and mud fell away. He pushed himself up to sit with his back against the wall, breathless and feeble. Found himself staring at a stove. Its cast–iron door stood open, its dark hole (where wood and kindling would be stacked) stared back.

Rap rap rap.

'Go . . . away,' he whispered, voice raspy.

It can't, something whispered back. *It wants you to open up.*

He wrenched his eyes from the stove and, under the cupboard nearest him, spotted something rolled against the skirting board. He found the energy to slowly scoot over and reach an arm under the cabinet. He held his prize stupidly in his lap.

A can of vegetable soup.

A few minutes of scraping boots, clanking metal and grunting effort later and he was at the stove. Fuel had already been piled in its belly.

Left-front pocket.

There, he found a Zippo lighter.

Another space of time later, as the soup began to bubble in a saucepan, it came again.

Rap-rap-rap-rap-rap.

He stubbornly ignored the tapping in his head and pulled himself up to slump at the kitchen table. He slurped hot soup, spoon clattering against his teeth as it rattled its way in.

It's long past time you opened that door, Pilgrim.

The rapping stopped.

CHAPTER 2

Pilgrim

The storm had moved off to the north, carrying the rain with it. An earthy smell – of grass and soil, dampness and wood – hung heavy in the air. He found he could breathe only in shallow inhalations, his lungs tight and wheezy as if he were recovering from a bad chest cold. When he lifted his face to the sky, he was met with a grey blanket of clouds. Everything was quiet but for the *drip-drip-drip* of water and the distant underground rush of flooding sewers. No cars, no people talking, no dogs barking.

The soup and rainwater he'd collected from the gushing pipe had steadied him, allowed him to walk in an almost straight line, but the world around him remained insubstantial, fluid; it shifted and moved in unexpected ways, making him misstep and curse.

The mound of earth waited for him in the centre of the yard.

'What was I doing?'

Digging for treasure.

God, it sounded so much like him, that voice in his head. There was a niggling sense of familiarity, and that made him wary. Because it *wasn't* him. It was something separate and inexplicable.

'I wasn't talking to you,' Pilgrim said.

He stepped down off the back porch, gripping the railing for support. The toppled wooden X, which he could now see was constructed from two chair legs lashed together, drew him closer. Hand out, his fingers met and traced the rough edging of the whittled markings, wanting to memorise them.

A rap didn't come this time, but a scratching did, as if whatever had been tapping at the inside of his skull was no longer content to politely knock; it would find its way in, even if it had to claw its way to do it.

He was so tired, and not just in his body. He was deep-down weary in the place his soul resided, if such a place existed. He was tired of trying to make sense of everything, tired of being lost. The suspicion that he'd done all of this before, that he was going round and round in hamster-like circles, was as strong as his sense of displacement. He was a person with one step outside of time and one step outside of himself, too.

Whose house was this? What had happened here? Everything was so jumbled. The fractured, abstract images that linked disjointedly in his mind mocked him, as if the lightning had lit up pathways of synapses in his brain and burnt them out in a flash. But, most of all, he was tired of the constant, nagging need to *go*. The act of not moving tugged at him like a kite tugged at its string. He sailed high with nothing but the wind for company and nothing to see for miles and miles. He didn't know where to go because he couldn't remember where he'd been. But going was the only thing that made sense to him. To stay still was to invite danger.

There was no rest for the wicked. Wasn't that what they said?

You need to let me help you. It sounded frustrated with him, angry at his resistance. *You're not alone. You haven't been alone for a long time.*

A tremble of something – not quite fear but close enough to be called its kin – ghosted through him.

'Who are you?' Pilgrim didn't know if he was asking himself that question or the voice.

You had a name for me once.

He laughed at the absurdity of it all. This must be what it felt like to go mad. Even worse, he couldn't muster the energy to care.

Sucking in a breath, Pilgrim gingerly lowered himself to sit at the edge of the ploughed and churned earth, teeth gritted at the stab of pain at the top of his chest. His hand went inside his shirt and he fingered the tender area below his collarbone. The skin there was hot, painful, thinly stretched and pulled taut. Earlier, sitting at the kitchen table, with the empty saucepan pushed aside and his back warmed by the stove, he had inspected the wound and found it to be healing nicely, no signs of infection. He recognised it as a gunshot wound, felt the sting and pull of tight and healing flesh on the back of his shoulder and knew the projectile had exited his body. It made him wonder if he'd experienced gunshot wounds before.

You've always been good at this, you know.

Pilgrim nudged at a heavy slab of mud with one boot, pushing at it, over and over, picking at it like a scab. 'At what?'

Hiding from yourself. What exactly are you afraid of finding? Nothing can be worse than what the voices made people do. Nothing can be worse than what you've seen these past seven years. Unimaginable things. Parents throwing children from rooftops. Brothers hacking brothers to pieces. So much death and fear, with no one to trust and nowhere to run. What can possibly be worse?

If it expected Pilgrim to have an answer, it would be waiting a long time. Instead, he pushed his toe into the side wall of the grave, watching as the mud sloughed away. He kept nudging, watching more collapse under the pressure of his foot, and found himself staring at tassels. Small, but definitely tassels. Like those on a scarf.

He didn't move for the longest time. The tassels were stuck

to the cleanly sheered-off wall, their colour lost in the smeared brown of wet soil, but something inside him knew they had once been red.

Red.

Red.

Red. The same red as the backdrop of his eyelids as lightning raged across the sky.

BURNING MADNESS DEATH.

He didn't remember moving, but the next thing he knew he was digging frantically, scooping great clay-like clumps out of his way, leaving scored caveman marks in the mud. He worked through the tearing pain in his shoulder, the lung-deep ache in his chest. And then his hands hit something that wasn't mud. They groped over something hard and stiff beneath the damp fabric of the scarf. He found its tasselled edge and pulled it aside and came face to face with a pale, sunken-cheeked young woman.

Red is dead.

'Who *are* you?' he demanded again, wheeling around to search the yard. 'What do you want?'

I want to help.

'You don't. No one does.'

I do. You heard it, same as I did. The words in the lightning.

Pilgrim shook his head, stubborn and silent. He'd heard nothing his delirious mind hadn't made up.

Burning, it said. *Madness. Death.*

His jaw clenched, pain stabbing his head. 'Don't you ever shut up?'

Not when you need to listen. There was pain in those words. Suffering. You heard it.

'Pain and suffering are nothing new.' Pilgrim stared down at the hole he'd made, at the messy tunnel he'd dug to the dead woman's face.

You're right, they're not. But that lightning didn't strike down from

84

the heavens, Pilgrim. I can still feel where it ripped through the air, like a burnt after-image. It's fading now, ghostly, but it's there, leading back to someplace. To someone.

He shook his head. He didn't want to hear this.

You don't get to hide from this any more. Neither of us do. I wish we could, I really do, but there's work to do. Work she started.

And as easy as that, the dead woman's name was on his lips. And with it came a howling gale that ripped through the door in his mind, leaving nothing but kindling in its wake.

Ruby, the voice breathed, a darkly intimate whisper in his ear. *See? I told you you were digging for treasure.*

Pilgrim fell to his knees in the mud and touched her cheek. It was stiff. Cold. The pain in his head sunk down to his chest, a ball of anguish so raw it felt like swallowing thorns.

Was this what grief felt like?

He brought his fingers to her mouth and, not knowing why, he peeled back her lips. Her gums were black, ravaged. Mulchy holes gaped where her teeth had been.

Pulled out. The voice sounded sad.

'What happened to her?'

The world happened to her, came the reply.

'I knew her.'

Yes. A while ago, but she found her way back to you.

The memory of her was patchy, imperfect, a faded and blotchy picture that had been left out on a sunny windowsill, its colours bleached from its palette. She was older, beaten in, a washed-out version of the young woman he'd met. He'd been standing outside a . . . store of some kind. A Walgreens? Yes, a Walgreens. He was wearing a fleece-lined trapper hat he'd looted from inside. It was cold in Wisconsin that late in the season and he never would have spotted her if he hadn't paused to tilt his face to the sun. Two bedraggled and lost souls shambling into view, going as far as the wide six-lane main street and stopping beside a short flagpole. The pole had been jammed randomly into the sidewalk, apropos of nothing, its ragged and dirty Stars and Stripes banner hoisted but flying for no one. Pilgrim had wondered if it had been placed there before or after all the killing.

He'd rested his hand on his holstered gun as the girl's head turned towards him. She stilled when their eyes met. And then she'd raised her hand, not exactly in greeting but in acknowledgement, of one human to another. Pilgrim had stared at her raised palm, at the sunshine that seemed to glow through her fingertips – like when you were a kid and pressed a flashlight to your hand and your skin glowed transparent, revealing the veins and capillaries hidden within, and there was wonder in the bend of your head, in the shine of your eye, because you never knew that they ran there, all those rivers and tributaries on the inside of your body – and he had nodded to her, and that was that.

Later, Ruby had offered that same hand to him, introducing herself and her brother Albus. Stuck her hand right out as if there were some civility left in the world and he'd best well acknowledge it. It had amused and irked Pilgrim in equal measure.

'I shook her hand,' he said out loud, staring at Ruby's dead and ravaged face. He didn't know why that memory had returned to him, knocked loose from his broken head and shaken free. It felt like a long time ago. He'd been a different person.

She disarmed you. It doesn't happen very often.

'You talk as if you know me.'

I know you about as well as you know yourself.

Pilgrim snorted softly, bitterly. 'Not much, then.'

For now. It's something we'll have to work on, it said, as if not wanting to get embroiled in the particulars of it right now.

Looking down at Ruby, Pilgrim didn't know exactly how long it had been since he'd first shaken her hand, but she'd suffered in the intervening years.

'What happened to you?' he murmured, and the blank it drew (and the silence from the voice inside his head) brought some solace, because he hoped it meant he'd played no part in what had befallen her.

He replaced the red scarf, covering her face, and reburied her. When he was done, he rested a hand on the mound and left it there until his muscles ached from cold and his teeth chattered.

He clambered clumsily out of the mud, a drunkard on his way home after a night filling his belly with cheap, burning liquor. He righted the slanted home-made cross so that it stood straight and true, jamming it back into the soil over her grave.

To the north, thunder rumbled, a rolling drumbeat that seemed to reverberate through the earth. The sky had darkened to dusk-red while Pilgrim wasn't watching. It flashed white as lightning burst a ragged seam across the heavens. Something tightened in his gut. It felt like expectation.

Listen, the sky seemed to whisper, and the air trembled, a gust of wind rippling across the grass to meet him, rocking him back on his heels. It flattened his shirt to his body.

You feel it. The storm, the voice said, and Pilgrim knew it didn't mean the weather. *People you love will die. People like Ruby.*

'Love,' he said, the word an ill fit in his mouth.

We can't run, it said.

He frowned, annoyed by the assumption that he would. 'No one's running.'

Good. Because I go where you go. You know that book you threw?

The change of subject confused him.

You should find it, it said.

'Why?'

Because it was given to you. And you shouldn't throw away gifts.

Pilgrim considered leaving the book where it lay, but the pettiness of the act didn't sit right with him.

It didn't take long to find it, the book's weight indenting the grass and marking its place. He rubbed his palm across the green-

and-black cover, smearing the dirt but clearing enough away to see the title. The words jagged to the right, dodging his attempts at reading them.

He flicked through the pages, the font ant-small and making his left eye ache. He stopped on the title page and stared. Handwriting. He brought the page close to his face, eyes following the dips and swirls of the pencil strokes. He traced a finger over them, his head hurting enough to make his eyes squint, but it was no use. The words wouldn't align.

'Can you read it?' he asked.

You broke your ability to read, and I can't use what's broken.

He grunted. Of course not. That'd be far too easy. Snapping the book closed, he slid it into the back pocket of his stiffened, mud-dried pants with some difficulty. 'Do you at least know who gave it to me?'

The same girl who wrote the note.

'Jesus. You're about as helpful as a bullet to the head.'

Pilgrim sensed its surprise, and also a faint hint of amusement.

You probably shouldn't joke about such things.

'Why give me a book if I can't read it?'

Because she knows you loved books, and she loves you.

Of its own accord, Pilgrim's hand went to his back pocket again, fingers brushing over the book's edge. A pulse of warmth entered his fingers at the touch and he quickly curled them into a fist, pulling them away.

She's the same as us. She hears a voice, just like you hear me.

Pilgrim didn't say anything. He gazed towards the house, its hulking presence more than the sum of its tiles and bricks and mortar. It breathed with him, wood and plaster creaking as it swelled and shrunk, breathed in and breathed out.

She'll end up like Ruby if we can't stop it.

'Stop what?' he murmured.

The storm. *Are your ears plugged up? You know: Burning, Madness, De—*

'I get the picture.' The pulse of warmth in Pilgrim's fingers had receded. Now he felt only cold and distant. 'Do you know where to go?'

You feel it riding your back, don't you? That urge to leave, to move.

'Where?' he demanded.

North, and as it said it, Pilgrim became aware of a dark, silent figure at the periphery of his vision, standing beside Ruby's grave. The figure was short, slim, girl-sized, and Pilgrim kept his head very still, even though a part of him knew it had to be the grave marker he'd righted and shoved back into the earth. Its arm was raised, its finger pointing, and he knew in which direction it was pointing him.

North, the voice said again. *Someone needs us there.*

CHAPTER 3

Haunted

Pilgrim found clean clothes in one of the upstairs bedrooms. The fit was a size too large but it wasn't anything that couldn't be fixed with an extra cinch of a belt. As he went through the house, rain lashing the windows and burbling down drainpipes, he found signs of recent habitation: balled-up clothes in the corners of rooms, empty food containers, wrinkled bedclothes, even nail clippings in the basin in the bathroom off the master bedroom.

Downstairs in the entrance hall he found blood smeared across the dark wooden floor. The blood was old but it began to glisten anew as he studied it, a wet rivulet trickling free to creep a slow, winding course towards his boot. Pilgrim eased his foot back before it could make contact, and in that single step the blood dried and browned and was old again. It was nowhere near his boot and he felt foolish for thinking it had been.

Running his palm over the smooth, varnished antique oak panelling, he discovered a lodged bullet. He dug it out and held it up to the sepia light filtering through the decorative glass above the main door. A dry clicking sound came from behind him and he recognised it for what it was – the hammer of a gun cocking. He turned slowly and was met with an empty foyer. Nothing waited for him but floating dust.

And me.

Pilgrim rubbed his aching eyes. Opened them. He wandered to the open doorway leading into the sitting room. No one was there. He was alone.

Holding the expended bullet up to catch what little light remained, he studied the blunt-nosed, squashed piece of metal. He couldn't say for sure it was the one that had passed through him but he felt a strong affinity to it, as if he recognised its face but couldn't recall the place or time they'd met. He put the bullet in his shirt pocket.

Turning a full circle in the middle of the foyer, he stopped when he faced a tall-backed chair and an old-fashioned telephone side-table.

Ruby sat there.

Pilgrim didn't say her name but mouthed it, making the shape with his lips.

There was a depth of feeling attached to her, but he remembered little more than a cold Wisconsin town, her raised hand and the silence of her brother, who hadn't uttered a single word, content to let his sister speak for them.

Albus. His name's Albus. Keep up.

Pilgrim bit down on a retort.

But their names solidified the images of them in his head, that one small act of recall sending a cramp of nausea through his gut. The scratching sensation took up on the inside of his skull again and a wave of vertigo forced him to lean against the stair's bannister. An unsettling weakness near buckled his knees.

Enough for now.

As soon as Pilgrim turned his mind from them, the trembling in his legs lessened.

Without consciously thinking about it, he went to the kitchen and to the key rack by the door. There, he plucked a set of keys from a hook and exited the house into the backyard.

Where're we going? It was innocently curious, but Pilgrim wasn't fooled.

Gratified that some things could remain his and his alone, he walked, far more steadily than he had up to that point, across the grass to the gate that connected to the back alley. He was without a weapon – which was foolish, he knew – but he didn't have far to go. Twenty yards along the alleyway and he turned into the neighbouring property, his feet taking him to a double garage.

A familiar smell of gasoline, engine oil and tyre rubber welcomed him as he entered. He had been in here before. The shelves and workbenches lining the perimeter of the garage were filled with all manner of work tools. The drawers overflowed with nuts and bolts and every mechanical part a petrol-head could ever need. And there, past the empty bay where another vehicle once sat, was a 1970 Dodge Charger. It was far from showroom condition.

The voice sounded cautious when it said, *We* are *heading north, aren't we? We're needed there, I'm sure of it. You aren't running?*

Wasn't it the same thing? It all meant leaving, moving, *doing*. Anywhere was better than here, and going was always better than staying.

'I told you,' Pilgrim said. 'No one's running.'

He spent the better part of a day getting the car ready. He did a final check of the house before they left. He ascended the first flight of stairs, having company for the climb, a new family picture greeting him on each of the fourteen steps. A man and woman smiling together; the man alone; the woman holding a baby not much past six months old. He didn't look too closely at them. Up another floor he went, climbing into the tower, and there he discovered a nest filled with dirty children's clothing, stuffed animals and chalk sketches of wildlife on the walls. In the far corner a drawing of a creature crouched, chalked in white on the dark wood wainscoting. Short and stocky-limbed, it was a hairless thing with big milky eyes that watched Pilgrim while he searched.

He ran fingers over a small section of wall where fingernail scratches had scored the wood. Bending close, he made out faint perpendicular lines. He pressed and heard a *click* and a secret panel opened. Inside, food cans (six in total), a photograph and a small cache of ammunition: .38 calibre. It was a shame he had no gun, but he took the cartridges anyway.

In the photo a family of women stood side by side on the front steps of this house. On the left, an older lady with greying hair had her arm wrapped around a kid in the middle, and the kid had her shoulder leant against the same broad-faced woman Pilgrim had seen in the framed photographs running up the staircase. The photographer had caught the broad-faced woman mid-laugh, her eyes crinkled up. Both her hands were wrapped around the kid's left one and she was holding it to the top of her distended belly. She was close to term, judging by her size, the unborn baby presumably the same six-month-old baby that Pilgrim had seen her with in the earlier picture.

It was a carefree family photo taken before the voices came. Which would make them all close to eight years older, if they were still alive.

Pilgrim stared at the photo, his attention catching on the kid. She looked to be around nine years of age, smirking with her eyes, mouth tipped up on one side. Her smiling eyes held secrets. He could see her lips move, forming his name, could almost hear it in his ear.

Pilgrim turned the photo over. Someone had written on the reverse, but the scrawl meant nothing to him. He folded the photograph in half and slipped it in his shirt pocket with the squashed bullet.

The white-chalked figure on the wall moved, subtly shifting to tilt its head in childlike inquisitiveness. Pilgrim didn't look at it. Looking at it would give it power.

Someone lived up here, the voice said, scratching for his attention.

From the corner of Pilgrim's eye, the chalk figure nodded in agreement.

The girl who gave you that book, she was here, too. She was looking for her family. It was pushing for a reaction, but it could push all it wanted. Pilgrim couldn't give what he didn't have.

'We lost her?' he said, because he couldn't help but ask.

No, she *lost* you. *I'm not a bully, Pilgrim, but tough love is love all the same. You need to dig all this stuff up. Just like you dug up Ruby.*

The clawing in the back of Pilgrim's head had abated, but it remained a constant source of aggravation. It was a creature that was desperate to dig its way out. He would need to feed it or else risk having it turn its claws inward, burrowing in instead of out, and who knew what damage that would cause?

'You said someone needed us if we go north. Is it her?'

A soft, thoughtful hum sounded in his ear. *All our roads lead back to her.*

Pilgrim grunted. It was a non-answer, and a mawkish one at that.

The chalk figure had returned to its original position, but its big eyes seemed to mock him. It was time to leave. This house was haunted.

It's not the house.

Pilgrim pretended not to hear.

CHAPTER 4

North

Pilgrim slept in the car when he wasn't driving. He slept more than he would have liked, his dreams filled with a red, pulsing static that ate into his head and ears so that all that lived inside him was a mad, boiling friction. Occasionally, the hushed roar of this red landscape would burst into a crackling so loud it would jerk him awake, and he would lie gasping and sweating in the back seat, blinking flashes of pain from his eyes.

The Dodge turned out to be a junker, lasting little more than two hundred miles. He put it down to the poor condition of the fuel he'd been forced to use. It stalled on him a few miles shy of Memphis, outside the once-famous Sun Studio. The streets were rain-slicked, humid, empty. The sky was amber. Storm weather. They were chasing it north.

From the trunk, Pilgrim lifted out the pack he'd filled with what little food he had left, a large bottle of boiled rainwater and the tool belt he'd taken from the neighbour's garage and rigged into a weapons belt. He shucked the pack on to his shoulders (folding a spare shirt under his injured shoulder to lessen the pressure). A modified nail-gun, fully loaded with six hundred nails, hung at his hip, along with a flat-head screwdriver that he'd filed sharp, and a hand-axe. He'd also picked up a box-cutter, which he'd slid into the top of his sock.

He was breathing more heavily than the activity warranted. His chest hurt.

He checked the street. Nobody. Good.

You can't ignore me for ever.

He hadn't spoken to the voice for nearly four hours. He'd taken a perverse sort of satisfaction in ignoring it.

Don't you have questions?

Of course he did. But the answers could easily be worse than his ignorance.

Some say knowledge is the key to the universe.

Pilgrim gave a soft, cynical snort. Sure it was. 'Have you always bugged me like this?'

It went quiet for a moment, either through offence or because it was considering its answer. *In one form or another. You remember what you used to call me?*

He did. It had snuck its way into his consciousness when he'd been driving, his mind drifting and distracted as his eyes followed the markings on the road. 'I'm not very original,' he muttered.

No, you're not. But we all have our strengths. Yours are giving me the silent treatment and a complete inability to remember anything of actual use.

Pilgrim shut the trunk lid with more force than was necessary. He gave the street another scan and went to the open driver's door.

I like the name Voice, it said. *It's simple. Self-explanatory.*

Hearing it say its name made Pilgrim's head hurt, a pain originating at the tender, fluid-filled bump behind his ear. So far, he had avoided touching it again. He pressed a palm over his left eye when it gave a dull, aching throb. Uneasiness stirred, a trapped feeling inside his chest as though fingers had hooked themselves into his ribcage and were pulling it down. His lungs slowly compressed, his breaths cutting short.

(Coldness. Darkness. Can't see, can't move, can't breathe.

Can't breathe. The weight, God, the weight, it's too much, it's crushing. There's no air. *No air*.)

Are you okay?

Pilgrim inhaled harshly, his chest rattling, and the fingers released their hold on his ribs. The sensation of being drowned in a weighted, ear-filled silence lessened a little. His arm was inside the Dodge, fingers wrapped too tightly around the ignition keys, their grated edges digging into the meat of his palm. But the pain was good. He squeezed tighter and felt the metal bite.

He abruptly let go, leaving the key dangling from the ignition, and started walking, fast, checking over his shoulder as he went. His feet made the barest of sounds, as if he were not really there, a man with no substance. Hollowed out and empty.

This is what being dead feels like, he thought. Having nothing in your head but ghosts. Memories make a person – if you can't remember who you were or who you are or who you want to be, then you're no one.

His legs felt weak under the heft of the pack and the tool belt. The nail-gun bumped his thigh on every stride. He broke his silence to wheeze a cough and had to stop to catch his breath, placing a hand on the wall beside him. The fast beat of his heart knocked into his breastbone, rocking him where he stood.

Calm down, Voice said, and Pilgrim didn't like the authority hiding under its concern, the belief that it could issue orders. *Your pulse rate is going crazy.*

So am I, he thought. God help me, so am I.

An invisible hand, the fingers of which had been latched on to his ribs, moved up to close over his throat. They squeezed and his breaths turned ragged, whistling as he inhaled.

Take it easy. Pilgrim? Do you hear me?

But he wasn't listening. He couldn't. The pounding in his head was too loud, the desperate sucking of his breaths all-consuming. There wasn't enough air, he couldn't draw it in fast enough, and he was drowning, a darkness rising up to swallow him like the oceans had once swallowed so many, tens of thousands of people walking or running or falling into the cold, churning waves, leaving no trace that they had ever existed until they washed up days and weeks later to dot the beaches like so many grounded whales, to crowd under piers and logjam tributaries, to catch in the reeds along the banks. You couldn't breathe without inhaling the liquefied stench of corpses. It had taken years for the smell of death to dissipate.

He couldn't do this, not out here in the open.

He fumbled for his seat pocket, digging under the tool belt, and he yanked the paperback out, ripping its back cover. He held it in front of his face and it was mud-smeared and tattered, but none of that mattered. It was his; someone had left it for him, someone who *knew* him, and that meant something. It did.

He almost dropped it as his numb fingers pawed through the first few pages, and there it was. The handwriting. He couldn't read it, but he traced the lettering over and over, fingers trembling, and eventually, after a hundred and three seconds of struggling to breathe, his lungs cracked open and the hand around his throat loosened its grip and fell away. His pulse stuttered, stuttered, slowed.

He pressed the coolness of the cover to his brow and closed his eyes, and a thought hit him, one so pure and simple it was if a needle had been inserted straight into the core of his brain and a cleansing fluid injected. He opened his eyes and pinned the paperback flat open against the brick wall. Tracing his fingers over the final word of the handwritten message, he plucked out the folded photograph from his shirt pocket. Turning it over, he pressed it to the brick, too, holding book and picture side by side, eyes going back and forth, comparing that last word the writer had signed off with to the same five-letter word on the back of the photo. They were the same. A name.

He flicked the photo over and stared at the girl.

You know me, her playful eyes say to him.

He scanned the rest of the book's message in a rush, but the words remained illegible and he drew in a slow, painful breath, his fingers tightening in their need to throw, to tear, to hurt. On his exhalation, he forced his hands to relax.

He glanced up and down the street, head turning this way and that as he looked for movement. Any movement. This time he wasn't so pleased to find everything so still.

Beware the fury of a patient man.

Pilgrim stopped, gathered his words, lined them up in a neat little row. 'What's that supposed to mean?'

At the back of his head, behind his ear, Voice curled inward, a snail sliding a retreat into its shell.

'Now look who's running.'

It paused in its retreat. *No*, it said, and there was weariness there, maybe even sadness. *I have nowhere to go, and no one else to speak to. Unlike you.* And, with that, it tucked itself into silence, leaving Pilgrim alone in the empty street.

CHAPTER 5

Notes

'*H*ello?' Pilgrim called.

He wasn't in the habit of searching people out. He felt it in the reluctance in his bones, in the beat of hesitance before his shout. This wasn't who he was and not what he did. It would bring trouble, because people always brought trouble.

He passed under a cable car. It hung from its wires between ticket office and raised docking platform, where sightseers would climb a set of rickety steps to debark and board, riding it to the mountaintop. On a clear day, the vistas would be spectacular from up there. Postcard perfect. At intervals along the cabling a further three carriages dangled like unpicked and unwanted fruit. He wondered if people had been trapped inside when the power failed. They'd never get to see the views at the mountain's peak, and neither would he. Today, it was hidden by misty, low-hanging clouds.

Exhaling a long, measured breath, he slipped a hand under the shoulder strap of his pack and gently massaged his shoulder.

You shouldn't push yourself too hard.

'Thank you for the excellent advice.'

Sarcasm doesn't become you. Besides, I'm serious. That wound isn't that old.

The way Voice said it made Pilgrim pause. 'How old?'

Sixteen days, maybe. Eighteen at most.

Pilgrim's massaging fingers stopped. They rested on warm, unbroken skin. 'You lie.'

I do not. It sounded insulted. *Can we move out from under the cable car? I'm worried it might drop on our head.*

'That's impossible,' Pilgrim argued. 'The wound's practically healed.'

If Voice had the ability to shrug, Pilgrim figured it would be doing it. *I don't know what else to tell you.*

'You know who shot me?'

Voice didn't reply.

Pilgrim took three steps to the right, centring them directly under the rocking cable car and cloaking them in its shade.

You're such an asshole. Yes, okay? I know who shot you because you *know.*

A movement caught the corner of Pilgrim's eye and he turned to find a girl standing in the parking lot with him. She was small, thin, solemn-eyed. There was a familial resemblance to the girl in the photograph, but this kid was a little younger, with dark, curly hair. She held an antique-looking revolver, and she lifted it to point at his chest. Pilgrim watched her struggle, using both thumbs to pull back the stiff, cumbersome hammer. He heard the dry cocking of it, a sound that echoed in his ears.

His heart clenched. His hand came up. 'Wait.'

She didn't wait. She squeezed the trigger. A horrendous *BANG!* smacked his ears. A punch to his shoulder shoved him back a step. He grunted and clamped a hand to his shoulder, but it was unbloodied, uninjured, no fresh gunshot wound and no more pain than he was already feeling. When he looked up, the girl was gone. Not run away or hiding, simply vanished. No girl and no gunshot wound. Neither was real.

Above his head, the cable car rocked, nudged by the breeze, creaking on its wheeled mechanism.

'What . . .'

So many memories are so close, I can almost reach out and touch—
'Don't!'

There was a resounding silence in the back of his head. *No need to shout. Jeez.*

Pilgrim stood on a precipice, a dark, unknown pit yawning at his toes. He leaned over to peer into the pitch-black darkness and could see no bottom. A howling emptiness called out to him and a chill swarmed up his body because the pit wasn't empty, it lied; it was filled with everything he'd ever hidden from, everything he'd locked away. Every chest secured and chained and thrown into the deep depths of the ocean, each injury stitched and bandaged and forgotten after it had healed, every last grave he'd dug, the dirt piling higher than the next, and the next, growing as tall as a building, taller than a *city* of buildings, everything buried so deep he'd never have to look at them again. They all waited for him down in that bottomless pit, the place he had buried parts of himself, or others had buried parts for him. They waited to eat him alive and spit out the bones.

It's okay. We'll tread carefully.

Or not at all.

You've had a lifetime to hide, Pilgrim. And another seven long years added on top of that. Stop being a coward.

He expected anger to rear up at its words but instead he felt only shame. Another shift of movement at the corner of his eye and he turned, expecting to see a second ghost, another lost moment returned to haunt him. Instead a man stood there. A young man. Dark-skinned and dark-eyed. His hair curled around his ears, a great mop of it, so much it seemed to overrun his head.

'Hari?' Pilgrim said.

Hari? Voice repeated, curiosity hooking in its claws.

But the brief, flitting memory passed before it could catch hold. This was a man and Hari had been . . . a boy. Definitely a boy. And Pilgrim had left him . . . someplace else. Someplace far from here, on the side of a road. *Scritch-scratch* went those claws inside his head. *Let us out*, they whispered.

Pretty sure this fella is real, Voice said.

The man held a bow with an arrow notched and aimed but not drawn. The bow confused Pilgrim, but confusion had been a steadfast companion to him since finding himself in the backyard of a strange house with lightning boiling the air around him, so he wasn't overly concerned.

At the man's hip hung a sheath where Pilgrim counted a further twelve arrows. Which made the arrow aimed at him number thirteen. He tried to not think about that.

'You're a Native Indian?' Pilgrim asked.

The man frowned. Offended, maybe, or perhaps as confused as Pilgrim was.

'No?' the guy said. 'I'm not that kind of Indian.'

Definitely offended.

Pilgrim nodded to his weapon. 'The bow and arrow give the wrong impression.'

'It's supposed to give the impression that I'll shoot you if you move.'

Pilgrim considered that a fair thing to suppose.

The guy's eyes flicked behind Pilgrim before settling on him. 'Was it you doing all the yelling?'

Pilgrim nodded.

'Do you need help?' The guy made a show of scanning the parking lot more widely. 'Doesn't look like you need any help to me.'

'Can you read?'

The man's face screwed up, moving past confusion and becoming outright bewildered. 'What?'

'Read,' Pilgrim repeated. 'I have a book I need reading.'

'Are you kidding me?'

'Does it look like I am?'

'No. You kinda look like you wouldn't know how, to be honest. So what I'm thinking is I'll go ahead and shoot you now, and check through your bag after you can't talk at me any more.' The guy pulled back on the bowstring.

'What's your name?' Pilgrim made sure to maintain eye contact. It was hard to kill someone when you were looking them dead in the eye. Harder still if you were making introductions. Pilgrim held out a hand, even though there was a parking lot's distance between them and he had no real interest in shaking hands with him; the memory of Ruby doing the same remained fresh in his mind, though.

The man's bow bobbed down, came back up, bobbed down again, an indecisive rise and fall as he debated with himself. He lowered the bow altogether, the tension on the bowstring releasing. He shook his head. 'What's wrong with you?'

'Brain damage, I suspect.' The dull pain behind Pilgrim's ear gave an answering throb in agreement. He didn't add that he thought he might be going insane.

No, I don't think that'd help our cause.

'You're hurt?' the man asked.

'Just having some trouble reading.'

'You want me to look at a book for you? That's it?'

'I need you to read a message. Then we're done.'

Unless he has a car.

'Unless you have a car,' Pilgrim added.

'No. No car.' The man looked around again, taking his time to decide.

Pilgrim could see the mechanisms of his thoughts, the suspicions, the irrepressible interest, see it all converging, meeting at a central point where this man's needs met his own. He felt it, like a crank slotting into place, locking them together.

The man's eyes came back to him. 'What book is it?' he asked.

A smile threatened but Pilgrim didn't let it slip free. He was still holding out his hand and let it drop. 'Looks to be horror.'

'Like Stephen King?'

If he'd once known who Stephen King was, he didn't any more. 'Maybe,' he replied.

'Okay, let me see.'

Pilgrim carefully, in slow movements, reached behind him and slid the book from his back pocket. He held it up, cover out.

The man's eyes brightened. Pilgrim could see it from twenty feet away. 'I think it's a Ray Bradbury. Can't see the title properly.'

Pilgrim took a few non-threatening steps nearer.

The guy read it in stops and starts. '"Something . . . Wicked . . . This Way Comes."' His soft brown eyes met Pilgrim's. 'I sure hope that's not prophetic.'

'Me, too,' Pilgrim said. 'Wouldn't that be a shitter?'

The corner of the guy's mouth twitched. An almost-smile. 'Sanjay, that's my name. But my family call me Jay. Which part of the book did you need me to read?'

They didn't move any closer to each other.

There was a moment when Pilgrim didn't want to be parted from the book, as if being separated from it might rob him of some form of mystical protection. Which was absurd. There was no such thing as magic.

But you believe in Fate?

He felt no instant need to dismiss the idea of it, so maybe that was all the answer he needed.

Fate's kind of like magic, though, right? Predetermined, unmeasurable, intangible.

'There's a handwritten message in the front,' Pilgrim told Jay, deciding not to get into any fatalistic philosophical discussions with the *unmeasurable, intangible* voice in his head just now. He threw the paperback underarm.

Jay caught the book neatly, having slung his bow over his head in readiness; it rested crossways from left shoulder to right hip like a bandolier. He'd sent Pilgrim a look when he'd done it. 'I'm putting my bow up,' he'd warned. 'But I have a knife. And I know how to throw it.'

We're on the Wild Frontier now. I always did like Westerns.

Jay started flicking through the pages. 'Where in the front, exactly?'

'Title page,' Pilgrim said.

'I can't . . . Oh, yeah. I see it.' He fell silent as he read.

A pain needled Pilgrim in the spot below his breastbone as he waited.

Jay glanced up. 'Who's this from?'

Pilgrim clenched his jaw. Breathed. Counted to five. Seemed he had to wait for the cable car to rot out of the sky and the ticket office to lose its roof, to cave in and join the garden of plant life already flowering inside it, before he got what he'd asked for.

'I don't know,' he said, careful to keep his tone neutral. 'I can't read it. That's why I asked you to.'

'It's addressed to someone called Pilgrim. Is that you?'

Pilgrim felt the ground tip beneath him. He closed his eyes, but that only made it worse. He looked away from Jay to a long-abandoned ice-cream truck squatting on rusted axles. They said that if you felt seasick, you should keep your eyes trained on land.

Who's 'they'?

Sailors. Pilgrim focused on the dirty, peeling penguin decal on the side of the van. Its flipper held up a popsicle, the joyous expression on its face designed to lure children in.

'Can you read it out?' he asked. 'All of it.'

'Oh, yeah. Sure.' Jay cleared his throat. '"Pilgrim, you were right when you said you'd know what book to choose just from the feel of it. I didn't realise you were being wise, because sometimes you were pretty dumb. But I love you anyways, and that's what's important, right? Loving someone despite their faults.'"

Breathe, Voice instructed.

Not realising he'd stopped, Pilgrim drew in a careful breath, the pain under his breastbone stabbing into him.

"'I wish you were here with us,'" Jay read slowly. "'I wish for it every day. Come find me in the next life, okay? I'll wait for you. I'll always wait for you. With lots of love, Lacey." She's put a bunch of kisses at the bottom.'

Pilgrim didn't need to pull out the photograph to see the girl, see her eyes. Smiling, serious, fearful, angry, shocked, remorseful, laughing, sad. He saw *all* her eyes.

'Lacey.' He said her name to feel it on his tongue, in his mouth, hear it in his ears, and it was as familiar to him as his own.

'That's a lot,' Jay said, looking impressed.

'What is?' Pilgrim asked, not sure what he was talking about.

'Kisses. I counted them. She's put ten.'

A solid number. Dependable. You could make a triangle with them: four on the bottom row, three above it, then two, then one. The strongest of shapes.

Pilgrim held out his hand for the book, ready to have it back, but Jay made no move to toss it. He was flicking through the pages. 'Who's this Lacey? She your kid or something?'

'It's . . .' Pilgrim searched for a word, not wanting to admit he didn't know what she was. 'Complicated.'

'Isn't everything ever?' Jay asked.

Pilgrim made a noise that could be taken for agreement, if that's what the guy wanted.

'You looking for her?' Jay asked, done with his page-flicking. He hefted the paperback in his hand, flipped it over to check out the back cover.

'Yes. No. Throw it back.' Pilgrim's eyes didn't waver from the tall-hatted character on the book's front cover.

Still, Jay didn't toss it.

Lacey. The double-syllable sound of her name sawed through Pilgrim's mind, the *Lace* part swinging in with serrated teeth, the *ee* ending slicing back out, cutting deep enough to spill blood, and his head turns in slow degrees and there she is, leaning against the ice-cream truck, the silly penguin reaching out its popsicle to her. She has that amused tilt to her mouth, innocence dancing in her eyes. She's older than in the photograph, has grown taller, stronger, but she is sadder, too. She holds herself with a confidence that has been hard won. She is all of seventeen.

'*You can't forget me,*' Lacey says, and he hears the smugness in her voice because she knows she has him trapped. '*I'm in you now, like blood, like bone. I'm not going anywhere.*'

She pushes herself away from the van, moving a few steps closer. She cocks her head to the side. '*They think they can "cure" us, you know. They don't understand that the voices we hear are a part of us now. They've seen an enemy enter their homes and their only thought is to set traps so they can rid themselves of us. Except we're not rats. And they can't take what isn't theirs.*' Her eyes soften, the smirk in her smile becoming affectionate. '*You'll come find me, won't you?*'

'Yes,' he said. 'I will.'

'Hey, man? You all right?'

'*I'm already in the eye of the storm, Pilgrim,*' she whispers, her voice fading from him. '*Don't stop. There's no time . . .*'

Pilgrim's eyelids fluttered as he blinked rapidly because the world was suddenly infused with whiteness, everything overexposed, too bright, painful. Jay's black negative eyes stared at him, had been staring for some time, judging by the slash of a frown cutting into his brow.

'You zoned out,' Jay said, and his mouth was a sucking void in the glaring white.

Pilgrim squinted at the ice-cream truck, the parking lot

crushing him in its blinding luminance. He spun around, searching, but she was gone.

She was never there, Pilgrim, Voice said, his concern a spotlight's beam pinning him in place. *You're seeing things.*

'Give me my book.' And the words rattled out of him, a scattering of midnight stones across the bleached-white ground.

'All right,' Jay said. 'Just let me—'

'*Now.*' The world shuddered on its axis, blurring so that all whites and blacks mixed to a washed-out grey. He didn't see Jay approach but the book was being pressed into his hands and Jay was saying something Pilgrim couldn't hear over the roar in his ears. He held the book so hard his knuckles shone white. But it helped.

It helped.

CHAPTER 6

A Wild Frontier

They were in a seedy part of town, walking past storefront after storefront (pawn shops, electrical stores, tattoo parlours, an adult store with dead neon lights in its windows in the shape of a spread-eagled woman on her back), and Pilgrim didn't know why Jay was still here. He'd expected him to leave as soon as they'd concluded their business.

Business would imply a transaction. You gave Jay exactly zip for his services.

'What do you want?' Pilgrim could have been speaking to either of them.

'Just making sure you're all right. You spazzed out.'

Pilgrim made no reply.

'Also, honestly? I kind of want to know what's going on.' Jay skipped around to walk backwards, levelling his dark, curious eyes on Pilgrim. 'I mean, who is this Lacey? Are you family? Is she a girlfriend or something?'

Pilgrim had become very aware of the book as he walked. It was in his rear pocket again and it shifted subtly against him at every other step. He felt better for having it, and that worried him. He didn't want a crutch, didn't need to become reliant on a wad of paper glued together. And he didn't like how Jay had seen him, disoriented, vulnerable, demanding that he hand the damn thing back.

Yeah. You seriously need to get a grip.

Pilgrim stopped walking and Jay stumbled into a puddle. The guy cursed and stepped clear, kicking his feet, cuffs dark with water. Standing this close, Pilgrim noted how tall he was, but he was too skinny to wear it well – too many angles and not enough meat. Pilgrim tried to gauge Jay's age and placed him somewhere around the drinking age for this state, possibly just under. Not that it mattered. There was nothing to imbibe.

'Go home,' Pilgrim told him.

'What? Really?' A large chunk of Jay's enthusiasm fell away and what was left was a deflated-looking man-child with bruised holes for eyes.

Pilgrim should have felt bad about that. He didn't. 'Really,' he said.

'It's just . . . I don't have much to go home to. I've . . . you know. Been on my own for a while now.'

You don't say.

'I don't have anything for you,' Pilgrim said.

'I know that. I'm not some naïve kid.' Jay frowned at him before dropping his eyes to his feet. He kicked his shoes some, sprinkles of water flicking free. 'I don't expect to be best buddies or anything. But maybe we can help each other out?' He jerked a thumb over his shoulder, up the street. 'The way you're heading? You don't want to go past Washington Heights. That territory's taken. You go in there, you won't come back out.'

'Washington Heights?'

'It's maybe five miles if you keep heading north.'

'Whose territory is it?'

'Theirs.'

Pilgrim let the word settle between them like disturbed sediment sinking back to the bottom of a pond. 'I see,' he said.

Jay shook his head. 'You don't see. You don't know what's been going on here. You can't go west through Interstates 45 or 55 any more. Can't cross the Mississippi without their say-so. Think you can slip around them? Maybe use the minor roads? Think again. They don't stay in the same place. They move around. You'll never know where they'll be until they pop up. There used to be half a million people in this part of Memphis, easy. Now? You're lucky if you see a handful in a week. And how many of them are like us?'

'Us?' Pilgrim said, watching Jay grow more and more animated.

'Yeah. You know, *normal.*' Jay shoved a hand deep into his mop of hair, eyes checking over his shoulder, checking over Pilgrim's shoulder, unable to keep still. 'Was a time they were scared of us, right? Locked themselves in their homes for fear they'd get found out. Rounded up and taken to some pit outside the city. Dumped there to rot. They had to be real careful. Keep themselves on the down-low. But not any more. Those times are gone. They got wise to us.'

'They did.' Pilgrim didn't know where the conviction in his reply came from, but it was there, sitting in the back seat of a car like an uninvited passenger: solid, irrefutable, going nowhere. Maybe because it was a universal truth that you could kick someone to the kerb only so many times before they picked themselves up and kicked you back.

'Probably figured if we can get all mobbish and flush them out, then why can't they? Surprised it took them so long. Could be more of them than us, for all I know.'

Oh dear. Poor lad thinks we're like him.

Voice was a passenger, too, turning up uninvited and unwelcome. Coming along for the ride, no matter what Pilgrim wanted.

Passenger? More like compadre. Mijo. Hermano.

'I'm going north,' Pilgrim told Jay.

'Is that where Lacey is?'

Pilgrim didn't like all his questions. Question after fucking question.

You don't like them because you don't have any real answers.

The truth of Voice's words only served to irritate Pilgrim more.

Jay filled the silence, incapable of doing anything else, it seemed. Standing still wasn't his forte, either; he shifted in place, moving his weight from foot to foot. Pilgrim would figure he was hopped up on stimulants or caffeine if there were either of those things left around here, which he doubted there was.

'When I heard you calling, at first I thought it was—' Jay gave him a sharp look and waved the words away. There was a quiet nervousness in him, hidden away under all his talking. 'It's not good being left on your own too long, you know? It makes you think things. Look, let me help you. You owe me that, at least.'

For reading a few words out? Nah, mijo. *Leave him. He talks too much.*

And *Voice* didn't? The last thing Pilgrim wanted was another talker hanging around, but two things stopped him sending Jay on his way. One, he didn't appreciate Voice telling him what to do. And, two, Jay had information that could prove useful.

Voice became wheedling. *Why do you insist on making things difficult for us?*

Pilgrim quit paying attention to him and started walking. Jay came along, matching him stride for stride. The guy's right boot squeaked with moisture.

'Tell me how you know about Washington Heights.'

'Well, I live here, don't I?'

Pilgrim stared at him until the guy looked away.

'My cousin, Manny. He told me most of it. We weren't

really so tight, me and him. Not before, anyway. Not so much afterwards, either, but we stuck together because it was the smartest move. To stick together. He had his girl with him. I knew her – well, I knew *of* her. My mom and auntie were forever talking about her because it'd caused some issues in the family. He'd been seeing her for a while back then, wanted to marry her. A real Romeo and Juliet set-up. You know about castes?' Jay asked him.

Pilgrim didn't know where this was going and likely his expression showed it.

Jay stepped around a puddle. 'It doesn't matter. She was technically a lower caste to my cousin. Kind of frowned on when it comes to marriage. But all that stuff stopped mattering pretty quickly, didn't it? One of the few decent things that came from everyone . . . you know . . . being dead. Whatever my mom and auntie thought, Manny and Suki were meant to be together. They really loved each other.' His voice went soft when he said it. Wistful.

Pilgrim hadn't missed Jay's use of the past tense.

'Anyway, it was always pretty obvious she heard one. A voice, I mean. Caught her arguing out loud to herself all the time. Sometimes she would laugh at nothing when she was in a room by herself. Sometimes she'd yank on her hair. I never got used to it and we never talked about it. Not really. It was . . . a problem for me, though. She'd say stuff when Manny wasn't around. Mean stuff that played on my mind. It was one of the reasons I didn't stay in their place with them. It was always there, hiding behind everything she said and did, in every look she gave me. I was scared of her – I won't lie. I was worried it might be, I don't know, contagious or something, or she might try and do something to me. So I stayed out of her way. But Manny, he just got on with stuff. Told me to get on with stuff, too. To not worry about it. So I did. It worked out pretty well, I guess. We mostly got along. And then she just . . . disappeared one night. Didn't leave a note or say anything. Just disappeared. It wasn't like her. She *loved* Manny. They'd stuck together all this time.'

'When was this?' Pilgrim asked.

Jay shrugged and rubbed the back of his neck. 'Maybe nine months ago? I'm not sure – it's hard to keep track. But Manny searched for her. He went out day after day, he wasn't about to give up. But where do you start with something like that? I mean, she could've gone anywhere. Not long after, we started spotting people passing through – more than we'd seen in a while. It was Manny's idea to take a closer look. We were careful who we talked to, but we started putting bits and pieces together from the snippets we heard. Found out they weren't passing through the city like we thought. And they were the same as Suki. Manny thought that's maybe where she'd gone, to be with her own kind, you know? So he started going in there. He was desperate to find her. He couldn't understand why she'd left without talking to him.

'He really wasn't the same after that. I went with him sometimes – to keep an eye on him mainly. We saw a lot of stuff. A lot of movement. But never any sign of her. It's such a big place, the chances of finding her were . . . Well, Manny didn't want to listen to any of that. He kept going in. He was gone for longer and longer. I wouldn't see him for days sometimes, and then he'd turn up and tell me what he'd found.'

Jay stopped walking, and Pilgrim stopped with him. They were coming up to an intersection. The roads leading to it, the sidewalks, the blackened stalks of the traffic lights, all were scorched black as if a bomb had been dropped. A fuel tanker lay on its side beneath the melted and ruined signal boxes and a mass of burnt-out vehicles was clumped around it, crumpled against its belly like suckling metallic piglets. There must have been multiple fatalities, but the fire had raged unchecked and most of the evidence had been lost to ash and time. Only a few charcoal bones lay scattered around. Pilgrim spotted a jawbone, too small to be an adult's. From the cracked concrete and fuel caps sprouted weed and vines, jungle-green against the charred backdrop.

'Then he stopped coming back,' Jay said, gazing towards the junction, his face creased around his eyes as if he were having trouble focusing. 'I haven't seen him in months now. I think they got him.'

Pilgrim wasn't sure what he was supposed to say. 'Sorry' was just a word, a dead, meaningless sentiment when voiced by a stranger. Still, he made an effort to be less brusque. 'I can't waste time going around. I need to go in.'

'Because you need to find Lacey?'

Pilgrim nodded; it was easier than trying to explain.

Jay was quiet for a while, eyes squinting, mouth straight. 'It'll be easier if I show you,' he said. 'Come on.'

For sixteen minutes Jay led him through back alleys and down accessways wide enough only for foot traffic. Occasionally, they would come out on to wider avenues where box trucks had once parked to unload their cargo, but only for a moment, before Jay slipped back into the narrow passages of the service corridors. Tall buildings hemmed them in, squeezing them tight, and Pilgrim felt that same constriction build in his lungs, a hand tightening on his throat again, throttling his breaths into gasps. Thankfully, Jay stopped them in the mouth of an alley that exited on to a double-wide cobblestoned main street.

They were in a restaurant-and-bar district. The street hung heavy with unlit neon signage, some as large as garage doors, others as small as manhole covers. Jay read them out for him: BB King's Speakeasy, Teeter Ree's Bar & Grill, Black Jack's Café, the Snake Pit Blues Lounge. Pilgrim spotted two music stores slotted in between eateries, in case anyone was tempted to pick up a Gibson Dot guitar on their way to dinner and drinks.

'There. See it?'

Pilgrim followed Jay's pointing finger and at first thought he was showing him the large Chicago Rock Café guitar sign hanging askew and seemingly about to fall at any second. Then he saw it. A street sign, green and bordered in white. Innocuous and invisible among all the garish signs and business boards. The street name wasn't of any interest to him (and unreadable even if it was) but the circular pattern drawn on to it with black marker was.

Next to the spiral design, five written characters.

'What's it say?' Pilgrim asked. He rotated his shoulder, trying to ease the discomfort, and pushed a hand under the strap of his pack to knead at the soreness. It didn't help.

'200y L. Let's go.'

Jay scurried out, keeping low.

Pilgrim forced his wooden legs to follow. He peered into the bars and restaurants, many open to the elements, their front concertina doors thrown wide as if business had been running as usual when calamity struck. There were desiccated corpses strewn inside, slumped over counters, tucked up against walls or under tables, but neither Jay nor Pilgrim commented on them. They were as much a part of the scenery as the neon signs and music stores. Less so. At least the signs and instruments were pretty to look at.

Jay stopped, his head going left, eyes searching. 'There,' he said, pointing.

Another circular pattern, this one daubed on the bottom corner of a café window in red spray-paint.

'*We've seen them before,*' Lacey whispers as she brushes past him, appearing out of nowhere. '*You're definitely heading the right way.*'

She crosses the street to stand in front of the café, her head tilting down, hair falling to hide her face as she looks at the red spiral on the window. '*They're tagging the places they've been,*' she

117

says, and glances back at him, worried eyes meeting his. '*Like last time.*'

He wanted to look away from her, but his eyes refused to obey. 'Like last time,' she'd said. He'd let her do this before. Investigate similar markings in another place, far from here, her curiosity tempered by a wariness new to her. That other place had worried her, too, and it should. Those spirals had been painted on automatic doors that had led into a cold, flooded casino. Both panes of glass had been miraculously unbroken, the doors lodged open by an upended garbage can tipped on its side. On each pane a painted head faced the other in profile. With the doors closed, their noses would almost touch, lips close enough to kiss. Inside each head, above where the ears would be, was a spiralled circle, going round and round and round.

'You see it?' Jay asked, bringing Pilgrim back to the cobblestoned street and the café.

Lacey no longer stood at the window and Pilgrim was unsurprised to see her gone, though the loss left a hollowed-out space in his gut. He pressed a hand to it. It had been a while since he'd eaten.

Sure, it's hunger pangs, Voice said dryly.

'What are they?' Pilgrim was finding it difficult to drag his eyes away from the red circular design painted so neatly on the plate glass. The longer he stared, the more it resembled a target.

'This is small fry compared to some I've seen. There was this one . . .' Jay trailed off and Pilgrim glanced over to find the guy staring into space. His voice took on a vague quality, as if he weren't quite present. 'It was over in Corkie's Park. Some sick bastard had gathered a bunch of old corpses, dragged them out there and laid them head to toe, head to toe, curling them around each other so some looked like they were hugging. In the middle he'd gathered a bunch of babies. Little kids. Heaped them up. An eye of the storm made up of dead kids, man. For weeks I couldn't stop seeing those babies. I couldn't sleep without seeing them.'

Eye of the storm, Voice whispered.

'What were they for?'

The frown he directed at Pilgrim was close to angry. 'It's *them*, leaving calling cards. Letting others know they're around. That they're done with hiding. There'll be something in there.' Jay nodded at the café. 'Instructions, maybe, or more directions. They're like an underground movement and their activities are ramping up. I've seen traffic on the roads. Not a lot, but more than I've seen in a long while. It's *them*.'

Pilgrim's ears perked up. 'They have vehicles? Gas?' Gas was the real attention-grabber. Fuel was near impossible to come by.

'Yeah. You can hear them, mainly at night. Manny told me they take people to camps, where they indoctrinate them. One in Illinois or Wisconsin, another out east. It's like a cult.'

'What do you mean, "indoctrinate"?'

Voice started singing in a faux-rap style.

> *Tin-foil hat, tin-foil hat*
> *Don't forget your tin-foil hat*
> *Don't drink water from that fluoride tap*
> *Keep your distance from the suits in black*
> *But best don't forget your tin-foil hat.*

'Not everyone who hears a voice wants to join ranks, do they?' Jay said. 'Same as how soldiers don't always want to enlist. But sometimes you don't get to keep your head down. Sometimes you get dragged into stuff even when you don't want to be.'

'Did Manny tell you that?'

But Jay shook his head, skittish as a buck as he scanned the street. 'Not here. It's not safe.'

'What if I wanted to find them?'

Jay's brows knitted together. He looked at Pilgrim as though he'd asked for his head to be set on fire. 'Why'd you want that?'

'You said they have a camp. In Illinois or Wisconsin.' Wisconsin was where he'd first met Ruby. That had to mean something. He didn't believe in coincidences. 'That's directly north of us.'

Connect the dots, Sanjay.

'They don't help anyone but themselves. You shouldn't get involved with them, not if you have a choice.' Jay got up, preparing to move. 'We can't stay here. We're too close.'

He didn't give Pilgrim time to reply but hurried away, falling into a jog, glancing over his shoulder to see if Pilgrim was coming. Pilgrim didn't want to follow. His legs hurt, his shoulder hurt and deep in his chest hurt, too. A gnawing pain rattled around his head like a hangover too stubborn to leave. His clothes stuck to him, damp from sweat and humidity, and a darkening sea washed in with his thoughts, muffling them under a wave of fatigue. Still, hanging around here wasn't a good idea.

Jay didn't stop for a further twelve minutes, and when he did, he didn't wind down his stride, didn't slow his pace to give Pilgrim a chance to catch up. He stopped as if he'd run into a wall.

They had approached the gas station from the rear, Jay skirting its side to pass by a set of smashed vending machines and newspaper distribution boxes. He didn't glance into their display windows, which told Pilgrim he'd come this way many times before. Familiarity bred complacency and Jay barely paused to check the gas station's forecourt before breaking cover.

'You! Hey! We see you!'

The shout stopped Jay in his tracks.

Pilgrim stumbled in his jog. He'd been too tired to stay on Jay's younger, healthier heels and hadn't made it past the gas station's restrooms – Jay was a full ten yards ahead of him, out in no-man's-land, bow on his back, knife in its sheath. In conclusion, he was fucked.

The fuel pumps ranged out to the left, the shelter of the gas station's roof casting Jay in shadow. The rain had dried up, the skies cleared. It was a few degrees hotter and the change from shade to sunshine marked a clear line around the island of the gas station.

'Where you off to in such a hurry, sweetness?'

Pilgrim couldn't see who'd spoken; they were off to the left somewhere, hidden by the corner of the station's store. Unmistakeably male, the voice had a melodic quality, the owner so close to falling into song he was practically flirting his way to the opening of a Broadway tune.

'Home,' Jay replied, breathless, sweating.

Pilgrim ghosted closer to the wall, hand out to touch the sun-warmed door of the men's restroom. He could turn and go back the way he'd come. He could skirt around the other side of the gas station to flank them. He could even stay where he was and hide; the restroom doors were probably unlocked, the dark toilet stalls the perfect place to tuck himself into and wait this out.

Go back, Voice said. *You don't owe him anything.*

'And where's home?' Another guy. This one a straight delivery with no fun inflections.

'Not far,' Jay answered cagily.

'You're out here on your lonesome? Oh, honey, that's just silly. Get yourself caught up in trouble that way. Come on over here. I want to see you properly.'

Jay wanted to glance back at Pilgrim – Pilgrim could feel it buzzing in the guy, the desperate need to send him a distress signal. The sour stench of sweat rode the air; Pilgrim could see Jay's neck and face drenched with it.

He's gonna bolt.

He won't. He wasn't stupid enough for that.

'Be a good kitty and keep your claws away from that knife I

see you reaching for. We don't want Kelley getting the wrong idea and hurting you by accident, now do we?'

Jay held his palms out and walked forward, eyes locked straight ahead. As he stepped out of view, Pilgrim slid the nail-gun from its holster, inch by inch, his tool belt creaking quietly. He'd seen Jay glance at it a time or two. Could plainly read how sceptical he was of it. As a weapon, Pilgrim could admit it was an impractical choice.

Might save his fool life now.

'What do you want?' Jay asked. Pilgrim could taste the dryness in the guy's mouth, the metallic tang of building panic at the back of his throat.

'What makes you think we want anything?'

'Maybe because your friend is holding a gun on me?'

Ah, clever lad.

At least two of them, one of whom had a weapon drawn. Pilgrim should go around back and approach from behind. It was the smartest course of action. But he wasn't here to play it smart or cautious. Since the Dodge had quit on him, he had come to a standstill, and all of this was taking too damn long. This whole place was a stopgap, a pass-through, and depending on how this panned out he would either get what he needed from these people – a ride out of here – or he would leave them behind and find another way.

'Oh, don't worry your pretty head of hair over my friend here. He's just being cautious. He doesn't like doing the rounds.'

'You're one of them, aren't you?' Jay said.

Voice blew out a sigh. *From clever to stupid in one breath.*

A beat of silence, so charged that Pilgrim felt the air molecules vibrate and saw vapours dance above the empty fuel pumps, hazy and hypnotic. He could almost smell the dried-up gasoline, the heat, the elements of combustion getting ready to ignite.

'One of what, honey?' And there was no show-tune-musical dancing on the stranger's lips now.

Jay didn't answer. The scuffing of feet ceased: theirs, Jay's – it didn't matter. They were finding their positions. Pilgrim breathed deeply, clearing his lungs of their clicking wheeze. He slid along the gas station's wall, keeping an eye on his shadow gliding two feet ahead of him. There was too much silence, the kind that lay foundations for violence.

'That's very divisive. Calling us "them".'

'I'm not like you.' There was bravado in Jay's delivery, but a waver crept in at the end to spoil it.

He doth protest too much, if you ask me.

Pilgrim wanted to tell Voice to can it. He was a distraction he didn't need.

'We don't like prejudiced people. We had enough of them in the old world, didn't we, dearest?'

'We did,' the second guy answered. 'We had ourselves a gutful of them.'

'What's your name, sweetheart?'

A scuff of feet again, further to the left. Theirs, not Jay's. Advancing. Pilgrim switched off the nail-gun's safety.

'It's just a name, my dove. It won't give us power over you, I promise.'

'Sanjay,' Jay said.

'Here's what we're going to do, Sanjay. We're going to give you a choice. You see how generous we can be? We're not so bad, really. Either you can come with us, all nice and breezy, and we take a little stroll together. Or you can apologise for being a bigoted little madam and we can leave you here where we found you.'

'I'm sorry.'

Even his laugh trilled high and song-like. 'Oh, darling, you're so quick to decide. Are you sure you don't want to reconsider?'

They're not saying everything.

Of course they weren't. Pilgrim had never expected them to.

'I'm just . . . I'm very sorry, okay?'

'Sorry for what?' Soft and light and deceptively sweet.

'I . . .' Jay floundered. Pilgrim didn't need to see him to imagine the frustrated crinkle on his brow or the darting of his eyes. 'I'm sorry for saying you were one of them. I didn't mean anything by it.'

'We *are* one of them,' the straight-talking guy said. 'Two of them, in fact. And when Roscoe said leave you where we found you, she meant right there, dead in the dirt.'

So many word games. Pilgrim would never understand why people talked so much.

He stepped on his shadow and followed it out. He didn't point the nail-gun at anyone but he held it ready in his hand. The big guy on the left swung his gun on him. It was silver nickel, a revolver, as far from antique as you could get. He wore a leather belt and holster slung low on his hips and a sweat-stained cowboy hat. No shit, they *were* living on the Wild Frontier. Except this guy wasn't playing at it.

The person next to him, the one called Roscoe, was . . . different. He had a perfectly coiffed mohawk and wore a number of wispy, diaphanous scarves that had nothing to do with practicality and everything to do with style. As were the numerous hooped earrings in his ears.

Pilgrim had had guns pointed at him before – the proof of it was in the soreness in his chest and shoulder – but if there was ever a point you got used to it, he hadn't reached it yet. That tiny muzzle-hole made you small. Made every step and word come harder, squeeze tighter, carry extra meaning. Another reason he didn't understand why people wagged their tongues so much in a stand-off.

His eyes fell on Roscoe's hands. They were empty but for the fingerless gloves he wore.

'Why, hello.' Roscoe smiled at him. He had a gold-capped tooth.

I think he's a she.

Pilgrim nodded in Jay's direction. 'He's with me.'

'You're a couple? How lovely.' Roscoe's smile appeared genuine; wide and full of teeth. 'And you are?'

'I'm one of you.'

Roscoe's eyebrow hiked up, her interest outshining her smile. The man beside her gave his companion a look, checking for her reaction, and the dynamics here were sealed. Pilgrim knew who was in charge.

Hmmm, Pilgrim, what are you doing?

He didn't have time to play games with these people. Any patience he had for such things had been left buried back in Vicksburg with Ruby. All that was left was a nail-biting, hair-tugging, digging animal in his head that wanted out, wanted him to get moving, the world spinning out so fast he felt invisible hands grabbing at him, eager to yank him along. The hard beat of his pulse pushed at his skin, throbbing with each second that ticked by. He stood perfectly still as he struggled to contain it all.

I don't think this is you being wise, Voice offered uncertainly, aware of everything he was feeling.

Pilgrim smiled, a grim curve of his lips, hearing the echo of Lacey's words in the observation.

Lacey. She was part of that scratching need, too, wasn't she? A mite under his skin, digging into his brain, itching like crazy. She was a half-buried presence, much like Ruby, and she was urging him to dig faster. Soon, the scratching to exhume her would draw blood. His, theirs – he didn't know.

'You've done well not to get strung up by your pretty neck,' Roscoe told him.

'I could say the same,' he said. 'And your neck is much prettier than mine.'

'Oh, I like you.' Roscoe's smile shone with delight. She turned it on her companion. 'I like him. He's one of those gentlemen I'm always telling you about.'

The man in the cowboy hat's expression didn't change. Neither did his aim.

'You're *one* of them?' Jay said, the look of betrayal on his face making Pilgrim uncomfortable.

The guy retreated a step towards the gas pumps, and the cowboy transferred his shiny revolver to him. Jay didn't seem to notice or care – he stared at Pilgrim as if Pilgrim had taken the nail-gun and shot him in the gut with it.

'I hear a voice,' Pilgrim said, as plainly as he could. 'I'm beginning to understand I've always heard one.'

There was a sigh, tickling deep inside his ear. *This won't end well, mark my words. You shouldn't be trusting him with this.*

Pilgrim shouldn't be trusting *any*one, period. That was one thing he didn't need reminding of. He didn't miss the hand that edged towards Jay's knife and briefly wondered if the guy's claim was true, if he really did know how to use it.

A mechanical *kerlick* came and Pilgrim briefly closed his eyes. He was getting tired of hearing that sound, imaginary or not.

Jay nervously wet his lips.

Rock beats scissors. A cocked gun beats a knife. And everything beats a nail-gun, in case you were wondering.

'Is it talking to you right now?'

Jay's wariness shimmered, blurring in the cloying heat as the eddies from gasoline vapours once had, and Pilgrim couldn't blame him for it. Pilgrim had lied to him, by omission if nothing else. He had every reason to be suspicious.

Pilgrim answered with a nod. The nail-gun was partly hidden by his thigh. He curled his finger around its trigger. 'He said I shouldn't trust you. That none of this will end well.' Pilgrim paused, not knowing exactly when 'it' had become 'he' to him.

'That's what it said?'

'Yes.'

'Then why didn't you leave me?'

Another good question. This guy's full of them.

'You helped me when you didn't need to,' Pilgrim said. 'You gave me Lacey's name, and anyway' – he shrugged and spoke louder – 'there could be an opportunity in this. For all of us.'

Roscoe had taken to running one of her scarves through her hands. A casual observer may have thought she was uninterested in the entire exchange, but Pilgrim didn't miss the sharp attentiveness in her gaze, how her eyes flicked to take in every detail.

'I'm all ears, my dear,' she told him pleasantly.

'You're part of a bigger group here?' he asked.

'Oh, there are lots more of us.'

'Are you going to make me go with them?' Jay cut in.

Pilgrim took his time answering. Not to be cruel or to make Jay wait, but because he had a decision to make. He noticed Jay had tucked what he could of his riotous mass of hair behind his ears. Its dark curls matched the colour of his eyes perfectly.

'You said you've been on your own a while,' Pilgrim reminded him. 'There's company to be had here.'

Jay's voice lowered with his brow. 'This isn't the kind of company I want.'

'They might know something about your cousin.'

Roscoe wasn't smiling any more. 'You pair are the cutest, I swear, but I'm getting super tired of all your whispering.'

Join the club.

'We'll go with you, nice and breezy,' Pilgrim decided, turning back to her. 'Isn't that what you said?'

'It was. And I only ever say what I mean.' Roscoe waved a hand at her companion, the first frown Pilgrim had witnessed on her marring her brow. 'Sweetheart, lose the gun-toting-cowboy act, would you? We all know you're the real deal. No need to labour the point.'

You're gonna get one of us killed, Voice muttered. *Or, knowing your luck, all of us.*

And Pilgrim thought *he* was the pessimistic one.

Voice sighed, unamused. *I hope you know what you're doing.*

So did Pilgrim.

CHAPTER 7

Resistance

Pilgrim spotted a number of spray-painted spiral tags on the way, tucked into corners, placed low or high in places your eye wouldn't naturally go to. Roscoe didn't pay attention to any of them.

She knows where she's going, that's why. Which is more than you can say.

She said she was taking him to someone in charge, and that was all he cared about. He didn't bother memorising the left and right turns. He wouldn't be coming back this way. The guy in the cowboy hat walked at the rear, and although the guy's gun wasn't drawn, and Pilgrim and Jay's weapons hadn't been confiscated, Pilgrim had the distinct impression he was in the middle of a prisoner convoy on its way back from litter-picking duties at the side of the freeway.

'Where do you boys come from?' Roscoe asked, looking over her shoulder. She wore beads plaited into her hair, two long strands in blues and purples, tipped with bird feathers. They trailed down her back, two tails hanging behind her ear.

'Not here,' Pilgrim said.

Jay said nothing.

Roscoe laughed. 'You're some chatty cats, aren't you? But I get it. That need for secrecy. From you, at least.' She pointed at

Pilgrim. 'Don't get it from you.' She gave Jay a look, brow arched. 'What you got to be so secretive about, my lamb?'

Jay looked away from her, mouth pressed in a tight line.

You choose to bring him along and now he's upsetting the natives.

'No need to look so sullen,' Roscoe told him, pouting. 'We're not *kidnapping* you. Your friend here has vouched for you, and that'll do.'

'For now,' the cowboy behind them added.

'Hush, you,' Roscoe scolded. 'All hiss and no strike, that's what you are. Still acting like a big scary alpha male when the time for it is *over*. We're all equal in each other's eyes now, my love.'

'Are we?' Pilgrim asked.

She smiled at him. 'We are here.'

A barricade of vehicles (trucks, ambulances, semis, a school bus) blocked the end of the street. Roscoe headed straight for it, leading them down the middle of the road, the beige-and-brown stucco frontages of pre-Civil War-era municipal buildings on either side. Pilgrim wouldn't have been surprised to spy gunslingers positioned up on the rooftops, waiting in ambush positions.

The vehicles making up the blockade were adorned with amateurish graffiti, the kind a class of teenagers might have made if they'd been set loose on a school project. It was only on closer inspection that Pilgrim could make out the hidden spiral motifs: in the pupil of an oversized eye; making up the centre and curling petals of a rose; incorporated into the thumbprint of a hand giving a thumbs-up; used in the place of the stars in a Stars and Stripes banner.

With a clatter, the side door of the school bus folded open. An older fella, silver-haired and grizzled, stood at the top of the steps. He was surprisingly well dressed in clean chinos and a sports jacket. Like Roscoe, he held no visible weapon.

'Sheila been by?' Roscoe asked as she stepped up into the bus.

The old-timer moved back to give her room. 'She's over at the shop. Working on the grid again.'

Pilgrim climbed aboard, ducking so as not to hit his head. All the seating had been ripped out, leaving a clear gangway to the rear of the bus; its back end was levered open like a can of soup. It led out to the street on the other side of the barricade.

'What were you expecting, son?' the old-timer asked him. 'Supplies for World War Three?'

'Something like that.' At the very least, Pilgrim had expected reinforced panels, guns, lookouts. Not a solitary old fella dressed for church.

'Our reputation precedes us,' Roscoe said, smiling. She smiled a lot. 'You'd be surprised how little trouble we get. Besides, this is only symbolic. You think we could barricade the whole of North Memphis off? We have more important things to do. This is part of a line, that's all, so folk know where we start and the divisions end.'

Two blocks further north and the buildings became less tall, were spaced further back. The streets were wider, flatter, dustier. The sky spread open above their heads and Pilgrim breathed it in, inhaling past the ache in his lungs. He heard the noise of work – clanking, drilling – and caught a hot, metallic scent in the air.

Welding? Voice asked.

Inside a concrete-floored, breezeblock-walled workshop, Roscoe introduced them to a middle-aged woman. Solid through the hips and broad through the shoulders, Sheila sat hunched on a stool at a workbench strewn with wires and transistors, shiny panels and screws. She had graced them with a brief, indifferent glance when they'd walked in and went back to her tinkering after the introductions were over.

She spoke to her hands. 'Either of you got any electrician experience?'

Jay looked at Pilgrim and Pilgrim told her he didn't. Jay shook his head.

It was just the four of them in here, the cowboy and his gun having chosen to wait outside the open shuttered door, leaning against a stacked tower of tyres. A waft of cigarette smoke hit Pilgrim's nose and his nostrils flared, a long-dead craving opening up his veins.

'We're rigging up solar panels to the electrics,' Roscoe explained. 'Sheila is a genius with that stuff.'

Which was all very interesting but not what Pilgrim was here for. 'I hear you transport people to camps up north,' he said.

It was either the abruptness of his words or the words themselves that brought Sheila's head up. She carefully placed the screwdriver she'd been using down and swivelled to face him. The stool beneath her let out an agonised squawk.

She should get some oil on that.

She eyed him from the crown of his head to the soles of his boots, plucking a dirty rag from behind her belt to wipe her greasy hands. A flicker of a smile crossed her lips when her eyes caught on Pilgrim flexing his fingers, catching them halfway to curling into fists.

Roscoe's and Jay's attentions shifted between them as the silence grew.

'It's just the one camp,' she finally said. 'And *I* don't transport anyone. Gunnar does all the running.'

Pilgrim transferred his frown to Roscoe. 'You said you were taking me to someone in charge.'

She frowned right back. 'I did. Gunnar is one territory over. Sheila is in charge here.'

He returned his attention to Sheila. 'I need to speak to Gunnar, then.'

She was still methodically wiping her hands. 'Oh, you don't want to do that,' she said, and that flicker of a smile passed by again.

'Gunnar's a real bastard,' Roscoe told him.

'Nasty as a rabid coon.' Sheila cocked her head. 'Why'd you want to go to a camp for? You got dissonance?'

'Dissonance?' Jay asked.

Pilgrim was surprised to hear him speak. He'd barely said spit since the gas station. From all the scowling he'd been doing, Voice had joked that the guy would end up with furrows deep enough to plant corn in.

'With the voice you're hearing,' Sheila explained. 'Do you have problems with it?'

Voice snorted a laugh. *Oh no, we get on splendidly.*

'I have lots of problems with it,' Pilgrim replied. 'But that's not the reason I need to go.'

Sheila's eyebrows tucked down. '"Need"? Must be important, then.'

Roscoe had wandered over to a back bench behind Sheila. An array of servos, wiring and electronics had been laid out in ordered piles. She went to poke at one.

'Don't touch,' Sheila reprimanded, not looking away from Pilgrim.

Roscoe froze mid-poke, her head coming up. A momentary look of surprise and then a smile. Caught out, she held her hands up and sidled to Sheila's side. A head taller than the seated woman, Roscoe slung a companionable arm around Sheila's shoulders and leaned into her.

'If you won't take me to see Gunnar,' Pilgrim said, 'I'll find someone who can.'

'Will you now?' Done wiping her hands, Sheila tucked the dirty rag under her belt and slipped her arm around Roscoe's waist. Gave it a squeeze. 'Found yourself a real asshole here, didn't you, babe?'

'But look how pretty he is,' Roscoe replied, slanting Pilgrim a sly glance. 'I couldn't help myself.'

'You have a funny idea of "pretty".'

Roscoe laughed and Sheila smiled, but only for a moment.

Seriousness wiped over her brief show of amusement as she got up, stepping out from under Roscoe's arm and coming towards him.

'I don't know you,' she told Pilgrim, stopping two feet away. 'I don't owe you anything.'

You have to give her something, Pilgrim. Make her want to help you.

But like she'd said, she didn't know him and Pilgrim didn't know her. He didn't see how being honest would help matters.

Come oooon, Voice whined. *Stop being so bull-headed. You should tell her about what we heard and where it was coming from.*

'No,' he said.

'You know who she reminds me of?'

Lacey stands at the end of Sheila's workbench, bent over and perusing the items gathered there. Her hood is raised and he can't see her face, but he knows it's her. Her posture, her movements, were like muscle memory to him. *'She reminds me of my grams. Bossy. Tough as old boots.'* She prods at a pile of screws. Nothing moves. *'But warm and gooey in the middle.'*

He wasn't so sure about gooey middles, but everything Lacey said rang with an echo of truth, as if she were speaking of things they'd already discussed, things she'd shared with him and he'd misplaced somewhere. She was prodding at him in the same way she was prodding at those screws.

He slid a glance at the others, but no one had reacted to Lacey's appearance. Jay was watching him, though, brow dug once more with furrows.

'You're no good at seeing these things,' Lacey tells him, and Pilgrim glimpses a smile from inside her hood as she abandons the bench to wander over to Roscoe. She lifts on to her toes to inspect the beads plaited into her hair. *'You're not used to people. You like to be on your own. But I trusted you, remember?'* She looks a question at him as she drops back to her heels. *'Sometimes you just have to let your guard down for a second and go with it. Because*

otherwise you get stuck – me at my lemonade stand, and you right here. Do you want to get stuck? Is that it?'

No, he didn't want to get stuck. He wanted to find her, because in finding her he hoped to understand the message of death and madness he had received in that strange lightning storm. In finding her, he hoped to finally have some peace.

His silence had lasted too long. When he looked back at Sheila her attention had shifted away from him, his reticence signalling an end to their conversation, as far as she was concerned.

'Roscoe, we're done here.' She turned away, dismissing him as she went back to her stool.

Pilgrim! There was such stern reprimand in Voice's tone that Pilgrim's eyelid twitched.

He forced his teeth to unclench and spoke to Sheila's back. 'I heard something,' he told her. 'Or someone. Calling to me. They spoke three words. *Burning. Madness* . . .' He noted her stiffness. '*Death.*'

Sheila's head swung back around and she stared at him. A hundred questions burned in her eyes. 'Where did you hear that?'

'I don't think you'd believe me.'

There was more than just silence in the workshop now; a taut stillness waited down by their feet, a poised cat that had its eye on a sneaking, scurrying mouse.

'From the sky?' she asked.

When Pilgrim didn't respond she approached him again, almost hesitantly, her eyes intent on his face. 'They wait for me in my sleep. Skies so vast and so angry they bleed red as far as the eye can see. The world *is* the sky, and all it wants is to devour us. I *feel* that, how it hungers.'

'You heard the same words I did?' he asked.

How uneasy she looked, how wary of him. She didn't like thinking on this, didn't like giving it life by speaking of it aloud.

'They came in the lightning?' he asked, pressing for an answer.

Her eyes had dropped to his lips. She blinked – a slow, languid blink, as if unsure whether she were dreaming – and forced her gaze back to his. 'No, not lightning. But the sky is alive. It runs hot with power. It's all white noise up there, crackling and hissing so you don't even know you're hearing it at first. It's just this relentless roaring static – everywhere, all at once, in your ears and in your head.' She had taken her dirty rag out and was wringing it between her hands, twisting it so tight it cut the circulation off to the tips of her bloodless fingers. 'But if you listen for long enough, that's when they come. That's when you realise you've been hearing them all along. *Burning, Slaughter, Madness, Death*. It *wants* you to listen. It's been waiting for us to.'

'Do you know what it is?' Pilgrim asked, unable to look away from her.

She was shaking her head. 'No, but there's so much pain there. You feel that, don't you? The pain?'

Pilgrim turned to Roscoe. A horrible weight of silence rested in her; it was in the slackness of her mouth, in the reluctance of her eyes. 'Have you experienced this?' he asked.

A headshake. 'No. But Sheila's heard her voice for longer than the rest of us here.' She glanced at the woman, seeking reassurance for revealing something that wasn't hers to tell. 'I'm not sure if that makes a difference.'

'There're only a few of us who dream of the red skies,' Sheila said. 'But the dreams, they're getting worse.'

'I didn't hear the words in a dream,' Pilgrim told her, and he saw her uneasiness sharpen, become guarded. 'I was awake. And they were coming from a place. North of here.' He could have taken out a map and drawn a straight line south to north from where he'd woken up in Vicksburg to Memphis, through Illinois and towards the place where he'd first met Ruby.

Onward, northbound, like he was a compass's needle, unable to waver. Ever since he and Voice had been struck by that message there hadn't been any other direction. 'This camp of yours,' he said. 'Where exactly is it?'

'I can't tell you that,' Sheila murmured, and her eyes lost some of their focus, shifting slightly to Pilgrim's right.

'An idea, at least.'

'In Illinois,' Roscoe told him.

Is this camp where it came from? Voice wondered, but his thoughts meandered off into a low musing that Pilgrim found difficult to follow.

Was Lacey there? Is that what she meant when she said she was in the eye of the storm?

'What are you doing to people there?' he asked.

Sheila's distraction had lasted a moment, a few seconds, if that. Her eyes cleared and she was looking at him again. 'Look, I'm sorry. I can't help you. Things are tense enough here as it is. All it'll take is the wrong kind of push and everything we've worked to build these past months will come crashing down. Gunnar and I didn't part on good terms the last time we spoke, and the last thing me or my people need is that twitchy bastard on our backs.'

'I understand,' Pilgrim said, and he did. He'd rather not get involved in other people's problems, either. It brought nothing but suffering. Sometimes, though, you had little choice but to suffer. 'I understand, but I think it's selfish of you.'

Sheila's lips thinned, and this time it was her fingers' turn to curl themselves into fists.

'Careful, sweetheart,' Roscoe warned him, and there were no smiles, no flashes of a gold-capped tooth from her.

'You're not the only one who's selfish,' Pilgrim said, feeling a decade's worth of tired, grubby baggage loaded on to the back of that one sentence. Words came slow and painful to him, tipping out, heavy as stones. 'All I want is to leave this place.

137

Just turn around and walk away and not stop until there's no one left but me and the knock of my boots on an empty road.' He could hear them now, a clear, rhythmic tap that was pleasingly countable. One, two, three, four. 'I wish I could be left alone, by the voice in my head, by the things I see and hear, by this constant nagging urge to find something I know I'm meant to find, even though I don't understand how or why. But as much as I want those things, I can't leave and I can't stop. Do you know why?'

Sheila hadn't taken her eyes off him. Her head gave the minutest of shakes.

'Because of a girl. A girl I can barely remember. She wrote a note and left it for me.' In his seat pocket, the firm wedge of Lacey's book nudged back into his awareness.

He felt Jay shift beside him. 'She put a bunch of kisses on it,' the guy said.

Sheila searched Pilgrim's face, her expression very serious and very still. 'This girl of yours, where is she?'

'North? In one of these camps, maybe? I don't know,' Pilgrim admitted. 'But I have to find her. She'll need me.' And saying it aloud landed the last thudding stone in the pit of his stomach. The weight of resignation, the weight of responsibility, all tied to a purpose he had little to no understanding of. It made him angry: not at the girl, but at a world and the people in it who were going to make his journey that much harder. He recognised the same sense of duty in Sheila – to Roscoe, to the people who had gathered in this place and looked to her for guidance. He wondered if she understood the terrible burden she had placed upon herself.

Around her neck she wore a gold heart-shaped locket and he wanted to ask if it held something inside it: a lock of hair or a small photograph of someone special. A heart she carried so close to her own. Perhaps it held nothing at all.

'*Show me to her.*'

He had lost track of Lacey for a time but with his thoughts so close to her again she reappears at his shoulder. Even with her chin tipped up to speak to him, her head barely reaches the top of his arm. If he closes his eyes, he'll be able to smell her – a hint of lantana flowers and fresh lemons. He doesn't close his eyes. Now isn't the time.

He feels a touch on his chest.

But Lacey's fingers weren't there. *She* wasn't there. But her photo was.

He pulled the picture from his shirt pocket, unfolded it and held it out. 'She's the one in the middle,' Pilgrim said as Sheila took the photo.

He knew when she found her. Her eyes changed, softened, as did her mouth. She flipped the photo over.

'Lacey?' Sheila asked, glancing up at him.

He nodded, the name sending a pang through his chest, too high to be ascribed to hunger pains.

'Someone's written the year.' She turned the photo back over and studied the girl. 'Why, she'd be sixteen or seventeen by now.'

'*I'll always need my family.*' There is such sorrow in Lacey's voice. She is so close she lives at the edges of him now, in his cells, in the lift and fall of each blink when that split-second darkness could open on to anything. '*Grammy, Karey. I miss them both so much.*'

He nodded to the photo. 'The two women are her grandmother and sister. They're gone now.'

Sheila said nothing for so long Jay shifted beside him again, shuffling his weight from foot to foot. Pilgrim sensed he wanted to speak, but he kept his thoughts to himself for now. Sheila pursed her lips and folded the photograph up, halves to quarters, a neat, compartmentalised memory.

'I'll take you to see Gunnar,' she said, handing the picture back to him. 'But once you're there, me and you are done. You and Roscoe are done. Are we clear?'

Pilgrim nodded and slipped the photograph safely back into the left-side pocket of his shirt.

'We're clear,' he said. 'Thank you.'

'Don't thank me,' she said. 'You haven't met him yet.'

Four roads fed into a rotary system. At its centre was a small, circular park with pathways, trees, grass pegged down with benches and five people who stood on sentry duty. Pilgrim, Sheila, Roscoe and Jay approached it from the south.

'We're moving into Gunnar's patch now,' Roscoe said.

She hadn't taken the lead this time but had fallen back to walk beside Pilgrim and Jay. Jay didn't give any indication he'd heard her. His head was down and his eyes on the photograph Pilgrim had passed over to him. He'd asked Pilgrim if he could see it and he couldn't think of a good enough reason to refuse.

'How come you're not all in the same territory?' Pilgrim asked her.

'It made sense for us to break off into smaller groups, especially when more and more people kept coming into the city,' she explained. 'Sheila speaks for ours. Gunnar here. Patty towards the Mississippi. Then there's Porco, Jessop, Michel and Iona. I like to think of it as a restaurant system – a greeter meets you at the door and directs you to a table and waitress zone she knows has space. We all know roughly how many people we have in each group. So when newcomers turn up, or we find them roaming around, depending on what they're looking for, they get taken to the right place.'

What they're looking for? Voice wondered.

'Everyone is let in?' Pilgrim asked, dubious.

Roscoe nodded. 'Most everyone, sure. At least at first. We're all heathens here, sweetheart, and proud of it. We allow people to shuffle around some if it's not a good fit, but generally it works pretty well. Everyone knows who will allow a non-voice-hearer in, for example. Some show up with a husband or wife in tow, that kind of thing, but that's surprisingly rare. We always let any kids in, of course. They get an open invite.' She glanced over at him, an expectant pause resting between them.

'Of course,' he said.

She nodded again, satisfied with his answer. 'We're a refuge here but we still have to be careful to protect our own. Sheila is mostly happy to have any non-hearers. Iona and Michel, too. We tend to scare the majority of them off, though.' She waggled her eyebrows. Grinned. 'The other groups don't welcome them so much. Another reason we split up into territories. Politics, you know?' An eye-roll, but she quickly became grave and touched Pilgrim's arm. 'I wasn't lying when I said Gunnar's a bastard. You should watch yourself with him.'

Pilgrim grabbed a couple of deep breaths, each one tickling closer to a cough that wouldn't easily be stifled if it took hold. He hoped they didn't have much further to go. 'Would you do something for me?' he asked her. 'If things don't go to plan.'

Roscoe's eyes widened. 'You *have* a plan?' She laughed when he gave her a mildly offended look. 'Go ahead and ask your favour, sweetness. I'll see what I can do.'

'Would you take Jay back to where you found him? If that's what he wants.'

Jay's scowl burned into the back of Pilgrim's head. 'I don't need you to speak for me, man. I'm more than capable of looking after my—'

'Oh, hush your complaining,' Roscoe told him, and Pilgrim felt sure she would have smacked Jay, if he'd been nearer. 'You're just sore he hears a voice, and that makes him a *bad person* in your book. Well, you need yourself some new books, honey. Not a single thing has stopped you from leaving since you got here, yet here you are, strolling along with us, nice as pie. You need to be quiet and think on *that* before you go shooting your mouth off.'

The checkpoint people had wandered out of the park to meet them. They were armed – guns, knives, an assault rifle – but it was the gravity with which they undertook their duties that interested Pilgrim. It was in stark contrast to how he'd entered Sheila's territory – right past an unarmed old-timer hanging out on a school bus. Roscoe had been right; the politics here were very different.

Feels like we've wandered into a war zone.

'Sheila.' The man with the assault rifle nodded. He was short, squat and sported a crew-cut. He had forearms beefy enough to crush beer cans.

A second guy, younger, his hair tied back with a bandana, smirked at Pilgrim's tool belt. 'Mr DIY!' he greeted. 'Awesome. I need my closet door rehanging.'

'Sure,' Pilgrim said. 'I can rehang your jaw from your face while I'm at it.'

The smirk dropped from Bandana Boy's mouth.

Voice sniggered.

'Hey.' Sheila sent Pilgrim a look that plainly told him to be quiet. She returned her attention to Crew-cut. 'I'd like to see Gunnar,' she told him. 'Got a couple more to go on the next ride out.'

'Leave them with us. We'll check them out.'

'No.'

Crew-cut paused in the middle of turning away, and Pilgrim couldn't tell which of his expressions the guy was feeling most keenly – disbelief or displeasure. 'Say again?'

'I'd like to see Gunnar,' Sheila repeated. 'We haven't spoken in a while.'

Crew-cut cast his gaze over Roscoe, Pilgrim, Jay. He turned to Bandana Boy and nodded, and that was all it needed – he took off running.

'You know where he is,' Crew-cut told Sheila shortly.

'I do.'

Crew-cut gave her a bow, theatrical and mocking, and waved them through.

The evening sun glowed on some distant horizon, lighting the sky like a strip club.

'There're a lot of birds here,' Pilgrim observed.

Lines of them perched on roofs, on windowsills, on the tops of dead streetlights. Black, shiny eyes watched them as they passed below. He counted as new birds fluttered in to roost and others took flight. Thirty-three. Three was a bad number, unlucky, like when you placed two left shoes together or a watch face down. And here there were two of them, side by side.

Along with the high number of birds, there were far more than the handful of people Jay said you'd be lucky to come across here in a week. A couple crossed the street with a small child between them. The two adults cast glances his way, their expressions closed and distrustful. By the time they reached the opposite kerb, the man was swinging the child up into his arms and they were hurrying away.

A street over, Pilgrim heard more signs of life. A modest buzz of activity. People were openly living here. He couldn't recall seeing anything like it.

Estes Park, Voice said.

It was the vaguest of memories and Pilgrim had to lever it up, a rock sunk thick into a mudbank. There had been a group of more than thirty people living near a large, mirror-like lake, mountains and woodland on all sides, and so much fresh air it hurt to breathe it in. It had been quiet except for the birds. They had nested in the trees, their calls trilling like a hundred tiny bells every morning at daybreak. Pilgrim hadn't stayed long. The people and their bustle, all those eyes and ears, their turning thoughts – it had been too much. There were too many things to keep track of and too many things that never stayed in the same place. It had disoriented him and so he'd left, abandoning it for the only form of solitude he could have: him and Voice.

'They came when we did,' Sheila answered, following his gaze to the birds' roosts. 'All this' – she gestured at the city around her – 'happened fast once news started filtering through.'

'News?' he asked.

Sheila gave him a look, as if gauging how serious he was being. 'That's right. News about the Flitting Man.'

A faint look of puzzlement must have crossed his face because Roscoe said, 'Surely you've heard of the Flitting Man?'

'Should I have?' He could see his reply troubled them.

'He told me he's got brain damage,' Jay said, as if that helped explain it.

They were passing under the grimy, striped awning of a candy store. Sheila put an arm out to stop them and lowered her voice, her frowning eyes meeting Pilgrim's. 'You'd best get your story straight before we go in there. He'll catch you in a lie. And you'd better do me the courtesy of explaining yourself. Everyone here knows about the Flitting Man – through rumour or elsewhere – but we know.'

Don't you dare say a thing about—

'I got shot and woke up in a backyard in Vicksburg,' Pilgrim said. 'I may have missed a few things.'

From the back of his head, Voice let out a frustrated sigh.

'Vicksburg?'

A look passed between Roscoe and Sheila.

You're an idiot, Voice told him.

'What were you doing in Vicksburg?' There was no friendliness in Sheila's tone; a shutter had come down over her eyes, making it impossible to read her.

'Digging for treasure,' Pilgrim said.

Her face tightened. 'Not only are you a smartass but you

expect me to believe you've never heard of the Flitting Man? That you don't know a *single thing* about what's been going on recently?'

Being the centre of Sheila's attention was like being gripped at collar and neck by two burly hands. Pilgrim was pinned, riveted by the pent-up annoyance radiating from her.

Pilgrim and Sheila sitting in a tree, K. I. S. S. I. N. G.

That almost tempted a smile from him, but he didn't want to rile Sheila further. She was no-nonsense and straight-talking – she said what she meant and she did what she said – and he had to admire that.

'Like I said,' Pilgrim said carefully, 'I must have missed a few things.' But, if he were being honest with himself, there was something about those two words, wasn't there? *Flitting* and *Man*. They slid together as neatly as a knife into a sheath.

'What about the name Red?' Sheila asked him. 'You ever hear of a girl called Red? Early twenties. No teeth.'

Ruby-Red.

Recognition rocked him to his foundations, cracking him straight down his centre. One side yawned away, collapsing and scattering in a pile of dust and disbelief, and the other side remained standing, staring back at Sheila as if nothing had happened.

And the shock resounding through his head wasn't his alone. Voice was as stunned as he was.

'There's something about you,' Sheila said, eyes narrowing on him. 'I saw it a mile off. Something I couldn't put my finger on at first.'

Pilgrim stayed quiet, not trusting himself to speak.

'You're trouble. It's there in the words you don't say. In the stillness of your eyes. Too much trouble, for my liking.'

She left him standing there, and he had to take three full breaths before he could follow.

THE PART
FROM THE PAST

The Man Who Saw Red

Chapter 1

Ruby-Red

Four years ago

Pilgrim had called himself another name back then. He didn't know why. Hiding had come naturally to him. He didn't think about it too closely; it was what it was, and he was who he was. A name meant little when you got right down to it.

It was cold here, colder than he'd expected. The temperature had dropped as he'd crossed the border from Illinois into Wisconsin. He'd found a long, flat stretch of main street, lined with looted stores and empty cafés, and had a mind to go shopping. An hour or so passed before he was stepping out of Walgreens, the chill air hitting his face, the sun warm on his skin, but it wasn't for shelter or warmth that he'd considered re-entering the store.

The girl spotted him and his opportunity to retreat was lost.

Haltingly, she raised her hand in greeting and it seemed to him it momentarily took on the red translucent glow of molten metal. He blinked and her hand went back to normal. Giving her a nod while cursing under his breath, he made his way over to them. His strides were measured, cautious, and as he went he took stock of what he was seeing. Neither the girl nor the guy beside her had packs or visible weapons. They had the clothes on their backs, the boots on their feet and very little else. He toyed with the idea they might be mentally deficient in some way. He never went anywhere without his pack. Or a weapon.

You may lack common sense but, no, you're never unprepared. Voice said it to no one but him, but Pilgrim murmured for him to be quiet anyway.

He'd been in town for a day so far, methodically searching the surrounding residences for food and water supplies, batteries, antibiotics. Anything useful.

'Hi.'

Pilgrim left a good, safe distance between them. He nodded a second time to the girl and, on closer inspection, saw she wasn't so much a girl as a young woman. The guy was the same age. Actually, they looked similar.

Siblings.

'Hm.'

The guy had his hands tucked into his armpits. He was shivering.

'It's cold, huh?' the woman said, small puffs of smoke leaving her mouth.

'You should get better jackets,' Pilgrim said. 'They have hats, scarves, gloves. In there.' He pointed back at the Walgreens.

'I like yours,' she said, and smiled; not a full-blown smile, just a curving of her lips. It squinted the corners of her eyes.

He wasn't sure what she meant and then remembered the new hat he'd pulled on. It was fleecy, with ear-flaps. Purple.

She lost her smile when he made no reply, with either words or expression. Her eyes dropped to the gun holstered at his hip. 'Look, we've had kind of a tough time of things lately. Lost our stuff this morning. Don't have any water. In fact, we don't have anything.'

She was a skinny thing. The guy not so much, but there was something fragile about him, too. Not weak fragile. Innocent. The guy was watching him silently.

Pilgrim relented. 'They have red, too,' he told her. 'I could show you.'

Oh, Hoyt . . . Voice said, because that was the name Pilgrim went by back then. There was sighing disappointment there because Voice disliked people almost as much as Pilgrim did.

A delicate wrinkle of skin creased the girl's brows. 'What?'

'Hats,' Pilgrim clarified. 'Purple, green, pink, red.'

You already said red, Voice said.

That small smile appeared again. 'You think I'd pick red?'

Pilgrim shrugged. 'Maybe. You seem like a red to me.'

By the time they were done shopping, the young woman wore a deep red hat in the same style as Pilgrim's, ear-flaps tied under her chin, and the guy sported a green knitted bobble-hat. They picked out scarves and stuffed gloves into their too-thin jacket pockets.

'That's my brother Albus,' she said. 'I'm Ruby, though sometimes I get called Red.' She stuck her hand out and Pilgrim looked at it for a long moment before reaching over. Her fingers were warm, not hot like he expected, and her palm was dry as she slipped her hand into his. She gave it a single efficient shake. Albus stuck his paw out, too, and Pilgrim transferred his hand to his, meeting the young guy's eyes as they shook. He hadn't said a single word.

As stoic as you. Just what we need.

'Who took your stuff?' Pilgrim asked, looking at the man but figuring Ruby-sometimes-Red would be the one to answer. He wasn't wrong.

'Some bald guy. He didn't want to hurt us. He was just . . . hungry.'

He watched how she and Albus shared a look, something passing between the two.

'It's fine,' she told Pilgrim, and shrugged. 'It's only stuff. Nothing that can't be replaced.'

'Food isn't easily replaced,' he pointed out.

'No, you're right. It isn't. I know you don't know us, and that this is going to sound strange but, please, don't jump to assumptions about us, okay?'

Uh-oh. Here it comes. She's going to confess to roasting the bald guy and eating him. They're raving cannibals. That's why they don't need to worry about food and—

'You're very good at concealing it. Really. No one would ever know.' She was staring at him as if he were some fascinating creature she'd found hiding beneath a rock. 'Which is a very good thing. You'd probably be dead twenty times over if you weren't.'

The muscles across Pilgrim's shoulders tensed. Beneath his purple hat his scalp prickled and flashed hot. His right hand tightened into a fist.

'You hear one, don't you?' Ruby-Red asked. 'A voice. It's okay that you do,' she added hastily. 'We won't tell anyone.'

He glanced at the brother. There was an intentness to his gaze, a benign curiosity that didn't alarm Pilgrim but did make him uncomfortable. The guy blinked a few times, as if clearing his thoughts, and raised his eyebrows in question.

Why don't they look scared? They should be scared.

'Who are you people?' he asked. He made a conscious effort to unfurl his fist. His fingers brushed the gun's holster.

You gonna shoot them?

He hadn't decided yet. It would depend on how she answered.

'I told you already. I'm Ruby, this is Albus.' The guy nodded and offered a small smile. 'And in here' – she tapped her head – 'is Jonah. He says it's nice to meet you, Hoyt.'

Holy fuck, Voice breathed into Pilgrim's surprised silence. *She's a mind-reader.*

CHAPTER 2

Letters

'What're you writing?' Pilgrim asked.

Ruby stopped mid-scribble and glanced up. On the counter beside her the artificial light from the lantern cast shadows over the shifting landscape of her face. They moved when she smiled.

'I'm an epistolary-journal writer. It's my thing.'

'You're a what?'

She broke into a full smile. It was one of her greatest assets and she was quick to use it. He wouldn't be here, in the dark bowels of this thrift shop, swallowed up by the overcrowded racks of clothing, if she wasn't so charming. It had been two full days since he'd met her and her brother outside Walgreens and he'd felt no great urgency to part ways with them yet.

'I write letters,' she explained. 'About what's going on, where I've been, where I'm heading, my thoughts, feelings, dreams for the future. I leave most of them behind for people to find. Sometimes, I gift them. Occasionally, I hold on to a few. Depends what's in it. This one is number . . .' She checked the top of the paper. 'One hundred and sixteen.'

Pilgrim whistled under his breath.

That's Virginia Woolf levels of letter-writing, Voice said.

'I guess I have a lot to say,' she said, eyes widening on a grin, as if she'd amused herself. 'This one's for you, actually,' she added.

Her head bent back to her task. Pilgrim wanted to move closer, to try to sneak a glimpse of what she was writing, but he didn't move. He didn't want to show too much interest.

Voice didn't have any such reservations.

Ask her what she's writing, he said. *Ask her, ask her.*

Pilgrim opened his mouth.

'You'll have to wait until I'm finished,' she said without raising her head.

Albus appeared from between the racks, wearing a new quilted winter jacket. He held his arms out and turned three hundred and sixty degrees, modelling for them.

'Lovely,' Pilgrim said.

'It suits you, Al,' Ruby agreed.

'Shame it's bright orange,' Pilgrim said.

Albus raised his eyebrows and looked down at himself.

'You'll stick out like a Halloween pumpkin.'

Albus's arms dropped, hands *whump*ing his sides. It was about as close as he got to complaining.

'Hoyt's right,' Ruby told her brother, the glow of the lantern adding a gleam to her eyes, highlighting her look of commiseration. 'You should find something darker.' Her head cocked as she listened. She smiled and looked at Pilgrim. 'Albus says you're stifling his sense of fashion.'

'It's either that or have someone use him as target practice. His choice.'

Albus pulled a face and turned around, disappearing back into the racks. Pilgrim heard the soft squeal of hangers as they slid along railings.

'You're a sourpuss,' Ruby told Pilgrim.

He grunted, unbothered. 'I've been called worse.'

'Makes me wonder what's happened to you, though, to make you that way.' She tapped her pen against her lips.

'What does Jonah say?'

'About you? Not as much as you'd think. Which is interesting in itself.'

'Not much of a gossip, then.'

'Hmm, no, not really. He's as tight-lipped as you. He's an utter pain in the butt, frankly. Between the two of you, I might actually lose my temper at some point.'

'How do you do that?'

'Not lose my temper? By being awesomely patient and saint-like.'

'No. With your brother. How do you hear him when he doesn't say anything?'

She considered Pilgrim for a moment and he couldn't work out if she was deciding to answer him or listening to Jonah. 'I have help,' she said finally. 'We're twins, you know – not sure if you picked up on that. Not identical, obviously, but similar enough. We've always had a connection. Weird twin shit you probably wouldn't believe even if I told you. But the hearing-him thing? That's mainly down to Jonah. I don't fully understand it myself. But you know what they say: "Never look a gift horse in the mouth."'

I've never understood that expression, Voice said.

'I can see you're chomping at the bit for more conversation, but you need to stop distracting me. I want to finish this.'

Pilgrim was happy to leave her to her letter-writing—

Epistolary-journal writing, Voice corrected.

—and wandered the store. He came across a framed piece of artwork as big as a flat-screen TV. He swiped a palm across the glass, clearing away the dust. It revealed a map of the United States, each state shaped from the licence plate of the region (the sunset colours of Nebraska, the green of Colorado, the bucking bronco of Wyoming). It was touristy and tacky and it appealed to him for reasons he couldn't explain. He rubbed a thumb over the stickered price-tag.

$124.99 (shipping included).

Buy two, Voice said. *One for you, one for me.*

A clanging crash came from outside and his head snapped around. A second of resounding silence when nothing moved and then he was heading for the front of the store. A hand snagged his arm, pulled him up short, stopping him before he could pass in front of the window.

Albus held a finger to his lips and pointed.

Through the plate glass a huge black bear had rolled a dumpster into view. It reared on to its hind legs and lifted the lid with one giant paw. It gave a brief look inside and, finding nothing it wanted, shoved the dumpster away. The container slammed into the thrift store's frontage and a long, jagged crack shot through the window from base to top edge.

Ruby joined them.

'It's a mama bear,' she breathed on Pilgrim's right. 'Look at her.'

There was no way Ruby's voice could have carried, but the bear's head turned and she stared at the store, as if she could see them in the darkness, three shadows backlit by lantern light.

Pilgrim held his breath and it felt as though Voice held it with him. His fingers slipped to the gun at his hip.

'Go home, Mama Bear,' Ruby whispered. 'Go home to your baby.'

The bear dropped to all fours and ambled closer. She swiped the dumpster aside with a rattling clatter and lifted back on to her hind legs. She must have been eight feet tall. Her front paws spread on the window and Pilgrim saw the wickedly sharp claws as long as his thumb. He also saw how thin the bear was. Too thin. She was starving. At this time of year, she should be well fed, solid all the way through, ready for hibernation.

The bear snorted and steam misted the window.

The pane creaked under her weight.

'It's going to break,' he muttered. He pulled his gun. Flicked off its safety.

Fingers gripped his wrist and Ruby held on to him and whispered, 'Go home, Mama Bear. Go on now. Time to go.' She said it like her words held power, like they were laced with animal magic. 'Go, go, go,' she whispered.

The bear opened her maw, incisors flashing. A sound came out of her that was somewhere between growl and yawn. She shook herself and dropped down, swung her large head back and forth as if saying, *No, no, you're absolutely right. I'm late for supper*, and turned on the spot and trundled away, rear end swaying.

Pilgrim released his breath and heard his two companions do the same.

Baloo isn't as friendly as I remember.

'We're close to a state park here,' Ruby said, almost too low for them to hear. She let go of Pilgrim's wrist and he could feel the lingering imprint of her fingers on his skin they had pressed so tightly. She looked over at him and her brother. 'We should be careful. There might be more wild animals roaming around.'

Pilgrim slid his gun into its holster. 'All the more reason not to wear orange.'

Albus huffed a laugh.

It was as they were leaving the thrift store – Albus wearing a dark forest-green jacket – that Ruby handed Pilgrim the letter she'd written for him. It was sealed inside a plain white envelope with the name Hoyt printed on the front in pretty, cursive lettering and a hand-drawn rose on the reverse where the letter was sealed shut. The rose swirled outward from its centre in a perfect unfurling of petals. His eyes followed the flowering whorl, the design appearing to have been made from a single, uninterrupted pen stroke.

'Don't read it now,' she told him. 'Not until we part ways. Do you promise?'

Pilgrim didn't like making promises. Didn't like dealing with the fallout when he was forced to break them.

She pinched the top corner of the letter and gave it a playful tug.

He didn't release his grip.

'If you don't swear, I'll take it back,' she warned.

Pilgrim gave her his promise.

CHAPTER 3

Names

Two weeks and three days later

'We're lost, aren't we?' Pilgrim said.

Ruby didn't answer, her head bowed over the rumpled roadmap as she walked, her other hand awkwardly holding on to Pilgrim's compass.

Albus trudged beside him, fingers curled under the shoulder straps of his pack. He smiled at Pilgrim and shrugged his shoulders as if to say, *I'm sure we're fine.*

'You wouldn't say even if we were,' Pilgrim said to him.

He couldn't if his life depended on it, Voice said. He sounded mean-spirited and crabby.

'What crawled up your ass?'

Albus raised his eyebrows and Pilgrim tapped his head, indicating he was speaking to Voice. It was liberating to be so open about him, to talk out loud to Voice as if it were the most natural thing in the world. But it was important Pilgrim didn't get used to it – a habit like that could have serious consequences if he did it in the wrong company.

Albus breathed an 'Ahhh' of understanding and went back to his walking, following his meandering sister. Pilgrim could hear her muttering to herself.

I have no ass. As you well know. I'm tired of traipsing around out here with barely a word of explanation. We should have stopped back when we had the chance.

It was well past midnight. The motel they had passed was more than five miles behind them, down a long, dark and winding mountain road. Their boots stamped on the icy blacktop, echoing through pine trees, deadened by the clumps of snow the sun had failed to melt during the day. The moon was high and bright in the star-speckled sky and the curving double-lane road was as black as oil but for the yellow centre lines. The freezing emptiness made Pilgrim shiver.

She's gonna walk us to our deaths out here. We'll be like those plane-crash survivors in the Andes who ended up eating each other.

Pilgrim's breath misted on a sigh. He wondered if he should be concerned with Voice's fixation on cannibalism.

'We're almost there,' Ruby said. She turned to give Pilgrim a look, though he knew it wasn't directed at him.

Voice grumbled. *And she needs to stop listening in on our private conversations.*

Pilgrim sent his thoughts deep, concentrating on conveying exactly what he wanted without extraneous thoughts getting in the way.

—You know it's not her doing the eavesdropping.

Whatever. They both need to stop. You hear me over there? Quit being a Peeping Tom. Or a Peeping Jonah. Whatever. It's creepy.

—You never hear anything from him? Not a stray word or—

No. I wouldn't be so annoyed by it all if I did.

—Well, I guess you partway understand how I feel, having you listen in and watch every single thing I do.

Don't exaggerate. It's not every *single thing.*

'Here?' Ruby whispered.

She was looking at Albus. The guy had stopped walking and was gazing off into the pines. He looked back at her and shrugged.

'This has to be it.' She stowed the map and compass away in her jacket pocket. Pilgrim would have to remember to ask her for it back later.

He didn't know why she was whispering, but he found himself treading more lightly, staying clear of the crisp, fallen pine cones on the sides of the road. She stepped off the blacktop and her feet crunched on to frozen grass. Pilgrim and Albus followed her to the snow-covered track that ran into the trees. They stopped to stare down the shadowy, wheel-rutted dirt road, the tall pines creating a dark, branch-enclosed tunnel. It looked like the road that led to a witch's house.

Oh, hell no.

'What's down there?' Pilgrim asked.

Red smiled and rubbed her mittened hands together, blowing a warming stream of air into them. 'Jonah's family,' she answered.

Twenty-three minutes later they came upon the log cabin. A single light glowed from the front window, a beacon in the frigid night. A plume of grey smoke drifted into the sky from a stone-stacked chimney. As they'd left the road behind, the air had grown chillier and Pilgrim's nose was numb by the time his feet hit the path leading to the cabin's front stoop. He longed to sit in front of the log fire that burned inside.

A shadow passed the window and Voice startled, a turning sensation in the back of Pilgrim's head.

They know we're here.

The door creaked open a few inches and snuffling noises reached their ears. At waist height, a dark snout poked out, and a voice, old and craggy, said, 'Anybody else with you?'

'It's just us,' Ruby replied.

'Good. Peggy won't hurt you, but she is likely to slobber you to death.'

Ruby's eyes sparkled when she glanced over at Pilgrim and Albus. 'Go ahead,' she told the woman. 'We don't mind.'

The door swung open and a sleek dart of movement streaked down the porch steps and across the lawn. The Doberman collided with Ruby and she started laughing – the closest Pilgrim had heard to giggling for years – as she crouched to fuss the dog. It attacked her with its long tongue, its rear end wiggling under her petting, tail *whump*ing Albus's leg on each wag.

'I thought Dobermans had pointed ears,' Pilgrim said, watching as Albus joined his sister in lavishing the animal with affection. Overwhelmed, the dog collapsed on its side, whining in pleasure, tongue hanging out the side of its mouth as Albus rubbed the Doberman's belly with his gloved hands.

'Only when they have been docked.' The old lady had ventured out on to the porch and had wrapped one hand around a porch railing. 'Which is a cruel and unnecessary practice.'

She wore a thick tied bathrobe over what appeared to be three sets of clothes piled one on top of the other. It made her appear bulky and cumbersome, but her face was thin and lined with years of living. Her grey hair had been pulled back into a loose bun. 'Don't think we have had the pleasure,' she said to Pilgrim. Her eyes were flecked with silver moonlight.

'Hoyt,' he said.

'Hoyt,' she repeated, and he heard the scepticism. 'That's not your name.'

He felt a spike of irritation. 'It's the only one I have.'

She made a noise, somewhere between a snort and a *pffft*. 'Nonsense. Anyhow, enough keeping an elderly lady outdoors. It's colder than *die Nase einer Hexe* out here. No more fussing my dog. Come inside. Quick now. Come, come.' She shooed them all in, waddling her way back across the porch, hobbling and favouring her right leg.

The interior of the cabin wasn't what Pilgrim expected; he felt the equivalent of Voice's nod.

Stench of wet dog, dirty crockery everywhere.

Instead, they were greeted with a neat, clean area where

everything had its place. The bookshelves were organised in colour order rather than alphabetically. The fireplace housed a roaring fire, the mantelpiece was bare but for two hand-carved wooden figures on opposite ends: two Dobermans, one sitting regal with its chest puffed, the other mid-run, limbs striding out. Looking around, Pilgrim spied a number of other whittled figurines: dotted on bookshelves, on side-tables, a parade of them lining the top of a stand-up piano at the back wall. Mostly animals but people, too, intricately carved with walking sticks and hats, champagne flutes and bouquets of flowers.

The cabin smelled of roasted coffee and woodsmoke.

'I am glad you've come.' The old woman shuffled her way to an armchair. She barely fit with her layers of clothing, but she squeezed between its arms, rocking and wedging herself in. Wood shavings flecked the floor at her feet, the only mess in the whole room. She picked up an X-ACTO knife and a piece of wood she'd left on a small, round table beside her and waved them to the couch and chair.

'Sit, sit. We don't stand on formalities here.'

The Doberman had stuck close to Ruby and Albus, and as they moved to take the couch, it went with them, placing its beautiful glossy head on Ruby's lap as soon as she'd settled herself. Pilgrim didn't immediately head for the other chair. He went right and walked a half-circuit of the sitting room, wanting a better angle so he could see everything in it.

'Boy, go get the coffee,' the woman told him as he stopped beside the last empty chair. 'Cups are in the cupboard over the sink.'

'It's been a long time since I was called "boy",' Pilgrim said. 'Or ordered around.'

'I'm too old to mince my words. Now, do you want coffee or not?'

He shucked off his pack and rested it next to the seat, taking a moment to stretch his arms and shoulders out. He wondered if he was doing it to waste a few seconds so it didn't seem as though he was jumping to obey her. It made him feel foolish and very much like the boy she'd called him. The tiny smile she wore implied she thought the same.

He went to investigate the kitchenette tucked around the corner of the sitting room. As he did, he heard her and Ruby begin to talk.

You think she wants us out of earshot?

Pilgrim didn't know. Didn't care, either, because the smell of coffee grew richer as he stepped into the nook. On the kitchen's work surface there was a coffee pot with a ghastly orange knitted sweater pulled over the top of it.

Tea cosy.

'What?'

It's a tea cosy. It keeps the pot warm.

Pilgrim touched a finger to each cupboard door and opened the one above the sink, finding the cups and hooking out four. He grabbed the coffee pot with its foolish-looking cosy and carried everything into the sitting room.

Conversation halted when he appeared. Both Ruby and Albus had removed their hats, jackets and gloves. It was quite the domestic scene.

Now *do you think they wanted us out of earshot?*

'Sit,' the old woman said. Pilgrim placed everything on the low table in front of the fire. He was getting warm and unzipped his jacket and unthreaded his scarf. He didn't take them off, though, and he didn't sit.

The woman smiled, her two front teeth crooked and overlapping slightly.

Snaggle-tooth.

'Aren't you staying?' she asked, clearly amused.

Ruby ran her hand over the dog's sleek head, stroking it over and over. She watched him. So did Albus. He felt a tension in them, an expectation. Of what, he wasn't sure.

'Why do I get the feeling you know what I'm about to say?' he asked the old woman.

She laughed, a husky, tickled sound. 'Oh, we are not so mysterious as all that. It's all very simple, really.'

The well-fed fire was turning his warmth into a sticky heat at the back of his neck and under his arms. He shrugged his jacket off, unable to stand it, and unfastened another button on his shirt.

'Making you hot, am I?' Another laugh, her eyes crinkling. 'Now sit, you're putting a crick in my neck, looking up at you. Albus, would you be a dear and pour?'

Albus did, the gentle clattering of cups and the liquid slosh of pouring coffee so homely in their sounds that Pilgrim felt a nostalgic twinge. He couldn't recall the last time he'd sat like this, warmed by a fire, in (mostly) pleasant company, about to drink freshly brewed coffee. He glanced at Ruby and found her eyes on him, affection in the soft smile on her face, as if she were observing the first, tentative steps of an injured wild animal she had nursed back to health.

'Stop,' he told her.

Her eyebrows shot up. 'Stop what?'

'Stop thinking whatever it is you're thinking.'

'She cannot help her thoughts, *Sonnenblume*. None of us can. Thank you,' the old woman said as Albus passed her a cup.

Albus offered Pilgrim a cup, and their eyes met over the steaming drink. The guy couldn't talk in ways Pilgrim understood, but he understood the message in his eyes loud and clear: *Quit being so prickly and relax.*

I tell you that all the time, Voice complained. *You never listen to me.*

Pilgrim paid neither of them any mind and turned to the old woman. 'You said it was simple.'

'I did say that, yes,' she replied, a twinkle in her eye.

'What did you mean?'

'The voices. Why they are here. Why you and me and Ruby hear one. Why so many of us did and still do.'

'And you have the answer.' He said it as though he didn't believe her for a second.

Prickly and *cynical*.

She took a sip of her drink and winced, either because of the heat or because of its bitterness. '*Ja*, I do.'

Pilgrim waited, barely aware of the burn of the scalding water through the cup's ceramic. The dog made a high whining noise as it opened its mouth to yawn.

'Why?' Pilgrim finally asked, the word pulled from him like a stubborn tooth.

'The same reason you have forgotten your real name and all the little details about yourself that you cannot bring yourself to find.'

His stomach tightened, an uncomfortable noosing, closer to dread than anything else.

Closer to fear, Voice said.

No, it wasn't fear that had led him to hide from himself, it had been done out of—

'Need,' she said, and winked. 'Now that *is* simple, isn't it?'

'No,' he answered. 'It's not.'

'You expect it to be something large and complex, and these things rarely are. The voices were needed, and so they came. Tell me, when did you start hearing yours?'

'I don't know.'

She gave him a narrow-eyed look. 'You lie. You know. But fine, we shall play it your way. I was in a hospital in Bamberg. Very ill. I was all of twenty-three years old and didn't have long to live. I was recently a mother to a little girl – Eva was her name – and not married more than two years. I was very much in love with both my husband and my new daughter. I didn't want to go. Didn't want to leave them. It felt as though God had turned His back on me, that He was being unspeakably cruel to take me away from those I loved so soon. I had everything and I had nothing. And *that* is when it came, as I lay in that hospital bed, with tears blinding me and the pressure of all those worries weighing down my chest so it felt like I would drown.'

'You heard a voice?'

'*Ja*, I heard one.' She sipped her drink.

'What did it say?'

'It told me to stop being a self-pitying fool. That not everything was about me.'

Pilgrim swallowed a hot mouthful of coffee. It burned a line down his oesophagus. 'Seems harsh.'

'Oh, it was. But it was also true. Being that close to death can make you incredibly self-centred.'

'Understandably.'

'Yes. But it is not very helpful.'

'You said you were dying,' Ruby said.

A crooked smile. 'And yet here I sit, drinking coffee and shooting the breeze?'

Ruby nodded. The dog's ears had perked up as they conversed. It looked from speaker to speaker. As if knowing its mistress was telling a difficult story, the dog left Ruby and padded to her, resting its chin on the arm of its mistress's chair. It huffed through its jowls and the old woman laid a hand on the dog's neck. Her knuckles were swollen and sore-looking.

'What happened?' Ruby asked.

'I *was* dying, but I had some lessons left to learn. And lessons yet to pass on. I had a . . . resurgence, you could say. It was quite remarkable. A miracle, even. The doctors were very surprised.'

'And the voice you heard?' Pilgrim asked.

'Oh, it stayed with me. And has been with me ever since. Much like Ruby's Jonah in that regard.'

The two women smiled at each other.

'So your point is it came when you needed it?' Pilgrim said, for some reason displeased by their camaraderie, displeased by the whole conversation. 'What about all the other voices? They weren't needed. Not everyone wanted to die.'

'Maybe not wanted, no, but they needed to. Your turn.'

His hand tightened around his cup, hearing a hidden threat to her words, but she continued to talk and he eased his hold enough to take another drink. The coffee was bitter, but still he drank.

'No name and no history,' she mused. 'Maybe we should call you Clint Eastwood, eh? The Man with no Name.'

He didn't smile; his face was too stiff for that. 'Hoyt is fine.'

She placed her cup aside and picked up the discarded carving and the X-ACTO knife from her lap. She went back to whittling. Tiny shavings of wood curled away and fell to her bathrobe. 'And where did Hoyt come from?'

'A book,' he said without thinking.

'Ah. Are all of your names from books?'

'Yes,' he said, again without much thought.

'I see. And do you know why you are here?'

He felt like they were in the middle of a dance and he was trying his best not to get his toes trampled. The room and the crackling fire, Ruby, Albus – as silent as ever – and the dog, all faded into the background as he watched the woman's arthritic hands deftly manoeuvre the blade along the grain in the wood.

'Ruby brought me here,' he answered. '*You* brought me here.'

'Almost true. It wasn't us, as such, but the voices we hear. Jonah and mine hear each other, you see. Speak, listen, *collude*. It's something they can do because they've been here many, many years. Much longer than yours. Much longer than anyone's voice. They're as old as the mountains and as wise as the trees.'

What's she talking about?

Pilgrim could feel Voice's bafflement.

'But I am an old woman, and mine shall die with me, the same as Jonah will die when Ruby's time comes. It is a pact they have. A promise made. It is how it *should* be. They have interfered long enough and understand it is time to leave the rest of us to our fates. But there is another who will not go so easily.' She lifted the wood to her lips and blew, clearing it of dust. She looked up into Pilgrim's eyes. 'It is natural to want to continue living, is it not? To grasp on with both hands and refuse to let go? Even when your grasp hurts others, even when it harms everything around it. Sometimes it takes an outside force to loosen that grip. To be the one to make it release its hold and say, *Enough — this isn't yours any more.*'

'You're talking in riddles,' he said.

'Am I?' She cackled, her old face creasing. 'And here I thought I was speaking plainly. That's the danger of listening to them for so long, I suspect. They are quite tricksome when you get right down to it. Let me be blunt, then. We have entered a new world, *Hoyt*.' The way she said his name was mocking but not unkind. 'And you have a role to play in it. As does Albus.'

'This has nothing to do with me,' Pilgrim said.

'Is that what you think? That you can change your name and lie low and everything will flow over you like a bedded stone in a river that will never be disturbed?' She leaned back, giving him a look of rebuke. She rested her wood and knife in her lap again. 'You have a part to play, whether you like it or not. *That* is one of the things we are here to discuss.' She held up a knotted finger when he opened his mouth. 'In the morning. You arrived much later than I expected and my bones ache. You have kept me up long enough. Sleep where you will and stoke the fire if you wish. Or not. Peggy will keep me warm.' She set her carving aside and levered herself stiffly from her seat, hissing in pain and holding on to her hip. 'Come on, girl. Bedtime.' The dog rose to its feet.

'Sweet dreams,' Ruby said as the woman went past.

She didn't reply but reached a gnarled hand out, cupping Ruby's chin in her palm. They looked at each other for the longest moment, and then she let Ruby go with a tender stroke to the cheek. As she walked behind the sofa, she laid the same hand on top of Albus's head and gave his hair a small ruffle.

'Your hair is far too long,' she told him.

Ruby smiled at her twin.

The dog padded after the old woman to the other side of the room, where they disappeared behind her bedroom door.

Pilgrim, Ruby and Albus were quiet for a time, each of them staring: at the fire, at the door the old woman had gone through, at the floor. At last, Pilgrim got up, crouching to add another log to the fire.

'All that talk,' he said, poking at the logs to feed oxygen into the flames, his face baking in the heat, 'and she never said her name.'

'Matilde.'

'What?'

'Her name's Matilde.'

'And how old is *Matilde*? She looks close to ninety.'

Albus hummed softly in agreement.

'Looks can be deceiving,' Ruby said. 'I'm sorry I didn't explain more about why we came here.'

Pilgrim poked the fire some more, hard enough to send sparks flying up the chimney flute. 'I didn't ask.'

'You don't ask *anything*,' Ruby said. 'What's up with that?'

He sat back on his heels. 'None of this is my business.'

'But surely it is if you chose to come with us. We've travelled together for – what? – three weeks now?'

Seventeen days, but he didn't feel the need to correct her. He didn't feel the need to explain to himself why he'd stayed with them for so long, either. It had felt right. There was something about them that . . . drew him. And he didn't just mean how Ruby's raised hand had pulled him back to childhood, when he'd shine a flashlight through the flesh and bones of his hands and make them glow, and how a small, warm body would come and lean up against him, pushing her cheek into his upper arm and demanding he do the same to her, and when he did, her hand was so much littler than his, her fingers so—

You're treading awfully close to those memories you're scared of remembering.

Not scared. *Needed* not to remember. There was a difference.

Besides, Ruby and Albus found jackets and packs and a few provisions in those first three days. Doesn't account for you choosing to stay for a further fourteen.

Pilgrim did his best to close his thoughts off from Voice, even though his best efforts were rarely good enough.

'And you've never once asked where we're from or where we're heading,' Ruby continued. 'Nothing. You never ask about Jonah, not like Albus does. How can you not be more interested in all this?' She gestured around the cabin, at Matilde's bedroom door, at herself and her brother.

He *was* curious, but not enough to want to get involved. He had no intention of dragging things out into the light when he might later wish he'd left well enough alone. You couldn't get burned if you didn't stray too close to the fire.

You're getting a little near to these flames now, though, aren't you, compadre?

He was. He threw dousing water over his smouldering curiosity and took a good, long step away from it.

Easy as that?

As easy as that. It was liberating not to care.

If you say so.

Pilgrim stood up. 'I'm going to sleep. And in the morning, I'm leaving. You should come with me.'

'You can't run away for ever,' Ruby told him, disappointment in her eyes. 'Someday there won't be anywhere left to hide.'

She didn't know him very well. He was excellent at hiding.

A hand on his arm woke him. Pilgrim's fingers immediately slipped under his pack to his gun, but it was only Albus who leaned over him.

The cabin was chilly – the fire had burned down to faintly glowing embers. It did nothing to illuminate the far reaches of the room. The sofa and chairs hulked in the darkness. Pilgrim could make out Ruby on the sofa, a shapeless lump beneath the blanket Albus had draped over her.

Albus's hand tightened on his arm.

'What?' Pilgrim whispered.

Albus backed off and beckoned him to follow. Pilgrim brought the gun out and tucked it under his belt at the small of his back. He copied Albus's example and stayed low as they crouch-walked their way to the same window the beacon of light had shone from the night before. A lace curtain covered the dual-paned glass and Albus pointed outside.

Pilgrim didn't touch the net curtain as he peered through it. The sky was lightening to cobalt grey and a fine frost covered the grass and leaves, giving everything a pearlescent glimmer. There was nothing out there but the pine trees, their coats speckled with melting dew, and the dark veins of roots threading through the frosted earth.

I don't see anything, Voice whispered.

Then they moved. Three of them, hunkered low to the east on the other side of the track that he, Albus and Ruby had followed in. They wore dark clothing, dark woollen hats, and two held weapons.

Guns. Have to assume the third has one, too. What're they doing here?

'Go wake your sister,' Pilgrim told Albus. 'Quickly.'

Albus scooted away, and Pilgrim heard rustling noises and murmurs as Ruby stirred from her sleep. In Matilde's room, the dog snuffled at the bottom of the closed door.

It knows something's up.

'What's going on?' Ruby asked. A warm hand settled on his shoulder as she dropped to a knee beside him. She followed his gaze outside.

'Three people,' he murmured. 'Armed and watching the place. They haven't moved any closer, but they will.'

Of course they will. What other reason are they here for?

Ruby cursed under her breath but voiced no questions as to why they were out there, why they were being watched, what they wanted. This cabin was thirty minutes off the main road. She'd had trouble finding the place with the aid of a map and a compass. There was no way these people had stumbled upon them by accident.

'Wake Matilde up,' Pilgrim said, not taking his eyes from the crouched intruders. The three were exchanging words, the small puffs of their breath visible only because he strained to see them. 'Ask if she has any weapons other than her sharp tongue and the dog. Another gun would be useful.'

Pilgrim had their only firearm – Ruby had no weapons that he'd ever seen and Albus had a hiking stick, the kind that 'serious' walkers preferred and would decorate with colourful enamel badges from the places they'd visited. It was four feet long, made of hickory, and ended in a knobbly ball of wood. Fine for when you were hiking around and staying out of folks' way, but no good for when armed people dressed in black came for you in the night. Neither brother nor sister seemed inclined to want to shoot or kill anybody. Pilgrim considered them short-sighted and foolishly optimistic.

Ruby said nothing more. Her hand left his shoulder and a few seconds later Pilgrim heard the *click* of a door and the frantic scratching of dog claws on the wooden flooring; Ruby must have caught the Doberman by its collar as it attempted to rush out.

'Can you use a gun?' he asked Albus, sparing him a glance.

Albus's eyes were wide, a kid caught out in class when the

teacher asked them a question and they'd been too busy daydreaming to have an answer ready.

Pilgrim didn't have time for it. 'Yes or no?'

The people out there were getting ready to move; he felt it in the shivering quality of the air. It was the frozen, anticipatory grin of a crocodile as an antelope grazed nearer to the water.

Albus made a soft affirmative noise, but they'd both heard the hesitation. It didn't matter. Albus didn't have a choice. Pilgrim pulled his gun from the back of his waistband and handed it to him, grips first, clicking the safety off as he did.

He spoke fast. 'It has twelve rounds in the clip. It's ready to fire. Simply aim and pull the trigger. Hold it with both hands if you can – it'll kick. Go for the torso – chest, stomach. Don't try to be fancy. And stay away from the windows. Say the same to your sister and Matilde.'

Another glance outside. They were on the move. Low and stealthy. They had no idea Pilgrim knew they were coming.

He didn't wait for Albus to reply but went to the front door and oh-so-carefully drew the bolt back, unlocking it. Next, he hurried to the sofa and stuffed cushions under the blanket, giving the illusion someone slept beneath. He gave Albus a last glance, the man's eyes having tracked his every move, and Albus nodded to him. He understood; their best chance was the element of surprise. Let them sneak in, let them think it was going to be easy. Shoot them before they realised they'd made a mistake.

Pilgrim ran for his pack. He grabbed the knife he'd unbelted from his waist before settling down to sleep. Unsheathed it. The blade was matte black. It wouldn't reflect light; it wouldn't give his position away.

The night before, when he'd collected the cups and coffee pot, he'd taken note of the back door, and now he slipped out of it. He didn't run across the backyard (where Matilde had rows of trenched earth and wicker trellises that would bloom into a sizeable vegetable patch come spring) because his boot prints, even from a distance, would alert the intruders that someone had left, and recently. Instead he went right, hugging the cabin's wall and placing his boots close against its foundations, moving away from where they would make their approach. Two of them would come, because that's what he would do. Send one to the front and two to the rear.

He reached the corner of the cabin and bent to pick up the ceramic gnome that sat perched on top of its ceramic toadstool and was reading a ceramic book. Pilgrim carried it with him as he cast a glance towards the front yard and ventured into open land. There might be more men in the woods, but he didn't think so. He didn't know how he knew this, but the certainty of it pumped hot and fast in his veins.

He sprinted for the trees, his feet breaking the iced dew on the grass, but not loudly. He didn't have the luxury to slow his speed. Time wasn't his friend today.

As soon as the trees swallowed him up, he veered left and began circling. He figured he'd have two minutes, tops, to skirt all the way back round to the far side of the clearing – the side the intruders would come from. They wouldn't know he was in the woods. They would be focused on their target: the cabin and the people sleeping inside it.

What will you do when you reach them? Voice whispered, and it amused Pilgrim that he made such an effort to be quiet.

'Kill them,' he said.

Voice made no reply. He knew as well as Pilgrim did that death was safer. Dead men didn't get back up and hurt you. Dead men didn't escape and bring more trouble down on your heads.

He was making too much noise, so he slowed, even though the mad beat of his heart and every hot surge of blood urged him to go faster.

No sounds came from the cabin, which was good. The man left to take the front hadn't made his move yet.

Pilgrim saw a blink of movement in front of him. A dark shape stepping between the trees. A second shape, slightly shorter, crossed the same path, following the first. Two of them. He felt no pride in having predicted their plan; they were heading for the last barricade of trees that would bring them out on to Matilde's backyard. There they would pause one last time on the tree line, the safe spot between woods and open land, and perform a final check to satisfy themselves that all was clear. Then they would commit to their plan and break cover, and it would be swift and silent and clean.

Pilgrim ghosted forward, light on the balls of his feet, breathing long and deep to avoid the gasps that wanted to burst from him. The sharp scent of pine opened up his sinuses so that the cold air bit, hurting the backs of his eyes, his throat. It nipped at his ears and neck. The ceramic gnome on its toadstool had frozen itself to his damp, chilly palm. His fingers were numb.

He saw the two figures stop at the edge of the pine trees; dark, faceless shadows. Their heads swivelled as they checked the lay of the land. They saw no one, because there *was* no one – Pilgrim was at their backs and they did not think to check behind them. He was not part of their plan.

It was impossible to be silent in an iced-over wood, and the two intruders both swung around to investigate the noise they heard, heads turning in the opposite direction to Pilgrim because he had thrown the ceramic gnome with its ceramic book far away from him. It crashed through the woods to their right. It distracted them from the rush of his feet, confused them long enough for him to reach the nearest intruder and stab him in the neck.

The blade sunk deep into his throat – Pilgrim had aimed to keep the blade away from the spine, away from bone where it could snag and catch. Scalding-hot blood gushed out, and it felt good on his icy hand. He ripped the knife free, twisting it as he did, and a wet gurgling accompanied it. The intruder crumpled to the ground.

The second figure was bringing a gun around, and Pilgrim grabbed their wrist, his knife-wielding hand coming in low, under their guard. The gun went off, shockingly loud next to his head, so loud he flinched and instead of sliding the knife in under their ribs, the blade skimmed along their side, slicing through their jacket and nicking them, but not maiming. Not killing.

From inside the cabin, the dog barked. Short and sharp, over and over. It warned whoever was in there to back the fuck off.

Gunshots – three of them – and the dog barked no more.

Quickly! Stop her already!

And Voice was right. Her grunting breaths, her height, the strength in her arm, pushing at his hold but unable to break it, desperate to get the gun in line with his head to deliver a killing shot, all revealed her to be a woman, and Pilgrim hesitated, and that was all it took. She suddenly stepped into him, turning and tucking herself close, and with a yank he was flying through the air, heaved over her shoulder. He crashed on to his back, breath blasting out, and she would have finished him right there and then, executed him at point-blank range, if he hadn't retained an iron grip on her wrist.

Her gun went off again as he jerked her hand aside. *Blat!*

Snow and dirt kicked up next to his head.

Blat! Blat!

A stinging burn scored a line above his ear. He swore and twisted away, wrenching down on her wrist. The woman cried out and dropped to one knee, and that was as close as he needed. He'd lost his knife when she'd flipped him; he grabbed her hair in his free hand, a fistful of ponytail hanging from under her woollen hat. He dragged her down with it and she cried out a second time as he pulled her to the ground, scrabbling for dominance, pushing, shoving, elbows digging out gasps, rolling to get on top of her. He was physically stronger, and that was the only reason he wasn't dead.

Someone called his name, but he had no breath to answer.

On top of the woman, he forced her gun-arm up. She squirmed, she growled, her teeth snapped at his face as she tried to bite him. Her furious breaths steamed hot, and it was intensely intimate, their bodies grinding together, breathing in each other's exhalations, and she was young, he could see that now. Younger than him. As young as Ruby, her eyes dark and furious, intelligence living there. Her arms shook, her hand strained around the grips of her gun, but he was stronger and it was aimed at her temple and he didn't hesitate. He hooked his thumb through the trigger-guard and blew out her brains.

When Ruby found him, Pilgrim was lying on his back, his head and upper body sheltered beneath the trees, his legs and feet vulnerable to sky and sinking moon. The two bodies he'd felled lay beside him. Their spilled blood had crystallised and stained the frost red.

'Hoyt,' Ruby gasped, and she was breathless from running but he was sure that wasn't the only reason she couldn't catch her breath. She fell to her knees and touched his arms, his shoulders, his face. Her fingers were ice-cold on his cheek. 'Are you okay?'

'Yes.' *No*, he thought. He was shivering uncontrollably. 'You? Albus?'

'We're okay. Just the dog.' She shook her head, grimaced, and he thought there might be tears close by but she didn't let them fall. 'We need to leave. Now.' She didn't wait for him to answer but grabbed his hand and tugged. 'Come on.'

He didn't move. Couldn't. Felt like he might turn into stone and become part of the scenery. A ceramic gnome with his ceramic, murderous hands.

It was them or us.

Words. Empty. Meaningless.

'Hoyt.' Ruby wrapped both hands around his and tugged again. '*Please.*'

He let her pull him into a sitting position. Stalled again.

'Will there be more?' he asked.

'Of them?' She looked at the bodies. A pause. 'I can't be sure. Possibly.'

And he thought about pulling his hand back. Taking it away from her and telling her to leave. He didn't want to be mixed up in this. In people coming for them in the middle of the night, in having to kill girls as young as her, with fierce, intelligent eyes.

'They weren't here to kill us.'

Could have fooled me. But there was no humour in Voice's tone, only a coldness Pilgrim rarely felt in him.

'Not all of us,' she amended.

So many questions teetered on the edge of his lips, more than he'd had for a long, long time.

Ruby changed tack and crouched, wrapping her hands around his as if it were something precious to her, drawing their combined hands close to her. She looked him in the eye and said, 'I would have told you everything, if only you'd asked. But I won't force answers on you, not if you don't want to hear them.'

Stay or go.

'Stay or go,' he murmured.

'Come with me,' Ruby said. There was a sorrow in her eyes that hadn't been there when she'd fallen asleep. Her hands were no longer cold, the act of holding them cupped around his generating a warmth between them.

He said nothing but climbed to his feet, moaning at the stiffness in his back. He extricated his hand from hers and she let him, but she stayed close as he searched for his knife, found it and cleaned it on the dead man's jacket. He took the man's weapon, a Glock 9mm. It had been well looked after. He searched the man's pockets, found a spare clip and pocketed it. Pilgrim did the same to the dead woman, although he didn't look at her face. He took her gun but found no spare ammunition. Neither of them had packs. No food or water. They had either hidden their supplies nearby so as to not be weighed down or there were others waiting for them.

Ruby's right. We need to get out of here.

Pilgrim offered Ruby the dead woman's gun, but she shook her head. Still she refused a weapon. They would need to talk about that.

Lanterns had been lit. Inside the cabin, two more bodies. One a man, the other a dog. Matilde was sitting with the Doberman pulled into her lap. Her nightshirt was drenched with blood and her grey bun had come loose around her face. Albus stood over her, a dazed, stricken expression on his face. The old woman crooned and rocked the dead dog, but when she saw Pilgrim, she set the Doberman aside and started to rise. Albus hurried to help her.

'You should be dressed,' Ruby scolded, and she sent her brother a look as if to say he should have sorted all this while she was gone. She went to Matilde and, between her and Albus, they steadied the woman.

'I'm not leaving,' Matilde said.

Ruby started to argue.

'I will not debate this with you, child. I'm too old to be gallivanting to Lord knows where. I have had all the adventures I need. *More* than enough. This is my home and I'm staying, and that is final.'

Pilgrim went to his pack. He shucked on his jacket, fastened his gun belt and slid his knife back into its sheath. He didn't care if Matilde came or not; she was not his responsibility. Although she would slow them down considerably if she did.

'Hoyt.'

Matilde's eyes were on him. He felt them before she even said his name.

'Listen to me carefully. You can forget your name, you can even forget the precious face of your mother and everything that has happened to you from the day of your birth to now. But you *will* remember what I say.'

When he looked at her, her eyes drilled into his, carving a space inside his skull. The air shivered the same as it had outside, as if something hot and slick had wormed its way between them, a predatory sensation that lifted the small hairs on his neck and raised gooseflesh on his arms. He stared at her mouth, at the ice-blue glow resting on her tongue.

'By the end, you will have led everyone to where they need to be,' she said, and he saw her words crystallise in her mouth, a blue-haze frost that shimmered in the lantern's light. 'Through deed or words, it does not matter, but all players will have gathered and everything will be coming to an end and everything will be starting anew. And on that day, it will feel like you have lost because you will have suffered greatly to get there. It will make you want to fall to your knees and beg your surrender. But that is the lesson you must learn. That it is only through great sacrifice that all will be saved. You *must* remember that.'

More riddles, Voice said.

'Not riddles,' Matilde snapped. '*Truth*. Many millions have already sacrificed. And it will be our turn soon enough. You must go now. He is on his way.'

Albus and Ruby led her to her armchair and wrapped the woollen blanket around her shoulders. With both the front and rear doors flung wide, the cabin was frigid.

'Pass me my work, *Sonnenblume*,' she said to Pilgrim. The frozen blue glow in her mouth had dissipated, as if she'd swallowed it down and it glowed inside her now; a cold, blue pulse beating along with her heart.

While the siblings hurried to gather their things, Pilgrim

picked up Matilde's carving and X-ACTO knife from the table and handed them to her. She pushed the carving back into his hands.

'It is not finished, but it's for you.'

The details were rough and ill defined, but the carving was of two people. The taller of the two had been worked on the most, its head, face and shoulders all intricately re-created. He looked at a miniature version of himself, complete with neckerchief and messy, windswept hair.

There's no way she'd have had time to carve this while we've been here, Voice said.

The smaller person standing next to him had no features, her face perfectly blank. The only thing he could surmise from its height and rudimentary shape was that they were younger and female. The single detail that *had* been carved was a rifle, slung over the figure's shoulder.

Who is that? Voice asked.

'A girl,' Matilde said before Pilgrim could ask. 'One you will go back to time and again. And you *must* go back. She is your centre – all your roads lead to her.'

He glanced over at Ruby. She and Albus wore their hats (hers red, his green), gloves and bulky jackets and were deep in conversation, their heads close together. Ruby's mouth moved or she was silent as she listened; Albus never spoke but wore a look of intense concentration on his face.

'Not her.' And the way Matilde said it brought Pilgrim's attention back to her. The lines had deepened around her mouth. She looked ancient, fragile, as if the weight of her years bore down with a terrible strength. 'You'll have put Ruby and Albus on their own paths by then, and you will be on yours.'

'You said he's on his way. Who?'

'Do you know what the Devil looks like, *Sonnenblume*?'

The idea of horns, tail and pitchfork came to mind. Pilgrim shook his head.

'He looks exactly like us. If it is you, the Agur, who sets us on our paths, then it is *he* who will throw us from them.' She smiled at Pilgrim's expression. 'Now that *was* a riddle, wasn't it? Listen: there is Ruby and Jonah.' She touched a crooked finger to her ear. 'There is me, and there is *him*. Three. There should ever only be three. A powerful number, I'm sure you know. When Ruby and I are gone, he will remain. Remember I said there will always be one who refuses to let go of what isn't theirs? Even when their grasp hurts everything around it? He is that one, and he is without conscience. Good luck, *Sonnenblume*. You are going to need it.'

They escaped into the night, the three of them (a powerful number but still an unlucky one), and they remained silent for the duration of it, even Voice, as if he understood that to speak would be to bring a spotlight to bear on them. They didn't follow the track that had brought them in but were guided by the compass Ruby held. Before they set foot into the woods, she hooked out a necklace from under her collar, kissed the medallion hanging from it and slipped it back inside her jacket.

It was only when their boots met the blacktop of the road that Ruby broke their silence.

'We have to stay away from other people for a while,' she said, the words rushed and breathless. 'If we see *anyone*, we go the other way.'

'When I met you,' Pilgrim said, 'you told me a bald man had taken your things. Was that true?'

Albus steadfastly didn't look at him. Ruby was braver; she held his gaze for three full steps before she faced forward again.

'Not entirely, no,' she admitted.

'They came for you, didn't they? Like they came for you tonight.'

'Yes.'

'Why?'

'It's . . . hard to explain. Here, let's cut through.' They were coming to an intersection where one road curved right out of sight. Ruby led them to the trees, cutting the corner and staying close to the pines for cover.

'You said I should ask if I wanted answers,' Pilgrim reminded her. 'I'm asking.'

A long billow of breath misted from her mouth. 'It works differently depending on the person, but the longer a voice has been around, the stronger it is. Think of it in terms of call reception on a cellphone. Mine and Matilde's have been here so long they are on the strongest signal. A powerful signal. They can speak to each other over distance. It's useful but it's also risky, because they chance being heard by others. And, if they can be heard, they can be traced.'

'What others?'

'Other voices.'

'Like the one Matilde said was on his way?'

'Yes, exactly like him.'

'My voice doesn't hear anything.'

'He will. You've had him long enough. But something happened to you, didn't it?' Ruby's words had softened and her pace slowed. Their feet crunched to a stop in the undergrowth as she turned to face him. Their breaths steamed. The greying light of dawn was fully upon them and it made Pilgrim feel exposed. He glanced around, but all he saw were dark conifer trees, as tall as the sky, and the black ribbon of road leading them to who knew where.

'Voice lives in your mind, and if your mind is broken . . .' Ruby smiled sadly and shrugged, leaving the rest unsaid. 'He's on a weak signal right now but he'll get stronger if you do. If you let him. They all will.'

'Sounds like we shouldn't let them.'

'You say that as if there's a choice. You can hinder them, but it won't stop them in the end. Not now they're here.'

A cold wind blew through him, passing through his clothes and cutting him to the bone. Voice had only ever been his. They were a team, a dysfunctional one, but a team all the same. This was like hearing your best friend had a hundred other best friends, all of whom he'd prefer to speak to over you if given a choice.

I'd never—

'No,' Pilgrim said. He didn't want to hear it.

'This is bigger than you or me,' Ruby told him. 'It doesn't matter what we want any more.'

Albus made a low sound. He didn't need to speak for Pilgrim to understand he was worried about them standing out in the open for so long.

Ruby's nodded. 'Al's right. Let's keep moving. We can talk while we walk.'

They crunched back to the road. Every sound they made was met by tree or ground or snow, swallowed before it had a chance to travel more than a few feet. It was eerie, as if nothing could stay alive out here, as if whatever words left their mouths were dead and buried almost before they were spoken.

'Matilde said he was coming,' Pilgrim said.

'Yes. He heard us. Sent others to find us. There was always a chance he might, despite how careful we were. But she wanted to see us before she died. She'd been waiting a long time for us.'

She's dead? Voice whispered.

Ruby nodded. She didn't stop walking. 'She won't wait for him to find her.'

Had Matilde used her X-ACTO knife to do it? The blade was sharp as a razor. Pilgrim doubted she'd have felt a thing as it opened up her veins.

'This is crazy,' he said.

Ruby laughed, but it was dead air. Humourless. 'Isn't it? How do you think I feel? I was thrust into this just as much as you are now. I have to say I took it better.'

'What does that mean?'

'What does it *mean*?' It was the first time Pilgrim had heard true anger from her. It melted through the deadening effect of their surroundings and echoed back to them. She had come to a standstill again, and it halted him and Albus, too.

'You think I wanted all this?' She threw her hands up. Her eyes were hot enough to thaw the frost in a perfect circle around where they stood. 'You think I knew what I was letting myself in for when I let this – this *thing* inside my head? You think I understood how it'd make me care about what happens to this fucked-up world and everyone left in it? It gave me a stake in all this, and I can't ignore it as much as I want to. I *can't*, because I'm the only one who knows where this is all heading. So I drag my brother around with me and hope to Christ I don't get caught by the wrong people because it means Albus gets caught with me. I stand back and watch people die because if anyone recognises what I am, what I *hear*, everything I do will be for nothing. Sure, having Jonah gives me hope, and I try and pass on that hope when I can, but all this extra knowledge that comes from having him makes me a target. Makes Al a target. None of this is what I wanted. Yet here I am. Sucking it up and doing what I have to do. What have *you* been doing these past few years?'

Pilgrim shook his head, already knowing she wouldn't like his answer. 'Surviving.'

'Surviving for *what*?' she cried. 'You have nobody – at least no one you talk about. The reason you've stuck with us this long is because you have nowhere else to go.'

He remained silent. What could he say? She was right.

She says it like it's a bad thing, Voice sulked.

'So where *is* this all heading?' he asked.

She huffed a disbelieving laugh. '*Now* you decide to ask all the questions? Your timing sucks, Hoyt. Seriously.'

'Sorry.'

'No, you're not. You're not sorry. And I can't tell you – I *won't* tell you. Some things aren't mine to tell and they're not meant to be known. It won't do you any good, anyway. It'll only fuck you up worse than you already are.'

Ouch. Touché.

Albus moved to rest a hand on his sister's shoulder, a comforting gesture, a caring one, and the anger drained from Ruby as quickly as it had come. She deflated, weary. She covered Albus's hand with her own for a brief moment and then reached to take Pilgrim's wrist and pulled him into walking with her again. Albus fell into step beside them.

Pilgrim heard her breaths, short and fast, as if she'd been running. She waited for them to calm before she spoke. 'I can't force you to care,' she told him. 'Seems that's beyond me. But someone important will come along when you least expect it, and surviving won't be enough for you any more. And you won't be able to forget about them. Not like you have everyone else.'

PART TWO

The Man Who
Went North

Chapter 1

Gunnar

Pilgrim knew who the small figure was that Matilde had carved standing next to him. All those years ago, long before Pilgrim had come across a lemonade stand on a lonely stretch of desert highway, Matilde had known he would cross paths with a girl and her rifle. A girl called Lacey. How much knowledge had Matilde taken with her when she'd died? How much had Ruby? Were the rest of them destined to fail now they were gone? No one had any real understanding of what was to come. *Who* was to come. Only Pilgrim, a man whose sanity was slowly unspooling from its less-than-secure mooring.

There's Albus, too, Voice said. *He was there.*

And where *was* Albus? Was he alive? Pilgrim had no idea and no way of finding out. He couldn't recall the contents of the letter Ruby had written for him. Maybe it held clues. Maybe it had everything he needed to make sense of it all.

The scratching at the back of his head sharpened to a tight, constricting pain. He ran a frustrated hand through his hair, gripped it and tugged on it hard. The pull and sting did nothing to rattle anything loose.

The third voice Matilde spoke of, it's this Flitting Man, isn't it?

As soon as Voice said it, Pilgrim's hand loosened its grip and fell away. His head hurt but the pain was a focused thing, a digging drill that was excavating into dark and dangerous caverns.

('You know what the Devil looks like, *Sonnenblume*?' Matilde had asked.)

'He looks like us,' Pilgrim whispered.

'You need to understand something about Sheila,' Roscoe said, cutting into Pilgrim's thoughts and drawing them out of the yawning pit they'd fallen into.

He, Jay and Roscoe were standing outside the Monarch Hotel. There were no bellhops, no limousines idling out front, but there was a revolving door with fancy gold ornamentation and faux-marble tiling under their feet. Pilgrim's backpack was on the floor, resting against his shins. He didn't remember taking it off.

After all these years, he's still looking for Ruby. They're all still looking for her. Voice fell silent, became watchful. Pilgrim imagined him studying Roscoe through his eyes.

It seemed the Flitting Man had made a name for himself since Pilgrim and Matilde had had their conversation.

They obviously have no idea what happened to her.

And it was going to stay that way. Pilgrim's shirt stuck to his chest and back, saturated with sweat. Keeping his face purposely blank, he sipped at his water bottle then casually offered it to Jay. The guy didn't take it straight away, but his thirst won out and he accepted the bottle, tipping his head back to drink. The chatterbox Pilgrim had met in the cable-car's parking lot had withdrawn, erecting a protective shell of silence around himself that was hard to breach. He still held Pilgrim's photograph, though, and would open it up from time to time to study the faces on show.

What's he looking for?

Pilgrim didn't know and didn't ask.

'She's not a power-hungry maniac like some here,' Roscoe was saying.

Pilgrim tuned into her, putting some distance between him

and his thoughts for now, between him and the fast-brewing paranoia that had awakened at hearing the Flitting Man's name and Voice making the connection between him and what Matilde had told them. Or maybe it was Voice's apprehension he was sensing; it was difficult to tell at times.

'She was homeless, you know. Lived round here most her life. That park we passed through, she told me she used to sleep on one of the benches in there during the week, then packed up and steered clear over the weekends. Said people were too ready to let loose come Friday night, too ready to let go of themselves. They'd drink themselves stupid, come stumbling into the park, looking for fun times. Now, to some, fun meant pissing on a bag lady, it meant smacking her around. Might've even meant setting her alight while she was still asleep in her sleeping bag. Look, she's a proud woman,' Roscoe said, folding her arms. 'She wouldn't appreciate me telling you this, not one iota. All I'm saying is she knows what it's like to be marginalised. Then. Now. It's all the same, it's just a different set of people. She wants that to change. *We* want that to change. And finally, the Flitting Man is offering that to us.'

'I see,' Pilgrim said, inflection carefully neutral.

'*Do* you?' Her gaze challenged, not allowing for such a flippant answer.

'Yes,' Pilgrim said. 'I see he's been very busy.'

Roscoe trapped him with narrowed eyes, as if unsure whether he were mocking her or not.

You narrow your eyes like that when you're taking aim at people, too, Voice said helpfully.

'This isn't a discussion for now,' Roscoe said. 'Sheila will help you if she can, but don't take it for granted. Don't take *her* for granted.'

Jay handed him back his bottle and Pilgrim offered it to Roscoe. She looked at it, at him, then took the bottle with a half-smile and a shake of her head.

The revolving door let out a juddering screech and Sheila appeared.

She crooked a finger at Pilgrim. 'Leave your weapons here. No, not you,' she said when Jay made to remove his bow. 'He'll have no time for you. We don't want to push our luck.'

'Don't lose that,' Pilgrim told Jay, indicating the photograph he held.

'I won't,' Jay said, eyes not quite meeting his.

Pilgrim left his tool belt, pack and water with him, too, and followed Sheila inside.

As she led him across the marble floor of the lobby, their footsteps tapping eerily, he eyed the wide, sweeping staircase heading upward. It was lined with plush carpet and brass runners. The bannister was ornately carved mahogany.

'How many flights?' he asked, feeling the heavy fatigue in his legs, the wheezing draw at the end of each breath.

'Four. You gonna wuss out on me now that I got you here?'

'Wasn't planning on it.'

'Just don't die on the way up. I'm not carrying you.'

She could if she wanted, Voice said. *Look at her shoulders.*

'And don't go telling him you were in Vicksburg, either. Not unless you want that trouble I mentioned.' She waited for his nod, and said, 'Good. Now let's hustle before he changes his mind.'

If he thought Gunnar would be occupying an executive suite with all its luxurious extras, Pilgrim had miscalculated. Bed, desk, lounging settees and other furniture had been dragged out on to the spacious fourth-floor landing.

Breathing heavily, Pilgrim grasped the bannister's newel cap and pulled himself up the last step. His thighs trembled and burned.

A man called over to them. 'Sit down before you fall down.'

Gunnar was adolescent small. Hair unwashed, beard unkempt and tied into a rat's tail under his chin, he could be anywhere between thirty-five to forty-five. The sore, flaking skin of his arms was on full display in a sleeveless tank; he suffered from some sort of skin condition – eczema, or scabies, maybe. He stood at a bureau with Bandana Boy and a second man, a number of papers and maps spread out before them. The armchair Gunnar meant for Pilgrim to sit in was on the opposite side of the landing to the bureau.

No chance of seeing what they're looking at from here.

Pilgrim had little interest in what they were looking at.

'I'm told Martin Luther King sat and worked at this desk,' Gunnar said, his hand caressing the bureau's corner as one might stroke the hip of a beautiful woman.

Pilgrim was too weary to be impressed. He was too weary to think about anything but crossing the six feet to that armchair and dropping into it. He rested hot palms on the hard, knotted muscles of his thighs and kneaded. Sheila, he noticed, hadn't broken a sweat.

'Looks like you've had a bad day, friend,' Gunnar said as he left the two men and came to join him. 'It's lucky you found us.'

Luck is a fool's currency.

For once, Pilgrim had to agree with him.

The overstuffed cushions swallowed Gunnar's slight frame as he sank into the seat opposite. He steepled his fingers and Pilgrim couldn't work out if the pose came naturally to the man or if he were attempting to project a picture of considered intelligence. Again, Pilgrim didn't care. A dagger was digging itself under his lowest rib and it was all he could do to sit straight.

'Not very talkative, is he?' Gunnar asked Sheila.

'Let him catch his breath. He'll talk.'

Pilgrim drew in a last, deep breath, held it, and then released it quietly. 'I'm hoping my luck holds out.'

'I'm sure you are.' Gunnar unsteepled his fingers and smoothed the sides of his beard in long, attentive strokes, the way great historical figures had once stroked theirs while considering important stately matters. Pilgrim glanced at Sheila, interested to see if she was being taken in by this small man's affected posturing.

Doesn't seem he has much to say, either.

Pilgrim felt Voice back there, a presence behind his eyes, observing, listening, thinking. There were times he wanted to plug his ears and wrap a blindfold around his head to stop his spying, but now wasn't one of those times. Now he felt uncharacteristically grateful to have him around.

Gunnar's hand paused mid-stroke. 'Voices interest me. The ones we hear, the ones others hear. The ones who think they cannot be heard. Do they interest you?'

Everyone's eyes were on Pilgrim: Sheila's, Gunnar's, the two men's by the bureau. He replied with care. 'They interest me insofar as they affect me.'

'And what if, at some point, they *all* will affect you?'

'Then I guess my interest in them will grow.'

Gunnar went to scratch at the inner bend of his elbow. Stopped. Briefly closed his eyes and moved his hand to the arm of the chair instead. 'I think you have a lot to learn.'

I think so, too.

For all Gunnar's affectations, he hardly moved. He sat straight-backed in the armchair, his feet flat on the floor, and Pilgrim realised he had misread the man. The considered way he stroked his beard and steepled his fingers weren't acts of aggrandisement, they were focal points. Distractions. The cracked, scaly skin at the bend of Gunnar's elbow looked painful. Itchy and inflamed. It made Pilgrim think of the scratching that clawed at the back of his head, wanting him to dig, dig, dig and not stop until all the dirt was removed and his insides laid bare.

'I'd like to learn more,' Pilgrim said, telling the man what he wanted to hear, what would get Pilgrim a place on the next ride out of this city. His breathing had calmed and he found it falling into a meditative rhythm. In, out, easing, *sinking*. He heard the rustle of papers on the bureau, he heard one of the men clear their throat, he heard a faint ticking, not of time (it wasn't as exact as that), but of heated wood, maybe, expanding and shifting with the dropping temperature as evening entered into night. He saw the tiny veins in the whites of Gunnar's eyes. The dark crescent skin beneath. The man hadn't been sleeping well.

Pilgrim felt a tickle at his shoulder, as if fingers were stroking over his collarbone and down his chest. The healing wound there tingled and grew warm. 'I think we can find peace in them if we ever allow ourselves to,' he said, and he hadn't intentionally dropped his voice but it came out deeper, softer, imparting secrets. 'A way to let them help with our pain. Soothe us when we hurt.'

The rustling of paper grew louder, and the men's voices murmured as they discussed some separate topic, growing bored with the esoteric nature of Pilgrim and Gunnar's conversation. But Gunnar hadn't lost interest. He leaned forward, his bruised gaze intent.

Pilgrim let his eyes drop to the man's arms and the patchy, red, flaking skin.

'There's capacity for great healing in them,' he said, the words flowing like warm honey; they had been biding their time in there, waiting to be shared at precisely this moment with precisely this man. Without knowing it, Pilgrim's fingers had slipped partway into his shirt to touch the warm, tender skin of his shoulder. It was smooth, the wound almost healed.

Voice had stilled and become silent, listening as closely as Gunnar.

Pilgrim's voice dropped even lower, the room no longer occupied by anyone but him and the space between his mouth and Gunnar's ears. 'There's more we're capable of. Pathways we never knew existed. Things they can show us if only we allow ourselves to truly surren—'

Something thumped to the floor and Gunnar flinched, breaking Pilgrim's spell. He exploded out of his seat.

'Would you *shut up!*' Gunnar screamed, and grabbed the nearest thing to hand – a ceramic vase – and threw it. It flew like a missile and cracked into Bandana Boy's head, sending him staggering into the wall. The vase dropped to the desk, smashing into pieces and scattering the papers and maps. The second man danced away from the carnage.

'Can't you see we're *talking* here?' Gunnar yelled. 'How about I interrupt *your* discussion by coming over there and jamming a piece of pottery up your *asses*? How would you like *that* for an interruption?'

They stammered their apologies, even Bandana Boy, as he clamped a hand to his head, blood seeping through the material of his bandana and dripping down his face.

'Out! I'm sick to death of you! GET OUT!'

The two men scurried away and, by the quickness of their steps, Pilgrim didn't think this was the first time they had been so violently banished from Gunnar's presence.

Gunnar's hands went to his head and his fingers dug deep into his hair, rubbing, scratching. His fingernails made a loud *scritch*ing noise. They were sure to be scoring welts into the man's scalp.

Gunnar drew in a deep breath and stilled. He combed back through his hair, neatening it, and turned to Pilgrim. 'I apologise for them. They have no manners.' He settled back down and intertwined his fingers and became still once more. 'Please. Where were we?'

Surrender? Voice offered, tentative.

'Surrender,' Pilgrim said.

'Yes.' Gunnar nodded, as if in complete understanding. 'The camp can help with that.'

'That's what I'm hoping for.' Pilgrim wasn't hoping for anything of the sort, but if this was the game he had to play to get what he wanted, then he'd play.

'They work on synergy,' Gunnar said, doing his salesman pitch. 'On how to move forward: you *and* your voice' – he interlocked his fingers together – 'together as one. It's a mindset we work on among ourselves here, of course, but a few of us need a little push. Something more . . . specialised, shall we say?'

Pilgrim frowned at that. Were these camps something the Flitting Man had a hand in, or were Gunnar and his ilk taking it upon themselves to round folk up and browbeat them into getting on side? It was getting difficult to see where the grand influence of one became the appropriated ethos of another. Pilgrim wasn't sure if it even mattered any more.

'We've never had the chance to really appreciate what's been given to us, have we?' Gunnar said. 'All we've learned is to hate and distrust, and because of that we've turned our ears aside; we've been in near-constant conflict with the very thing we should be closest to. That's a lot of short-sightedness to undo, and not all of us are willing or ready to do it. The camp doesn't allow for such prejudices. It's a safe place, with a single purpose.'

It sounds like some brainwashing hippy camp, Voice said.

'What purpose?' Pilgrim asked.

'To help us accept who we are now. That we are better for having the voices we hear. How can we fight those with hatred in their hearts for us when we are so busy fighting with ourselves?'

Pilgrim let that sink in. 'And what if someone isn't ready to accept what they are?'

'Then we help them to reach an understanding. One way or the other.' Gunnar smiled, and his gaze slid over to Sheila, and was there a tilt of scorn to his smiling mouth? A slyness in the cast of his eyes? 'Isn't that right, Sheila?'

They definitely have bad history.

Yes, and Pilgrim wanted no part in it.

'How exactly do you do that?' Pilgrim asked, unable to mask his suspicion. 'Is there pain involved?'

'I understand your concerns, friend. I do. But so often it's only through pain that the most profound changes can occur. Be comforted by the fact that many of your fellow voice-hearers have gone, myself included, and found the greatest of benefits in doing so. I made a promise when I left that I would gladly send anyone who needed help their way. They have been doing great things. *Great* things. Now,' Gunnar said before Pilgrim could ask anything more, 'you said there's capacity for healing in them.' A finger snuck out to scratch daintily at the back of one scaly wrist. 'Explain what you mean.'

Pilgrim decided not to explain – words were Gunnar's forte, not his. Instead, he showed. He slid forward in his seat and pushed his shirt aside to bare his shoulder. The skin beneath his collarbone displayed evidence of some faint bruising and redness, but no scabs and very little scarring. Gunnar's eyes were like an unwanted caress, lasting far too long, but Pilgrim let him look his fill.

'Bullet,' Pilgrim explained.

A small intake of breath. 'When?'

'I don't know exactly. I'd been unconscious some time, I think, but from what my voice told me it's been no longer than three weeks.'

Gunnar's gaze sharpened as he leaned closer. It was all Pilgrim could do to not lean away. He sensed that the man wanted to reach out and feel for himself. Slide that same scratching finger over Pilgrim's unbroken skin. The thought made his flesh crawl. This man wore his malignancy on the outside, his skin eaten up by it, and Pilgrim didn't want any bit of it touching him.

'Completely healed, give or take,' Gunnar murmured. 'It went straight through?'

Pilgrim twisted to show him the faint exit wound at the back.

The man was silent as he inspected it.

'There are possibilities in this,' Gunnar said quietly. 'Yes. But first you must learn to *listen*, like I learned to listen. To shut out discomfort and distraction. The Flitting Man gave us the courage we needed, showed us that to be strong we have to be united. We're capable of such strength. *You* are capable of it.' Pilgrim shivered as he felt a brush of a finger over his shoulder. 'I know it's what he wants for us. For us to reach our full potential. How can we strike out at our enemies if our arms are not connected to our fists, yes? We must work as one, with no exceptions.'

Pilgrim shrugged his shirt back into place and shifted a few inches back, wanting to put some space between them. 'You speak as if you know him,' he said.

'We will *all* know him, like we will know each other soon. I don't need to have met and spoken with him to understand what needs to be done. It might not be *his* voice I hear' – Gunnar placed a finger to his ear – 'but the message remains the same, and it comes through loud and clear. Freedom comes at a cost. It always has. And we must be ready to pay it.'

Pilgrim, Voice whispered. *I think he might be mad.*

Maybe he was and maybe he wasn't, but even mad people could speak the truth on occasion.

Gunnar addressed Sheila. 'You said he needed two places?'

'Yes,' she replied. 'Potentially. He has a companion with him.'

'*Companions* aren't allowed.' Gunnar spat the word like a profanity. 'This isn't some daytrip we run to the beach.'

'He's useful to me,' Pilgrim said, not wanting to play his hand too hard. 'He helps me to . . . focus.' Which was an outright lie.

Gunnar frowned at Pilgrim's shoulder. Lost in thought, the man was quiet for so long that Pilgrim looked to Sheila, but she shook her head at him, a tiny movement that discouraged him from pushing further. Pilgrim caught hold of the fraying threads of his patience and focused on the firm, physical wedge of Lacey's book jammed under his right buttock. He imagined counting its pages, one by one. By the time he got to sixty-three, the pages were starting to tear from the spine.

'You don't like having to wait, do you?' Gunnar said softly. He hadn't looked up from Pilgrim's shoulder, but he did slip forward in his seat, edging back into Pilgrim's space. Their knees touched and Gunnar pressed a single fingertip to the top of Pilgrim's knee. Tapped it there in a gentle drumming rhythm.

'If I send you, you are to learn everything you can about how that gunshot healed so fast. Do you understand? And once you have, you will be returned to me here.'

Pilgrim, I don't think this is the kind of guy we should be making deals with.

Pilgrim didn't see as they had a choice.

We could walk away? That seems like a fine choice from where I'm sitting.

And spend a week or more searching out a working car? And another week on top of that looking for gas? No. No one was walking away.

'I understand,' Pilgrim said, and Gunnar's finger ceased its tapping, coming to rest on his knee. Pilgrim didn't know how one digit could weigh so heavy.

The man leaned even closer, creating an intimacy Pilgrim immediately wanted to escape.

He breathed his next words in his face.

'*Burning. Madness. Death.*'

There was a sudden stillness from the back of Pilgrim's head, and then Voice whispered, *She* told *him!*

Sheila met Pilgrim's eyes with a slight eyebrow raise, as if to say, *How else did you expect me to get him to see you so quickly?*

'You're like Sheila and me,' Gunnar said, smiling a smile that welcomed him into the fold. 'You've seen blood in those skies. You know what's coming.'

Pilgrim didn't know anything about any blood, but his

curiosity was piqued all the same. 'Is it connected to the camp somehow?'

He knew he'd said the wrong thing as soon as the smile dropped from Gunnar's face. A hot flush flooded the man's cheeks, battling for dominancy against the splotchy red skin of his eczema.

'Don't be *stupid!*' Spit sprayed and Gunnar's hand clamped down on Pilgrim's knee, hot and damp and too tight. 'It's there to *help* us! He *wants* us to be ready! The words we hear and the dreams we see, it's *all* about what's being done to us by those who want to *wipe us out*. We're being burned and brought to madness. *Killed* when they don't get what they want from us. How do you think we're *hearing* it if it's not coming from our own kind?'

Pilgrim had no answer and wouldn't have spoken even if he had.

'Gunnar.'

Sheila said it quietly, deferentially even, but there was a firmness in her tone that broke through Gunnar's fury. The man sat back, wiped spittle from his mouth and chin, his hand finally leaving Pilgrim's leg.

'Yes, yes,' Gunnar said, his chest swelling on a heavy breath. He smiled an apology to Sheila, teeth very yellow in his flushed face. 'Forgive me. We sit here, waiting for our chance to strike, and I grow impatient.' He turned his smile to Pilgrim. 'Now, what was it we said? Two places?'

Gunnar slapped Pilgrim's thigh as he stood, leaving him there to go back to the bureau. Pilgrim stared at his leg, at the spot where the man's spit would now be seeping into the fabric of his pants. He listened as Gunnar swept broken bits of pottery to the floor, the clattering noise so loud it made his jaw clench.

'Remember, I'll be hearing about your progress.' Gunnar scribbled away on a piece of paper. 'I have ears and eyes in places, too, you know.' He stopped to glance across the room at Pilgrim.

'I won't forget,' Pilgrim replied, jaw still tight.

Gunnar smiled slowly, using the pen to scratch at the side of his neck. 'Good man. Now, what's your name?'

'Hoyt,' Pilgrim said, the name slipping from his lips. He didn't know why he lied.

'I won't be forgetting about you, Hoyt. You should remember that, too.'

CHAPTER 2

North

The transport was due to leave in the dead of the night. Pilgrim didn't consider how fortunate their timing was; if he'd arrived a day later, Roscoe said he'd have had to wait as much as a week before another ride was sent. But these things swung on a pendulum, one not weighted with good or bad luck. All it did was swing.

Sheila and Roscoe walked them two streets over to what was little more than a serving hatch, sandwiched between a chain coffee shop and a bank. Sheila spoke to the man inside for a few minutes and, not long after, Jay and Pilgrim found themselves with bowls of stew cupped in their hands and aromatic steam dampening their faces. They spooned the food hungrily into their mouths. There was no meat in the broth, but plenty of vegetables. Pilgrim ate every bite.

Sheila didn't part with any fuss. She waited for them to finish and returned their bowls, pausing to watch Pilgrim buckle on his tool belt and pick up his pack, shaking her head at him as if he were already a lost cause. 'I hope you find her – your girl in your photograph,' she said, and then she left without another word. Pilgrim wished more people were like Sheila.

Roscoe stayed to escort them. They only had a short distance to go to find a transit van parked, five people huddled at its rear around a fire lit inside a metal brazier.

'Not everyone comes back,' Roscoe said. 'You need to be careful.'

No one needed to ask what she meant.

'What do they do to people there?' Jay asked. He'd been chatting more since Pilgrim had returned from seeing Gunnar.

They must've had a heart-to-heart while we were gone, Voice said.

'Whatever works,' Roscoe replied. 'Solitary confinement. Meditation. Starvation. It's different for different people – I've heard lots of stories. It's not all bad. I mean, I've seen plenty come back and they're . . . better. Less conflicted. It takes work to be at peace with what we are now. We find our own ways of getting there.'

'Or you're forced to find them,' Pilgrim said.

Roscoe glanced at him. 'Yeah, that, too. It's why Sheila doesn't send many out. Not unless they want to go. Speaking of which, you might not like this next part, but if you want to get where you're going, you'd be wise not to kick up a fuss. You have Gunnar's note?'

Gunnar had handed Pilgrim the slip of paper he'd scribbled on before dismissing him.

'Pass it over. And you,' she said to Jay, 'what's your decision, my dove? Last chance to back out. I'll take you back to that dump of a gas station if that's what you want.'

Jay's dark eyes shifted to Pilgrim, searching for something, perhaps a sign to tell him he was doing the right thing. If so, he'd be searching for a long time.

RIP, Jay.

Pilgrim said nothing, not to convince Jay to stay or talk him into leaving. This was a decision Jay had to make on his own.

'He's like a loose ball-bearing in one of those puzzle games.' Lacey is crouched near the burning brazier with the others, hands held out in front of her to warm. The men to either side of her have

no idea their number has increased by one. '*The ones with the little holes that you have to get the balls into. You tilt it and lean it*' – she mimes holding one, cupped in her hands, rocking it back and forth – '*and have to be reeeal precise and careful so those little balls drop into each slot. Know the ones I mean?*'

He nods. He knows the type.

'*That's what he is,*' she says, and nods at Jay with such sympathy in her eyes that Pilgrim can't help but feel an echo of it. '*It's hard for him to find a place to fit.*'

'I don't have my stuff,' Jay said.

'Trust me, honey,' Roscoe told him. 'You won't need anything where you're going. And it won't disappear – it'll be right here when you get back. It's good you have each other, you know.' She looked from Jay to Pilgrim, her lips pursed. 'You both seem so . . . I don't know. *Lost.* Jay told me about his cousin,' she told Pilgrim.

Did he? Voice said, surprised.

'I couldn't help with that, but the woman. Suki.' She was saying all this to him, so he figured he'd best pay attention. 'It's an unusual name. Not like Jane or Anne. I might've heard something about someone by that name getting a ride out to this place you're going to. I don't know. It was a while ago so it's a slim chance. I told Jay I couldn't be sure. But maybe you can each help the other find what they're looking for, huh?'

Pilgrim doubted it.

'If Manny got told the same,' Jay said, 'he could've gone looking for her there.'

'You can watch each other's backs,' Roscoe added, as if that would sweeten the deal.

Pilgrim didn't need someone to watch his back.

You've got me for that, Voice said sweetly. *Why don't you just tell him he's not wanted? He knows he's not gonna find his cousin – you can tell by how he says it. He'll only get in the way. Let him go back to where he came from and we can—*

'Gunnar said two places,' Pilgrim said, cutting Voice off. 'It's up to Jay if he takes one or not.'

Voice trailed off into disbelieving silence. *I don't even know who you are any more.*

The five people gathered around the burning brazier (none of them Lacey — she, of course, had long since disappeared) stopped talking as Roscoe came forward to hand Gunnar's note over. A suspicious-looking guy read it three times before passing it to the only woman in their group. A second man took Pilgrim's pack and emptied it on the ground. Jay protested, but Pilgrim sent him a look which closed his mouth.

Pilgrim lost interest in the man pawing through his meagre possessions, his eyes drawn to the back of the van. He stared, transfixed, its presence more real to him than anything else in that street, himself included. Colours drained away from him, the people and their noise became indistinct and ghostlike, but the van was solid, a corporeal keystone that locked the earth in place with it at its centre.

Listen, Voice murmured. *I can almost hear them. Rats trying to chew their way out.*

'The tool belt, take it off.'

It took Pilgrim a moment to realise the man was talking to him.

'Take it off or I'll cut it off you.'

Roscoe held out her hand. 'I'll look after it.'

Pilgrim unbuckled the belt and laid it over her palm. 'Keep it,' he told her. 'Never know when you might want to lay down some flooring.'

She smiled, her gold incisor winking, and fastened the belt around her waist. He wasn't too proud to admit she wore it better. He could imagine her tying a silk scarf to the haft of the hand-axe to add flare.

The woman who had pocketed Gunnar's note unlocked the rear doors of the van and notched them open.

Inside, heads swivelled towards them.

Two low benches had been fitted along the van's walls and were currently occupied by ten backsides, five on each bench. The burning brazier spilled a shifting, undulating firelight over them. The two people nearest the doors stared back at him – a weedy guy in a football jersey, chinos and socks, and a harsh-faced woman with bushy hair and bare feet. It felt somehow obscene to see her naked toes with their too-long nails.

Pilgrim heard a soft *chink*. Metal on metal.

So that's *what Roscoe meant about not liking this part.*

Looking into the rear of that van with its absence of windows and shifting shadows, those sneaky bastard fingers hooked into Pilgrim's ribcage again and began pulling down, his chest crumpling and his lungs crumpling with it. He didn't know he'd taken a step back until a hand gripped his arm with fingers that were firm but gentle. Roscoe's voice murmured in his ear.

'Remember why you're here, honey. Remember the sweet face of your girl.'

He didn't need the photograph in his hands to picture her any more. Child or teenager, Lacey slipped easily into view – no piecemeal images, no struggling to recall details. She was as clear as ocean glass washed up on the shore.

The weedy guy in the football jersey burst from the back of the van, leaping to the sidewalk amidst surprised cries, running as soon as his socked feet hit concrete.

He got maybe six yards before he was tackled and brought down. Two men lifted him by the arms, and he set to kicking and railing at them as they dragged him back to the van's open doors. The kicks didn't quit until he took a hard punch to the gut. He groaned and folded. A shout came from inside the van, calling to leave him alone, but it was a lonely voice. Nobody else's joined it. He got heaved into the back where he'd come from.

'Lock him up, for chrissake,' the woman ordered, sounding

pissed. 'Didn't I tell you to cuff him in the first place? "He's cool," you said. "He'll be fine," you said. Fucking idiots.'

They held the moaning man upright as one of the men took out a pair of handcuffs and cuffed his wrists behind his back. The guy slumped in his seat, chin to the chest of his football jersey.

It wasn't the spectacle of them detaining and forcibly imprisoning a man that troubled Pilgrim, it wasn't even the manhandling or the way they'd stripped Pilgrim of his belongings (although being stripped of his boots was worse than any rough treatment they could have doled out – worse even than losing the box-cutter he'd slipped into his sock). No, it was the dark interior of that box they were pushing him towards that was the problem. It was the hot bodies all squeezed in tight, leaving no space to breathe. It was the multiple *clinks* of metal that told him the jersey-wearing guy wasn't the only person cuffed in there, and the hard finality of the bench under his rump, the cold metal panel against his back and cold floor under his socked feet. He could feel his throat close up, caving in on itself as the stench of unwashed bodies, vomit and shit closed over him.

He heard his own sucking breaths, the wheezing that became panicked *clicks* in his throat. The animal claw as he gripped at the underside of the bench with white-knuckled fingers.

In the seat opposite him, Jay stared, wide-eyed, and Pilgrim saw himself as Jay did: a tensed, quaking creature. He glimpsed Roscoe standing back from the doors and her eyes were wide, too. With fear for him, with shock, who knew – Pilgrim was past the ability to tell.

The rear doors of the van slammed shut and there was nothing but darkness, inside and out.

CHAPTER 3

Nightmares

Pilgrim dreams of floating. He dreams of light in the darkness. It has blinked on. Wavering. A speck hanging in the black nothingness. It isn't warm like the sun but glaring white. Artificial. It doesn't draw any closer, but Pilgrim is captured by it. Fascinated. He sweeps his arms forward in a gliding pull, and the more he sweeps and pulls and kicks with his slow, deliberate feet, the closer the light comes, until he realises that *he* isn't the one moving, *it* is. It bears down on him, inexorable, unescapable, saturating his world with a light so bright it sears his retinas and courses fire through his veins so that nothing but an imprint of him remains, the rest of him burned away. A ghostly impression on the still of a negative. And with his disappearance, the sense of floating vanishes, too.

He drops, freefalling, and lands on a bone-rattling impact, hard enough to make him cry out.

Polished white tiles, white walls, white cabinets. A hospital room, two beds, only one occupied. He gets unsteadily to his feet to better see its occupant. A man carved from palest wood, full-sized, limbs whittled into smoothness. He is frozen in a statue of agony, his back arched and fists clenched. Detailed veins stand out in his neck and ligaments lift stark from his wrists. The face is knotted with so much pain it's unrecognisable.

Could even be you.

Pilgrim looks closer at the grotesque countenance, its carved eyes squeezed shut and lost in woodgrain creases. Mouth stoppered up and grimacing around a gum-guard.

A machine stands at the head of the bed, sprouting wires that lead back to the figure, attaching like roots to the perfectly smooth skull, whorls of grain going round and round.

Pilgrim grabs the rooted cabling, wanting to rip it free, but it's like touching searing metal. Something zaps in his head (*BURNINGMADNESSDEATH*), a loud crackling that jerks him, and he snatches his hand away.

No one can change the past, Pilgrim.

Reluctantly, he backs away, and with a last look at the carved man in the bed, caught in mid-seizure, he escapes the room.

The corridor is disconcertingly silent. More frozen people wait for him, some in the middle of running, others on the floor where they'd fallen. He walks around them, looking at faces, their rigid, unmoving panic something they all share. He turns the corner and comes upon a staff counter tucked into an alcove. Three nurses are behind it, dressed in blue scrubs. One has a phone pressed to her ear, arm up and out in a stopping gesture to a man leaning over the counter – a civilian by his rumpled T-shirt and jeans. His mouth snarls mid-shout and he is swinging a tyre iron at the second nurse's head. It hangs motionless, but Pilgrim knows it will connect with her jaw, smash through it and punch her teeth from her head. The third nurse has shoved herself into the tiny leg-space beneath the counter, hands tight over her ears, the horror in her eyes captured for all time.

Pilgrim bends closer to look at her name badge. The picture is of a young blonde, smiling slightly, proud to be where she was but also self-conscious. He can't read her name, can't read any of it (even here his ability to read is missing), but he lets his eyes linger on the emblem in the bottom-right-hand corner of the ID badge and the writing beneath it.

'*You're almost home, you know.*'

Pilgrim looks up, slowly straightening when he sees Lacey sitting on the counter, her feet swinging. She's munching on an apple. He can't remember the last time he'd seen an apple. She seems to be enjoying it, juice dribbling down her chin before she wipes it off with her sleeve.

'*It's why you're in that van. Why you're here.*' She waves her piece of fruit at the nurses and the white corridors of the hospital. Her chewing slows. '*You left people behind, Pilgrim. You left and forgot all about them. You almost forgot about me, too.*'

'No. I didn't.' The thought of it fills his throat with bile.

She looks down at her lap, at the half-eaten apple she holds, except it's not an apple any more. It's a small round tomato, its skin wax red. '*You need to help them. It's the only way you'll find your way back to me.*' When he doesn't respond, her eyebrows lift and she holds the tomato up. '*You want it?*'

He shakes his head. It makes him feel ill to think of its juice and slimy seeds.

He expects her to pop the fruit into her mouth whole, but she doesn't. She holds it cupped in her palm. '*I'll be waiting for you, Boy Scout.*'

A piercing pain impales Pilgrim's hand. He hisses and unfurls his fingers, not knowing when he balled them into a fist. Staring at a black dot at the centre of his palm, he leans closer as his skin writhes.

Tiny black antennae wriggle as an ant pushes its way out and crawls across his palm. Pilgrim shakes it off, fast, swallowing past the dryness in his mouth, the edges of his sanity peeling back to reveal something gelatinous and fluid.

'This isn't happening,' he mutters.

The skin under his palm ripples, shifts, and more insects squeeze from the tiny hole, one after the other, five, ten, twenty, they teem out to cover his hand. He cannot control his breathing. A tickle brushes behind his ear and he spins around, ready to strike out, but dizziness drops over him and he's forced to lean against the counter or fall.

Something drips from his ear and he bats at his head. Insects fall to the floor, small specks dancing on the white tiles. A deluge bursts from his nostrils, worms as well as bugs, and he gags, staggering against the counter as a flood of writhing bodies rushes up his throat. He vomits creatures on to the paperwork scattered across the countertop, hundreds of them, *thousands*. Pressure builds behind his eyes, pushing until something trickles from his eye ducts, insects swarming for his pupils, the light growing dimmer, dimmer, dark. Pilgrim strangles out a cry as he sits bolt upright.

Jerking awake with a suddenness that startled those nearest him, he found himself sitting in pitch-darkness. His shoulder ached from where he'd slumped awkwardly against the cold panel of the rear door. The van's engine ran steady and monotonous; they were cruising at speed. Small noises came from around him. Murmurs, rattling handcuffs, quiet sobs. Someone snored.

A breathing body was pressed to his other side. Too close. Too hot. He squeezed his numb hand into a fist, its circulation cut off while he'd slept. He jammed it against the door, pushed, wanting it to move, to give him space. He was being crushed. His breathing turned ragged and he shoved at the metal, not feeling any pain. Shoved a second time, bumping into the person next to him. The woman swore and shunted him back.

Pilgrim, be still. It's okay. You'll only hurt yourself.

He couldn't stay in here. There wasn't enough air. He had to get out.

We will. It's okay. Just breathe. Your eyesight will adjust. Just give it a few moments. It's not as bad as it seems, I promise.

Pilgrim forced himself to listen, to relax his fingers from their fierce clutch, and his racing heart eased a few notches. He lifted his hand to his mouth and bit hard into the meat of his palm. He

214

barely felt it. 'Something's wrong with me,' he murmured into his skin.

You've been through a lot. More than you're ready to know. But it's all there, under the surface, and it wants out. Don't be afraid, okay? I'm right here.

'You being here is part of the problem.'

Don't be mean. I'm trying my best. You're feeling better, right?

He was, a little. 'No,' he said.

Voice laughed at the lie.

Pilgrim had believed they were in total darkness, but Voice had been right. He was beginning to see the faint outline of the people in here with him, swaying with the motion of the van. He felt eyes on him, staring at him in the dark. A line of daylight at ceiling level marked the badly sealed partition between them and the driver's cabin.

Daylight.

It had been night when he'd been bundled in here.

Pilgrim counted heads. It made him feel better. Twelve, including his own. Twelve souls on their way to Camp Salvation. Another three people possibly up front in the cab made a total of fifteen. He almost laughed. Fifteen was a lucky number.

'I thought you were dying.' Jay's voice, coming from directly opposite him. 'You stopped breathing a bunch of times.'

Pilgrim grunted and shifted on the hard wooden seat. It did nothing to ease the ache in his shoulder. 'Is everyone in here missing their shoes?' He was still sore over his boots being taken from him.

'Yeah, by the looks.'

Pilgrim brooded on the line of shadowy feet. 'How long have I been out?'

There was a low, dull *clang* as Jay straightened away from the van's wall on his side. 'Not sure, but I've been needing to pee for the last three hours.'

Three hours. They could have covered a hundred and fifty

miles during that time. Pilgrim's eyes may have adjusted but he hadn't grown accustomed to the smell. If anything, he could now discern notes of nervous sweat and stale ammonia underneath the stronger stench of shit and vomit. Someone had already beaten Jay to it and loosened their bladder in here.

'We've been stuck in this can for more than six now,' said a woman with a heavy New York accent. She added an *aw* sound on her Os. More became *mawr*.

'We're right on the Missouri–Illinois border, not far from East St Louis,' a guy said. He sat at the opposite end of the van to Pilgrim, near the seam of light. 'I can hear them chatting up here. I don't think we have far to go. Another hour. Maybe two.'

The sobbing from earlier grew louder; a woman, not the New Yorker, further along Pilgrim's row.

Talk started up. A confused din. Pilgrim heard a mixture of fear and restless excitement; they weren't all cuffed, after all. Some were here of their own volition.

You are, too, remember.

Pilgrim didn't answer. He was staring hard at the guy who'd spoken. The one who'd said they were closing in on East St Louis. Down in his lap, Pilgrim's hand tingled and buzzed as blood prickled it back to life. His breathing picked up but it wasn't due to the close confines of the van or the rank, too-warm air. He was seeing that ID badge again attached to the scrubs of the blonde nurse with the terrified eyes. She'd been stuffed under the white hospital counter, huddled on the white tiled flooring, white corridors leading away in both directions. Everything so white. He shifted in his seat, antsy, an underlying urge to *do* something coiling tight in his limbs. That same gnawing need he'd felt back in Vicksburg – to move, to go, to not sit passively by – leapt up inside him, and he wasn't sure why. He *was* moving; or, at least, the van was.

The shadowed figure of Jay leaned forward, and after a

moment Pilgrim realised he was waiting for him to do the same.

Jay kept his voice low. 'What's the plan?'

'Plan?'

'Yeah. We haven't had a chance to talk. At some point they're gonna figure out I'm not like you. They might not be happy.' Jay's voice had petered to a whisper during that last part and he'd glanced at his neighbour to make sure he wasn't eavesdropping. The neighbour was the weedy guy who'd attempted an escape back in Memphis. His head hung low and he swayed back and forth with the van's gentle rocking, his arms tucked awkwardly behind him. Pilgrim didn't think the guy had the wherewithal to listen or care about anything right now.

Jay's eyes shone dimly in the darkness. Pilgrim tried to decide whether or not to share the sudden creeping uncertainties he had about where the van was taking them. He didn't think Jay would be happy, either.

'Want to wait and play it by ear when we get there?' Jay asked. This close, Pilgrim could feel the nervous energy in him. It was like sitting too close to hot, fast-working machinery.

He flashed back to the hospital room in his dream. To the occupant in one of the beds with their contorted face stretched round a gum-guard. Why had the cabling sent such agonising spasms through Pilgrim's hand when he'd grabbed it? Why had it snapped loose those words in his head? *Madness. Burning. Death.*

What are you thinking on? Voice asked, hovering at the edges of these musings, his inquisitiveness pressing close.

Lacey had said something to him, her mouth full of apple, its juice shiny on her lips.

'It's okay for you,' Jay was saying, breaking into his thoughts. 'You can just sit and talk to yourself like it's not the craziest thing in the world. What am I supposed to do?'

'Do the same,' Pilgrim answered. 'You'll fit right in.'

'This isn't funny.'

'I'm not joking.'

Jay released his breath and shifted in his seat. 'I'm freaking out here, all right? There's a part of me that thought maybe going to this place would help me, and I don't mean with finding my cousin. But now I'm thinking it was a really, really bad idea.'

Pilgrim hadn't known Jay very long, but he knew that if he stayed quiet long enough and let him chatter away, he'd work it out of his system eventually.

'I told you how Suki liked playing with me sometimes, saying stuff she knew I hated hearing. Stuff that kept me awake at night.' Jay's voice dropped and Pilgrim had to cock his ear towards him in order to hear. 'I told you I'd been alone for a while, ever since Manny went and disappeared on me. So what if I sometimes talk to myself when there's no one else around? Who doesn't, right? Everyone talks to themselves. Out loud, inside their heads. It's only natural. Sure, it might've gotten worse, but I still think that's pretty normal, right? To talk to yourself. Even if it's in here.' Another shift as a shadowy arm came up. Pilgrim assumed Jay was pointing to his temple. 'But I got to worrying, about all those things Suki told me. What if it's not *me* I'm talking to? What if I've been lying to myself all these years? How do I deal with that? I mean, how'd I know the difference between talking to myself and talking to—'

'You're not hearing one,' Pilgrim said, cutting him off.

The dim outline of Jay didn't move. 'How'd you know?'

'Because you wouldn't need to ask.'

Pilgrim could feel his eyes on him, the silence widening to a gulf as Jay slowly leaned back against the wall of the van, away from him. He didn't last long, though, only a minute or two before he was sitting forward again.

'You talk in your sleep, you know,' he said. 'Mumbles, mostly, but I caught some of it.'

Pilgrim stared at him in the darkness, saying nothing.

'Something about going home.'

Pilgrim stopped breathing. *That's* what Lacey had said to him. ('*You're almost home, you know.*' Her cheek bulging with the apple she was eating. '*You left people behind, Pilgrim. You left and forgot about them.*')

A shock of energy shot through him, a flash of electricity that lit up his brain. Home. He'd been heading for this bear-trap all along, hadn't he? It had waited for him to step close, for his foot to come down, and *SNAP!* Sliced through flesh to hook in its teeth, doing its damnedest to stop him from walking away.

Voice burst forward, excited. *What is it?*

'We have to get out of this van,' he muttered. 'Before it's too late.'

But . . . we're not at the camp yet? Now Voice sounded confused. The guy at the front had said there was an hour or two to go before they reached their destination.

They were never meant to go there.

From shoving at the van's door earlier, Pilgrim knew it was solid, that no amount of kicking would get it open. Any latches had been removed from this side, too.

Doubt filled Voice's pause. *Are you sure about this?*

The only dreams Pilgrim had had up to now were filled with red static spaces and the endless rushing of white noise. The fact they'd changed now, here, and that Lacey had said—

Voice interrupted. *Look, I've been letting this go, Pilgrim, because I know what a big motivator she's been in getting you this far. But the Lacey you've been seeing isn't real. You do understand that, don't you?*

Of course he did. He wasn't completely crazy. Not yet. But real or not, she was telling him something he needed to hear.

The things she says aren't anything you don't already know. Voice fell into a mumble. *In some part of your cheesecloth brain.*

Which was why they needed to get out. Pilgrim patted down his pockets, searching for his Zippo.

Your lighter isn't there. They took it. Another pause, this one assessing: of Pilgrim, of the van. *What about the gapping by the cab?*

The seam of light towards the front of the van was pencil-thin. Pilgrim didn't see how it could be prised apart without some kind of tool. He recounted the figures sitting around him. They were twelve in total. Twelve people carried a lot of weight.

Someone lifted their voice above the woman's sobbing and the muted conversation.

'Everyone shut up and listen to me for a minute.'

The man who'd spoken sat three people down from Pilgrim. From the size of his shadow, he wasn't a small man. He had a British accent.

'You muppets really think we'll be spending our time sitting in meditation circles and weaving flowers in our hair when we get where we're going?'

'Not this again,' someone muttered.

'Keep your voice down.' That came from the guy nearest the cab.

'None of you are the least bit worried about what'll happen if they can't brainwash you into line? I have no doubt they get their fair share of crazies and spacks brought in, but what if *you* can't find a way to jive with that little voice in your head? You think they'll go easy on you and let you go?'

The talking had died down. The sobbing woman was still crying and sniffing, but she was listening. Everyone was listening. Maybe because they knew they were on the last leg of their journey and time was running out.

Time was running out for Pilgrim, too.

Listen to him, Voice whispered. *Maybe we can use what he's saying.*

The British guy answered his own question. 'Of course they won't let you go. They're gonna use you as *bait*.'

'What *are* you talking about?' the New Yorker asked.

Jay leaned forward to touch Pilgrim's leg and Pilgrim leaned forward to meet him.

'He was going on about conspiracies and experiments and stuff earlier. You missed it all while you were napping. This skinny fella who tried to escape?' He indicated the weedy guy beside him. 'Seems like he made a believer out of him.'

On the other side of the weedy guy, the shadow of someone small and quiet sat unmoving. A woman? Pilgrim wouldn't have noticed she was there if he hadn't felt her eyes on him.

The British guy was still going. 'This camp wasn't put up here for no good reason. There've been plenty of shady goings-on up in this neck of the woods before all this *camp* business started up. Why'd you think I kicked up such a storm when they came to put me on the van? Think I *wanted* to get myself locked up to this nutjob?' The shadow of an arm rose, the clinking of cuffs coming with it. His neighbour's arm lifted, too. The sobbing woman. They were chained together.

'You're talking out your rear end,' the guy next to the cab said, sounding as if he'd heard all this before. 'None of this means anything. It's just rumours.'

'Let him speak,' another man said.

'What did you hear?' a small voice asked, anonymous in the darkness.

You feel it? Voice murmured. *The shifting?*

Pilgrim did. It wasn't a physical shift but a bending of the dark, as though the shadows were bleeding outward, swallowing those around him and morphing them into a single amorphous form.

'I shared a flask of soup with a bloke over near Jefferson City,' the British guy said. 'He told me that folks like us have been going missing up here for a long time. Way before anyone got their act together and sent someone off to set up this camp. I'm thinking it's the real reason it was put there. To keep an eye on things.'

'We've been going missing for years,' the New Yorker told him, impatient. 'I don't see why anyone would care now, or even what your point is.'

'*My point*, darlin',' he said, 'is that nobody hides what gets done to us, do they? Our kind don't "go missing" – we get displayed in all our dead glory so the rest of us crap our pants and know what'll happen if we ever have the brass balls to poke our noses out of our pits. But that's not what's going on up here. I heard we're getting nabbed off the streets so's our skulls can be sawed open and our brains pawed over. Even heard tell they scoop out the bits they don't like.'

I think he's talking about me.

'You're saying someone is performing lobotomies on us?' The New Yorker might as well have scoffed in disbelief. 'Well, that's certainly a new one on me.'

'We've all heard how some of us don't return from this place they're taking us – don't pretend like you haven't. So where exactly do you think we go?' A persuasive wheedling had tiptoed its way into the British guy's voice. 'Seems to me, smartest thing to do would be to gather those of us who can't get along with their *synergy programme* and use us as bait to figure out what the hell's been going on all this time. Knowledge is power and all that. No matter how you go about getting it.'

'You're so full of shit,' said the woman beside Pilgrim. She was all jutting elbows and sharp ribs. She burned hot against his side, a stewing rancour scrunched up inside her like a stove with too much fuel in its belly. 'So much shit I can smell you from over here. The camp is gonna make us *better*. No way in hell Flitting Man'd ever use his own like that. No way, no how. He's been sent by God, and we're gonna be done right by for the first time since these demons got trapped in our heads, and *none* of your filthy lies are gonna change that.'

'Whoa there, Westboro Baptist.' Pilgrim heard the mockery in the British guy's voice. 'All I'm saying is that, in all these years, you don't think one educated man's tried to figure out what the fuck's going on with us? Not *one* mad scientist out there hasn't laid us out on a table and cracked open our heads? Open your eyes, love. They've been cutting us open *long* before this Flitting Man fella came on the scene, and long before any *voice-behavioural* camps got founded. They're far from being done with us, too, I bet.'

'He'd never let those . . . those . . .' The woman blustered. '*Science men* take us. Not *ever*. He's on God's side and we're on his.'

In the dark, someone muttered, 'Speak for yourself.'

'Either way,' the British guy said, and Pilgrim could hear the easy shrug in it, 'if you don't end up with pins shoved under your fingernails until you cave and fully accept the most holy of voices into your life – *hallelujah, brothers and sisters!* – then you'll find yourself wandering the streets, waiting to be picked up by some quack doc who wants to open up your skull and start slicing and dicing. Good luck, folks.'

Well, Voice said when he'd finished. *I think that about did it.*

Pilgrim agreed. It was his turn now.

'I asked to be put on this van. I'm here voluntarily.'

Two rows of shadowy heads turned toward him. Even the weedy guy raised his eyes to look.

Pilgrim kept his voice slow and even, rolling it out as the rumbling wheels rolled out, the vibration working its way up through the floor and through the benches they sat on, settling in bones and in ears. He was calm and he was convincing, because he wasn't spreading hearsay. He spoke nothing but the truth.

'There have been times recently I've heard someone calling out to me. Terrible messages about madness, about burning and death. I've spoken to others, people like us, and they told me about the dreams they've had. Dreams that scared them. Of vast, powerful, bloody skies that whisper to them those same words that I heard. Maybe some of you have already seen these red skies. Maybe you haven't. But it's the reason I'm sitting here.' Voice did a strange thing, then, something he'd never done before. He started speaking along with him, repeating his words, laying an echo over them so that they sounded eerie and elongated, lingering in Pilgrim's head a fraction after leaving his mouth. 'All that noise, the things I heard, it's coming from somewhere. From some*one*. Maybe lots of someones, exactly like us.'

Exactly like us.

'I don't know this man,' Pilgrim said, indicating the British guy. 'Don't know anything about the rumours he's heard, but he's right when he says there's something very wrong happening here. To voice-hearers. I feel it. It's what I came here to find. It's what we're heading straight for, all of us, right now, in this van. Burning and madness and death.'

Burning and madness and death, Voice finished.

The tyres spun out as their words had spun out, clean and free-wheeling, taking them all to the same dark destination. Silence while what had been said sank deep as deep could go. The British guy whooped in triumph and clapped his hands, handcuffs rattling. 'See, I *told* you! Madness and death!'

At her spot at the front of the van, the sobbing woman jumped up, dragging the British guy who was tethered to her along with her. A series of metallic bangs took up as she began to hit and kick the dividing partition to the driver's cabin.

'Let me out! You can't do this! You *stole* me!'

An answering thud accompanied the shout from up front. '*Shut up back there!*'

'Jesus,' Jay muttered. 'What did you do?'

'I want out!'

'*No one's getting out!*' roared the woman in the cab. '*No one's seeing the light of day till we get there! Now SHUT IT.*'

This served only to spur the hysterical woman on. She screamed and hammered the metal with bangs that clanged as loud as a hammer on an anvil. Those nearest to her tried to calm her down, but she was past listening. A second voice joined the shouting, as scared as the sobbing woman, and the decibels in the back of the van increased with the building hysteria.

Pilgrim got to his feet. He stood stooped as he held on to a metal bracket welded to the ceiling. The British man's head angled his way. He was partly hunched in his space next to the hysterical woman, trying to alleviate the pressure on his chained arm as she continued to bang and yell. Seeing Pilgrim stand up, he straightened further and nodded to him.

How'd I know he'd be the first to sign up? Voice said.

Pilgrim felt the uncertainty in Jay as he rose across from him. 'What's happening?'

'I was wrong about where I needed to go.' Pilgrim had to raise his voice over the din. He flexed his numb, tingling fingers, working the last of the feeling back into them, and gripped the bracket harder. 'We need to get out.'

'But we're *moving*.'

'Not for much longer.' Pilgrim nodded at the British guy.

A slash of teeth. A grin. 'Oh, I'm with you, mate.'

'Pilgrim?' Jay sounded like a scared kid.

'We have weight between us,' Pilgrim told him. 'If we shift it enough, the tyres will lose traction.'

'You want us to *crash*?' the New Yorker said, incredulous.

'It's either that or let them finish taking us to this camp of theirs.'

'A crash could kill us,' she said.

'The van isn't going more than thirty-five. And the driver will brake when she realises what's happening.'

'How can you possibly know how fast we're going?'

It was in the engine note, in the thrumming of the wheels. It rushed by in the wind on both sides and above their heads, pushing downward and inward and closing over them at the rear.

Pilgrim reached over to grasp Jay's shoulder, brief and firm, everything in the grip that he had no words for.

The woman beside Pilgrim yanked on his arm. 'Sit *down*! I'm fine with where I'm going! You're ruining *everything. Hey!*' she yelled at the top of her lungs. '*These shitheads back here are messing around!*'

'Shut up, lady,' Jay hissed.

'*They want you to crash the van!*'

Pilgrim's hands might have been occupied with the bracket, but his feet weren't. He jerked his knee up and slammed it into her side. He felt her breath blast out, hot and humid on his leg, and she folded over his thigh.

The van tilted imperceptibly and Pilgrim had to quickly shift his weight, spreading his feet to keep his balance. Now. They had to do this now.

'The road's curving,' he said, raising his voice.

'Are you sure?' Jay said, and Pilgrim knew he wasn't asking about the angle of their turn. The combination of his anxiety mixed with the hysteria filling up the enclosed space of the van made Pilgrim light-headed.

'I am. I'm sorry.' The apology may have sounded flat and meaningless to Pilgrim's ears, but he *did* regret that Jay would never get closure on his cousin. There was nothing he could do about that now, though.

More people had stood up, their silhouettes tall in the dimness. One of them was the weedy guy, which made seven in total. It might be enough.

That guy's going to get his head caved in with his hands cuffed behind his back like that.

It was a risk, but Pilgrim wouldn't attempt to dissuade the man from taking it. As if sensing their intentions, the calls and thumps from the two hysterical passengers rose in volume. Pilgrim shouted over them. 'On three, we throw our weight against my side of the van, high as you can.'

'Okay.'

'Hurry it up, mate. This wildcat is tearing my arm off.'

'I can't believe we're doing this.'

'I'm ready.'

'Jesus,' Jay said.

The van would finish taking the turn at any moment. The woman he'd kneed was recovering – he felt her shuffling around beside him – and he knew in another few seconds she would be on him, clawing at his hands and arms, scratching at his face.

'One. Two. *Three*.'

Pilgrim used the ceiling bracket and the strength in his arms to propel his weight, yelling through the wrench in his shoulder as he threw himself sideways, body-slamming the metal wall. The impact clacked his teeth together. Jarred him. Jay's knees battered into his side and hip as he jumped after him. The van rocked alarmingly. Wheels squealed and the vehicle swerved, throwing them into each other.

'AGAIN!' Pilgrim yelled.

He pushed to his feet, shoving bodies away, treading on them and ignoring the pained yelps. He leapt at the wall. Slammed it. He didn't know if anyone else threw themselves with him, but the van tipped, and Pilgrim felt the wheels lift, felt them rotate freely in the air, felt the driver's panicked response, steering into the lift instead of away from it. She braked, just like Pilgrim said she would, and a heavy body smashed on top of him, punching out his breath. He heard Jay grunt in his ear. The van tilted off its axis, leaning past any angle it could ever recover from, and screams rang out as people tumbled towards Pilgrim's side of the van, a surge of bodies and flailing limbs. Pilgrim caught a foot in the mouth.

The vehicle crashed on to its side and Pilgrim crashed with it, a thin sheet of metal the only thing separating the shuddering, screeching road from his shoulder. He was buried beneath the hot weight of squirming bodies and he had to grind his teeth against the panic that stampeded through him, a clawing horde of animals that wanted to tear and kick, to scream at him until he scrabbled his way free or lost his mind.

The squeal of ripping metal was deafening, overriding the cries. The engine roared. The van began to spin, a nausea-inducing carousel ride.

And then it stopped. *Everything* stopped. An abrupt and violent inertia that threw everyone forward. Pilgrim flew with them, a grinding thud as his shoulder struck a panel that had crumpled inward. The agony that shot through him was enough to short out his brain and switch it off.

CHAPTER 4

Surrender

The walls of the pit are made of bodies heaped in rings, one on top of the other, towering above him. The top of the pit is high. It's like looking into the sun down a long tunnel (if the sun was an eye, red and dark as flayed open flesh).

He is by himself yet he isn't alone. Whispers come from the walls. They rise and fall like the wind, and the wind whistles in his ears, in his mouth, in his chest. No, not the wind. It's *him*. He breathes deep and his lungs whistle some more. They're trying to speak to him.

He turns his head until his cheek presses the ground. It looks like mountain ranges, his eye is so close. Two ants crawl towards him, traversing the mountain passes. Pilgrim exhales and the ants shiver, struggling as they brace themselves against the wind. He holds his breath and the ants' antennae twitch. The ant on the right tilts its head at him.

'You're not a cave dweller,' it says, its voice so small it isn't there. 'You shouldn't be here.'

'No,' Pilgrim answers. 'I must have fell in.'

'Climb out, then. You're in our way.'

'It's too high. And the sky is red.'

The second ant turns to his companion and says, 'Sounds like excuses to me.'

The first ant nods, its shiny black compound eyes studying Pilgrim. 'You don't see us giving up when we have hills and mountains to pass. When thousands of our kin have been crushed and murdered. We are endless. We are one and we strive. We will show you.'

The two ants run forward, legs chittering across the mountain-capped ground, coming at Pilgrim's face, and he couldn't care less, not when they tickle over his chin and *tip-tap* their way over his closed lips, not when one after the other they slip into his left nostril and crawl inside.

The commanding voice of God speaks.

Open your eyes.

Pilgrim opens them, not realising they'd been closed. He gazes up at the blazing red sky, all the way above his head. It hums with a terrible power, and he waits to see lightning flash, hear words crash in the flare, but instead something large slips over the tunnel's edge and enters the pit with him. The thing's dark body partly blots out the red sky. A second thing enters the pit, and both creatures begin a fast, skittering descent.

The god in his ear sighs in awe. *Not a pit. A hole.*

Thick, stick-like hairs sprout from the fleshy ridges of the hole's walls, and a deep pink glow pulses from outside, glowing through skin. The hairs quiver and bend as a wailing gust of wind passes down the tunnel, and the things—

Ants. They're ants.

—the biggest ants Pilgrim has ever seen, as big as black bears, lie flat against the walls until the gust passes, and then they are up and running again. They make alien-like *chitters* as they dart towards him, faster now, their ovoid heads twisting to keep him in sight, and it's their chittering that turns them into words, stalking him, saying things like *Listen* and *Thanatos* and *Madness* and *Death*.

They want him. He is food. They will drop on top of him

and stab their funnel mouths into his chest. Suck out any goodness he has left.

There's no pause between their scurried darting and their leaps, no warning before they are airborne and falling from the sky. The ground under Pilgrim's back softens, becomes gelatinous, and he feels himself sink, the surface membrane stretching, thinning, giving way, and he doesn't struggle as he sinks deeper, the cushioned fluid embracing him and closing over his head. The ants land and the viscous liquid shudders. Their tarsal clawed feet dimple the surface but don't break it. Their mandibles snap at his face but their bites meet fluid and nothing more.

Breathe.

The sonar beat of his heart consumes him, pounding in his ears, in his head, quivering through the fluid. He sinks deeper, the blood-red light darkening, the frenzied skittering of the giant ants growing dimmer and dimmer until everything becomes a hazy red-tinged black.

Pilgrim, breathe.

He opens his mouth and fluid rushes in. He panics and thrashes, his movements slowed to an astronaut's floating. A wall of noise rises steadily in his head, a cacophony of whispers that leaves no room for anything else.

All is darkness.

He's afraid and he won't breathe. He will suffocate if he does.

Breathe. The word eases out, gentle in his ear, overriding all sound, and God's voice is tender. All it wants is to protect, and Pilgrim floats deeper, darker, the storming of the whispers settling, but still he can't bring himself to surrender.

Light flickers as his eyelids flicker, the final flashes of consciousness blinking by.

A *click* sounds, more felt than heard, and his lungs open, expand, and fluid rushes in. Panic seizes him, but that's okay. *He's* okay. He doesn't drown. Doesn't convulse. He breathes and his lungs automatically pump in and automatically pump out, and he is revitalised, each pocket of air bursting with life

with peace

and calm.

God has saved him.

Pilgrim stills at the thought, floating in the dark. He doesn't believe in God.

But you hear him.

He doesn't believe in God.

Then what *do* you believe in?

He drifts, no sense of time or place, no sense of anything but the beating of his heart and the liquid intake of breath.

Me, he thinks.

That's good enough, the voice says.

Pilgrim awoke with a great sucking breath, gasping through his open mouth. He blinked at the grey concrete of the overpass and struggled to sit up, holding back a groan as a jagged spearhead stabbed into his shoulder.

Jay had startled back at Pilgrim's first breath. 'Why can't you wake up like a normal person?' he complained.

The van was laid out on its side, its nose crumpled against a concrete abutment, the only thing that had saved it from careening off the road and taking a nosedive to the highway thirty feet below. It lay on its left flank, the back door levered open. Noise filtered back in. Moans and soft crying. A few bloodied people were lying, sitting, wandering around. A waif of a woman in a knee-length summer dress perched on the kerbside two lanes over. Another woman, her hair a birds' nest, had meandered away in her bare feet, muttering to herself, hands gesticulating wildly; she turned around and screamed:

'*What did you do? You killed us, you bastards! You damned us!*'

She whirled around and continued to stumble her way to the end of the overpass where it met an intersection of three roads.

Pilgrim frowned around at the Meccano-type gantry built across the furthermost-right lanes, holding up directional signs. He frowned out to where a stack of three chimneys jutted into the sky, and then he frowned back at the crashed van. 'How'd I get out here?' he asked.

'Managed to drag you out, but it wasn't easy. I had some help.' Jay nodded past Pilgrim to a trim woman in her late forties, hair plaited in a thick braid over her shoulder. Flares of pain lit up all over his body when Pilgrim turned to look at her.

'You're quite the heavy lump,' the New Yorker said. She caught him checking out her flannel shirt and jeans, her socked feet. She plucked at her shirt. 'Don't let the cowgirl get-up fool you. I'm a city girl.'

An Indian and a cowgirl, Voice said. *Now all we need is a horse.*

'*That's pretty racist, you know,*' Lacey says. She sits cross-legged a few yards away on Pilgrim's right, her rifle laid out across her lap. She is cleaning its long barrel. '*I'm not entirely sure if that crash was one of your better ideas or not. But it got you where you need to be, so . . .*' Her shoulder pops a shrug.

Here or not, real or not, he was relieved to see her. He was in the right place if she was waiting for him.

'*How're you doing, Tonto?*' she asks, her gun-cleaning put on hold. Genuine concern furrows the skin between her eyebrows. '*That was a real doozy of a nightmare you had.*'

He opened his mouth to answer and caught himself. The New Yorker was looking at him, waiting for him to speak. Her shirt had a rip down the left seam, over her ribs. It flashed a patch of milky-white flesh at him.

'It's a fine shirt,' he told the woman.

'And you're a fine liar.' With a musical *clink* (a gold charm bracelet dangled from her right wrist), she offered her hand. 'Clancy.'

He glanced at it, wondering if she'd already gone through this process with Jay. She had nice hands, long and fine-fingered.

An artist's hands. And that prodded at him a little, a gentle scratch of déjà vu at the back door of his brain.

Lacey has craned her neck to look. *'They're like Alex's hands. She's someone else you've forgotten.'* Sorrow lays a heavy blanket over her.

'It won't bite,' Clancy told him when he didn't move to take her hand. 'And manners don't cost anything. We did pull an act of teamwork back there, for good or bad. That has to count for something.'

He hears the roll of Lacey's eyes. *'It's just a handshake. Jeez. She's not asking you to make a baby with her.'*

'Give me a hand up?' He changed it to a request at the last second and one of the woman's eyebrows and one side of her mouth tipped up.

'Sure.' She grasped his hand in a strong, no-nonsense hold and pulled him to his feet.

Jay rose with them, hovering like a mama bear.

Pilgrim stood stock-still for a count of six, swaying but upright, his bruises and pains pulsing bright behind his eyes. Clancy moved to cup his elbow, steadying him.

'Take it easy,' she said, letting him go right as he was about to pull away. She looked past him to Jay. 'You boys know each other well?'

'Yep,' answered Jay.

'No,' Pilgrim said.

'Ah.' Clancy wisely refrained from saying anything more on the subject. She nodded to the van. 'Don't know what your plan was but no one's hanging about. The three up front are dead.'

Lacey now stands on top of the overturned van. Pilgrim hadn't seen her move. *'She's not wrong. They're like canned dog meat in here. It's pretty gross.'* She looks like a pioneer up there, the dawning sun lighting her up, rifle slung over her shoulder. Seeing her makes his shoulder hurt.

Or your heart, Voice said. *It's pretty close to there.*

Pilgrim's head hurt, too, but that was a whole different kind of ache.

'You meant what you said in there?' Clancy asked. 'About terrible things being done to people like us? About others dreaming about it?'

'I meant all of it,' he said.

'It's happening to women, to children?'

'I don't think anyone's safe.'

'He's looking for a girl himself,' Jay piped up. 'A teenager. Name of Lacey.'

Pilgrim gave him a look. The guy's lips flapped as loose as an old woman's.

Jay shrugged. 'Don't worry about Clancy,' he told him. 'She's cool.'

Voice sniggered. *Yeah, Pilgrim, chill out. She's cool.*

Pilgrim didn't know what she was, but he had things he needed to do before anyone else thought of doing them.

'Is there anyone else dead?' he asked, limping away from them and heading for the van.

Not counting the four survivors who were a distance away from the wreckage and still going, Pilgrim did a headcount of those left present. A dishevelled guy who was crawling back inside the rear of the van; a second man who was sitting with his arms wrapped around himself, rocking back and forth and muttering to himself; the woman in her summer dress, sitting on the kerbside and taking turns looking over at them and squinting against the sun towards the straggle of people who had now reached the end of the overpass. The woman who'd screeched back at them was among them.

'Two more,' Jay confirmed, trailing after him. 'The skinny guy who was cuffed next to me and the woman who wouldn't stop crying.'

That stunt of yours killed five, Voice said.

They weren't terrible numbers. Ten had survived. The sheer number of people packed into the rear of the van most likely saved the rest of them from any serious injury. Their bodies had cushioned each other when it rolled and tipped.

'What're you doing?' Jay asked, following him all the way to the overpass's concrete safety barrier. Pilgrim boosted himself on top of it.

'Boots,' he replied, voice strained as his shoulder wrenched at the abuse, his healing injury aggravated by all the recent rough treatment. Level with the top of the van, he hiked himself on to its side, metal dimpling under his hands, then his knees. He rose to his feet and paused to catch his breath, standing in the same spot Lacey had been in. He looked down at Jay.

'You coming?'

Not waiting for him, Pilgrim made his way to the cab's passenger door and was busy levering it up when Jay arrived.

He had been putting off looking inside the cab, and for good reason. Only the driver had been wearing her seatbelt. The windshield was gone, and the passenger nearest Pilgrim was half outside the van, his upper body mashed into the concrete abutment. He wasn't recognisable as human any more, he was just a broken mess of splintered bones and exploded gore: a water-bomb filled with meat and dropped from a fiftieth-storey window. The body from the waist down was still in the cab. Pilgrim could see its shoes, tucked under the middle passenger's corpse.

That one hadn't fared much better.

Ugh, where's his arm?

The corpse's right arm was missing at the shoulder. Ripped clean off. Pilgrim didn't want to think about where it might be.

The driver had been crushed by the steering column. Her face was grotesquely swollen and a deep purple.

'Do we really need shoes so bad?' Jay asked, helping to hold the door open. There was a hint of green under the dusk of his skin.

Pilgrim didn't reply. It wasn't just shoes he needed.

He climbed down, placing his feet carefully. But not carefully enough that he didn't feel a warm, moist squish between his toes. It took some digging and manoeuvring, but he got the two sets of shoes off the men and passed them up. The nauseated look on Jay's face when he took the bloody items was enough to make Pilgrim smirk. Anybody would think he'd never seen torn-up bodies before.

Maybe he got into the habit of staying away from bodies while they were still leaking everywhere, Voice said.

With his hands on the door's ledge, all Pilgrim wanted to do was to climb back out, but his search wasn't over.

Haven't you had enough body parts and viscera for one day?

Pilgrim sighed under his breath and went back in. It took a lot more effort, digging into the footwell under the broken steering column to get to the driver's shoes. His nose filled with the stench of blood and bowels, his head filled with Voice's loud complaints and disgusted groans. Wetness smeared his arms. Something moist and fleshy touched the back of his neck and he moaned under his breath as he finished untying the sports shoes and pulled them off. Finally, he checked the last place left to him, having already exhausted his search elsewhere.

He fought against the crushed dashboard, prising open the glove compartment and snapping the plastic handle off in the process. Inside was an ice scraper, vehicle paperwork, a pair of woollen gloves and a folded-up road map. He grabbed the map and climbed out of the cab quickly, breathing properly only once he was sitting on the side of the van, his legs dangling over the edge.

Jay didn't waste any time climbing down, leaving Pilgrim with a small pile of bloody shoes. There were red smears on the back of Jay's shirt.

'Did you hurt yourself?' Pilgrim asked, frowning.

Jay seemed confused for a second, twisting around to look. 'Oh. No, I'm okay.'

'How'd you think that British crackpot got out of his cuffs?' Clancy asked, squinting up at Pilgrim, a hand shading her eyes. 'Jay's already been in that cab once to get keys.'

Pilgrim looked at Jay, but the guy wouldn't meet his eyes. *Huh. What a hero.*

'You're not looking any less bloody,' Clancy said as Pilgrim finished his descent and his feet touched the ground.

'I've seen cleaner abattoirs,' he said. The stench of death stuck fast in his nose, likely to hang around for a day or two. He held the driver's smaller shoes out to her. 'They're yours if you want them.'

Clancy looked at the shoes silently. Her mouth opened, closed, a guppy fish floating in its tank. 'Are you sure?' she asked.

He wouldn't have said it if he wasn't. He pushed the shoes into her hands and she cradled them like newborns.

'Thank you,' she said, soft and surprised.

He nodded and turned away, finding Jay hopping around, measuring a sole from each set of boots against the bottom of his foot.

'What size foot are you?' Jay asked.

Pilgrim went to answer and found he had nothing to say. He didn't know what size shoe he was.

Jay passed over the pair of scuffed brown boots. They were roomy in the toes but fit well enough. Pilgrim stepped them out to the centre of the road, a booted foot to either side of a rubber-burned skid mark, and stared north. He let his eyes fall closed to the sun and heard a dull rumble of distant traffic that no longer ran. Saw sparkles of sunlight, rippling gold on water. He could almost smell it, the exhaust fumes and the cold, muddy banks of the river.

'Who says you get all the footwear?'

Pilgrim recognised the British accent. The dishevelled guy who'd been crawling around in the back of the van was now standing in his socks by the levered-open rear door. He'd torn a strip of cloth from somewhere and wrapped it around his forearm in a makeshift bandage. Blood was seeping through it.

Pilgrim met the man's stare, waiting two long beats before answering. 'I do. I did the dirty work of getting them.'

'So that's it? End of discussion?'

He didn't see how this man's lack of shoes was his problem. Didn't care to spend time debating it with him, either, so he walked the tyres' skid marks, following them back to the van. They led to the British guy, too, and Pilgrim noted how the man's eyes got skittish and his body fidgety as he drew nearer. Pilgrim didn't say a word as the guy stepped aside, moving out of his way. Pilgrim walked right on by, going around the rear of the van to the roof that was laid out on its side.

The roof panel was dirty, a mixture of grime and dust residue from countless downpours. He rubbed a finger through it, leaving a mark. For a moment he let his fingertip hover above the dirty metal, and then he began to draw. It took five attempts, working the shapes he'd seen on the name badge pinned to the blonde nurse's uniform out of his mind and into his fingers. He could only get part of it right, no matter how hard he tried.

'What's that supposed to be? "Lols"?'

Jay was standing behind him. Pilgrim didn't know how long he'd been there. The guy gazed at his scribbled marks with his head tilted to one side and his face scrunched up.

'Looks more like "Lois" to me,' Clancy said, joining them. The blood-spattered Nikes were tied nice and neat on her feet.

Louise? Voice asked. *Is it the nurse's name?*

No, that wasn't right. But it was close. Pilgrim cast his gaze around, his thoughts turning, turning, turn—

His eyes caught on the woman in the summer dress.

She hadn't moved. Her knees were drawn up, her dress tucked under her thighs and her arms wrapped around her legs. Her right arm ended in a narrow stump above the wrist.

'Tyler.'

The British guy was perched on the van's rear door, using it as a seat as he wound what appeared to be part of a torn T-shirt around his foot. Done, he used a belt he'd appropriated (probably from the same person the shirt had come from) and secured the rag in place. It wouldn't last five minutes once he started walking.

Pilgrim frowned at him.

'Her you're staring at,' the man explained, 'got picked up in a music shop down on Beale Street, I heard. She was playing harmonica, loud as you please, if you can believe it. Mad as a hatter, that one.'

A part of Pilgrim knew that the old him, the Pilgrim he'd been before he'd woken up to the storm and the lightning and the wet grass of that Vicksburg backyard, would have taken one look at that woman and walked in the opposite direction, never giving her another thought.

Pilgrim, do we have time for this? We're so close now. We shouldn't get distracted.

The same resolute urgency that had told him to get out of the van worried at him, insisting he move, leave, go, and yet there was something in the woman's posture, in the vulnerable bend of her neck, in the small bumps of her knuckles across the back of her only hand, that stayed him.

He slapped the road map he'd swiped from the van's glove compartment into Jay's hand as he passed him. 'Work out exactly where we are,' he said over his shoulder. 'Get help if you need it. I'll be right back.'

Two minutes. That was all he needed, then they were out of here.

As he approached, the woman dropped her eyes to his boots.

In turn, he dropped his to her feet. They were bare. Toenails so tiny they were like those of a child. Blood had caked dry in smears on her legs. A solitary ant crawled over her right foot.

He stopped two yards from her.

'Waiting on a ride?' he asked, having to close up one eye, the morning sun glaring at him from above her head.

She didn't lift her gaze from his boots, but her eyelashes flickered. Her arms squeezed her knees tighter to her chest.

He glanced along the off-ramp in the direction traffic would once have appeared. 'Hitchhiking isn't such a reliable enterprise these days.'

Her lips were cracked and dry. Her tongue came out to moisten them. She said something he had to strain to hear.

'No cars,' he said.

The slightest of headshakes. Sunlight made her hair ignite.

'A camel, then.'

The faintest of smiles. A wing of hair had fallen in her eyes, obscuring the angles of her jaw and cheekbone, but she didn't push it aside.

'Hot-air balloon?'

She finally looked up at him. 'No.'

'I know. A tandem.'

That faint smile again. 'You're kind of crazy,' she said.

She didn't know the half of it. But he didn't need to strain quite so much to catch her that time.

'I recognise your voice.' She spoke softly, with great precision, as if she considered every word before saying it. 'You're the one who's searching.'

Funny word to choose, but it fitted, he supposed. 'Why are you sitting alone over here?'

'I'm not alone.'

Now that she was looking at him, she didn't look away. He found the directness of her stare as intense as the sun, but not uncomfortable.

He crouched down and the sun slid down with him, hiding itself behind her. His knee cracked, and the slow creak of a ratcheting mechanism answered from inside him, an invisible antique clock notching another increment of time that he'd lost.

The sunlight shimmered and peeked over her head, the top crescent of the sun inching its way into view.

Tick-tock, Voice said.

Sweat dampened Pilgrim's upper lip and he gripped fast to that burning insistence to get up and go, pinning it down and holding it calm even as it twisted beneath him. 'You're called Tyler?' he asked.

'Did *he* tell you that?' She made the slightest gesture with her head. Even her movements were considered.

Pilgrim knew she meant the British guy. 'He did.'

'You shouldn't trust him. I wasn't found on Beale Street playing a harmonica. He can't help but lie. It's all he knows.'

A wall of silence came down inside Pilgrim's head.

How does she know that? Voice whispered. *We're too far away for her to have caught what he said.*

'I know because we hear him.'

Pilgrim frowned. 'We?'

'Me and Tommy.'

More silence, from outside as well as in. She didn't elaborate and Pilgrim was forced to ask. 'Who's Tommy?'

'The alien inside my head.' A delicate frown. 'It was the TV sets that did it. Beamed them straight off their motherships and into our eyes. We loved our TVs, didn't we?'

The tension he felt at the back of his mind loosened. *Riiiight. An* alien. *Of course. Let's get out of here, Pilgrim. Stop wasting time on this fruitcake.*

'You don't believe me.'

'I didn't say that,' Pilgrim said.

'You didn't, but *he* did.' She pointed one slim childlike finger at Pilgrim's head. 'He called us a fruitcake.'

Voice didn't say anything, but Pilgrim could sense his astonishment. A part of his skull had cracked open and an infusion of cold seeped in, like when you peeled off a Band-Aid and, for the first time in days, felt fresh air touch the wound.

Just like Ruby, Voice breathed.

Ruby had warned of this, hadn't she? Likened it to cell signals, saying that Voice was on a weak signal but would get stronger if Pilgrim let him. All voices would.

'It's one of the reasons we were being sent there,' Tyler said. 'To that camp.'

Pilgrim wondered when this conversation had become so strange. 'I don't understand.'

'Didn't that itchy little man explain it to you?'

Gunnar?

A second later she made a soft noise. 'Is that his name? Well, Gunnar might use the Flitting Man's name to preach and sermonise – most of it dressed up to serve his personal needs – but the part about us needing to accept our voices, to be open and receptive to them, that isn't a lie. It really is the only way forward for us.' Her eyes flicked to his left, but only for a moment. She licked her dry lips again. 'We live in such vast, open spaces, and yet we know of the Flitting Man, and he undoubtedly knows of us. Tommy hears others like her now, and more are learning to do the same. News and information are being passed on and on from voice to voice, like a long chain letter. A great big interconnected network. Every time someone says the Flitting Man has his eyes and his ears everywhere, that's what they mean. And we can't be a part of that if we don't learn to listen.'

Tyler regarded him across the few feet of grey concrete, oblivious to Jay and Clancy kneeling over the map spread out on the road, oblivious to the ruin of the crashed van and the dead people inside it. They could be the last man and woman left alive in the world. 'Tommy says your voice is intermittent, like a radio with a broken aerial. It makes her think you've been resisting.'

'I'm not resisting,' Pilgrim said, feeling oddly defensive.

Voice wanted to argue; it was there in a wound-up stiffness at the back of Pilgrim's ear. But Voice didn't say a word. Not now he knew he could be overheard.

'The camp would have probably helped you with that if we hadn't crashed the van. I've heard it called dissonance, when you resist your voice, but you shouldn't resist. It'll only end badly. You're either with the Flitting Man or you're against him.'

She didn't say it as a threat – there was nothing even vaguely threatening about her. If anything, she sounded concerned for him.

Pilgrim. Voice didn't need to say more than his name. This girl, as harmless as she seemed, was screwy. But that didn't mean she couldn't be useful.

'If Tommy can hear others,' Pilgrim said, 'hear voices like mine, can she tell where they are? Can she find the people with them?'

A pinch of frown came and went. 'Somewhat. No great distances for us. Maybe a couple of hundred feet. It tunes in clearer the closer we get. We can hear the lying Brit's over there, for example. His talks *a lot*.'

'And the woman?' Pilgrim asked, curious.

Clancy, Voice reminded him.

He glanced over his shoulder.

Clancy was pointing out something to Jay on the map. Jay was sitting back on his heels and frowning down at it. Clancy talked, her expression earnest, kept on pointing, obviously trying to convince him of something, and Jay leaned down to look closer.

The British guy stood separate, staring at Jay and Clancy, some emotion Pilgrim didn't like very much darkening the man's face.

Why is he even still here?

'She has a voice,' Tyler said. 'But it's . . . stifled. It doesn't like her very much.' Her head was turned, ear towards Clancy, as if it helped her to hear. It put her in profile. Her nose, like her toenails, was as dainty as a child's. 'There's a lot of sorrow in her. Unhappiness. About herself. She's done things she regrets.'

Pilgrim wanted to ask *what* things, but they all had regrets, didn't they? He'd killed people. He'd erased parts of his life and cast aside others that deserved to be remembered. Who was he to ask what anyone else had done?

What if she becomes a problem?

'She's not a bad person, I don't think,' Tyler said thoughtfully. 'Good people do bad things sometimes. When they're hurt or angry or scared.'

Pilgrim stared at Tyler, unnerved at hearing her answer a question that hadn't been voiced.

Lucky for you she's not a mind-reader, Voice said. He sounded bitter. *It's only me and my kind her Tommy-alien hears.*

'You'll hear them, too,' Pilgrim told him, a quiet condemnation in his tone. 'At some point.'

Voice hesitated. *I don't know about that.*

Tyler was watching him with interest. 'He will if you ever let him.'

And there was no doubt as to the similarity between what she said and what Ruby had told them all those years ago in the mountains, the snow and the frost and the fir-trees dampening her words.

It's not so simple with us, is it? Voice said sadly.

'Tommy says your voice sounds just like you.'

'He's nothing like me,' Pilgrim said, an immediate surge of denial grinding the words between his teeth.

'Maybe. It's time to leave. We're close to what you're looking for, aren't we?'

Pilgrim straightened from his crouch – felt like a giant as he towered over the small woman at his feet – but before he could answer, her gaze moved past him and a ghost of concern passed over her features.

Clancy's voice had risen with annoyance. 'Buzz off and get your own. He's already done enough for you.'

Pilgrim turned in time to see the British guy pounce.

Jay was kneeling by the map when he was tackled. He wasn't given a chance to stage a defence; the British guy was heavier and had the height advantage. He shoved Jay to the ground, digging his knee into Jay's side, pinning him to the road. Jay cried out, his face twisting in pain as the bigger man snagged his ankle and dragged Jay's boot nearer. He was yanking on it when Clancy attacked from the side. She yelled as she pushed at him – two-handed shoves to his shoulder, his neck, even to his head. But the British guy growled and hit out, his hand striking her across the face. The blow knocked her back. Her hands came up to cup her nose. Her eyes streamed.

Jay struggled and whimpered from under the man's weight but couldn't squirm free. One boot was off by the time Pilgrim reached them, and he didn't attempt to extricate Jay or ask the man to kindly stop what he was doing. He stomped the British guy in the ribs, boot sinking deep, caving him in. There was a subtle shift and he felt a snap under his foot, and the British guy shrieked and fell away. The precious boot he'd stolen was dropped in favour of grasping his side. He bleated something about broken bones, to stay back, that he was sorry, but Pilgrim wasn't listening. He gripped a fistful of the man's shirt and a handful of his hair and dragged him across concrete, still not listening as the British guy babbled more apologies interspersed with warnings. The DIY belt-and-rag covering on his foot unspooled itself.

At the rear of the van, Pilgrim stopped only long enough to adjust his grip, his shoulder ripping with pain as he lifted and threw the man inside.

'Don't!' There was the barest hint of an accent in his garbled whines. 'Don't do this! *Please*. There are dead people in here!' His voice went up at the end, panic lifting its pitch.

Pilgrim slammed the door shut, muffling the cries behind a solid panel of metal.

Thumps sounded from the other side. A louder, shuddering thud as the guy threw himself against the door.

No more thumps came after that. Pilgrim figured he must have hurt his busted ribs on his last attempt.

Clancy had helped Jay to his feet and was holding his arm while she talked to him. With one hand, she pushed a thick wave of his hair out of his eyes as Jay nodded to whatever she'd asked and said something in return. Pilgrim noted the smeared blood above the woman's lip, carelessly wiped away. The British guy had given her a good whack.

'He thinks he's going to die in there.'

Pilgrim hadn't heard Tyler, her bare feet silent as she'd crossed the highway's lanes. She stood with her arms held neatly at her sides, her handless right wrist almost lost in the folds of her summer dress.

'That door won't hold him an hour,' Pilgrim said. He'd have liked for it to hold for longer – a day or more – but wishing for something didn't make it happen.

He kneaded at the pain sawing at his shoulder. Swung his arm back and forth a few times, but it did little to alleviate it.

'Sorry,' Jay said to him. 'I didn't mean for you to get hurt.'

Pilgrim told him it was fine. His shoulder wasn't meant to ever fully heal, it seemed.

Clancy had collected the map from where it had been spread out on the ground and was folding it back up. Jay's boot lay on the road where it had been dropped, and Jay stood in one socked foot, his attention caught on Tyler. He had spotted her stump.

'Jay,' Pilgrim said, and the guy startled. 'Get your boot. We're leaving.'

Shifting, furtive noises had started up inside the van again.

Clancy joined them, the folded map in her hand. 'Honey, I think you'd best come with us,' she said to Tyler. 'You don't want to be left alone out here if he gets loose.'

She's not alone, Voice whispered.

Pilgrim might have normally argued against more people tagging along. The group seemed to be multiplying faster than made him comfortable (having Jay around had been more than enough company for Pilgrim's liking). But Tyler could be useful to him, and Clancy was perhaps doing him a favour by inviting her along.

Tyler offered her a small, grateful smile. 'Thank you. You're right – I'm sure I'll be a lot safer with you.'

I wouldn't bet on it, Voice muttered, but quietly, so as not to be overheard.

CHAPTER 5

Arrival

Jay hadn't pulled on his boot when Pilgrim had instructed him to; he'd instead insisted that Tyler wear his shoes. They were too big for her and they flopped on her feet, knocking the sidewalk in hollow clops.

Two blocks east from where the intersection met the end of the overpass they came across a fishing and tackle store. The sky had darkened, the sun disappearing behind a grey army blanket of clouds, and they had each picked out a rain slicker and a sweater to wear. (Clancy discarded her ripped flannel shirt, torn even further from her altercation with the shoeless Brit.)

No more cowgirls, Voice had lamented.

They swapped out the rudimentary weapons they'd gathered (a forearm-length piece of rebar, a hunk of concrete that fit inside the hand, a broken piece of glass) with a selection of sheathed and folding hunting knives from inside a display cabinet. There was a whole wall of hiking boots and walking shoes. Thirty, at least. The British guy had missed out.

As they continued north-east towards the Mississippi, Pilgrim checked the map often. He stared at the meandering line of the river on the paper, at the way the I-55 seemed to kiss the bend in the Mississippi as it curved slightly to the right, and he could almost hear the low drone of the nearby highway again, the whoop of sirens and screeching tyres, could smell a hint of smoke overlaying everything, as if the city were on fire. He searched the overcast sky, scanning for smoke.

Nothing's burning, Voice told him. *You've been here before.*

He'd told the others as much but in fewer words, unable to answer the barrage of questions Jay threw at him. Once they hit the river, he knew they needed to follow it north. Always north. To the bend in the river where the highway touched the water.

'Hey.' He felt a touch on his arm. 'Where do you go when you faze out like that?'

He blinked from the map to Clancy's face, realising he'd been staring at it too long. He could confess to her that he went to the past, a place he seemed to be slipping into more and more these days, but he didn't think she'd be pleased to hear it. They believed he knew what he was doing and where he was going, and to explain that a large portion of this was based on feelings and intuition wouldn't bolster anyone's confidence.

Clancy sighed when he failed to reply. 'You make me feel like a buzzing fly circling your head and it's all you can do not to swat me away.'

Pilgrim's attention drifted to his boots. Their sides bulged slightly on each step, his weight stretching the leather. They'd belonged to another man before he'd plucked them off his dead feet without a single thought given to the miles they'd walked or whether someone important had gifted them to him – a loved one, perhaps, one who was, even now, waiting for the dead man to return home.

'Did you hear what I said?' Clancy asked him.

Pilgrim hummed an acknowledgement.

'Really? Because this whole thing is starting to feel suspiciously like it's just another crash site to you. One more bump in the road before you head off into the sunset, with none of us getting a name-check before you go.'

He considered her, noting the effort she'd put into braiding her hair, some of it unravelled since the crash, tendrils of it wispy around her face. He noted the neat turn-ups of her jeans and her clipped fingernails, the faint scar on the tip of her chin. She was a whole story, years in the making, walking beside him and matching his stride. An entire world of complex life systems that had combined to create something that could never be replicated.

She refused to look away from him during his study.

'I know your name,' he said finally.

A frown creased her brow and she shook her head, mouth opening as if she wanted to say something more to him. She closed it again and turned away, effectively ending their conversation. And that confused him. He'd told her he knew her name. She'd be getting a name-check in this story, if that's what she wanted. What more did she expect from him?

Jay and Tyler walked ahead of them, their heads close together as they chatted back and forth.

I hope she's not filling his head with talk of aliens, Voice said.

'What are you doing here?' Pilgrim asked the woman at his side. 'You understand where I'm going won't be safe.'

'And that right there's the problem, isn't it?' She didn't bother looking at him when she answered. 'Nowhere is safe. Not for us. I could walk off by myself right now and be dead within a day. Doesn't matter where I go.'

She'd missed a smudge of blood from where the British guy had hit her. It had dried to a crust under her nose.

'You have dried blood above your lip,' he told her.

She shot him a glance, and he felt a momentary nudge of satisfaction for getting her to look at him. Her hand came up and she wiped at the spot, rusty flakes falling to dot her sweater. At her wrist, her bracelet tinkled. A horseshoe charm dangled from a link, a four-leaf clover next to that and, further along, a wishbone, tiny and delicate. That was a lot of luck to pile on to such a thin chain.

'A gift?' he asked, nodding to it, curious despite himself.

Seeing where his gaze was, she lowered her arm, tugging her sleeve down to hide the jewellery. Her hand remained clamped around her wrist; an extra barrier against his prying eyes.

That's a yes, Voice said.

Out in front, Tyler laughed at something Jay said, and the guy grinned down at her. Displeasure tugged Pilgrim's brow low. He would need to have a word with him about that. Distractions, especially female ones, could get you killed.

Clancy's grip fell away from her wrist and her arm settled back at her side. She exhaled through her nose, loud enough for him to hear. 'The woman who gave it to me is gone,' she said. 'Like everybody is gone. They're whittling us down, one by one.'

She was like us? Voice asked

Pilgrim relayed the question.

A nod, stiff-necked and curt. 'She called hers Chocky. It was from a book. About a kid who talked to an imaginary friend.'

It sounded familiar, but Pilgrim couldn't say if he'd read it or not, and thinking on it rattled too many chains, chains that had kept things locked up for a long time, their clanking chasing themselves into echoes, the same ringing questions bringing back the same empty answers. *I don't know. I don't know. I don't know.* They scored sharp fingernails into his brain.

'She was everything to me. Everything.' Clancy's eyes closed and, when she opened them again, Pilgrim expected to see the shine of unshed tears, of grief that had long settled in, but instead he was greeted with fierceness. 'There comes a point when we have to say, "No more," doesn't there? When that's all that's left to us? To say, "No more."'

Pilgrim offered a nod, because everyone had their limit, no matter who they were. A line that shouldn't ever be crossed.

They fell into silence after that, neither of them wanting to talk. Voice worked through a repertoire of songs, most of them agreeable enough to not make Pilgrim want to stab needles into his eardrums. It was like listening to his own private radio station. It also kept Voice from chatting to him, which suited Pilgrim.

The breeze picked up, bringing with it rain and the scent of stagnant water and the faint sewage smell of rotting fish. Pilgrim walked faster, until everyone's breath panted, leaving no room for anyone to talk.

Upon seeing the tall, off-white Christian cross on its stone plinth, Pilgrim's pace slowed to a stop. Markings had been inscribed in the stone. It made him think of the lines gouged into the rigged-together wooden grave marker he'd straightened over Ruby's grave.

'St Louis Hospital,' Jay read, his head tilted back to stare up at the cross.

Not Louise, Voice said. *You were trying to write 'Louis' for 'St Louis'.*

The original red-brick hospital sat stately on its vast lawns, a sanatorium of an era lost long before even the voices came. Black window-paned and dark shale-roofed, it exuded history in its decorative cast-iron downpipes and projected a long-worn pain in the crumbling façade beneath its eaves. The western side of the hospital was a huge new addition with none of the character of the older wings. It was all grey concrete set at right angles and blank glass panels and stood like a sprawling set of interconnected blocks a toddler had left out after play. A dark, feathery contingent wheeled in the sky above the modern section, a collection of ravens and crows that had refused to stray far from the hospital's dead.

Voice started singing, a mournful dirge that did nothing to improve the depressing view.

> *When the birds died first, falling from the spires.*
> *The rooks and the starlings heaped on their feathery pyres.*

Heads tipped back as they tangle in phone lines
We watched,
We watched,
In silence, grateful it wasn't us.

'Are there signs for staff parking?' Pilgrim asked, talking over the end of the song.

Jay's hair was flat and drenched. That fine, drizzling rain had fallen on them for the last twenty minutes. It felt colder now, compared to when tens of thousands of cars had chugged on their daily commutes through the city and people milled in every open space. Pilgrim didn't know if it was his imagination or if the seasons had changed over the years, but there was a chill in his bones here, an empty coldness that he didn't remember feeling before.

Jay sniffed and gathered his jacket closer to him as he looked around for a sign.

Tyler beat him to it. 'There.' She pointed. 'Staff Lot B.'

A narrow road with speed bumps headed to the old eastern wing. As they followed the marked route, their boots loud on the asphalt, Pilgrim's head remained permanently turned, his gaze on the hospital. The eyes of its windows tracked him. The mouths of its doors were grimly set, unhappy at seeing the intruders. It wasn't a welcoming sight.

This place is massive.

Pilgrim looked at Tyler. Her hood was up, her face obscured. 'Do you hear anything?' he asked her.

Jay's head turned in interest. He was curious about her, maybe even a little wary. Pilgrim could understand why. He didn't know what they'd talked about as they'd walked together, but he assumed she'd been as forthright with Jay as she had been with him.

I hope she told him that no aliens beamed themselves into his head. Might help him sleep easier at night.

Tyler considered the hospital for long moments and finally gave a vague shake of her head. 'No. Nothing so far.'

Best be careful anyway. Doesn't mean there aren't any non-hearing kinds of people around, Voice said.

The road ended in a large parking lot, big enough to accommodate a hundred cars or more. It was a quarter filled. The vehicles were all in disrepair, tyres rotted to rubber stubs, wheel-rims oxidized, grass and weeds grown through cracks in the blacktop and twining around axles and exhausts. It was a graveyard for vehicles. And beyond the graveyard was the birdcage.

The birdcage, Voice breathed.

Pilgrim didn't know how he knew its name, it was just *the birdcage*. And it *was* a cage, all right. A fenced-in enclosure attached to a back wing of the hospital. Metal stairs ran up to its roof as part of the fire escape to access the floors. They staggered their way up four flights, but it was the birdcage that was of interest to him. A grilled gate at the near end stood ajar, a chain hanging from its sliding bolt. The padlock was missing.

How'd you know there was a padlock?

Pilgrim was picking at the bones of a past that even Voice didn't have access to. A slab of unease shifted in his gut, a deep space opening up inside him, gaping into the unknown. They were roaming into places both new and old at once and with it came a sense of jarring dislocation.

'You've been to this hospital before?' Tyler was peering all around, her face open and full of interest inside her hood.

On some subconscious level Pilgrim knew it, the same way he subconsciously knew there were sixty-two railings from one end of the birdcage to the other and that the padlock had been rusted long before it went missing. Also, that someone had been here before them – they had broken through the chain and padlock to get in.

Or out.

Pilgrim pulled open the gate and it squawked at him, the friction as abrasive on his nerve endings as it was on the gate's hinges.

'Would you look at that . . .' There was wonder in Clancy's voice. She was staring off towards the parking lot, at the overgrown grass between them and the derelict cars. It shimmied and swayed as something tunnelled its way through it. Pilgrim glimpsed fur, ears, the flick of a tail, and out popped a ginger cat as big as a dog. It sauntered over to them.

'Jenks,' Pilgrim said, and he barely had to search for the name before it was there. The cat looked mangier, tufts of his fur missing in clumps. There was a notch in one ear where something had taken a chunk out of it and his tail was bent at the tip, but there was little fear in the way he padded up to them, despite any past skirmishes.

'He knows you,' Clancy said.

'I don't think I ever touched him.'

First time for everything.

'Pet him now,' Tyler said, the hush in her voice sounding eager. 'Go on. He wants you to.'

Pilgrim went to one knee, unmindful of the dampness soaking through his pants. He held out a hand and the cat stopped, one paw up, green eyes steady on him.

'Jenks,' he said again, and the cat's ears twitched. Jenks let out a deep meow, his head lowering, eyes pegging each of them in turn. He let out another low keening yowl, and it sounded more like a warning this time.

'Back up, guys,' Clancy said. 'See if he'll go to him.'

Pilgrim heard the shuffle of their retreat.

The cat edged forward, wary now, alert to them but seemingly too tempted by Pilgrim's outstretched hand to back off. He wished he had something to give him. A chew toy, maybe.

He's not a dog.

Or a treat. Judging by his size, Jenks enjoyed his food.

He has his pick of birds here, doesn't he?

The cat was three yards away when he lifted his head. His nose and whiskers twitched.

'Come on, then, Jenks,' Pilgrim murmured. 'Don't make me wait.'

The cat stalked forward the last few feet and sniffed at Pilgrim's fingers. He stilled as Pilgrim slowly ran his hand over the cat's head. Ears flattened under his palm, the fur damp and mostly soft but with a couple of rough patches where something had stuck in the fur. The cat remained frozen for a few strokes, assessing the hand and the person attached to it, and then he submitted, tilting his head into Pilgrim's rubs, eyes narrowing in pleasure.

'Jeez, listen to that,' Jay said. 'He even purrs like a brute.'

'He's happy,' Tyler said, a smile in her voice. 'Look at him. He's found his friend.'

The animal's hefty body vibrated with his deep purring and Pilgrim took his time petting him, rubbing his fingers under Jenks's chin, stroking his chest, rubbing his velvety-soft ears between his fingers.

'We should get inside,' Clancy said, and Pilgrim knew it was his cue, and yet he couldn't bring himself to move. It felt like avoidance, this pause on the grass, his hand stroking the mangy cat. It felt like running away, even when he'd expended so much energy on getting here.

The rain had stopped and the clouds parted over the parking lot. The sky had turned a deep desert yellow, a strange, oppressive colour that painted everything in a muted light.

Storm's coming? Voice asked.

Pilgrim forced himself to his feet and Jenks shrunk back, green eyes watchful. The cat darted past, dodging around Pilgrim's legs and flashing through the gated door and into the birdcage. Pilgrim hadn't noticed the fire-exit door was wedged open, but Jenks slipped through the gap and disappeared inside.

'There goes the welcome party,' Jay said.

Tyler was hugging herself, the too-big cuffs of her windbreaker hanging over her hand. She hadn't complained, but she was shivering with cold. Clancy looked pale and miserable. And Jay – well, Jay looked like a drowned rat. They had all waited long enough.

'Let's go in,' he said.

He had been in this hallway before. Where the corridor deadended to his far right, a frosted window lit up yellow, as if a fire raged outside. The corridors' floors, once shiny, were carpeted in blackish-green moss, sprinkled in places with chunks of plaster that had fallen from the high ceilings. Jenks had vanished around a corner at the top of the corridor, at what looked like a nurses' station. It wasn't the same countertop as in Pilgrim's dream – this one was enclosed in its own protective box of wire-meshed glass.

'What kind of ward is this?' Jay asked, and even in his attempt to talk quietly his voice echoed ahead of them, announcing their presence.

'No one ever called it by its proper name,' Pilgrim said. 'It was just the Unit.'

They passed room after room, little more than two beds and two small bedside tables in each. Wires trailed from collapsed ceiling panels, thick spiders' webs netted the windows and dozens of dead flies dotted the windowsills. Three shower stalls, their doors swung wide, sported impressive algae life spreading from their shower trays up the walls. The smell coming from them reminded Pilgrim of sewage drains after a hard downpour.

'A woman killed herself in the middle one,' he told them. 'Back at the start of all this. Scalded herself to death. Her skin peeled off like a snake's.'

'God,' Clancy whispered.

'Yeah, thanks for sharing,' Jay said.

At the threshold of one bedroom, a gummy black smear as wide as a person stained the flooring. Pilgrim stood and stared at it for too long. The room the smear trailed into had sprung a leak, transforming it into a self-contained jungle; thick rope-like vines climbed once-yellow walls now blackened with mould. This room had a fungal smell to it, rich with plant life.

Jay sneezed.

'Let's keep going,' Clancy said, touching Pilgrim's back. Jay may not have understood what kind of ward this was, but she did; Pilgrim felt it in the brief rub she gave him before lifting her hand away.

She touches people a lot, Voice said. *She's like a mother hen.*

Pilgrim heard the phantom rattle of dinner trolleys and their racks of trays – plastic trays with recessed areas for each food group. They'd used plastic cutlery and cups, too. There were no rails in the closets, only shelves on which clothes could be folded and placed. Scissors to trim nails and beards had to be signed out from the nurses' station, and you were watched while you used them. If you wanted to shave, that was supervised as well.

Look.

The corridor opened up on a communal area, delineated by dark parquet flooring.

The day room.

Four walls, three couches, one TV set and twelve assorted chairs. Four shelving units that held one hundred and thirteen bits of reading material separated into seventy-two magazines and forty-one books (forty-two at full count). Eleven board games, including Scrabble, Monopoly, Checkers and Battleship. One stereo, two speakers, and no potted plants. And Pilgrim knew he could walk the circumference of the room in exactly sixty-two paces. He could walk all sixty-two paces right now without needing to detour for a broken chair or a smashed TV set, because the space was neat. In fact, it was *too* neat. Somebody had tidied up.

'Don't any of you move a muscle,' someone said from behind him. 'I haven't shot anyone for two straight days, and my trigger finger is getting twitchy.'

Pilgrim didn't have to see her to know who spoke. He felt her like a grey raincloud gathering at the back of his head, smoking wisps curling around his ears from the cigarettes she used to smoke. Her voice had come from the branching corridor which Pilgrim knew led to the men's rooms, the dining room, the crafts room and the bank of telephones, and when he turned his head it was as though she were smouldering, too, tendrils curling off her shoulders and the top of her head. Jenks twined his body around her booted feet, unaware of the swirls of smoke ghosting around him. She held a gun on them, the hold-with-two-hands type that could blast a hole clean through you. Pilgrim's shoulder gave a twinge at the thought. The weapon was a clean piece. Shiny. Well looked after.

As he watched, the tendrils of smoke dampened themselves and sank down, her body absorbing them until there was no trace left of them.

'Katherine,' Pilgrim said.

Her eyes backtracked to him. Widened. Looked him up and down. Her gun slowly lowered, a disbelieving smile spreading across her face.

At least she seems happy to see you.

'You know that's not my name, you motherfucker,' Abernathy said.

CHAPTER 6

Abernathy

Abernathy closed the distance between them in five long strides. She leapt and he caught her on reflex. She wrapped her arms tight around him, hugging so hard he felt his neck crack.

'I thought you were dead, Sol,' she said, her breath warm on his ear.

'That's not so far from the truth.' He winced. 'You're breaking my neck.'

'You're *lucky* I don't break it.' She loosened her hold and unwound her arms. She smiled into his face as her feet touched back down. 'It's been almost *eight* fucking years. Where the hell have you been?'

'Busy forgetting this place.' He'd expected the smoky scent of cigarettes to linger around her, but she smelled only of storms and rainwater and starch. She was dressed all in black, her hoodie, her T-shirt, her fatigues, all as neat and clean as her gun. She wore a webbed belt and holster around her waist.

Looks almost like a uniform, Voice said musingly.

Abernathy punched Pilgrim in his chest. 'You owe me a better explanation than that. Who're these losers?'

He made the introductions. 'Jay, Clancy, Tyler. Everyone, this is Abernathy.'

'What's up?' Jay said, nodding, and Pilgrim was relieved his hands stayed at his sides, no handshakes offered. He was frowning at the gun Abernathy held. 'It's Abernathy and not Katherine?' he asked.

Abernathy lifted the handgun and pointed it at his face. 'It's never Katherine.'

His hands shot up, palms out. 'Whoa, okay! Jesus, I'm sorry.'

'I'm not Jesus, either. Although we're way past due a Second Coming. Anything else you want to know?'

'No.'

'Good.' She lowered the gun and smiled around at them. 'Welcome to the Unit. Prime accommodation for the lost and disturbed. Sol definitely knows how to treat his friends. Brings them to all the swanky places.'

'You haven't changed much,' Pilgrim said. She talked the same and, mostly, she looked the same. The years had shaved off the softness of youth and replaced it with something tougher, leaner. Her hair was chopped shorter and she carried a few extra scars. She looked good but . . . dangerous. Then again, there had always been something dangerous about her.

Unpredictable.

Yes, that, too.

'*You've* changed, though,' Abernathy said, looking at him with an assessing eye that he didn't entirely like. 'A lot,' she added. 'I mean, you're talking more, for a start.'

'This is him talking more?' Jay asked, eyebrows going up.

'For sure. The bastards here were good at stripping parts of us away,' she said. 'Drugs, therapies, treatments. Sol here used to wander round, doing his counting thing. You remember that?' she asked him. 'It was like you were looking for something you could never find.'

Counting had always brought a semblance of order to a world that, to him, severely lacked any. There was a peculiar sense of dislocation being here, as though two versions of him occupied the same space – Pilgrim and Sol – one superimposed over the other. But it was impossible to hide from your past when you were standing right in the middle of it.

'*Did* you ever find it?' Abernathy asked.

'No, not yet,' he said. 'But maybe you can help me with that.'

'Yeah, maybe.' The way she said it, though, mouth unsmiling and eyes cautious, said that he probably shouldn't hold his breath. 'You shouldn't have come back here, Sol. None of you should be here.'

'I'm not sure we expected to find anyone so soon,' Clancy said.

'The cat definitely took him by surprise,' Jay added.

Pilgrim couldn't take his eyes from Abernathy. He watched her small tics: her jaw clenching and unclenching, her fingers readjusting themselves on the grips of the handgun she hadn't yet holstered.

'Jenks is the only decent thing about this place, aren't you, old buddy?' The cat yawned at Abernathy, two sharp incisors flashing, top and bottom. He seemed to be missing the rest. 'But I meant what I said.' Her eyes came back to Pilgrim. 'You shouldn't have come.'

'Why not?' Clancy asked.

Pilgrim surveyed the day room again, but nothing was out of place and nothing screamed out 'Trap' or 'Danger' or 'Run'. The ward was empty but for them.

He looked to Tyler and she met his gaze, giving him the tiniest of shrugs.

She doesn't hear anything either, Voice said.

Abernathy's frown cut deep into her brow. 'Come on, we can walk and talk. Or rather eat and talk. I was in the middle of supper before you guys interrupted.'

'Supper?' Tyler asked, unable to disguise her stark look of hope. 'Is there enough for all of us?'

Abernathy took her time giving Tyler a once-over. 'You don't look like you eat much, little rabbit. So, sure, I can let you have a nibble.'

The dining room wasn't as tidy as the day room, but it wasn't a disaster site, either. Abernathy had cleared the detritus from one half of the room to the other and where they sat on benched seating was serviceable, if not exactly spotless. A converted metal garbage can sitting on two house bricks worked as a cooking grill. Abernathy added more fuel to its fire when they entered.

'You still choose to eat in here?' Pilgrim asked, taking a seat opposite her. Tyler and Jay settled themselves at his side of the table while Clancy went around and sat beside Abernathy. Jenks stayed on the floor, disappearing under the table. Pilgrim felt him brush up against his ankle.

'Supper, sure. I come back in the evenings sometimes to see Jenks.' She passed out food: corn on the cob, carrots, unshelled peas, a package with meat in it – chicken, by the look and smell. 'You're lucky you caught me. Man, I can't believe this. Jackson is gonna shit when I tell him who strolled in here.' She shook her head, smiling in disbelief to herself.

'Jackson's here?' Pilgrim said, looking over his shoulder, expecting to see the man waltz in.

Jackson, Voice breathed.

'Not in the Unit, but yeah, he's alive and kicking.'

'Where did you get all this?' Clancy asked, hunger clearly outweighing any suspicion as she sampled her first bite.

Jay mumbled something unintelligible, his mouth already full.

Abernathy had picked up two roasted corn on the cobs and handed one to Pilgrim. It was hot and he wrapped his fingers around it for warmth. She didn't look away from Clancy, though, and he felt it, even if the others didn't, how she was gauging how much to say.

264

'It's grown,' she said. 'Everything's grown from scratch. Same as the meat. Chickens, dogs, cats. I won't tell you which you're eating.' She winked at Jay when he stopped chewing. She bit into her corn to cover her smirk.

'Who grows it?' Pilgrim asked, yet to take a bite of his own food.

Abernathy wiped juice off her chin and carried on chewing for a few seconds. 'We can get into that if you really want, but first I need to ask: who of you hears one?' All smirks were gone.

Pilgrim felt a shift in the atmosphere, a cold draught sweeping in to cut through their rain-dampened clothes. Food hung forgotten halfway to mouths. No one spoke.

'We won't get very far if no one owns up.' Abernathy set her corn aside, wiping her fingers on her pants. Clean, starched pants, same as her shirt.

Clean as her hair and fingernails, Voice murmured.

Tyler finished licking chicken grease from her fingers and into the silence said, 'We all hear a voice, to one extent or another. Except for Jay. He doesn't hear a thing.'

Jay's mouthful of food bulged in his cheek. His eyes flicked to Pilgrim and he saw the hope flare bright there, painful and oh so fragile. He was afraid to be like them. Not least of all because of what might be done to him if he was.

Abernathy's eyebrows had lifted. Pilgrim suspected it took a lot to surprise her. 'Who needs secrets with this one around, huh? Look, it's fine,' she said when Clancy opened her mouth to speak. 'I'm not any sort of voice-hater or anything. But when I said you shouldn't have come here, now I *really* mean you shouldn't have come.'

'Who else besides Jackson is with you, Abernathy?' Pilgrim asked quietly. This was why he'd been drawn back here, why the words and the lightning had singled him out – *Burning MadnessDeath* – as he lay inert in the grass next to Ruby's half-buried corpse. This place *wanted* him. It knew him and wanted him home.

'The doctors think they're on their way to curing you, you know,' Abernathy said just as quietly, the table's edge pressing her stomach as she leaned in. Her face was lit by the flickering of the grill's firelight, though Pilgrim felt no warmth from it.

Voice was so silent a stone could have been dropped in the dark well of Pilgrim's mind and no sound ever rebound back to him.

'Of course, in curing you they cook your brains,' Abernathy continued with a shrug, 'so it's not a foolproof technique or anything. But they're not giving up. Fuck no. If anything, they're trying extra hard, because they're doing *such important work*.' A mocking curve of her lips. She leaned away again and went back to eating her corn. No one joined her.

'Which part of the hospital are they in?' Pilgrim asked.

Clancy pushed to her feet, the bench's legs scraping. Words spilled from her mouth before she'd finished standing up. 'They're in the *hospital*? They're here right now? What are you doin—'

'*Sit. Down.*' Abernathy's command threw a wall up against Clancy's ire and the women stared at each other.

In the following stretch of silence Voice's sigh whistled through Pilgrim's ears. *Unless you want a standoff till Christmas you'd best say something.*

'Clancy,' Pilgrim said.

She threw him a glance, and he saw more than hostility in her. More than fury or hatred. He saw anguish. He nodded to her, and slowly, stiffly, she settled back in her seat.

Jay had placed a reassuring hand over Tyler's arm on the table-top. Tyler was pale, her eyes large and dark in her face.

'You *really* don't want to go wandering off anywhere,' Abernathy continued, as if nothing had happened. He hadn't missed how her hand had slipped under the table, though. How she'd moved it near to her gun. 'You might stumble somewhere you're not welcome.'

He picked apart her words, tried to determine whether there was a threat in them or not. Her eyes were serious, but there was nothing malicious in them. Nothing combative. It could just be Abernathy playing her games.

You need to be careful with her. She's not the same person you knew.

Pilgrim didn't move, leaving his hands on show, forearms resting on the table's surface, fingers loose and casual. 'That's where you get your food from,' he said. 'It's all on-site.'

'Everyone's found ways to survive,' Abernathy told him, her eyes never leaving him.

'We have,' he agreed.

'And if I wanted to hand you over, I wouldn't be feeding you my hard-earned supplies now, would I?'

'That wouldn't make sense, no.'

Her attention moved around the table. Everyone stared at her, their food growing cold.

'I always liked you, Sol,' she said, her eyes returning to him. 'There was never any bullshit with you, and I can appreciate someone who doesn't bullshit.'

'You're hurting people here, Abernathy.'

'Not me,' she said. Her cheek twitched. 'Well, *technically*, not me.'

He looked at her shirt, at the perfect line of her pressed collar. 'You're helping the people who do. And that's just as bad.'

Her faced hardened. 'You don't know anything about me,' she said coldly. 'You don't know where I've been or what's happened. Don't walk in here and start throwing accusations around when you don't have the first fucking clue what I've had to do to keep me and Jackson alive.'

Unconsciously or not, her hand had reappeared and her fist was clenched on the table. Her knuckles were white. Peeking out from beneath the cuff of her hoodie's sleeve, the colourful inks of her tattoo did a good job of disguising the fine silvery lines of scarring Pilgrim knew travelled up her forearms.

'I need your help,' he told her.

'I didn't figure you'd come here for a vacation, Sol.' She tilted her head towards the rest of the table. 'Do they even know that's your name? Because every time I say it they get this weird fucking look on their faces.'

'His name's Pilgrim,' Jay said, protective, prickly.

Abernathy's right eyebrow went up. 'Pilgrim, is it? That's . . . pretty enigmatic. It suits you, though.'

'It's the only name I have now,' Pilgrim told her.

'That's not strictly true, though, is it?' Abernathy's smile was slow and knowing. It made his stomach tense.

Her fist unfurled and she rested it palm flat on the table. Back to being easy, in control. She looked at the others, cutting him free from her gaze, and *there* was the mischief he remembered from the old her, the Abernathy of the Unit who was solidifying in his mind with every passing minute of being in her presence. Except the playfulness he remembered had tempered with age, developed a sharp, slicing edge.

'There were rumours about him on the ward,' she said. Her tone had changed, become mysterious, as though she were telling them a secret bedtime story. She cast him glances as she talked, but this performance wasn't for him. 'Things like he was a serial killer whose victims talked to him and had sent him mad. Or he was a junkie that the government had pumped full of illicit experimental drugs. I liked the time-traveller one best – that must've come from someone who'd watched *Twelve Monkeys* too many times. It was all horseshit, of course. I know why he was in here. I know who he is.'

This time something twisted in Pilgrim's stomach, a sharp, painful clench of muscles. But he didn't stop her. He let her talk.

'We used to chat a bit, you and me,' she said to him. 'Whenever I'd get admitted, you were here. I don't think they knew what to do with you – you had no family, no friends. Not that anyone knew about, anyway. We talked when I first came in. I was so young back then, not much past my eighteenth birthday that first time. But hanging around you seemed to keep the truly fucked-up ones at bay. And you never wanted anything from me. I could tell you were safe,' she said softly, a faint frown on her face as she looked at him from across the table. The wicked gleam in her eye had snuffed out. 'Then, each time I got readmitted, you were a little less talkative. A little less present. You still let me sit with you and talk to you, but you didn't interact so much any more. Birdy called you a lifer – said you'd never get out of this place. You were down to a couple of sentences a day by then. You always looked out for me, though. In your own way.'

Birdy.

'I remember him,' Pilgrim said. 'Birdy. He was always smoothing back his hair.' The distaste he felt at saying the man's name was a physical thing, a squirming worm under his tongue. It made him want to spit. 'He liked you.'

'He was easy in a lot of ways for me. A lot of men are. They see a pretty girl, smile at the pretty girl, pretty girl smiles back and asks for something in return for a favour, pretty girl gets what she wants. He wasn't a nice man, but I'm not very nice, either, so it's all fair. You beat three lumps of shit out of him that day we broke out of here.'

Pilgrim looked down at his hands, at the knuckles, thickened and chipped with scars. Violent hands.

'You don't remember,' Abernathy said, disappointed.

He shook his head, no.

'Oh, well, it doesn't matter. I was one of the few who'd dare go up and talk to you. You cut quite the figure prowling around the day room, doing your thing. Your memory was totally busted, of course. You'd been having ECT since you were a kid.'

'ECT?' Jay asked.

'Electro-convulsive treatment,' she told him. 'They pass electricity into your brain through electrodes and *ZAP!*' She smacked the table, making Jay jump and Jenks streak out from under it. The cat vanished into the hall.

Pilgrim could feel Clancy's gaze on him, her sympathy a cloying hand that clamped him in its grip. He wanted to prise it free.

'That's barbaric,' Tyler said softly.

'Not really,' Abernathy said. 'It's not like in the movies. At least, not modern techniques. It was all very humane: muscle relaxants, general anaesthetic. No pain. Although God knows what it was like when he was young.'

Pilgrim shook his head. 'I don't remember.'

Abernathy shrugged. 'And why would you? You'd had more than a decade of it. That would mess anyone up.'

'What else did you find out back then?' Jay asked, too eager and too interested. 'When you talked to him?'

'Enough,' Pilgrim said. 'This isn't what we're here for.'

Abernathy leaned forward on her elbows, eyes on him. 'I know more about you than you know yourself, by the looks.'

She likes that she does, too.

Pilgrim's heart did a slow contraction, a hard *lub-dub* in his chest that he was convinced everyone at the table heard.

'You've been hiding behind names for a long time, Sol. Pilgrim. Whatever the hell you call yourself these days. But, like you said, you're not here for reminiscing, no matter how good a storyteller I am.' Abernathy sat back again and folded her arms, back to business. 'So what do you want?'

'Information,' Pilgrim said. 'I was brought here.'

A flicker of uncertainty passed over her face. 'Brought by who?'

'I'm not sure any more. Jay, do you have the photo?'

Jay removed the photograph from his pocket and unfolded it, leaning over their half-eaten food to flatten it on the table in front of Abernathy. Jay pointed. 'Lacey,' he said, as if her name were a spell that could unlock all gates.

Abernathy didn't speak for a long time as she studied the picture. She looked up, her eyes going from Pilgrim to Jay and back again. 'Is this some kind of joke?' she asked.

'Joke?' Jay asked, confused. 'No, it's no joke. Why would it be a joke?'

'Am I supposed to know who this girl is?'

Jay tried to not look crestfallen, he really did. 'You don't know anyone called Lacey?'

She turned to Pilgrim. 'Is *this* why you've come? For this girl? You've come a hell of a long way for nothing, then.'

'Are you sure you don't recognise her?' Pilgrim asked. 'She'd be around seventeen now.'

I warned you, Pilgrim, Voice said softly. *I warned you she was never really talking to you.*

Abernathy's patience teetered on a blade's edge – it was in the jut of her jaw and the furrow between her brows – but something in his face stayed her tongue. She sighed and looked again.

'Look, I'm sorry, all right? I don't know her, and I don't know anyone called Lacey.'

At the low, complaining creak from the table, Pilgrim released his grip on its corner. 'Someone called me here,' he told it. 'I *heard* it. I feel it. The same words over and over. They've led me to this place.'

Abernathy stared at him, looked to each of the others sitting at the table with her. She didn't appear impressed with what she saw. 'I just got done telling you you weren't a bullshitter and now you're coming to me with *this*? You haven't given two craps about anything or anyone here for the last eight years. You left and didn't look back. I get it, I do. But there's *nothing here* for you any more. Do you understand? Nothing for *any* of you.'

'"Burning", "Madness", "Death",' Pilgrim said. 'Do those words mean anything to you?'

Her eyelashes fluttered in a rapid three-blink. 'No. They do not,' she replied, flat and final.

She's lying, Voice said.

Clancy swivelled in her seat to face her, the movement verging on aggressive. 'We're not leaving. Not if you're hurting people here.'

Abernathy latched on to the distraction, turning in her seat, too. 'It's either leave or I shoot you in the face. I know which option I'm liking the sound of more.'

'You're a *murderer*,' Clancy spat.

'Oh, I'm going to be one in exactly one minute's time, lady, if you don't back the fuck off of me.'

This was the Abernathy who'd been lost to him for close to eight years. Hard, angry, and willing to follow up that anger with violence if she had to. But he couldn't help but remember the cigarettes she'd pass to him out in the birdcage, or the pieces of pie she would slide his way during dinner. He wanted to try to get her on side. He didn't want to make an enemy of her.

'Abernathy,' Pilgrim said.

'*What?*' she snapped, turning on him. 'I swear to God, Sol, I'm about to lose my shit.'

'I know. But, like you said, I've come a long way.'

'So what? Want me to do a congratulatory dance for you?'

'No. I want you to stop lying.'

She glared at him, and he sat unmoving, waiting her out. Finally, she threw up her hands. '*Fine.* Christ almighty. What do you want? Fuck it. Come on, I'll answer whatever questions you have.'

CHAPTER 7

Intel

Pilgrim stood in the corner of the day room, at the one window that would unlatch, and breathed in the night air. It held no hint of carbon monoxide, no pollution; it smelled fresh and clean, it smelled of river water and grass. At his back, the others slept, the occasional shift in their position and their sleepy mumbles the only things to break the stillness.

He hears her breathing before she speaks, a soft, rhythmic ocean tide in his ear.

'You and your sister would sit on the floor, so close to the TV you'd have to tilt your heads back to see. You'd watch cartoons while your mom did laundry. You told me her name. Do you remember?'

He does. He's remembering so much now, being back in this place. Stepping into the Unit's corridors, seeing the birdcage, the day room, having Abernathy sit across from him in the dining room. There was no tearing down of doors, no splintering explosions as memories ripped their way free. This door had swung itself open, silent and smooth.

'Violet,' he murmurs, and stops, because even with the name he can't picture her face.

Lacey slips her hand into his and her palm is so warm, her fingers so tight in their clasp, that he has to close his eyes and tell himself they're not real. *She's* not real. Abernathy hadn't been lying about that; Lacey was an unknowable number of miles away, unreachable, untouchable, lost to him, like his sister was lost to him.

'*I thought you were wrong to forget about her,*' she says. '*Because I'd never let myself forget my sister or my niece. It's unthinkable to me. But I want you to know that I understand now. I understand why you found ways to push them away. And it's okay, Pilgrim. You don't have to remember any more. You can stop. You can let me go.*'

'No,' he says.

Lacey turns to him but he keeps his eyes closed.

'*I've hurt you enough. You don't have to hurt any more.*'

'I remember a roofless barn,' he says, not knowing if he was talking to her or himself. 'I remember the warmth of firelight. You told me that you don't forget your family. That's what you said.'

'*And you said you only remember people for as long as you need them. You don't need me, Pilgrim. Not any more. And I . . . I don't need you. I have Voice now. You gave him to me, remember? I'm not alone.*'

He looks at her, then, and her face is missing, like his sister's face is missing. A blank nothing. He doesn't know how she has spoken to him all this time without lips. How she breathes without nose or mouth. She has no eyes – only endless space from chin to forehead.

'No,' he says again, the word stabbing its way out. 'No. I won't forget you.'

Her voice comes from that empty, blank space. '*What if I'm already dead? What if this is all I can be for you now? A figment of your imagination.*'

I'm sorry, Voice said, small and sad.

The ghostly hold on his hand disappeared, and Lacey with it.

'You knew she wouldn't be here,' Pilgrim said, but there was no accusation in his tone.

I suspected it, yes. I'm not sure you'd have made it even halfway here without thinking you were doing it for her. You must have known that deep down. It's why she came with us.

Pilgrim heard Abernathy approach, much like she had that night all those years ago when they'd stood in this exact spot and watched the *whumps* of explosions light up the night sky along the highway.

'Any more car fires out there?' Abernathy's voice was soft; she didn't want to wake the others.

The moon was hidden tonight, clouds shrouding the sky and leaving the highway and distant Mississippi in darkness. It was a dead world out there, filled with the crumbling monoliths and gravestones of a civilisation long gone.

'There's nothing,' he murmured. 'Not a single thing.' And he felt the yawning truth of his words, a swell of despair so overwhelming it stole the beat of his heart, its thud sinking into his chest until he could barely feel it.

She might not be here, Pilgrim, but Lacey is out there somewhere. We'll find her. I promise.

'Are you thinking about her?' Abernathy asked. 'This lost girl of yours?' She moved to lean against the wall next to the window so she could face him.

He didn't answer, but maybe she didn't expect him to.

'It's funny the things we do for the people we love. I'm not sure I even know what love is, besides obligation and responsibility. And I was never any good with either of those. I'm kind of a fuck-up.'

'You've done right by Jackson,' he said.

She'd told him about what Birdy had done. How he'd hooked Jackson up to an ECT machine and fried him for so long there wasn't a hell of a lot left of the man Pilgrim had known. 'He'd started on you when I got there,' she'd said. 'But I was too late for Jack.'

She'd lost Pilgrim at some point after unbuckling his restraints. He'd wandered off and she'd been too distracted to notice. She'd shouted for him, she said, but it had been no use. Pilgrim couldn't tell her why he'd left, or where he'd gone. That was a part of him he didn't think he'd ever get back.

'I couldn't leave him,' Abernathy said quietly. Her face was veiled with darkness, but she sounded mournful, regretful even. Maybe a part of her wished she *had* left Jackson behind. 'He was grabbing at me and gibbering, spit drooling down his chin, but he had this look in his eyes. Like he knew who I was. Like he was trapped in there. I couldn't leave him like that. We'd have been long dead, if not for this place. He needed the doctors and their drugs, and it turned out they needed him, too. Without him, they wouldn't still be here, doing what they're doing. What Birdy did damaged him, sure, but Jack woke up hearing *nothing*, Sol. The voice he'd heard was gone. Burnt out. They won't let me take him out of here. It's too late for that.' The shadowed shape of her head turned to one side, looking away from him. 'You don't know these people like I do. They're dangerous. This isn't some amateur set-up like it was in the early days. We have resources now. I'm wearing a *uniform*, for fuck's sake.'

'We have time to work it out.'

She let out a heavy, frustrated sigh, but seemed to decide on something. 'There was talk of you at one point, you know,' she said. 'You were the other one; the other patient Birdy had strapped in that room besides Jack. They wanted to look for you. They thought you might be a key to unlocking part of the puzzle. A lost piece.'

Lost piece to what? Voice said. *No one cured you of anything. I'm right here.*

Pilgrim didn't say anything. He could feel Abernathy's eyes on him and he wasn't discomfited by it. He was curious about her, too. She had done terrible things, must have, if she'd been living among these people, working with them.

'It was good you changed your name. Got away when you

did. But you couldn't stop running, could you? It's in your bones.'

'I'm not running now.'

Her face remained in shadow, the day room darker than the world outside it, but he got the impression she was studying him. 'I found your hospital records. They weren't hard to find. It has your medical history in there. Your background. Sol wasn't your birth name. How many names have you had? Do you even know?'

Pilgrim didn't raise his voice, but there was a warning in it. 'None of this is yours to tell.'

'And I haven't. I haven't said a word to anyone. Never told them what I found. But you should know, I think Christopher is a nice name.'

Your name's Christopher, Voice said, more whispering breeze than sound.

Silence settled over them. It breathed with them, in and out, more swells of an ocean.

'There were news clippings in there, too. One said you didn't speak for almost two years after they found you,' she said. 'They called you the Mute of Little Mount. Did you know that?'

Pilgrim let his vision soak up the night, let it bleed in from the edges until darkness crowded him, blotting out the day room, blotting out Abernathy, leaving him standing alone. 'You think what we've seen since the voices came is the worst we humans can do. It's not. It wasn't the voices who did those things. It was us. No one else.'

She murmured an agreement, but in the dimness, her head turned as if she could no longer bear to look at him. Her arms folded around her body, for warmth, maybe, or for comfort. To his left was the table she had sat at with Jackson on their final morning here. It had been swept clear and a game of Solitaire set up.

'Matilde was right,' Pilgrim said. 'Voice came to me when I needed him most. He saved me, and cursed me, too. But without him I wouldn't be here.'

Abernathy joined him in staring at the playing cards tiered out on the table.

'I'm sorry,' she said, and her apology felt like it encompassed a million trespasses, none of which were graspable to either of them.

His nod was a minute thing. Unnoticeable.

She finally stopped staring at the table and straightened away from the window. For a moment he thought she would reach out, touch his arm, but her arms remained folded across her body. 'You should get some rest.'

'No.' He was done with sleeping. 'We have things to discuss.'

She frowned into his face, and her eyes weren't so far off his; she was taller than he remembered.

'Christopher,' she said, and he didn't correct her, although hearing the name pained him. 'This isn't some game. If you're found here, you're as good as dead. All of you are.'

'I thought you said they could cure us.'

'No. I said they *think* they can. Jackson is their one and only success so far.'

Their only *one?* Voice said sharply. *What the hell does that mean?*

It meant none of it was working.

Pilgrim stepped closer, wanting to see her better in the dark. She didn't flinch, but he felt her breathing stop, heard the tiny shift in the fabric of her clothes as her muscles tensed. She had an inch-long scar beside her left eye that hadn't been there before, and a second one – a slim, almost invisible slice – that followed the line of her jaw. The small mole near the corner of her mouth had always been there, though.

He didn't touch her. He didn't have to. His closeness held her in place, his gaze locked her in.

Through the window, and far in the distance, a fork of lightning lit the tar-black sky. The flash threw silver on to the Mississippi and, for the briefest instant, the water rippled with sparkles. A fine palsied tremor passed through Pilgrim's hand, the one Lacey had held, the same hand he had grasped the wiring in his dream with, its cabling running hot and electric.

'If Jackson's their only success,' he said carefully, the tremors in his hand getting worse, 'how many have they killed trying to get it right?'

Abernathy winced. She glanced over Pilgrim's shoulder at his sleeping friends. Her voice dropped so low he had to watch her lips to read the shapes they made. 'Don't be naïve, Christopher. They've been trying to claw back what was lost for *years*. They don't want to share any part of this world with you. They don't want you muttering to yourselves or doing your little eye-shifting thing whenever Jiminy Cricket whispers in your ear. They're *terrified* of what you did, of what you still might do. You really think this small Podunk hospital is the centre to all this? You think so many of us here could've stayed undetected and underground for so long without help?' She angrily tugged at the collar of her shirt. 'Where exactly do you think this uniform came from? This isn't the only place that's been trying to perfect a treatment that works. They report back to each other all the time. Everything gets shared. *Everything.*'

A needle of freezing steel slid into his skull, right over the place where Voice lived. The hair on the back of his neck stood on end. He turned to look at his companions: Jay stretched out on the floor at the foot of Tyler's couch; Tyler curled up under his jacket, the sleeve of her hoodie dangling down, close to touching Jay's shoulder; Clancy on the couch beside it, flat on her back and ramrod straight, as if even in sleep she was unable to relax. He wondered if Tyler's and Clancy's voices fell into silence at night, like Voice did, if they rested along with them, the inactivity of their minds a blessed reprieve after all the thoughts that careened and shot through them during the day.

'How many more places like this one?' Pilgrim asked Abernathy, still gazing towards the couches.

'I don't know. Three, that I know about, for sure. One larger one out east. But listen, I don't rock the boat. I don't ask questions or stick my nose in where it's not wanted. I'm good at fitting in. I get water, food, a clean bed and clothes. It suits me and it's the only place Jack can be. So I pull my weight.'

'Pull your weight?'

He got a stiff pantomime smile for that.

She's one of them, Pilgrim. Open your eyes.

They stood close, two feet separating them. He couldn't see her gun but he knew it was there. He could grab her if he had to, pin her to the wall before she could move. He was stronger, if not faster. He could slam her head against the window-frame and crush her skull before the others had even fully roused themselves.

'You *are* good at fitting in, aren't you?' he murmured. 'You're good at getting people to trust you. Like that kid whose ear you bit. You'd even won him over by the end.'

There was a hint of what might have been remorse in the set of her mouth, possibly even unhappiness in the fine lines at the corners of her eyes. But it was hard to tell with her.

'But you're not a doctor,' Pilgrim said. 'Not a scientist. You're not a leader, either. You said what you are. A fuck-up.'

The frown that crowded her brows was full of offence. 'Screw you.'

He didn't want to ask the question, didn't want to hear what her answer would be, but it hung in the air between them, too big for either of them to ignore.

'How many of us have you taken to them?'

'I didn't—'

'*How many?*'

She clamped her bottom lip between her teeth and shook her

head once, an angry shake. A cornered one. 'I don't know,' she hissed. 'Too many to count.'

Pilgrim's chest deflated, his breath leaving him on an endless exhalation. He couldn't bring himself to breathe in again straight away.

I told you you needed to be careful with her, Voice said. *She's not the same person you knew.*

But she was the same. More than he'd thought. Abernathy's morals had always been fluid and ambiguous. She did what she pleased when it suited her; that's the way it had always been. The only thing that had changed was the circumstances. Back then, there had been institutions to keep her in check. Medication, doctors, therapists, laws and rules and consequences, and more consequences heaped on top of those. She had nothing to hold her back here. She'd had no one to tell her to stop.

'You're going to help me fix this, Abernathy. Do you understand?'

She opened her mouth but nothing came out.

'I shouldn't have left you here alone,' he said. 'I'm sorry.'

She rubbed at her face. Combed her fingers through her hair. It was an agitated gesture, if Pilgrim had ever seen one. She looked past him to the couches before bringing her eyes back to his face. 'You really have changed,' she told him. 'You never gave this much of a shit before.'

The truth of her words hit their mark. He'd been well practised in staying out of people's way. No one to worry about, no one to mourn. It was a safe existence; a solitary one (if you didn't count Voice), but safe. Forgetting about everyone he cared about had been his way of protecting himself. And it had worked.

Until Lacey.

Until Lacey. She had ruined everything. So had Ruby and Albus, in their way. Ruby had sown her seeds, down in the very heart of him where they couldn't be seen, and Matilde had provided a sprinkling of water. He had a role to play, she'd told him, and he'd dismissed her because he'd wanted no role. He didn't get involved. His tool set comprised avoidance and indifference, and he had wielded both with skill.

And yet here he was.

Lacey could have easily been one of the people Abernathy had rounded up and brought here. She could have had electrodes attached to her head and had every single thing shocked out of her mind that these doctors believed didn't belong, and maybe she'd have died, or maybe she'd have woken up a drooling zombie – a zombie like Pilgrim had been, walking and counting everything in the Unit, riding a motorbike across the desert and talking to no one, a man who had been dead for longer than he'd been alive. If he couldn't protect Lacey by being with her, he could protect her and everyone like her by doing this.

'You're going to help me fix this,' he told Abernathy again, talking over her when she started to object. 'And I'll help you get Jackson out.'

She glared at him. 'You're completely nuts.'

'I am,' he agreed. 'I used to live here, remember.'

Her glare cracked and the corner of her lip twitched upward. '*God*, you're such an asshole for coming back.'

'I know. You missed me.' He said it straight-faced.

She fought against the smile a second longer before giving into it. It died not long after reaching her eyes. 'They'll do worse than kill us if they find out what we're doing.'

'Us', she'd said. 'We'. Pilgrim almost smiled. 'Then we'd best make sure they don't find out.'

Oh my God, Voice said. *You're both completely nuts.*

PART THREE

The Man Who Remembered

CHAPTER 1

Groundwork

Once Abernathy had decided on a course of action, she didn't let anything hold her back. Pilgrim had asked for full disclosure from her, and his request was taken seriously. Over the next day and a half she armed them with information.

The Unit's day room had become a planning room. They had packed away the playing cards and, in their place, hand-drawn maps and notes lay scattered across the Formica table-top. There, the five of them sat, afternoon sunshine casting warm rays of light across the mess of paperwork. The parquet flooring gleamed as though it had recently undergone a buffing. If not for the peeling paint and bubbled walls, Pilgrim could have been fooled into thinking he was still a patient here; soon, the rattle of lunch trolleys from the dining room – a ghostly echo from the past – would interrupt their meeting.

'No,' Abernathy was saying to Clancy. 'Everything goes through them. Every scrap of data gathered, they see it first.'

She had explained that every decision made at St Louis went through four people and four people alone. A head council that consisted of two doctors: a clinical psychologist called Dr Robbie Lloyd, and neurologist and surgeon Dr Elizabeth Jane May. The security and defence representative came in the form of a colonel in his late fifties who everyone called, rather boringly, the Colonel.

'The two doctors have been here from the start,' Abernathy said. 'They were on the staff. Liz was one of the doctors who refused to leave when things got bad. Dr Lloyd . . . well.' She pulled a face, a decidedly unimpressed one. 'Who the hell knows what goes on with Dr Lloyd. Narcissism, mostly. Look, you have to understand, it wasn't like this place shut down overnight. Even with everything going on, departments in here carried on working. For weeks and weeks there was activity here. People came for help, for medication and supplies, and when they couldn't find what they wanted . . .' She shook her head, her eyes following her finger as she ran it along the table's edge. 'Things got ugly pretty fast.'

It took a moment for her gaze to lift and, when it did, it rested on Pilgrim. 'I'll never be convinced that all that ugliness was down to the voices, you know. People, they've always been selfish. Selfish and opportunistic.'

Pilgrim nodded. He agreed with the sentiment.

Abernathy drew in a breath and sighed it back out. 'Anyhow, I'd holed up with Jackson in a ward just off here. I couldn't move him much – he was in a bad way. By the time I'd run out of drugs and went searching for more, I came across Liz. It was by sheer luck I found her. She was in her lab coat, just like on any other workday. She convinced me to let her take a look at him. And that was it. That's how it started – for me and Jack, at least. Back then, there were only twelve of us, Drs Lloyd and May included.'

'What about the Colonel?' Jay asked. He'd taken the seat next to Tyler. He had a notepad on the table in front of him and he'd been twiddling a pen non-stop for the last twenty minutes, intermittently drumming it on the pad. Pilgrim wanted to rip it out of his hands and stab it into a part of his body that would hurt but not necessarily kill him. 'Sounds like he's military.'

Abernathy snorted. 'I seriously doubt that. Pretty sure he's one of those guys who stockpiled supplies and readied themselves for the end of the world. You know, a *prepper*.' She said it with a hint of loathing, even though the world *had* kind of ended and the Colonel and his ilk had been right to prep for it. 'He came afterwards. He's lived in St Louis all his life – he's not an outsider or anything. We were actually self-contained for a good while – as long as two and a half or three years – but then the Colonel and a few of his buddies got those long-range radio-transmitter thingies up and running, and, well, that opened everything up. Made it official, if you like. We have around seventy people now. Peter would know the numbers.'

Peter. The fourth person on the council, and the man Abernathy was required to report to. Peter Bird.

No one called him Birdy any more.

Peter Bird's credentials for holding a respected place within the facility were lacking but for the obvious: he was the only one so far who had treated someone who heard a voice and successfully cured them of it. For that reason alone, he had considerable standing here.

'Will we need to deal with him?' Pilgrim asked Abernathy. 'Birdy?'

'He's still a massive jerk,' she said. 'He's proud of this place. Of what he's achieved, though he's had fuck all to do with the building of any of it. He'd definitely recognise you if he saw you, though. So we won't be crossing paths with him if we can help it. He's harmless by himself. His kind of power only works when he has others to lord it over.'

'Okay. We stay out of his way, then,' Pilgrim said.

Three months prior, though, a fifth person had arrived to shake up the hierarchy.

Clancy had her head down as she perused the list of names Abernathy had written out. Her finger tapped over the name at the bottom. 'Vanessa Mendoza,' she read.

'Right. Vanessa.' Abernathy had picked Jenks up and draped him over her lap like a comforter. He was so long his legs dangled over the sides of her thighs. She stroked him absently as she answered. 'She's the wild card in all this. God knows where she came from – no one has ever given me a straight answer, but I suspect it's from one of the other facilities. None of the council were surprised when she showed up, at least. They knew she was coming. And she didn't come alone, either. She was *escorted* here, like some princess. Things have been tense around here since her and her goons arrived. She's been mainly focused on the kids. Anyone under the age of sixteen. She found me not long after arriving, said that if I ever had the opportunity to grab any kids while I was out, that I should do it and bring them to her. Preferably no older than ten, she said. I *didn't*, of course,' she added, fielding off Clancy's outrage before it spilled over. 'I'm not the best at taking orders, and especially not ones that might end up with little kids being poked and prodded at. But I'm not the only one who rounds folks up here. Treatments in general have stepped up a gear over the last few weeks, regardless of what I did or didn't do. They're acting like they're running out of time.'

'Are they?' Pilgrim asked.

'*You're* here, aren't you?' she replied, giving him a meaningful look. 'So yeah, maybe they are.'

'What does she want with them?' Tyler asked. 'The children?'

Abernathy shrugged. 'No clue. She asks them weird stuff. Like if they dream a lot and about what. Or if they like to read and what kinds of books. I hear she gets them to draw or paint pictures sometimes. Asks them what games they enjoy playing. Occasionally, she does some simple logic and math puzzles with them. And then they all get a physical examination. That's pretty much it. Harmless stuff, by all appearances. She doesn't really get involved with the treatments or speak to any of the adult patients. She observes and assesses, sure, but mostly she makes her notes on the kids and that's it. Faye likes her – she's one of the teenagers here. All the kids seem to.'

'What about the adults?' Clancy asked. 'Do they like her?'

Abernathy shrugged. 'How can you like someone you don't know? She doesn't mingle. She sits with her little cohort during mealtimes and walks everywhere with them. She spoke to me that one time, and that was it. Everyone falls over themselves to assist her, though. Even Dr Lloyd. I can't decide if it's because she's hot as hell or if everyone's afraid of her. You should see Birdy when he's around her. It's painful. So far up her butt you can practically see his feet sticking out.'

'You think we can get a chance to speak to her?' Pilgrim asked.

Abernathy gave him a half-disbelieving, half-amused look. 'Because I said she's hot or because you're interested in what part she has to play in all this?'

He let her stew on that for a minute, until her amusement gave way to full-blown annoyance. 'The latter,' he said finally.

She shook her head. 'Like I said, she always has her goons with her. It'd be almost impossible to get her alone. I'll tell you something else weird, though. You see those patterns dotted around now? Kind of like spirals and circles? They get graffitied all over the place. Cars, windows, buildings – you name it. I see them a lot when I'm out.'

Out rounding people up to be killed, Voice finished snidely.

Voice had been unfailingly disagreeable since they'd found out the specifics of what had been going on in the hospital and Abernathy's role in it, but Pilgrim had allowed for his disgruntlement. Being in a place where work was underway to permanently eradicate you from existence would upset anyone.

Abernathy got nods from all of them. They had seen the signs in one form or another.

'Well, I'm almost positive one of her guys has the same pattern tattooed right here.' She drummed her fingers on the back of her hand. 'He keeps it hidden. Is careful to wear gloves. But I caught a glimpse when he got sloppy one time. I'm ninety per cent sure it was the same.'

'*Almost positive,*' Voice griped. '*Ninety per cent sure.*' *I wouldn't bet my butt on it, if I were you.*

'Those signs are for voice-hearers,' Jay told her.

'Yeah, well, whatever it was, he doesn't want anyone seeing it.'

It was odd, if she was right. Was this guy a voice-hearer who'd sided with what was being done here? It seemed like a dangerous game to play – what if Abernathy had decided to oust him? He might have found himself strapped to a gurney, along with all the other voice-hearers in this place. Yet Vanessa had to be aware of the tattoo, if what Abernathy claimed was true, and that only made Pilgrim want to speak to the woman more.

'Why didn't you tell anyone what you saw?' Pilgrim asked her.

'I was going to,' Abernathy said. 'As soon as I found a way for it to benefit me.'

Clancy made a disgusted sound and Abernathy smiled curtly at her.

'So, who exactly *is* running the show here?' Jay asked. 'The hot chick?'

'Vanessa's definitely considered important,' Abernathy said, 'but I'd say Dr Lloyd is top of the list, for sure.'

'Isn't the Colonel going to be a problem?' Pilgrim asked.

Abernathy was busy lifting Jenks up and cuddling him. The cat didn't seem to mind. 'Ah, he's just a dumb grunt, isn't he, Jenksy?' She scratched behind his ears. 'He's the muscle around here, but he doesn't have anything to do with the treatments. He wouldn't know his ass from his elbow when it comes to that stuff.'

Clancy turned the sheet of paper around and pushed it towards Abernathy, a deliberate, confrontational shove. 'And what about Dr May? Liz, I believe you called her.'

Here, Abernathy got quiet. Her hand paused mid-stroke down Jenks's back as she stared at Clancy.

Here they go again, Voice murmured.

'Liz is a mediator, not a fighter,' Abernathy said. 'And she's been having some serious reservations recently about what goes on. Her daughter might be a voice-hearer. They're doing tests on her at the moment. So, no, I don't think Liz will be a problem for us.'

Tyler leaned forward, interested at hearing they might have a potential ally. 'Could we get her on our side, do you think?'

But Abernathy was already shaking her head. 'She's scared of you. Scared about what's going on – she's heard the rumours being bandied around, like everybody has.'

'What rumours?' Pilgrim asked.

Abernathy's lip curled. 'Flitting Man this and Flitting Man that. There's been a lot of movement out in the city over the past few months. More of your kind seem to have turned up. Easy pickings, you could say, but even so, it has everyone worried.'

Maybe that's something we can use, Voice said thoughtfully.

'Okay, read out what we have so far,' Pilgrim told Jay, and Jay stopped chewing the end of his pen and picked up his notepad. He read out their shopping list. At the last two items, the biggest ones by far, Pilgrim turned a questioning look to Abernathy. 'You're sure you can get them?'

She nodded, seemingly unconcerned. 'I'm good, don't worry. You might not like what car I have in mind, or what I'll have to do to get the gas for it, but I'll get them. Oh, and put bolt-cutters on there,' she told Jay, pointing to his notepad. 'I broke my last pair.'

And spray paint. I have an idea of how we can use those Flitting Man rumours to our advantage.

Pilgrim passed on Voice's instruction and Jay added both items to the shopping list.

'Anything else we need to worry about?' Pilgrim asked, mostly aiming the question at Abernathy.

She ignored him and picked Jenks up, holding him so they were eye to eye. She baby-talked to the cat. 'Uncle Christopher will see for himself soon enough, won't he, Jenksy? Maybe then he'll wish he never came up with this dumb plan in the first place.'

CHAPTER 2

Infiltration (Part 1)

Abernathy led Pilgrim and Tyler down a fungus-carpeted hospital corridor; it did a fine job of muting their footsteps. All the corridors so far had been the same, any familiarity Pilgrim might have had with them lost in their uniformity. That was until Abernathy led them past a staff counter nested in the corner of two merging hallways. He recognised the emaciated body of one of the nurses from his dream draped over the countertop in her mouldering scrubs. She was little more than bones and papery skin. A few wisps of her hair sprouted from the white cap of her skull. Her jawbone hung crooked, evidence that the man with the tyre iron had indeed finished his swing.

There were no signs of the two other nurses, but, further up the corridor, the man's body lay slumped against the wall. The tyre iron was jammed into his eye socket and Pilgrim felt the judder of metal in his hand, its pry-bar end connecting with the man's face, the shuddering slide as it pushed deeper. The man had already been swinging his tyre iron when Pilgrim chanced upon them, the crunch of the metal rod connecting with the nurse's face enough to make Pilgrim stop mid-stride. Undoubtedly, the man would have moved on to the nurse with the telephone pressed to her ear, and then found the one hiding under the counter – the blonde who'd smiled self-consciously on her ID badge – and smashed their skulls in along with their colleague's. Pilgrim didn't recall closing the distance. He didn't recall his and the man's scuffle. But he did remember how much force it had taken to shove that tyre iron through the man's eye and into his brain.

'I've been here,' Pilgrim said, staring down at the guy he'd murdered.

Not murdered. Self-defence. He'd have tried to kill you, too.

'I'm not surprised,' Abernathy said, stopping to see what the hold-up was. 'You were practically named on the lease here. Listen, I'll have to tie you up when we go down a floor.'

'Already?' he asked. He didn't think it would be so soon.

'We talked about this. Tyler is fine with it. Right, little rabbit?'

'If it's the only way to get us in, then yes,' Tyler said. 'I'll do it.'

Abernathy raised her eyebrows at Pilgrim. 'See? She's half your size. Stop being a pussy.' She pointed at the body with the tyre iron sticking out of its face. 'Are you done staring at your boyfriend?'

Pilgrim was more than done with him.

Abernathy led them left at the next intersection, their shoes moving from cushioned moss to crispy, peeling linoleum that crunched underfoot. They went down a long walkway that connected one section of the hospital to the next, grimed-up windows running alongside them, and turned right at the next cross-section of corridors. Fifty yards further on and she shoved open a door, putting her weight behind it. Its bottom edge scraped an arc through the mould.

'Through here,' she said, grunting. 'And keep your voices down.'

Any outside light that had filtered through the high windows and skylights was left behind as they entered the dark, damp stairwell. Abernathy dug into the pack she'd brought along with her and removed one of the new flashlights.

'Watch your step,' she warned, flicking it on.

The smell of stagnant water grew stronger as they descended. A subterranean chill crept through Pilgrim's body, entering at hands and feet and slowly seeping its way into his lungs. It felt like they were visiting a crypt rather than the bowels of a hospital.

Seems unlikely anyone's set their hideout up in such dank surroundings, wouldn't you say?

It did. But Abernathy said it was down here, so down they were going.

And you believe her one hundred per cent? This is our last chance to rethink any of this.

He meant rethink *her*. But this was perhaps the first time Pilgrim had experienced wanting to believe someone, despite having few reasons to. Logically, she held the only gun. If she'd wanted, she could have led them all down here at gunpoint two nights ago when she'd found them wandering the Unit. She could have lied about what she'd been doing all these years. She hadn't known how Pilgrim would react to discovering she'd aided in what was, essentially, mass murder, but she hadn't hidden the truth from him. More than once she'd told him to leave this place. It had taken some convincing to get her to bring him down here at all.

Of course, neither Jay nor Clancy had been happy about this part of the plan. Clancy shared Voice's reservations over Abernathy's loyalty and she'd argued on and off for most of yesterday until Pilgrim told her she was giving him a migraine.

Jay had kept his protests to himself around the others, but they'd come flooding out as soon as he and Pilgrim ventured outside on their shopping trip. His complaints had mainly centred on him being left behind. 'But I'm your wingman,' he'd said, to which Pilgrim had replied that they weren't fighter pilots and they weren't in a movie.

Jay's protests had eventually been overruled when Abernathy

pointed out that she'd never brought more than two captives in at once; any more would raise suspicions. Besides, Pilgrim didn't need four people to have to watch out for, traipsing around and potentially getting themselves hurt. Tyler was one more than he'd have liked, but he needed her and she'd wanted to help.

Descending the slippery, fungi-slick steps, Pilgrim stuck to the right, giving Tyler room to hold on to the railing with her left hand. She glanced over at him, as if she could hear all his churning thoughts. Her face was porcelain white in the backwash of Abernathy's flashlight. It made her seem ethereal. Less than human. She had removed her rain slicker and wore only a thick hoodie with a pouch in front.

She sent him an encouraging smile. It trembled at the edges.

Abernathy splashed into the bottom of the stairwell and turned to face them. She tucked the flashlight under her arm and reached inside her jacket. The bottom dropped out of Pilgrim's stomach when she came out holding a bunch of zip ties and threaded two out. The rest went back in her pocket.

Neither Pilgrim nor Tyler moved any closer.

'Think of this as our first exercise in trust, Christopher,' Abernathy said.

A small pain stabbed his chest again when she called him that.

Right. And it has nothing to do with the fact you're about to put your life in the hands of someone who's been killing our kind for God knows how long.

'I've already trusted you by leaving all my weapons in the Unit,' Pilgrim said, stepping down off the last step, water sloshing over his boots. The chill was as bracing as walking into a snowdrift.

'And I'm trusting you to not mindlessly kill everyone when I take you in. I have people I vaguely like down here, believe it or not. You talked *me* into doing this, remember, not the other way around. Now, your wrists.'

Pilgrim, I'm really not sure about this.

'Pilgrim.' Tyler whispered his name at the same time Voice did. 'Last night, I dreamed of the people they have locked up down here.'

He listened but didn't take his eyes away from Abernathy.

'They think they're going to die. Alone. In the dark. They were so scared they held each other's hands.'

At the hollow of Abernathy's throat the fluttering shadow-beat of her pulse told him exactly nothing about what she was thinking. He looked past her to the closed door, warped by water, the paint peeling and flaking away. From its bottom hinge, rust stained a shape like a question mark lying on its front. On the wall next to it, a small clump of white-capped mush-rooms formed the question mark's dot. Stepping through that door was the equivalent of being blindfolded and led towards a cliff's edge, hoping that each footfall found solid ground.

And that you get pulled to a stop before the land runs out, Voice said.

That, too.

Pilgrim met Abernathy's eyes. They were steady on his.

He held his hands out to her.

A zip tie was fed around his wrists. 'There *is* a technique to getting out of these things,' she said as she pulled the cord tight with a *zzzzzppppt*. A wince ticked in his cheek as the plastic bit into his skin. 'Tense your wrists and drive your clasped hands down at your hips. Short and sharp. It'll snap if you do it hard enough. And I mean *hard*.' She left him and went to Tyler.

'You might've said that before,' he said, testing the zip tie. She'd left no give.

'Where's the fun in that? Holy shit, where's your hand?' Abernathy had pushed Tyler's cuffs up to reveal the stump of her right wrist. She glanced over at Pilgrim, as if he'd performed some magic voodoo trick.

'I don't have one,' Tyler told her.

'This whole time you've been here, you've been missing an entire *hand*?'

Tyler frowned. 'Yes?'

'God, I never noticed. Who took your lucky rabbit paw?'

'No one. I was born without it.'

'So God took it, then? Shit. How am I even supposed to . . .' She ran her eyes over her. 'Here, turn around. I'll have to zipper you to your belt.' Abernathy fastened Tyler's left hand to her belt loop. 'That'll have to do. Man, you guys.' Abernathy shook her head. 'You're full of surprises. Right, you' – she pointed at Tyler – 'don't talk. And you' – she pointed at Pilgrim – '*definitely* don't talk. It's best you leave all the talking to me.'

Pilgrim raised his tied hands and mimed zipping his lips.

'Yeah, I know. You've had a quite a bit of practice with that.' Abernathy reached up and tweaked his nose. Her fingers were ice-cold and he began to realise that all her talk was perhaps more to do with battling her nerves than because she enjoyed the sound of her own voice. 'Okay, let's scoot,' she said.

It was a further ten minutes of walking before the need for Abernathy's flashlight became redundant. The service corridor they followed ended in a flood of artificial lighting, its source originating from around the next bend. The dirt and detritus that had littered their way up to now disappeared, a stark line delineating where years of neglect met walls and flooring that had been scrubbed clean. Clinically so. The red brick and ceramic tiles of the old hospital ceased and became the concrete breezeblocks and industrial panelling of the modern block. Clean lines and bare, vinyl floors.

That final walk towards the light was a long one for Pilgrim. It gave him plenty of time to think about whether their plan would work, or whether it would end with all of them dead.

Abernathy had gone over the maps she'd drawn of this part of the hospital, but it hadn't prepared Pilgrim for the noise or the brightness. The strip lighting burned with an intensity that made his eyes water. He couldn't recall the last time he'd seen fluorescent tubing working. The hum of activity had also increased, and not only from the buzzing lights and the distant rumble of working generators.

They were on a wide, concrete-floored concourse large enough to accommodate two full-sized cars. Pristine metal tubing, wiring and red-painted pipes ran above their heads. Vents made a soft *shush*ing sound. Everything was so shiny and new and in stark contrast to the peeling, filthy, decaying carcass of the world Pilgrim lived in; down here, they had made their world neat, made it run seamlessly and efficiently while everything above it was falling into ruin. It jarred his brain, made him think that, if he reached out and touched it, the veneer would crumble away to reveal the rotted innards beneath.

'How many more guns do you have down here?' he asked, his voice resonating in this world of man-made steel, conduits and concrete.

They'd gotten through the secure entrance without any trouble. Abernathy had flirted shamelessly with the guards on duty there, both of whom seemed to know her. The men had held military-grade assault rifles and had eyed Pilgrim and Tyler with the kind of disdain normally reserved for hardened criminals.

Abernathy shrugged. 'The Colonel would know. If I had to estimate, I'd say at least half are armed in some way. So, around thirty-five-ish?' She walked behind them, her gun shoved into Pilgrim's side. She'd assured him its safety was on, but you never knew with Abernathy. He was careful not to make any sudden moves.

Tyler leaned closer, her shoulder bumping into him. 'Tommy can hear them,' she whispered.

Abernathy's ears perked up. 'Hear what?'

'How many?' Pilgrim asked Tyler.

'Ten, maybe? Tommy says it's hard to separate. There could be more. She says they're very frightened.'

Abernathy was frowning at them. 'Who the fuck's Tommy?'

With perfect timing, the tube lighting flickered.

They stopped walking, faces tilting up to the ceiling.

'They can only treat patients every few days,' Abernathy said.

I can't believe they call them patients, Voice muttered. *What complete bullshit.*

They'd agreed before coming down here that it would be safest if Voice remained quiet unless he had something absolutely vital to say. Pilgrim didn't class the observation of something being 'complete bullshit' as essential information. Voice must have sensed his disapproval because he slunk back into his hole without saying anything more.

The lights flickered again, making little *tink*ing noises, and cut out completely, plunging them into darkness. The soft electronic whirring and the *shush* of vents geared down, too. Pilgrim held his breath for the three long seconds it took for the light to blink back to eye-watering life.

'The ECT machines take up a lot of juice,' Abernathy explained, eyes falling from the ceiling to find him. 'They have to schedule their use. It took years for them to stop overloading the generators and shorting everything out. They have a lot of motivation to keep going, though. It's not like their goal has changed.'

'*Their* goal?' Pilgrim said, intrigued by her choice of word.

She nudged him with the gun to get him walking again. 'Look, I honestly couldn't give a shit if you hear a voice or not. I've had plenty of bad experiences with people who didn't hear anything at all. All I care about is where Jack and I end up. But none of it takes away from the fact they have food down here, power, water purification. I'd have been an idiot to walk away from that.'

Tyler's head was twisted round and she was giving Abernathy

a strange look. 'You have no problem at all handing innocents over to them?'

'What "innocents" are you talking about, little rabbit? There's no such thing, not any more. And, believe it or not, some come here under their own steam. They *want* to be rid of their pesky little head-friends.'

The sound of voices had all their gazes shifting up the corridor. A man had stepped out on to the concourse. A woman and child followed him. The adults' black outfits matched Abernathy's, but where Abernathy and the man wore a black hooded jacket (and he carried a flask), the woman wore a white lab coat that hit her above the knee. The kid wore matching grey sweat pants and a hooded sweater. Her running shoes were very white.

He couldn't see any weapons, but that didn't mean they didn't have any.

Abernathy cursed under her breath and checked over her shoulder. There was nowhere to go.

'We couldn't have been a couple of these willing volunteers?' Tyler whispered. 'You wouldn't have needed to tie us up, then.'

Abernathy shook her head, eyeing the approaching trio. 'I'm not exactly known for bringing in the willing ones by the time we get to this stage. Now shut up.'

She herded Pilgrim and Tyler to the side, towards a long wall made partly of opaque glass bricks. Dark, indistinct shadows drifted on the other side like sea predators in a murky tank. The faint sound of animals came from in there – Pilgrim thought he heard the *cluck* of chickens. He caught a whiff of faeces, sawdust and dried pet food.

Pilgrim tested the zip tie again, pressing his palms together and tensing his hands. The plastic sawed into his wrists.

The man in the hooded jacket passed a cold, critical eye over Pilgrim and Tyler. 'Two more already, Abbie?' he asked. 'You're batting above your average.'

Abernathy offered an easy shrug. 'What can I say? Murphy was beating me. I needed to pick up my game.'

'Did this one cause you trouble?' The woman was checking out the bloodstains on Pilgrim's clothes, caked dry from the crash. When her mouth crimped with disgust, he wanted to tell her where he'd got them from, describe the torn, split bodies of the driver and her two passengers, and watch her reaction. She had a stiff, formal bearing, her hair scraped back and pinned in place, her hands folded neatly in front of her.

'Oh, he was a problem, all right.' Abernathy tightened her hold on Pilgrim's arm and dug the gun barrel under his ribs. It hurt, and he was sure she meant it to. He let the discomfort show on his face. 'But he's still here with his hands tied up and my gun in his side. Isn't that right, dipshit?' She dug the gun in harder.

'Abbie, language, please,' the woman murmured.

'What? Faye's heard worse. Haven't you, you little dip-shit?' Abernathy smiled at the girl, and the girl grinned back. She was maybe twelve years old. Abernathy had mentioned this kid in relation to Vanessa Mendoza; she said Faye had liked her.

The woman in the lab coat frowned down at the girl at her side and the kid immediately wiped the grin from her face. Pilgrim noted the resemblance between the two. He also noted how the kid had folded her hands in the same neat fashion as her mother.

'Why isn't this one secured properly?' The man in the hooded jacket was gesturing to Tyler, looking less than pleased.

Tyler had her eyes on the ground. She was playing the good, timid prisoner. Pilgrim took note and shifted his own gaze to the floor.

There was a silence from Abernathy, and Pilgrim got the impression she was pissed at her methods being questioned. 'She only has one hand,' she said. 'I had to improvise.'

'You cut off her *hand*?' Pilgrim heard the shock in the woman's voice.

An exasperated sigh came from Abernathy. 'I know you think I'm unhinged, Liz, but I don't actually go around cutting people's hands off.'

Liz. Dr Elizabeth Jane May, one of the two medical professionals here who performed the treatments. Keeping his eyes steadfastly downcast, Pilgrim stared at the hands responsible for such acts. A muddied beat of contempt sloughed through his veins at seeing the neat, pale coral varnish she'd applied to her nails.

The doctor rapidly backtracked. 'No, no, of course not. I didn't mean to suggest—'

'Yes you did.'

'Peter was looking for you,' the man said, impatient with the women's back and forth. 'Liz put one through the machine yesterday and the results were . . . good.'

'Better than good,' Liz said. With his gaze directed at waist level, Pilgrim couldn't gauge their expressions, but he could watch how the doctor's long, fine-boned fingers interlocked and released. Interlocked and released. She wore a slim gold band on her wedding finger.

'He was excited to show you,' Liz said.

'Ah. I'll catch up with him after I make my deposit at the human bank.'

The guy in the hooded jacket didn't seem to appreciate her flippancy. 'You shouldn't make him wait.'

Silence.

Pilgrim glanced up from under his eyebrows and, yes, they were both staring at each other. Tension held the air. Nobody moved.

'I said I'd catch up with him,' Abernathy said.

'You're heading to the morgue first?' Liz asked, keen to change the subject. 'I'll come with you. I need to take Faye to Testing.'

Testing. Abernathy had said the daughter might be a voice-hearer. Pilgrim wondered what that would mean for a kid in a place like this.

Abernathy's grip on his arm tightened. 'You don't have to do that. You lovebirds look like you're in the middle of something.'

'Nick's on duty at nine. I was just walking him to his post. You're okay from here, aren't you, darling?' She looked a question at the man and Pilgrim could tell he wasn't happy about his wife spending more time with Abernathy. He kissed her cheek – a dry, sterile brush of his lips – and left without answering.

'Yeah, see you later, Nick,' Abernathy said to his back. 'Fucking asshole,' she muttered.

'Abbie, don't. Please.' Liz smoothed her hands over the front of her lab coat, straightening herself. She took a deep breath and held her hand out to the girl beside her. Managed a smile. 'Shall we?'

The girl took it.

Abernathy smiled, too, all teeth and sarcasm. 'Oh gosh, yes. Let's.' She gave Tyler a small shove that got her moving and Pilgrim went without needing to be prodded. See? He could be a good prisoner.

Liz left more than six feet between them, walking on the other side of the concourse with her daughter. Her shoes clicked. She was wearing stiletto heels. Pilgrim hadn't seen anyone in heels, female or otherwise, in a long time. The girl's trainers were silent. Every few steps, she threw him and Tyler a glance. Not curious ones, but suspicious and wary.

'We have one more test to go, don't we, my darling?' Liz said to her daughter.

The girl nodded.

'EEG?' Abernathy asked. She was a step behind Pilgrim, the gun a presence in his side, touching him on each even-numbered step. They had walked eighty-four since passing through the guarded entrance.

'That's right,' Liz replied.

'It's looking positive, then.'

Liz's nod was small; it gave nothing away. 'She's done very well. Where did you find these two?'

Abernathy didn't hesitate in her answer. She was good at this. Playing games. 'Wandering over by the east wing. Probably looking for medical supplies. Tends to be the way.'

Pilgrim could feel the woman's eyes on him. 'Do they speak?'

Abernathy snorted a laugh. 'Why wouldn't they speak?'

'You know what I mean.' Liz seemed a lot more relaxed now that her husband was gone. 'Did either of them say anything about what's going on out there?' Again, Pilgrim felt eyes on him – the doctor's this time. 'More and more of them spread their lies when they come in here,' she said.

'Lies?' Tyler asked in a whisper.

Pilgrim lifted his head and Liz's eyes were waiting for him. Two spots of colour had bloomed on her cheeks and he didn't know if it was temper at Tyler having the audacity to speak, or apprehension over the subject they were discussing. There was such tightly held control in her, fastened together by her perfectly pressed clothes and the immaculate arrangement of her hair. He imagined her in front of a mirror, meticulously applying her armour each morning, passing a brush over her hair for exactly a hundred strokes before tying it up. One crease marring the fabric of her shirt, one stray tendril breaking free from its pinned place, and her entire composure would crack and collapse – a mirage falling to reveal the strained, shivering creature beneath.

'Silly ghost stories,' Liz said, glancing away from him and talking to the space in front of her face. She pulled at the girl's hand for her to keep up and the kid did a quick hopping skip to draw level. 'They say he'll come for us. That he's already here, lying under our beds at night, standing in the shadows every time the lights cut out. They say there'll be nowhere to hide from him soon.'

There was no tremor in her voice, and she made sure to hold her head high, but ghost stories, silly or otherwise, were designed to scare. And they were especially potent when you'd locked yourself in the subterranean level of a hospital, where the bodies of deceased patients had once rolled through on their way to their resting places on the cold slabs of the morgue.

He said, 'There's power in stories if enough people believe them.'

Liz's eyes darted to him and, although her composure didn't slip, he noted how thinly her lips were pressed together.

'Enough chit-chat,' Abernathy told them with another jab of her gun. 'You're giving me earache. Here, go left.'

The service corridor rolled on and on for what seemed like another half-mile, but they went left at the next junction. This corridor wasn't as wide, but it was busier. Pilgrim sensed the spike in fear in Tyler as people stepped in and out of rooms that fed into the main hallway. Pilgrim didn't miss the guns strapped to waists or the disciplined way they went about their business, and he couldn't deny that he felt a sharp scratch of nerves drag over the back of his neck, too. The narrow corridor and the too-low ceiling hemmed him in. Sweat pricked his brow and a hot rush raced up his neck to press hot and tight through his face.

Voice hummed quietly, a reassuring sound, and the dull vibration brought a strange comfort. Pilgrim breathed through his nose, concentrating on his surroundings, focusing on the details. They had come a hundred and twenty-seven steps.

A tiny percentage of the people wore lab coats like Liz's. A few more were in medical scrubs. They carried folders and paperwork and they talked between themselves with a studied seriousness that bordered on parody. Pilgrim and Tyler attracted curious glances, but they didn't last long when Abernathy and Liz were spotted accompanying them, although they were given a wide berth, as though they carried a deadly contagion.

'Hold up a sec,' Abernathy said. She shepherded them out the way as a group of four men marched towards them, their strides almost synced, eyes hard and watchful. They, too, were dressed in black. Each held an assault rifle. Pilgrim felt Tyler press closer to his side. She looked paler than she had, her skin almost translucent. Her eyes darted left to right in small saccadic movements, as if fast streams of data were passing in front of them. Pilgrim hoped her nerves weren't going to cause a problem for them.

The door opposite was no different to any other except for the shape nailed above its frosted window. To Pilgrim it looked like a cross coupled with a tepee. Liz waited for the men to pass and then crossed to it. Unlike the wall of opaque glass bricks, nothing moved behind the opaque glass.

'Good luck, dipshit,' Abernathy said as the girl followed her mother.

The kid grinned back at her. 'Thanks, Abbie.' It was the first words she'd spoken.

Liz nodded a farewell to Abernathy, but then seemed to hesitate. Pilgrim got the impression she'd been about to say something different to what came out. 'Don't forget to check in with Peter when you have a moment.'

Abernathy pulled a face, all rolling eyes and sighing breath. 'Yeah, yeah. We can't forget Peter, can we?'

Liz smiled faintly and went inside, taking her daughter with her. And through the open doorway, along the back wall – glimpsed only for a moment – Pilgrim saw a line of cages. Spacious, sturdy, the kind you'd keep large primates in. Which was exactly what they were doing. Young teenagers, three of them (two girls and one boy), were locked inside. Then Liz blocked Pilgrim's view and closed the door in his face.

A man, dressed in a black baseball cap and black fatigues and polo shirt, with a black box-shaped device strapped to his belt and a baton on his hip, stood guard outside a double-wide steel door. It was set back from the corridor in its own alcove.

Pilgrim couldn't read the sign but Abernathy had told him what room this was.

The morgue.

'Hi, Glen.'

Abernathy had also said she hoped Glen would be on duty. Seeing the man eagerly step away from his station, Pilgrim understood why.

Glen immediately brightened upon seeing her. 'Abbie-go-nathy! How's it hanging? Everything good? You been busy up top again?' His face sported a serious case of razor burn.

'Sure have. Got two more for you. Can you open up?'

'Okey-dokey.' Glen began rooting around in his front pocket. 'Hey, you know, I was thinking . . .' he said, bringing out a set of keys and taking his time picking through them, '. . . about how you and me should grab a bite to eat together later. Everyone's still talking about who stole Dr Lloyd's personal journal. I thought you could finally spill on how you posted all those pages over the mess hall without anyone seeing.'

'Such spurious claims, Glen. No one ever proved it was me.'

Glen slotted in a key. 'Oh, yeah? I'd bet my dessert it was.' Finished with the unlocking, he pulled open the heavy door. He had a grin on his face when he turned back to them.

'You'd give me your dessert either way, Glen, and we both know it. In.' Abernathy jabbed the gun into the small of Pilgrim's back and he and Tyler preceded her into the morgue. It was a large space, large enough to have fitted four pathology tables and their accompanying equipment, back when that was the room's purpose. It had been cleared out but for a long steel trough-like tray running at waist height along the right wall. At the back was a bank of cold chambers where corpses would be stored; tall, refrigerator-like doors, twelve in total.

Pilgrim felt a claustrophobic horror creep up on him and tap its chilly finger on his shoulder. He knew what Abernathy had said, but some part of him had hoped it wasn't true.

'Lucky for you, we got us some empties.' Glen went to the refrigerator doors furthest left. Got as far as unlatching one and opening it up (revealing a dark well, five feet high and maybe eight feet deep) when Abernathy stepped up behind, pulled the black device from Glen's belt and jammed it into the guy's armpit. A crackling sound emitted from it and Glen jerked, a strange gurgling sound blurting from him, and crashed into the refrigerator door. Abernathy went after him, pressing the Taser into his side and holding it there as Glen went into spasm, mouth gibbering, his feet dancing as he slid to the floor. His eyes rolled up into his head.

Pilgrim had taken four long strides back to the morgue entrance and was swinging the heavy door shut as Abernathy leaned over and pushed the Taser against Glen for a further five seconds. He slumped, unresponsive but for the occasional twitch. His baseball cap teetered and fell off his head.

Abernathy straightened up, expelling a breath. 'Sorry, Glen, but that's a hard pass to that dinner date.'

The commotion had alerted the occupants of the morgue refrigerators. Thumps and calls came from at least eight of them.

'No,' Abernathy said as Tyler started towards them. 'Not yet. They'll try and make a run for it if you let them out straight away.'

'But—'

'No buts.' A flip knife materialised, and Tyler threw Pilgrim a skittish look.

Abernathy rolled her eyes. 'I'm not planning on gutting you, little rabbit. See?' Abernathy came to Pilgrim first and cut the zip tie fastening his wrists. He rubbed the soreness from them quickly and started stripping out of his clothes as Abernathy went to free Tyler.

Even wearing another man's duds (the material retaining the warmth from Glen's body), Pilgrim was relieved to be out of his blood-splattered clothes and in clean ones. They were a perfect fit, too.

He and Abernathy picked the unconscious man up and stuffed him in an empty cold chamber and clunked it shut. Abernathy swiped the baseball cap and Glen's keys off the floor and plonked the hat on Pilgrim's head.

'Spiffy,' she said, pulling the bill low. 'You ready?'

'Nearly.'

'Hurry it up. We're on the clock now.'

While she handed Tyler the keys and dug out a spare flashlight from her pack, Pilgrim emptied the pockets of his old clothes, making sure to retrieve the photograph of Lacey from his shirt and the paperback from the rear of his discarded pants (he could have left both with Jay, but he'd felt the need to keep them close to him while he was down here). Both went into the corresponding pockets of his new clothes. He found a flip lighter in Glen's pocket – replacing the Zippo he had lost – and a strange green plastic toy, no bigger than the last joint of his thumb. A frog. It had a little tab on its butt. If you pressed it, it would make the frog hop.

'When you've locked the morgue door,' Abernathy was saying to Tyler, 'go ahead and let them out. I'd advise you to do it one at a time, though. Give them a chance to calm down before setting them all loose.' She was still digging into her bag while she talked.

'I can do that,' Tyler said, nodding.

'It shouldn't take us long, so if we're not back inside the hour it means we got caught and you're pretty much screwed.' She went to pass her a rattling aerosol can but, seeing Tyler's hand already occupied with holding on to Glen's keys and a flashlight,

Abernathy inserted it into the front pouch of Tyler's hoodie. 'Don't forget your homework,' she added, and gave the bulging pouch a pat.

'I won't,' Tyler said.

'She has a map you drew,' Pilgrim pointed out. 'She can get out if she needs to.'

'True,' Abernathy said, frowning thoughtfully at Tyler. 'Maybe you'll only be partway screwed, then. Good luck.' Abernathy picked her pack up, shouldering it as she went to the morgue's door. She stuck her head out to make sure the way was clear.

Pilgrim paused by Tyler. It felt wrong, somehow, leaving her here. 'We'll be back,' he told her.

'I know.' She offered him a small smile.

Abernathy looked over at them. 'We're good to go.'

'Hand over the Taser,' he said to her, holding his hand out.

Abernathy didn't move. 'What're you talking about?'

'The Taser. Give it to Tyler.'

'Why does Tyler need it? She'll be locked in here, safe and sound.'

Pilgrim waited her out.

'You're being serious?' she asked.

'Yes.'

A second's silence. 'But I want it.'

'You have a gun.'

'So?'

'Abernathy.'

'*Fine.* Forget it.' She marched over and slapped the device into his hand, and a short, sharp electric jolt zapped up Pilgrim's wrist. Every muscle in his hand cramped. The pain, although brief, was excruciating, and it catapulted him back into his dream and those damn wires he'd grabbed hold of. He growled and snatched the Taser away from her.

'Sorry. My finger slipped.' Abernathy turned away, but not fast enough to hide her smile.

A soft brush of air fluttered inside his ear; Voice was trying not to laugh.

When Pilgrim passed the Taser to Tyler, she was smiling, too. He shook his hand out – it ached unpleasantly – and she offered a commiserating shrug. 'You really should have seen that coming,' she said.

Shaking his head, more at himself than anyone else, Pilgrim followed Abernathy out of the morgue and listened for the *thunk* of the locking mechanism as Tyler engaged it behind them.

CHAPTER 3

Infiltration (Part 2)

Leaving the morgue and Tyler behind, Abernathy and Pilgrim walked fast, backtracking past the door Liz had disappeared through. Pilgrim kept his head low, the bill of Glen's cap shielding his eyes, but he must have slowed when he spotted the tepee and cross symbols on the door, the gait in his stride giving him away, because Abernathy caught his wrist and pulled him along.

'Don't even think about it,' she said. She smiled and nodded greetings to a couple of people that went by.

Pilgrim picked up his pace, allowing her to draw him away.

They'd almost made it back to the main concourse when Voice broke his silence.

Do you hear that? he whispered.

Abernathy's grip tugged on Pilgrim's wrist again, but this time he pulled back. She threw him an exasperated look.

His ears picked up on something. He lifted his eyes to the ceiling.

A low moaning – so low it could have been mistaken for wind in the vents if not for the wretchedness living inside it – bled through concrete and piping, settling under the general bustle of the corridor.

'We don't have time,' Abernathy said.

Pilgrim ignored her. 'What is that?' When she didn't reply he lowered his gaze to her. 'Abernathy,' he said. 'What is that?'

'Recovery,' she said, and was already shaking her head at the look he gave her. 'No. No way. If you want to get this done, we have to go.' She tugged at his arm again, wanting him to move.

He stayed where he was. She hadn't put Recovery on any of the maps she'd drawn, and he told her so.

'I didn't put it on for precisely this reason.'

They stared at each other, standing in the middle of the corridor, a number of people going around them and shooting curious looks their way. Finally, Abernathy muttered something under her breath and towed him with her as she reversed course, taking him right, down the next corridor. They went maybe thirty yards before she stopped. She pressed her ear to a door. There were no shapes nailed to this one; it was unmarked and unremarkable.

Six seconds of listening and Abernathy pushed inside, the suction around the door unsealing with a soft, sticking sound. They entered an observation room. A narrow, unlit space separated by a wide glass panel from a much larger room next door. Lights blazed in there.

Twelve hospital beds were set up, seven of them occupied. Muted through the observation window, the tortured moans he'd heard were coming from a woman in the bed nearest the dividing glass. She writhed in her bedsheets, head digging into her pillow. She had no hair; it had been shaved off. Horrendous burns marked her scalp.

'Why haven't they dressed her wounds?'

'They won't waste medical supplies on someone who won't be here for long.' Abernathy stood in profile to Pilgrim, staring through the window. Her arms were folded. Her face was blank. He had no way of telling what she was thinking.

The low cries petered out, replaced by a long run of silent

mouth movements. Pilgrim began to feel a dull ache across his brow from focusing on her lips so hard. He didn't catch all the words, but he caught enough. 'Listen' and 'Pain' and 'Burning' and 'Slaughter'. He looked away when she got to mouthing 'Death'.

Abernathy had *heard those words,* Voice said, low and accusing.

'This is how you're trying to cure us?' Pilgrim murmured.

Abernathy didn't reply, but her arms tightened in their fold and her shoulders drew up.

In the next bed over, a man stared vacant-eyed at the ceiling. He also sported a shaven head. A stream of drool wet his chin and cheek, and his hands were curled spastically against his chest. A third patient, their sex indeterminate, lay curled foetal-like on their side, legs drawn up, hands over their ears. They, too, talked to no one but themselves, lips writhing, a non-stop stream of words.

This is what we heard, Pilgrim. It has to be. We heard *them. So many miles. How did we hear them from so far away?*

But it was the patient four beds along that caught Pilgrim's attention. A teenager, bound to her bed. Lacey's age. The four-point limb restraints must have been a new addition because her face, neck, arms, hands, legs – every inch of skin Pilgrim could see not covered by her hospital gown – was scored with hundreds of raw, painful-looking scratches. She had shredded herself with her nails.

She didn't stir as those around her moaned out their misery.

'They've all had treatment?' he asked, surprised when his voice came out steady. Nothing around him felt steady any more – the world was tilting off its axis and they were tilting with it.

'Yeah. They'll be monitored for a while. Tests done. Notes written up on them.'

'Then what?'

'Then they'll try again.'

'Which ones are yours?' She was a presence at the edges of his vision, so still and so quiet. She could have stopped breathing for all he knew. Maybe she hoped he would forget she was there.

'The drooling guy,' she said quietly. 'He was wandering around Union Station, giggling to himself. I asked if he wanted some food and a place to stay the night.'

'You didn't lie.'

Her reflection in the glass showed she was frowning, but it wasn't directed at him. 'No, I didn't lie. But I knew what I was doing, bringing him in.' Her eyes met his in the window's reflection. 'We can't all be heroes, Christopher. It's hard enough looking after ourselves. And who's to say this isn't for the best?' She lifted her chin to the drooling, burned, bedridden man she'd helped put in here. 'What's wrong with wanting to protect ourselves? We can't always be wondering if they'll let their voices talk them into killing us again, can we?'

'From what I see, you're the only ones doing the killing.'

Her jaw tensed and she shut herself down. Her chest rose and fell in a slow, measured breath and she dropped her arms to her sides. 'Doctors – *specialists* – people more educated than me, made this place what it is. I didn't ask questions because I didn't want to. I even believed they could do it, too. For a long time I believed. They'd cured Jack, after all. It wasn't impossible.' She shook her head, a quick shake, dismissing her own arguments before she could voice them. 'Maybe if I'd tried, I could have got him out. But what good would it have done? He'd have had one of his seizures, maybe one as bad as the last one, when I thought he was dying. We'd have ended up as two new corpses, or else been caught within a week. What did you expect me to do?' she demanded, turning on him. 'Walk away just because what we do here is *ethically wrong*? Well, I'm sorry to break it to you, but there's no such thing as ethics any more.'

It was the first time she'd said 'we' since they'd finalised their plan to come down here, placing herself firmly on the side of the people who'd been performing these atrocities. Qualified doctors and scientists may be in charge, people of intelligence and status – and perhaps they'd even had the best of intentions at the beginning – but what they'd done, the suffering they had caused, it had made monsters of them all.

When he failed to respond Abernathy walked by him, her passing a cool draught on his skin. The door suckered shut behind her.

Pilgrim lingered, looking out into the ward, at the girl, red raw from her scratches, at the writhing woman, alone with her pain. He knew he wouldn't be able to take them with him, that he couldn't save them. They were beyond that now. He could do nothing for them except stop the same thing happening to somebody else.

Voice stirred but didn't speak. He didn't have to. Pilgrim could feel his distress, his helplessness.

Abernathy was waiting for him in the corridor when he came out, and they walked the rest of the way to Dr Lloyd's office in silence, Abernathy staying two steps ahead of him. She went straight in without knocking, the door almost banging off the wall; Pilgrim caught it before it hit.

No one sat behind the grey metal desk or in the armchair opposite it. A whiteboard on the wall behind the desk was covered in colour-coded text, and the desktop was lost under a pile of paperwork. An In–Out tray bulged with files.

Abernathy stopped him before he could take more than three strides into the room.

'You weren't bullshitting me about not being able to read?'

He'd had to ask her to read out the words she'd scribbled on maps and notes and it was only after much convincing that she'd relented and dictated everything she had written down. She'd sent him a number of looks as she did, as if expecting him to reveal that it was all a massive joke and she the brunt of it.

317

'No, I wasn't,' he told her.

'Then you're zero use to me in here. Go guard the door or something. If anyone wants to come in, say . . . I don't know, say Dr Lloyd's in the middle of a very important meeting and isn't to be disturbed. I'll be as quick as I can.'

Dismissed, Pilgrim stepped outside. He straightened his baseball cap and stood tall, unmoving but for his eyes.

'*She's not mad at you,*' Lacey says. She stands across from him, her shoulders leaning casually back, one knee raised and bent, foot resting flat on the wall.

He closed his eyes and concentrated on the hard beat of his heart. It was too loud and too close to his breastbone. 'This isn't a good time,' he murmured.

Voice stirred, a flowering, unfurling sensation that transmitted the unease he felt at Pilgrim choosing *now* to see Lacey. As if Pilgrim could control it.

'*She's mad at herself. You've made her face up to a lot of things since getting here and she's not too happy at what she sees.*' Lacey's expression turns grave, her eyes sliding left. She presses a finger to her lips and straightens up, mimicking his pose, hands flat to her thighs, head held high. At full attention. '*You're in the hornet's nest now,*' she whispers.

Two men approached, one dressed in scrubs, the second in civilian clothes. Neither of them spared Pilgrim a glance as they went by, too engrossed in a sheet of paper the man in scrubs handed to the other.

Lacey waits for them to be a full fifteen paces away before relaxing her stance and speaking again. '*Pilgrim, a little sabotage isn't going to cut it with these guys. They're going to go straight back to what they were doing before you came.*' She leaves her station and crosses the corridor to him. Standing at his shoulder, she peers up at his face beneath the bill of his cap. '*You need to get your hands dirty.*'

He spared her a glance and she looks so solemn, so sad for

him, that it almost made him reach out to her. 'I know what I need to do,' he said shortly.

'*Okay*,' she whispers, and her fingers skim over his, a touch as light as air. She nods past him. '*You're up.*'

A third person was walking towards him, an older woman, heavy around the hips and looking comfy in her corduroy pants and brogues. She had a rosy complexion, a blush less to do with glowing health and more with the bottle of alcohol she likely had stowed somewhere discreet.

By the time she reached him, Lacey was no longer standing with Pilgrim.

'You look to be new.'

Pilgrim nodded to her. He was indeed *very* new.

'Got you working already, have they?' The rosy-cheeked woman raised her eyebrows, a slight smile on her face. 'They don't hang around.'

'No, they don't.' She was looking him up and down, and he did his best not to do the same. She had a red pen tucked behind her right ear.

There was an awkward silence when he wished he was better at this. Talking. Like Abernathy was. But she saved him by indicating the door at his back. 'Do you think I could pop in for a second?'

He tried out a regretful expression. 'Dr Lloyd is in an important meeting right now. He's not to be disturbed.'

'Ah, I see. In that case, do you think you could give Dr Lloyd a message for me?'

'Of course.'

'Could you say that I'm extremely sorry to report that even after decades of civilised discourse and modern Women's Rights movements – never mind an almost mass-extinction-level event – that innate sexism is still alive and well.'

Pilgrim exhaled a breath as he glanced both ways along the corridor. Thankfully, it was a fairly quiet stretch and no one was in sight. He returned his attention to her, his hand slipping behind him. He nodded a greeting at her as if they were meeting for the first time. 'Dr Lloyd.'

She smiled politely. 'Indeed. Hello.'

'I'm sorry about this.'

'You should be.'

'No. I mean I'm sorry about *this*.'

Pilgrim grabbed her soft chambray shirt, opened the door behihd him and dragged her inside the office.

He heard Abernathy's surprised curse when she saw them, and the quick rush of her feet. Pilgrim steered the doctor to the armchair and pushed her into it. She landed with a grunt. Abernathy hadn't drawn her gun, but her fingers were hovering over its butt as she came back from closing the door.

Dr Lloyd's clear blue eyes regarded her evenly. 'This will be the last stunt you pull here, Katherine. On my word, I'll have you thrown out for this.'

'You think I care?'

'Yes, I do. If not for yourself, then for Jackson. And Mr Bird will not be able to save you this time.'

'He already knows you're a cold-hearted bitch who has it in for me.'

'Regardless what you think he knows, let me give you a piece of advice – from one cold-hearted bitch to another. You'd best get out of here while you can. Before I bring this whole facility down on your head.'

'No one's leaving,' Pilgrim said. 'Not until we've done what we came for.'

Dr Lloyd smiled a thin-lipped, patient smile, as if she were dealing with two simple-minded children. The sharpness in her eyes, however, was keen enough to draw blood. 'I'd ask who your friend is, Katherine, but we both know you don't have any.'

'We're old friends,' Pilgrim replied, eyeing her with interest, wondering why so many of her words seemed to be hitting their mark; Abernathy's feathers were fully bristled.

'Before-the-voices old?' Dr Lloyd asked him.

'That's right.'

'How interesting. And what are you doing here, Mr . . . ?'

Pilgrim didn't fill in the blank, but Abernathy did. 'This is Sol. Bet you never thought you'd see him, did you?'

Dr Lloyd's demeanour changed. Her eyes widened slightly as she reappraised him, her stare becoming coldly analytical. The plump, harmless, rosy-cheeked woman from out in the corridor was long gone. Pilgrim held in a sigh. Revealing his identity probably wasn't the wisest thing Abernathy had ever done. Not that it would matter in the end.

'Higher functioning than Jackson,' the doctor murmured to herself. 'No signs of dysphasia. No motor-function issues. Do you experience audial hallucinations of any kind?' she asked him. 'Disembodied voices?'

'No questions,' Pilgrim told her. 'No more examinations or treatments. It's over. All we need from you is information. Locations. People. Abernathy said there are at least three more operations like this.'

'Even if I were to give you information, what could you possibly do with it?' There was a penetrating intelligence in her, sterile and emotionless, and he could tell she was used to people shrinking before it. He had no doubt her intellect was scalpel-sharp, that it was capable of cutting incisively and with great skill, yet all she had used it for was to inflict pain. He'd taken stock of her *and* her office. There were no little mementos, no accessories, no picture frames or inspirational quotes cut from magazines. Instead there was a stark display of learning, in the textbooks on the shelves and the charts on the walls – even the ergonomic grey furniture didn't distract from it.

'All those turning thoughts,' Dr Lloyd said, watching him. 'Are they yours? Would you tell me even if they weren't? They stole that from us – the one place in the whole world that was supposed to be ours alone. Our minds should have been sacrosanct, an inner, private place that nothing could breach, not if we didn't want it to. In the old world, my job was to unlock that secret part of us, to delve deep inside, where our most forbidden thoughts lived. And I can safely say those places are far more terrifying than anything you or I have seen. Down in that darkness, when I held up my light, I could see them for what they truly were.'

'What's that?' Pilgrim asked.

'Monstrous.'

'You speak as though the voices were never the problem.'

She laughed, a high-pitched, girlish sound that didn't suit her. 'Humans have *always* been the problem, my dear. We spend so much time looking outward, looking for something *other* to blame, when we should be looking far closer to home. The voices brought the most terrible aspects of ourselves to the surface. We had a very robust set of parameters, programmed into us via our parents, via institutions, by the laws of civilisation and society. What can and can't be done, what is polite to say and what is not. Extremely complex patterns of conditioned behaviour, developed over hundreds, even thousands, of years. Then the voices came and, in one fell swoop, ripped all those controls away. They broke our conditioning and rewired our brains.'

'And what?' Abernathy asked. 'You're saying you've known all along what the voices are? Where they came from?'

'I'm saying we should be one thing and one thing only. We were never meant to be more.'

A thought formed, a vague recollection of something Pilgrim had once read. '"There is no coming to consciousness without pain."'

Dr Lloyd smiled, pure delight softening her intensity for a moment. 'Oh, yes. I'm positive Jung would have *lots* to say on the subject. But this isn't a phase of enlightenment for us. They are forcing us to regress to a baser, more primitive self.'

'I think,' Pilgrim said, 'that you've wasted all this time and energy trying to fix the wrong thing.'

Something in her eyes tightened and the starburst wrinkles around her lips deepened. He should have been satisfied that some of his words had hit *their* mark – he got the feeling it didn't happen too often – but all he felt was weary. Seven long years and all her IQ points, and she still hadn't learned anything.

He looked to Abernathy. 'Did you find it?'

She smiled, smugness and victory. 'Yep.'

Polite artifice peeled away and the doctor glared at Abernathy, her loathing an ugly, immeasurable thing. 'You don't have anything, you idiot girl.'

'*Au contraire, mon docteur.*' Abernathy reached under her jacket and brought out an A4-sized manila folder, its many loose sheaths of paper held together by an elastic band.

Dr Lloyd's eyes tightened even further. 'Where did you get that?'

'Didn't think I knew where your private files were, *Roberta*? I stole your journal, you dumb bitch. I know where everything is.'

The rosiness of Dr Lloyd's complexion darkened. Her mouth opened and Pilgrim knew she was about to huff and puff and blow down this whole house, and in this windowless, subterranean world, the corridors would carry the noise far further than either he or Abernathy wanted.

He leapt forward and clamped a hand over her mouth. He felt her jaw move, her lips part, and snatched his hand away as she chomped down, small white teeth snapping at him.

Abernathy dropped the file – it slapped the floor like a hand-clap – and snatched a cushion from under Dr Lloyd's arm. 'Out the way!' she snapped, and Pilgrim moved. The doctor shouted, but the sound was cut off as Abernathy shoved the cushion over the woman's face, leaning her weight into it, hiking her foot up on to the chair's seat for leverage.

The doctor squawked and flailed. She slapped at Abernathy's arms, clawed at the cushion, desperately trying to rip it off. Her hips humped off the seat, but Abernathy was strong and her face was twisted with effort.

Pilgrim went to the door, placed his hand flat to it. The wood was still and cool under his palm. No vibrations, no dull beats of running footsteps. No one was coming. They wouldn't be interrupted. Not in time to save anybody.

He kept his back to Abernathy, listening to the doctor's hits grow weaker, her muffled cries quieter. When all was silent, he looked over his shoulder.

Dr Lloyd had slid partway off the chair, her butt hanging over the edge of the seat, legs spread wide. Her arms dangled limply.

'Abernathy,' Pilgrim said.

Abernathy held her position, the strain in her arms and shoulders clearly visible.

He counted to five and said, 'Abernathy, it's done.'

She lifted the cushion off the doctor's face and exhaled, blowing a stream of cooling air up at her brow. 'That's way harder than it looks. My forearms are burning.' She dropped the cushion and bent to retrieve the folder. Dusted it off. She didn't look at him. 'That room with the cages?' she said. 'That's where they transfer the kids to as soon as their bloodwork shows hormonal changes. Faye is getting monitored daily right now for signs she's hearing anything she shouldn't. Only reason she's not locked up with the others is because her mom's a big deal round here.' Abernathy stuffed the folder under the waistband of her pants and covered it with her shirt. 'Dr Lloyd might not understand why puberty is such an important factor in hearing a voice for the first time, but if she finds out *any* of the kids here have one, she rolls them into the treatment room, just like all the rest. And it's worse for them, because they know exactly what's coming.'

The doctor's mouth gaped wide, her tongue a fat, porous muscle lying obscenely still. Even from across the room Pilgrim could see the red spider-web bursts in her eyes where capillaries had popped.

Abernathy nudged the dead woman's foot with her boot. 'She says not having children of her own helps her "maintain her objectivity". Personally, I think she gets a kick out of it when the kids started crying for their moms.' She checked her watch. 'Help me lift her? We've been in here too long.'

With some difficulty (Dr Lloyd was not light), they lumped her over to her desk and laid her out on the floor. Abernathy positioned the office chair on its side to make it look like she'd fallen from it. Pilgrim grabbed some sheets of paper off the desk and scattered them by the doctor's outstretched hand.

'Nice touch,' Abernathy said. 'If they find her before we're done, they shouldn't immediately think foul play.'

As she rolled open the bottom desk drawer, Pilgrim went to the whiteboard and uncapped a red marker pen. He returned to the doctor and stood for a moment, considering her, then leaned down and moved her hair aside. Behind her ear, he drew a swirling circle, starting small and winding out to the size of a dollar coin, and then he smoothed her hair down to cover it.

'Here.' Abernathy was holding out a compact, snub-nosed revolver to him. 'It's loaded,'

He dropped the marker pen into the open drawer and accepted the gun. It went into his right front pocket with Glen's tiny plastic frog.

Abernathy stopped by the armchair to pick up the fallen cushion and replace it, giving it a quick plump for good measure.

'Do me a favour?' Pilgrim asked, following her as she made her way across the office.

'What?'

'That hand cannon of yours, don't shoot anyone in the head with it.'

She sent him a quick frown. She'd made it to the door but had paused with her hand on the handle. 'Why? I didn't take you for the squeamish sort.'

'I'm not. It's just best you don't. It can be . . . risky.'

For a second, he thought she would push for more, but all she said was, 'Fine. Whatever.'

She paused again before pulling the office door open, as if fortifying herself before taking a plunge into cold, unfamiliar waters. She didn't stick her head out into the corridor to check before stepping into it, she marched straight out as if she owned the place.

Pilgrim followed her example and closed Dr Lloyd's office door firmly behind him.

Abernathy tapped at the sign at head level. It was blue with white piping. They were passing through a sizeable breezeblock alcove where the corridor opened up to accommodate an array of pipes as wide in diameter as boa constrictors. They ran along the left-side wall, gauges and spigots sprouting from their tubing.

'Emergency meeting point,' she said. 'One of two. The other is at the juncture of the main concourse we came in on. If we get split up, meet me back at this one.'

Walking at a steady pace, Abernathy threaded them deeper and deeper into the warren of corridors. Pilgrim had memorised the map she'd drawn, but even he experienced a reeling sense of disorientation. He missed the sky, the sun and the stars, the anchors with which he gauged direction. Down here there was nothing. Only endless uniform walkways. He had been set adrift in a sea of concrete and shiny grey flooring.

'Almost there,' she said, as if sensing his disquiet.

The set of double doors they were closing in on had porthole windows that had been painted over in black. Pilgrim didn't need the ability to read to recognise the lightning bolt on a yellow background. The universal sign for an electrical or high-voltage hazard.

No one was in sight, but he lowered his voice anyway. 'Why is the treatment room so far from Recovery and the morgue?'

'It was originally set up much closer,' Abernathy answered, casting her gaze around to make sure they were alone, 'but the patients could hear procedures going on and it upset them too much. To be honest, it upset a lot of people. So they moved the equipment over here. No one really comes down this corridor unless there's a treatment scheduled. Can't hear the screams from all the way over here, can they?' The left door swung inward. She held it open for him.

There were no lights on inside. The faint glow of white tiles and the stench of burnt hair dumped ice into Pilgrim's blood-stream.

Abernathy misread his reluctance to enter. 'We won't be interrupted. They did one yesterday. It'll be at least another day or two before they attempt another.'

He forced himself to step over the threshold and she swung the door closed behind them.

Everywhere, darkness.

Immediately, Pilgrim knew they weren't alone.

He didn't hear movement but he felt it. A space in the centre of the room that breathed the dark, absorbed it into itself like it was eating it up and growing larger with every bite. It was tall and it was motionless, its head bowed in order to fit beneath the ceiling. It knew they were there. It had been waiting for them.

It rushed forward through the gloom, a fast-moving skiff in black seas, and horror froze Pilgrim in place. It glided fast and stopped so close a breeze touched his face.

He could have lifted his hand and touched it, if he'd wanted.

He didn't lift his hand.

The thing peered into his face, its head tilting, tilting, tilting

327

to the side in animal-like curiosity. A chitinous clicking sound, furtive and quiet, the type that insect wings made when they flexed. Something whispered in the soft hiss of the overhead vents.

'*I see you, Agur . . . I see you, and soon . . . you will see me . . .*'

A loud clank and Pilgrim flinched away.

Abernathy swore, and Pilgrim's hand became her hand as it slid along cool tiles, searching for the light switch, and he wanted to tell her not to turn it on, not to flood the room with light because something awful was in here with them and to bare it would melt the flesh from their bones, would burst their hot eyeballs in a rain of fluid, a nuclear detonation that stripped away their sanity in a single, blinding flash.

She flicked the light on.

White tiles, an operating table, four bulky pieces of machinery and the lingering stench of burning. And that was all. No monsters, no figures hulking in front of him.

'See? Empty,' Abernathy said.

He was left standing there, trembling, as she made quick work of plugging in the machines. She glanced over at him a few times as she set everything up. 'You okay? Being in here probably isn't good for you.'

He coughed his voice back into place. 'I'm fine.'

'You don't look fine.'

He couldn't tell her that his imagination had conjured a boogeyman that unnerved him far more than the quiet whirs of the machines Abernathy was powering on.

'You're one hundred per cent certain this will work?' he asked.

'Nope. But we have a Plan B, so it's all good.'

He looked at her and said nothing. They had no Plan B. He also wouldn't tell her that his unease had tripled since stepping foot in here. Everything seemed painfully sharp, the corners of counters tapering to deadly points, the edges of doors and sidings honed to blade-like lines able to cut as cleanly as a razor. Every part of this place was dangerous.

He held out a hand. 'Give me a can.'

Abernathy set her bag between her feet and rooted inside. She removed two aerosol cans and began to shake them vigorously. They rattled loudly. 'What colour do you want?' she asked.

'It doesn't matter.'

'Black or green? Tyler already has the brown.'

'Black,' he said, just to speed things up.

'Figures.' She threw him a can of black spray paint and he caught it neatly. 'You do the arty stuff and I'll handle the writing.'

The people in the west wing were already worried that the Flitting Man was closing in – Abernathy had told them as much.

So why don't we tag the place to make them believe he's snuck right up to their doorstep? Voice had suggested. Freak them out enough and they'd be too scared to rebuild what Pilgrim and the others planned on destroying. Blow open their whole operation and make them feel so vulnerable and exposed they would never repeat the same atrocities again.

Pilgrim and Abernathy spent a minute or so graffitiing the room. Across the walls, Pilgrim sprayed a series of dripping spirals, including an eyeball with a spiral for a pupil. He finished with an unhappy face painted four feet wide on the tiled floor, its two eyes made of circles within circles. He tossed his can back to Abernathy and she dropped both into the bag.

'What's it say?' he asked, pointing to her handiwork.

She had scrawled a message in block capitals across the back wall. It would be the first thing anyone would see upon entering.

'"THE FLITTING MAN HAS COME FOR YOUR TOWN OF RATS." It'll scare the shit out of them.' She returned to the ECT machines and finished sticking the medical electrodes to the electrical outlets on the wall. Their umbilical cords trailed all the way back to their mother-machines. She cranked the dials up to their highest settings. 'Want to do the honours?' she asked him.

He shook his head. He just wanted it done. 'Do it already.'

She flipped a series of switches, one after the other. An accelerating whir started up, a whining buzz that needled his ears and tingled through his teeth's fillings. An almighty *CRACK* snapped through the room, the charge of electricity so great it shot through his skin and fired every muscle with a bolt of energy. His heart swelled and contracted. The whirring ceased and the lights shut off, throwing them into a dense, unforgiving black.

Burnt-out circuitry and molten metal singed his nostrils. It smelled like Sheila's workshop.

'Where'd you go?' Abernathy's voice floated to him.

For a second, Pilgrim couldn't answer her. He felt the strain in his eyes as they widened in their attempt to see, but there was nothing. Only darkness.

'Christopher?'

He spoke through the dryness in his throat. 'Here. Keep coming forward.'

Her feet scuffed in the dark.

Something touched his stomach and he drew in a sharp breath.

'Just me,' Abernathy whispered, and patted him.

'It worked.'

'Fuck yeah, it did.'

'They can't be fixed?'

'The generators maybe, but the machines are toast. We've not only shoved a fox in the hen coop, we're chopping the cock's head clean o—'

The wail of an emergency siren overrode her. It rose and fell, a haunting dirge that echoed and rolled through the lengths of corridors, filling up the spaces as water would fill up a sinking submarine. A shiver prickled his back.

Everything fell into silence for a count of three, and then the siren began anew.

'Can all personnel please report to the emergency meeting points,' Abernathy intoned in an announcer's voice. She tugged at Pilgrim's shirt. 'Come on. Time to blow this joint.'

CHAPTER 4

Retreat

Abernathy handed him a slim metal Maglite. 'Keep your head down and don't talk to anyone,' she told him.

The corridor was as pitch-black as the treatment room. Pilgrim studied the darkness, convinced someone was hovering close by, concealed in the shadows, in the walls, their hands reaching out, inches away from brushing his face. He stared so long, the dark seemed to shift and roll in fluid-like whorls, an oil that something was wading through to get to them.

A light blinked on. At the end of their corridor, someone with their own flashlight. The beam of light bobbed, swung back and forth and stopped on Pilgrim at chest level.

'What's going on up there?' someone called, and Pilgrim's belly broke open, a frigid cold washing in. He slipped his hand into his pocket, fingers curling around the butt of the revolver.

The flashlight's beam shifted higher, hitting him full in the face, and he twisted his head aside, eyes squinting closed.

The words came slow and condemning. 'I know you.'

'God*damn* it,' Abernathy hissed. She grabbed Pilgrim by the shoulder and yanked on him.

'Abernathy?' Birdy's momentary confusion turned to hard suspicion. 'What's going on? Hey!' he snapped when they broke into a run. 'HEY!'

Pilgrim was impressed by how fast Abernathy could move. Within a dozen steps, however, the frantic leaping of their flashlights had Pilgrim reaching for the wall, shapes jumping out at him, shadows fluttering in his eyes. The mad beat of birds' wings swung at his head, screaming faces leered into his, a dark skitter of insects swarmed in from all sides, devouring the corridor around him. Lightning flashed and a deep rumbling of thunder built beneath his boots. They were in the bowels of a storming ship, the decking an unsteady gangway; it dipped from under him and swayed back to meet his clumsy feet.

Keep it together, Voice snapped, panic making him sharp, and Pilgrim didn't rebuke him for talking. They were past that now.

Abernathy grabbed Pilgrim's arm when he stumbled into her, holding him steady.

'Don't make me run you down, Abernathy!' Birdy's shout was loud and too close, but Pilgrim's ears roared with tidal waves of blood and the concrete walls ricocheted sounds like steel drums (the wailing sirens howling over all of it); it gave the illusion Birdy was gaining on them when, in fact, he must be more than thirty yards back.

Abernathy ducked around a corner, Pilgrim crowding behind her, and a small throng of people was clustered outside a set of wedged-open doors. A handful of them held strip lights, the kind you snapped and shook to illuminate. Their insipid yellow glow cast everyone in a ghoulish, jaundiced light, eyes hollowed out into pits, cheekbones cut with shadows. Pilgrim didn't care, he was simply glad to have some of the darkness banished.

Abernathy headed straight for them.

'—heard it's tripped out again,' someone was saying.

'Toby said it was pissing out gasoline last week—' The rising volume at the tail end of the siren cut into their conversation.

'—oughta get on top of this stuff before we end up living like goddamn mole people—'

'—sure there weren't any drills scheduled for today—'

Talking stopped and heads turned. Abernathy threaded her way through them, fending off questions as Pilgrim followed the route she opened up for him. ('What're you running for, Abbie? What's going on back there?') Hot bodies pressed too close, hot breaths scalded the back of his neck, hot hands burned as they touched his skin, searching for reassurances, for answers. Pilgrim wanted to push them all away, his breaths turning ragged, his throat closing up.

He glimpsed the dull shine of aluminium between arms and torsos. Metal benching. Long lines of tables. Canteen–like serving hatches. His nose caught the scent of toast and brewed coffee and his stomach gave a nauseous clench. These people had come out of a mess hall.

Despite every instinct screaming at him not to, he clicked his flashlight off as he and Abernathy elbowed their way free.

She panted lightly as she threw her parting words back at them. 'Be careful of Peter. He's swinging his gun around like a madman.'

That knocked a few of them silent. Others reached for their own weapons – a collection of nightsticks but Pilgrim spotted at least two firearms. Those who were unarmed stepped back and flattened themselves to the walls, their sickly, yellowed eyes swivelling to scan the dark corridor in time to see Birdy barrel around the corner. And in that unwashed, jaundiced glow, with his teeth bared and his black hair stringing his eyes, he looked like a crazed ghoul who'd dragged himself up from the bowels of hell.

The ground had steadied under Pilgrim's feet, the nightmarish shadows pulled back. He broke into a run after Abernathy and she clicked off her flashlight, copying him. New shadows flittered past, a spectral dance projected on to ceiling and walls by the people behind them.

The siren was winding up again but he could hear Birdy's shouts. 'What are you *doing*? Get out of my way!'

Any answering shouts or resultant scuffles were obliterated by a massive, eardrum-battering explosion. It rocked through the facility and ripped the ground out from under Pilgrim's feet, punching him to the floor. An almighty *CRACK* rent the air and an inch-wide fissure drew itself rapidly along one wall. Concrete flaked as the crack split and shot upward, arrowing across the ceiling. A bracket popped loose, a pipe sheered free, and Pilgrim grabbed Abernathy's ankle (she lay flat out in front of him, arms laced over her head), and hauled her back, his shoulder wrenching as she slid towards him. The broken piping smashed down where her head had been.

'Fuck!' she yelled.

The sirens had cut off but Pilgrim could barely hear beyond the ringing in his ears. He fumbled for his flashlight and switched it on. Masonry dust sifted through the air. He coughed and twisted to direct the beam back up the hallway. The group of people had toppled like bowling pins; they were a groping mass of arms and legs. There were no signs of Birdy, but Pilgrim knew he was in there somewhere.

'Was that us?' Pilgrim asked.

'Are you kidding me?' Abernathy coughed and swiped hair out of her face. 'Overloading the generators wouldn't make anything explode like that.'

Drunkenly, he got to his feet, working his way up the wall. Abernathy lifted her hand to him and he half dragged, half lifted her up next to him.

'We need to get out of here,' she said.

'We're not done. There's still Vanessa Mendoza.'

Deep in the facility a number of smaller *whumps* sounded. Mini explosions, one after the other. He and Abernathy instinctively ducked against the wall as their repercussive detonations shivered through the corridor. More masonry dust rained down. Abernathy's hair had turned grey with it.

She angrily pushed away from the wall, away from *him*. 'No.

I'm done. I never signed up for a suicide mission. I'm getting Jack and I'm getting out of here.'

He was aware this hadn't been part of the plan. A facility collapsing around their ears would make everything a hundred times more difficult. But they had come down here to kill a beast. They had delivered an incapacitating blow to its head by taking out Dr Lloyd, and they'd broken its legs when they'd destroyed the ECT machines, but its pained wails were meant to bring the queen out from hiding, to separate her from her entourage in the ensuing chaos.

'The plan—' he began.

'The plan was to *potentially* deal with Vanessa when the lights went out and everyone was distracted, because *we weren't going to blow the whole fucking hospital up and* kill *everyone. That* was the plan.'

A howling whistle erupted and a cloud of steam blasted out. A dozen yards away the hallway filled with mist.

Abernathy shouted over the noise. 'You do what you have to do, but I need to go! Jack could be hurt! He needs me!' She waited for a beat, perhaps expecting an answer, or at least an argument, but when neither came she gave an angry shake of her head and spun away and left him there, disappearing into the steam.

Pilgrim was still staring after her when Voice surged into his awareness, loud enough to startle him.

The words, Pilgrim! The words! *I hear them!*

Pilgrim heard the cries of the injured. He heard shouts and screams. And he heard the shifting earth and the creature that lived inside the walls; the thing that had been in the treatment room had climbed inside them, its hunger awoken by the explosion, but also by the pain and terror that ran like floodwater through the hallways. Now it was turning over, stalking the corridors, readying itself to burst into its new subterranean home and devour whoever it could find.

The whistle of escaping air became a whispering voice and the whispering became a grumble in the concrete all around him, and then the words found him, exploding in sparks so bright they blinded. He reeled back, hand lifting to protect his rapidly blinking eyes.

'*Burning,*' they hissed and sparked.

'*Madness,*' they groaned and flashed.

Death, Voice said. *I know where they're coming from, Pilgrim. Run! I'll tell you when to turn.*

CHAPTER 5

Caged

Following Voice's instructions, his eyes squinted against the lingering prickle of static, Pilgrim made it all the way back to the main concourse without incident. No one stopped him. In a crisis, shared community values were the first thing to be struck off a person's list of priorities. No one wanted to die down here.

He hoped Tyler had taken those she'd rescued from the morgue's storage refrigerators and got the hell out.

She's not stupid. She wouldn't hang around.

A scattering of maybe a dozen people had assembled at the emergency meeting point, the beams of their flashlights combining to create a strobing effect that cut pillars of light through the dusty air. Judging from the jitteriness and the general air of agitation, it wasn't simply their training that had made them gather here. They stood in a loose semicircle and, as Pilgrim drew nearer, he could see what they were all staring at. At their feet, painted on the floor, was a huge spiral as big as a crop circle. It was shiny, as if it had recently been painted.

Did Abernathy do that?

And chance being caught? No. She'd wanted to find Jackson and get the hell out. So much so she had left Pilgrim behind and fled. She wouldn't waste precious time stopping to create a piece of freestyle art on the floor when Jackson needed her.

Another rumbling groan eased through the walls. A tremor shook the concourse. The pipework clanked overhead and a rain of chalk-like dust shook loose. The buried creature was creeping closer and it was all Pilgrim could do not to check over his shoulder. The mouth of the corridor he'd left yawned at his back. If he looked, he was afraid he might see two insect eyes blink back at him, glistening as they stared from the dark.

A distant crash reverberated through the passageways as something heavy collapsed. A subtle secondary light-source, weak and flickering, bathed those standing in the semicircle in a burnished orange. Slipping along the side of the group, Pilgrim craned his neck to see.

At the far end of the concourse hot, hungry flames ate at the darkness.

The fire will spread if no one gets it under control, Voice said. *We need to hurry.*

'He's here,' someone whispered, fear curled up in their throat. 'He's come for us, just like they told us he would.'

Pilgrim tensed, expecting all eyes to be on him. But, of course, they weren't talking about him.

'Shut up, Benson. Jesus.' It came from a man who was cradling a child in his arms, one hand cupping the back of the child's head, keeping his or her face buried in his shoulder.

But Benson couldn't shut up – his fear had a hold of him now. 'No! He *knows* we're here! He knows what we've been doing!'

'We need to evacuate,' a woman said.

'And go where?'

'M–maybe we should wait,' someone else said. 'I mean, we were told to wait here if—'

'Half the facility is gone!' Benson cried. 'They're murdering us!'

In answer, a scream tore through the gloom. The walls

enclosed them, buried them together down here, making it sound like the scream came from all directions at once.

Four people broke away from the group. Turned tail and ran up the concourse, away from the fires, the erratic light from their flashlights slicing through the dust-misted darkness.

Those who remained took a collective step back as something lurched through the flames at the far end of the burning concourse. It brought fire with it, the torches of its arms swiping at the air, their shambling steps faltering. It stopped dead, turned to face them. More arm swipes. No more screams came – the flames had eaten all those. The figure's head was engulfed in a hood of fire. Its knees buckled and it fell to the ground, sprawling on its front. It lay there, twitching as it burned.

The woman beside Pilgrim moaned, a deep, horrified sound. She backed up two steps, four, five, then turned and bolted, no flashlight to light her way. The darkness swallowed her by her thirteenth step.

'I came from B17,' a second woman said, her voice lifeless, numbed to a monotone. She stared into the fires, tiny flames flickering in her eyes. Her face was streaked with dirt and the scrubs she wore were filthy. It wasn't all grime; some was blood. 'People are trapped. I couldn't get them out, so I ran. The fires are raging everywhere.'

Maybe the Flitting Man really is down here with us, Voice whispered, and Pilgrim had to fight looking over at that black cave of a corridor again, at the shiny eyes he knew were waiting for him there.

A man tugged on the arm of the woman next to him. 'We can't stay here. Let's go, Marie. *Let's go.*'

The woman was staring at the burning body, the small conflagration throwing shadows on to the walls, the floor, the ceiling and its pipes. Gleeful fire spirits leaping and twirling. When she didn't move, the man gave up and left her. Two more went with him, the man carrying the child included.

Pilgrim, Voice said. *I don't hear anything any more. Do you?*

Pilgrim pulled his attention away from the fires and focused on listening. The crackling, electric words that had been hiding in wait in the hissing of the pipes and the grumbles of the earth were gone.

I have a bad feeling about this . . .

Pilgrim cleared his mind enough to concentrate solely on Voice, sending him a direct question that was in no danger of being overheard.

—It wasn't coming from Recovery, was it?

No. No, it wasn't.

—I should go straight ahead?

Yes. Keep going that way.

And Pilgrim felt the urgency in him, a taut cable that ran down the back of his head, pulling at the muscles in his neck and shoulders. Pilgrim ghosted past the few people left standing around the graffiti painted on the floor. Silent and fleeting, he elicited only the briefest of glances.

As large as the concourse was, it was already filling with smoke, and he stuck close to the wall as he entered the corridor that led back to the morgue. He trained his flashlight's beam at foot level, not wanting to trip over broken pipes or fallen debris. Its bulb was dim, the batteries fading. Or maybe it was his eyesight.

The dark had leached all familiarity from the surroundings – for all Pilgrim knew, he was walking down a featureless, nameless tunnel that ran on for eternity, one he was destined to walk for ever, unable to escape.

A skitter came from his right and he snapped the flashlight around. A dart of movement shot past his foot and he jumped back, smacking his shoulder into the wall.

A rat, Voice said. *It's okay, it's just a rat.*

Wheezing and coughing, Pilgrim covered his mouth and nose with the crook of his elbow. The temperature had noticeably risen. Sweat drenched the material at his armpits and trickled down his ribs. The back of his neck was hot and humid. He checked behind him, half expecting the fire to be chasing after him, and instead two smoke-shrouded figures darted out of the darkness. Pilgrim ripped the gun from his pocket, but the two men ran by, wordless but for their fast, panting breaths, their weak flashlights quickly fading into the gloom.

Look! Voice blurted.

Pilgrim fumbled his Maglite, the metal tube clonking the gun, knocking it from his hand. It spun away, his grip lost, and he knew it would smack the ground head first and break. Knew it as soon as the flashlight left his hand, the angle of its fall all wrong.

It hit with a *crack* and the light shut off.

The dumb blindness of his eyes gaped wider, but there was nothing to see, only complete, impenetrable blackness.

He went after the flashlight, groped it back into his hold, stabbed at the button, clicking it on, off, on, off. Shook it and pounded it against his thigh, but it did no good. He growled, a panic he despised crawling from his stomach to pack itself into his chest and throat. He wasn't sure he could find his way through these tunnels without light.

Sweat dripped off his nose, his chin. He wiped his face dry with a sleeve and looked left, right, left again, his heart jack-rabbiting under his ribs.

He blinked.

An anaemic, candle-like radiance hovered at eye level a dozen feet away, and upon seeing it he remembered Glen's flip lighter in his pocket. He'd had a means of light all along.

He felt his away along the wall and the light grew clearer, materialised in shape. A frosted glass pane and, above it, two shapes. A cross and a tepee. A winged shadow passed behind the frosted pane and he stopped breathing. He quietly placed the broken flashlight on the ground, swapped his gun to his empty hand and wiped his sweaty palm on his pants. He grasped the door handle.

It turned under his grip, and the door swung inward.

The girl stared up at him. The one from before – the daughter of Dr Elizabeth May. Her eyes were puffy and red.

In the dull light, he could tell she didn't recognise him with his new clothes and baseball cap. Puzzlement drew her brows together, and then a dawning fear as the realisation of who he was and where she'd seen him settled over her. Her eyes dropped to his gun.

He stepped into the room, forcing her to retreat, and kicked the door shut behind him. A single battery-operated lantern did little to illuminate the space, but he did a quick scan of the five cages in front of him. Three of them were occupied. Two of the children stood at the front of their enclosures, fingers curled around the bars, watching him. Like Liz's daughter, they wore grey sweat pants, grey hoodies and white sports shoes.

The teenager on the left rattled the bars of her cage. 'Can you get us out of here?'

'Please, mister. You gotta help us,' the boy next to her said.

'I got a baby sister down here,' the first one said, with another rattle. 'I need to *go*.'

The third kid was huddled in the shadows at the back corner of her cage. Pilgrim had to strain to see her sitting with her legs crossed, arms up as she braided her hair into a tight plait. He glanced at the daughter, at the dried tears, at the way she clasped her hands in front of her, fingers white from her grip, just like her mother.

Pilgrim . . .

He felt the direction in which Voice wanted him to look. It was like having a crank behind his eyes, notching them left, left, left.

A cot was set up next to a bunch of plastic boxes filled with medical supplies. On it, covered in a crisp white hospital sheet, was a bald man laid out on his side. All that showed was the top of his shiny head.

'What's happening out there?' Liz's daughter asked. 'Did you see my mom?'

He didn't take his eyes away from the man. 'No.'

Suspicion clipped her words short. 'Did *you* do this?' When he didn't answer, the pitch of her voice rose. 'Did you hurt Abbie? ''Cause if you did—'

'She's fine,' he said. 'She left.'

There was real astonishment in her intake of air. 'No way,' she said. 'She wouldn't do that. She'd never leave without him.'

Before the kid could say another word, Pilgrim went to the bald man, snagged a corner of the hospital sheet and yanked it off.

It wasn't only the man's skull that was hairless; he lacked eyebrows, eyelashes, stubble. His resting face, oddly youthful despite the burn scars at temples and crown, was one Pilgrim recognised.

Jackson, Voice breathed. *It was him I heard just now. He led us here.*

Liz's daughter appeared at Pilgrim's side, swiped the sheet out of his grip and re-covered him.

'What's he doing here?' Pilgrim asked, staring down at the man.

'He came bursting in,' the girl said. 'Kept rambling about something over and over, but I couldn't tell what. He was so confused. Kept showing me his hands and pointing over there.'

Pilgrim followed her finger to the cages. The kids stared back, trapped, their fingers clutching the bars of their holding cells.

Tears had filled the girl's eyes. Her mouth quivered. 'My mom left us in here. She went out there and left me alone.'

Jackson continued to sleep, undisturbed by their talking.

His face twitched and his limbs twitched with him, a slumbering dog dreaming about chasing chipmunks. One of his hands fell out from under the sheet. It was wrapped in a messy bandage.

Exactly like that lawyer Jackson found in the shower. You remember her? Do you remember what Abernathy said all those years ago about what she did?

Trapped and burned her colleagues to death. Pilgrim remembered a lot of things now.

'What happened to his hand?' he asked the girl.

'It was burned up. I wrapped it best I could. Not sure if I was supposed to.' Her damp eyes gazed up at him. 'We heard the bangs. It shook the whole room. *Was* that you?' she asked. Her bottom lip trembled. 'Did . . . did *he* send you here?'

The kids in their cages were still staring. Even the girl with her newly plaited braid had crawled to the front of her enclosure. They were spooked animals, shivering and tensed, ready to snap and bite in self-defence or else bury themselves in a hole where nothing could reach them, not even the sunlight.

'No one sent me,' he answered. 'And I didn't do this. Not all of it, anyway.'

Voice gasped. *Look!*

Jackson twitched, his face clenching. Twitched again, tensing up through his shoulders, his chest, his stomach. His hips lifted. His entire body shuddered. It shook the cot, knocking it into the wall on a hard *rat-a-tat-tat*.

The daughter quickly knelt and tugged at Jackson's shoulder, pulling him on to his side as the seizure took over. 'He's having another one.' Her voice was taut with the strain of holding him in place.

Pilgrim began to feel strangely weightless as Jackson's lips writhed, the words that had dogged Pilgrim's footsteps from the day he'd woken up in Vicksburg forming on this man's lips, grinding out between clenched teeth.

A hissing rustled at the base of Pilgrim's skull, a building static that raised the hairs on his neck and sent prickles scurrying over his scalp. Every inch of him tingled. He was made of air and electricity, the grounded soles of his boots the only thing preventing him from exploding into a million molecules, each cell self-destructing in a flare of purest white. He stared at those godawful words taking shape, watched them crackle with power, and he wanted to smash his fists down into Jackson's face, pound and pound until they stopped.

He lifted his insubstantial, feather-light hand, unfurled his fingers and laid his palm on Jackson's head. He expected a burst of electricity to spark between them, to light up his flesh so he could see through the bones and veins of his hand to Jackson's scalp, but the man's skull was hard and smooth and scorching hot, and that was all.

Jackson's eyes snapped open and the pupils expanded fast, eating their irises. His gaze locked on to Pilgrim, and the perfectly formed words that had been spilling from his lips broke apart. He stuttered his way through them, but the sounds were fractured, meaningless.

'You can stop now,' Pilgrim said quietly. 'I'm here.'

Under his hand, the heat of Jackson's head chased away any remaining feeling of unreality. The tingles passed and the fizzing static at the base of his skull withdrew.

Voice's nervous energy told Pilgrim how affected he was by what had happened. *All the pain and suffering in this place – it's like he's a conduit for it.*

'He brought us here,' Pilgrim murmured.

Yes. Jackson lit the trail and then you did the rest. It came so far. What Birdy did to you both in that room – something was born in that electricity, Pilgrim. Something powerful. Ruby said we'd eventually hear each other, find each other, but this . . . It . . . I don't know, it seems to only happen when he's having a seizure.

The shaking that had animated Jackson's body had eased back

to a fine tremor, and now his fine trembling ceased altogether. He slumped, boneless, head sinking down to the cot, and only the painful swivel of his eyes, turned all the way right to keep Pilgrim in sight, indicated he was aware of his surroundings.

Pilgrim removed his hand from Jackson's head.

'K . . . k–kuh,' Jackson said.

'That's what he kept saying when he came in,' the girl said. 'But he never finished. I've never seen him have two fits in a row like that.'

'Ey . . . K–k–k,' Jackson stammered, and his arm flopped, a rubbery-fingered hand swiping over his thigh. Patting at it. Pat, pat, pat. '*Eeeeee*,' he whined loudly, frustration evident in his tone.

Pilgrim pushed Jackson's hand aside and smoothed the material of the man's pants where he'd been patting. He reached around to his butt and did the same there.

What are *you doing?* Voice asked.

Pilgrim paused when he felt something small and hard. He went into Jackson's seat pocket, fingers meeting a dulled serrated edge. Metal, warmed by the man's body heat. He pulled out a brass key blackened at its edges as if it had been plucked out of a fire.

'He's trying to say "key".' Pilgrim held it up to the girl. 'You know how to open the cells?'

She nodded, eyes wide on the burnt brass key, and took it from him. The kids in their cages set to shouting and calling out, rattling the bars, eager to be free. Liz's daughter scurried over to the wall-mounted lever mechanism on the other side of the room, unfastened the padlock and flung it to the floor. She ripped out a metal bar that had locked the controls in place and pumped the lever on the right, then grasped the one next to it and yanked on that one, too. All the cage doors sprung open.

The two girl captives darted out and ran for the door.

'Wait!' Liz's daughter shouted.

They didn't wait. They threw the door open so violently the frosted pane of glass shattered on the wall, and with it came a second explosion, the percussive blast rocking through the room. *Everything* leapt – the cages, the cot, the plastic boxes packed into the corner. Pilgrim threw an arm over Jackson to stop him being shunted off the bed. The tower of containers toppled and the boxes burst open, bottles rolling and bumping into Pilgrim's legs.

The daughter had fallen to her hands and knees and was scrambling back towards him. The boy, the only kid who hadn't run, was wrenching at the open door of his enclosure, his eyes wild. But no amount of tugging would close it.

Pilgrim strode over to him. The kid was making small, animal grunts, and Pilgrim had to prise his hands from the bars and grab his chin, forcing him to look up at him. '*Stop.*' He clamped the kid's face harder. 'Stop it, I said. You can't stay here.'

The kid bit his lip, his eyes flooding with tears.

'Simon!' Liz's daughter looked about as lost as any person Pilgrim had seen, but she held out her hand to the boy and Simon pulled free from Pilgrim's grip and ran to her. They clasped hands and held on.

Both kids turned to him, and he knew that look, that desperate need for someone to take ownership of their safety and tell them what to do. Pilgrim gave them his back and returned to Jackson.

But you're good at telling people what to do.

A thought occurred to him. 'Grab the lantern,' he said to the girl, over his shoulder. It was their only source of light and he couldn't carry it if he had his hands full with Jackson.

See?

It was oven-hot and getting hotter. The air had thickened and smoke was trickling in through the open doorway. Sweat stuck his shirt to his chest and back. Pilgrim picked up one of the bottles that had rolled across the floor, gave the contents a quick identifying sniff and dumped the rest over Jackson's head and shirt. The man spluttered and flailed and Pilgrim grabbed his arms and yanked him up to sit. The guy was heavy. He wouldn't be able to carry him.

'Get over here,' he told the kids.

Two more bottles of water got dumped over their heads and Pilgrim ripped off his baseball cap and doused himself, too. The water wasn't cold, but it felt good in the stifling heat. He retrieved the fold-up knife from his boot and made quick work of cutting the hospital sheet into four strips. They got soaked in water, as well. He tied a piece around Jackson's mouth and nose while the kids helped each other with theirs.

'Let's go,' Pilgrim said, his voice muffled under his own mask. He pulled Jackson up, lifting and wrestling him to his feet. He wasn't a dead weight, and he tried to help, but his legs were as rubbery as his arms had been, and Pilgrim had to drag him to the door.

The smoke got worse. It drifted around them, coiling over shoulders, twining in hair. It blanketed everything in a hazy smog and carried with it a strong smell of melting plastic and scorched metal.

The two kids stood close behind him. He could only see the gleam of their eyes above their bedsheet facemasks.

'What's your name again?' Pilgrim asked the girl.

Faye, Voice said, enjoying the fact he'd retained the information when Pilgrim hadn't.

The white cloth moved, the outline of her mouth opening. 'Faye,' came her reply.

'Turn right, Faye,' he told her. 'We're going to the morgue.'

They were coughing and gasping within seconds, even with the damp hospital sheet wrapped around their faces. A dull roar as if someone had opened an airplane hatch at high altitude joined the shifting and creaking of the dismantling world. Somewhere not too far away, a thousand candy wrappers were being scrunched up.

Fire, Voice said. *It's burning through everything.*

In the recessed entryway to the morgue, he left the children with Jackson and quickly sidestepped through the heavy door; its top hinge had sheered away from the wall, leaving it hanging crookedly. He led with Glen's flip lighter, its wavering flame barely reaching the back corners. The refrigerated units were dark, open holes, including the one they had stuffed Glen into. The guard, in nothing but a pair of briefs, was laid out on the tiled floor, displayed in a crucifix form. His throat had been slashed open. A messy spiral was daubed on his chest and stomach, and dark drips had run down his sides like black candle-wax, dried to the contours of his ribs. There was more of his blood smeared on the tiles below his feet.

A second body lay slumped against the wall, and it was so petite and birdlike something gripped at Pilgrim's throat.

It's not Tyler.

The man had long, flowing hair. His shirt was unbuttoned, revealing a sunken, bony sternum and a concaved belly indicative of starvation. Something poked out from under his hip, black and boxy. The Taser. Pilgrim went to collect it. He stared at the device, wondering what had happened here.

He slipped the Taser into his pocket and called for Faye.

'Read this for me?' he asked when the girl appeared in the entrance. He crouched to hold the flame near to the bloody smudges smeared at Glen's feet.

The girl stared at the dead man. He couldn't see her mouth, but he imagined it hanging open.

'Faye,' he said, trying to be gentler with her. 'Just look at the words.'

Her eyes shifted downward. '"*No more*,"' she whispered. 'It says "*No more*."'

A piercingly loud report ricocheted, a single gunshot that

echoed into many gunshots by the time it reached their ears. A shrieking cry came after it, and then repeated, even louder. A name ringed with desperation.

Faye's eyes popped wide. 'Mom!' She dashed from the room.

Cursing, Pilgrim went after her.

Jackson had regained some strength and was able to stand and walk on his own, but he remained a listless shadow of a man. He was leaning against the alcove's wall and squinting against the lantern light when Faye ran by. The boy holding the lantern called after her and darted in pursuit. Jackson made a grab for him but swiped at empty air.

'Stop!' Pilgrim barked at them.

A second gunshot. Closer. Four echoes.

There were more shouts, a confusion of voices, not close, but the corridors were narrow and designed to carry sound. A sudden barrage of return gunfire found Pilgrim as he came out into the open: the *pings* of deflected shots zinged past and bullets cracked into concrete. He dropped flat to his stomach and a number of solid, muted thuds sounded. He hastily reversed course, shimmying back into the cover of the alcove.

Breathing heavily, he peered around the corner.

It was smoky and dim, but Pilgrim could make out a white lab coat. Liz hadn't managed to reach her daughter. She lay face down. Dark, seeping blood spread across the back of her coat. It pooled beneath her, a slow oil spill creeping outward. One arm was outstretched, her fingers almost touching those of her daughter.

Faye was sprawled out on her front, too. The hair at the back of her head was a sopping mess of brain and skull fragments.

'*Shit*,' Pilgrim hissed.

The boy who'd chased after her had flattened himself to a wall. His eyes gleamed in the lantern light, huge black holes above his facemask. It billowed in and out over his mouth. Their gazes met.

Pilgrim held a hand out. 'Put the lantern down,' he told the boy. He didn't believe the shots were aimed at them – they had originated from some way down the corridor – but if they spotted the movement of light there was every chance they would open fire again.

The kid didn't put the lantern down. He stepped away from the wall, tentative.

'*Put the lantern down,*' Pilgrim repeated.

The kid reached his hand out for him, took another step, and Pilgrim stretched further. Snagged his sleeve. A report rang out and the boy jerked away. A second report quickly followed, and a bullet zipped past Pilgrim's head.

The lantern swung and spun, transforming the corridor into a whirling zoetrope. The boy had gone down and Pilgrim went after him, keeping low, and seven Shadow-Pilgrims went with him. He snatched a handful of the kid's hoodie and dragged him back into the alcove.

The boy had released his hold on the lantern and was clamping both hands around his throat. Blood leaked through his fingers, his grip slipping. He choked on his words and dark stains bloomed on the pale facemask. Pilgrim ripped the material away. Blood poured out of the boy's mouth and down his chin.

'It's okay. Everything's okay.' Pilgrim closed his larger hands over the boy's, but it was no use. Hot blood pumped fast with the kid's heartbeat.

The boy stared into his eyes, afraid to look away, his face a rigid mask, teeth grimaced red. Terror beat in sync with the blood gushing from his neck. Pilgrim met his gaze, didn't flinch from it. It was all he could do.

'It's okay,' he said again, the lie thick on his tongue. 'You're all right.'

The terror faded rapidly and the kid grew slack and still. Pilgrim's grip was the only thing keeping the boy's hands gripped to his throat.

From above them, Jackson let out a long, low moan.

Pilgrim, Voice said, softly hesitant. *We need to go.*

He unclamped his gory fingers and the kid's hands dropped heavily, bumping to the ground. Pilgrim roughly wiped his hands clean on the bottom of the boy's hoodie and, leaving the lantern where it lay, got to his feet and hooked Jackson by his elbow.

'Let's go,' he said, gruff and too sharp.

The man did as he was told.

CHAPTER 6

Daylight

In his mind's eye, Pilgrim visualised Abernathy's map and took the first right after the morgue, keeping low and moving as quickly as possible, towing Jackson behind him. The metal casing of Glen's lighter was becoming uncomfortably warm in his fingers, its trembling flame failing to illuminate more than a few feet ahead of them. He followed the conduits overhead, checking for blue-stickered labels, the sense of something in the darkness coming for them, snapping at their heels. He had to fight the impulse to run all-out and leave Jackson behind.

Their own footsteps pounded through the corridor, and he began to imagine footsteps behind them, chasing, running them down.

Pilgrim released Jackson's arm and dropped his hand to the solidness of the revolver in his pocket. Jackson's pace faltered, began to slow, and Pilgrim grabbed his wrist again and pulled him along. The man mumbled to himself as he ran.

Watch where you're going! Voice snapped.

They veered around a corner, following the blue-stickered pipes, and then there *were* no pipes, and no ceiling either. Pilgrim stumbled to a stop. Jackson bumped into him, gasping, and Pilgrim reflexively caught hold of him, taking the man's weight when Jackson lost his footing. His shoulder wrenched and he grunted in pain. The flame snuffed out and darkness crowded in, a piling of earth that packed them tight.

The hot metal of the lighter burned as Pilgrim thumbed the wheel. He thumbed it again, sparks flying off but not igniting. Hissing in frustration, he released Jackson's arm to cup a shaky hand around the lighter; thumbed the wheel a third time. Amorphous shadows stuttered to life, flitting their way across the walls. A warm, flickering glow burned in the centre of their two-man huddle.

Jackson moaned again, low in his throat, a dejected, fretful sound.

In the corridor ahead, pipes had torn loose from their supports and had brought down a huge chunk of the ceiling. A mass of metal and concrete blocked their way. Jackson left their cocoon of flickering light to place his hands on the blockade. He pushed but, other than a skittering of loose rubble, nothing shifted.

Dead end, Voice whispered, breathless, as if he'd been doing all the running. *What are we gonna do? We can't go back.*

The exit Abernathy had described wasn't far. Pilgrim could practically feel the trickle of fresh air on his face. He looked back the way they'd come, gazing into the darkness, the smoke spinning in lazy eddies where they'd run through it.

Now their feet had fallen silent, he knew he wasn't imagining the running footsteps any more – they were faint, muffled in the enfolding smoke and rumbling earth, but it wouldn't be long before whoever they belonged to came hurtling around that corner.

He went to Jackson, drew his bandage-free hand up and made him take the lighter. The man made a soft, pained sound at the heat, but he didn't drop it.

Pilgrim pointed to the top of the barricade, taller than both of them. 'You need to climb it,' he said. The bulk of concrete and piping climbed to seven or eight feet, leaving maybe a two-foot gap at the top. Jackson was smaller than Pilgrim. He might be able to squeeze through if he was lucky.

Jackson blinked, his mouth working under the mask Pilgrim had tied to his face. 'Y–y–you?'

'I'll be right behind,' Pilgrim told him. 'But you – you start climbing.' He gave him a small push to get him going and stepped out of the muddy pool of light.

With the flame at his back, Pilgrim's vision instantly dimmed. He ran his hand along the rough-textured wall, following it as he navigated the corner. Through a myopic blur, he saw a ghostly, strobing light sweeping through the smoke. It seemed to be moving fast. He snuck forward, his boots soundless, his wheezing chest silent but for the wild thudding of his heart. It was hard to breathe so he dragged the mask off his face.

The swaying light came closer.

Pilgrim pressed himself into the depression of a closed door and reached a hand into his pocket, finger sliding to the trigger.

A figure dashed through the smoke and Pilgrim stepped forward, grabbed them by the throat and shoved them into the wall. A gust of expelled air hit his face as he jammed his weapon into their stomach and depressed the trigger—

'*Christopher?*' Abernathy gasped, and grabbed for his shoulder.

But it was already too late. He finished firing and a crackling discharge of electricity lit the space around them in their own mini lightning storm. A pained garble erupted from her before he could lift the Taser away.

'*Unnngh,*' she groaned, folding over as he let her go and grabbing on to her stomach as if he'd stuck her with a blade. 'What the fuck's *wrong* with you?'

Now she knows how it feels, Voice said.

Pilgrim agreed, but didn't say it. 'Do you still have the files?' he said instead.

She straightened painfully, coughing and groaning. '*Yes*, I still have them. It's nice to see you, too. Jesus.' She threw a cautious glance behind her. 'I can't leave yet. We need to double-back and find Jackson. I'm not the only one looking for him.'

Going back would be suicide. He spotted faint bouncing beams of lights. Pursuers.

'What did you do?'

She frowned at him. 'Why do you assume I did anything?'

He said nothing as he grabbed her jacket and dragged her after him.

'Okay, so maybe I stumbled across Vanessa and her henchmen and popped off a few shots,' she admitted as she winced into a run, one arm still hugging her stomach. 'And before you say anything, *no*, I missed. And it's your fault I did – I was trying not to hit anyone in the head.'

What Pilgrim had wanted was to speak to Vanessa Mendoza (she didn't have any handy files to steal that Abernathy knew about. Not like Dr Lloyd). But shooting her was a reasonable second option given the circumstances, he supposed.

As when Birdy had chased them, the pipes and walls, the hot, suffocating darkness, all lent a strange acoustic resonance to the subterranean tunnel they ran down, making everything sound nearer, closer, an arm's length away. Each time Pilgrim looked over his shoulder, he saw flickers of shrouded torchlight, but the owners of the flashlights remained lost in swirling smoke.

When they reached the blocked part of the corridor, Pilgrim was relieved to find Jackson gone. Abernathy's mouth opened to blurt out what he strongly suspected was an expletive, but she was cut off by a vicious bout of coughing. She bent over and hacked something up. Spat it on the floor. Pilgrim's chest was heavy and congested, his breaths so short they ran into one continuous wheeze. They couldn't do this for much longer.

Neither can they.

'Climb,' he said.

'I'm not going anywhere without Jac—'

'I already have him. He's on the other side.'

She stared at him. 'I don't believe you.'

All patience lost, Pilgrim growled, 'Would you just fucking *climb?*'

She angrily slapped her flashlight into his waiting hand and began her ascent. Pilgrim retreated to the bend in the corridor. He pulled out the revolver, stuck it around the corner and, without discrimination, fired it, unloading shot after shot. The gunfire roared louder than anything on earth, repeating back to him, a rumbling thunderstorm that followed from the lightning he'd discharged. But nothing else sounded: no rushing footfalls, no return gunfire, no shouts, no screams of pain. They were there, though, hunkered in the dark, sweaty hands clasped around weapons, one set perhaps encased in gloves, a spiral tattoo imprinted on his skin.

A muffled cough sounded in the darkness. Ten yards away? Thirty?

'*Christopher,*' Abernathy hissed. She was at the top of the blockade, squirming her way sideways through the narrow gap to go legs first. 'Come *on.*'

His empty gun clattered to the floor and he sprinted for the collapsed pile of concrete and pipes. He tossed the Maglite up to her, the world spinning in a dizzying lightshow before she caught it. He found handholds and clambered up, boots slipping under the rubble, shins barking against jagged metal. It wasn't until he was eye level with the gap that he saw the space for how tiny it was. He wasn't going to fit.

You will.

'I won't.' His heartbeat lived in his head and pounded an awful fear into him. He would be trapped, with heavy concrete above and unmoveable concrete below. Sweat dripped down his face. His breaths whistled in his ears, the pipe they passed through narrowed to a straw.

You will! Jackson fitted.

358

Jackson wasn't as big as him.

Perspiration stung his eyes. He blinked rapidly to clear them.

Pounding feet and hoarse breathing filled the corridor at his back.

Pilgrim!

'Christopher!'

Abernathy's face was there, a hand space away from his. She grabbed his shoulders and pulled. Sharp edges dug into chest, his ribs, and multiple points poked him through his shirt, grazing painful lines across his skin, but he was going up, he was squeezing through, head first, and a thunder of bullets came, smacking the concrete – he felt their juddering impact next to his knee, his hip, cracking into the caved-in ceiling above him (it's going to collapse!) – but Abernathy didn't stop pulling and she hauled him through and all his weight was on the wrong side of the cave-in and they were falling through space, wind rushing by. The impact of hitting the ground was like being in a car crash all over again, only softened by the airbag that was Abernathy's body. She let out a squeaking grunt.

Get up! Voice yelled. *Up, up, up!*

The flashlight had died but Pilgrim was scrambling up, bringing Abernathy with him, and there were no sarcastic comments, no groaning complaints. She dragged at him, a hefty weight, either seriously injured or winded and hurting, but he felt fresh air, a cold trickle on his hot, sweaty skin, and he aimed for it, stumbling, taking her with him, his outstretched hand skimming along abrasive breezeblocks, breezeblocks, more breezeblocks, then smooth, painted wood and, further down, a cool metal bar. It depressed inward and they fell through the fire door and on to a raised platform, cross-hatched with yellow hazard paint.

They were in a small underground lot, once used by private ambulances to collect the bodies from the morgue. No one used it; the security barriers to gain access to the area had been chained and locked (until yesterday, when he and Abernathy had cut them open with the set of bolt-cutters Jay had appropriated from Home Depot. Number eleven on their shopping list). The rest of the time the fire door lay flush against the wall. Closed and inaccessible.

Daylight streamed in from the single-lane ramp sloping upward to the outside, and he had never been so relieved to see it. He'd dragged himself up through layers of dark, wet soil and, after hours of digging, had finally broken through to the surface.

But there was no one here. No vehicles, no Jackson, no Clancy or Jay. The space was empty.

No Tyler, either.

Only two dozen empty parking bays and a meagre forest of concrete columns.

Pilgrim pulled in a sharp, dry breath. 'I don't see them. Where are they?'

Abernathy straightened up with a groan. 'She better not have—'

A shout.

He had to squint through the smoke-sting of his eyes to see Clancy hurrying towards them, waving. He hadn't seen the vehicle – she'd parked it in a corner, behind a concrete abutment (he also blamed the colour – it was largely an unwashed black, with oxidised patches on hood and roof).

Abernathy tugged and they half stumbled, half ran down the slope and off the concrete apron. She was holding on to her side, but she pulled away from him and started limping under her own steam, picking up speed, because she'd spotted Jackson by the car.

She ran past Clancy without a word of greeting.

Clancy reached his side, breathless, and took his arm. The worry etched on her brow and bracketing her mouth would likely take a while to fade. 'Are you okay?' she asked.

'Sure,' he muttered, and checked over his shoulder.

The fire door remained closed.

Not for much longer.

Pilgrim moved faster, his stride hitching into a lurching jog, every muscle and bone jolting in protest.

'I had to move the car,' Clancy said, panting as she hurried to keep up. 'I was concerned someone would come bursting through that door and spot us.'

'Did you see Tyler?' he asked.

He caught her nod. 'She and Jay went back to the Unit to get everything ready. We heard the explosions, and you were taking so long. We didn't know what was happening.'

Stop talking, Voice snapped, *and move faster.*

Abernathy had Jackson wrapped in a bear-hug. 'Where *were* you?' She took the man by the shoulders and shook him. 'I looked everywhere for you!'

He stammered, 'I was huh, huh . . .' Stopped, started again. 'Here.' His voice rasped, damaged by the smoke.

As Pilgrim reached the car, Clancy's supporting hand left his arm and she skirted around to the driver's side.

'Get in,' Pilgrim told Abernathy, and he was unable to halt the cold, superstitious shrivel of his stomach as she stopped fussing over Jackson's injured hand and bustled the man into the back seat with her. She had told Pilgrim that this was the most reliable vehicle they had; she'd used it before and it hadn't let her down. All the same, it took some faith to slide into the hearse's passenger seat.

The old, cracked leather hadn't finished creaking under Pilgrim's weight when two men burst out of the fire door.

'Go!' Abernathy yelled.

And here was the moment, the place in every movie where the getaway car refuses to start, leaving the heroes stranded as the enemy closes in. It always happened. It was predictable but necessary. It was—

The engine fired up first go.

The men were running, closing the distance far more quickly than they had any right to, coming from the same smoke-filled catacombs Pilgrim had been in. But the hearse was pulling away, accelerating, wheels squealing, as Clancy steered them at speed at the ramp.

The men gave chase, something frighteningly alien in how their eyes had locked on to the car, in how the pistons of their arms and legs pumped.

They look like they could run like that for days.

The hearse soared upward, leaving the men behind, and a nest of birds burst free from their hidden roosts as the car swept through the exit. Strident caws and the dark beat of wings came with them as they escaped into the sunlight.

CHAPTER 7

Lacey and the Bear

Clancy didn't park next to the rusting staff cars but drove the hearse up the kerb and bumped it over the tall grass to the birdcage. They piled out and Pilgrim found himself standing face to face with Jackson. It was the first time he had seen him in natural light.

The shorter man reached up. Rested his hand on Pilgrim's brow, much like Pilgrim had done to him back in the Testing room with the cages. Jackson had a squint to his right eye that Pilgrim didn't think was due to the mid-morning sun.

'It's Sol,' Abernathy said, coming around the hearse to them. 'You remember Sol.' She said the name twice, the way you did to old senile relatives who were hard of hearing.

'Sol,' Jackson repeated. There was a hint of recognition there, a faded and ripped memory, and it saddened Pilgrim in ways he didn't quite understand.

Maybe because you know what it's like to forget people.

Jackson continued to stare. 'Sol,' he murmured. He pursed his lips, fighting to get his words out, and got going again after a few false starts. 'Roman god of the sun. The currency of Peru. Acronym for Sh–sh–shit Outta Luck.'

Ha. That last one's pretty accurate.

Pilgrim sensed Voice stretching and flexing. An expanding

awareness across the back of his mind, the way you stood and stretched after sitting for hours in a cramped chair at the movie theatre.

It was hard listening to Jackson, a once-eloquent, intelligent man trapped inside a burnt-out, damaged mind. It was hard to look at him, too. He reminded Pilgrim of the woman Abernathy had roomed with, the one who'd habitually plucked every hair out of her eyelids and brows.

'Let's get out of the open,' Pilgrim said to him quietly.

Abernathy came to take Jackson's uninjured hand and drew him along with her to the birdcage. 'We shouldn't hang around here long,' she told Pilgrim over her shoulder. 'We're a fair distance from the west wing here, but everyone who got out will be around here someplace.'

By the time Pilgrim followed, Abernathy had moved ahead of Jackson to pull open the smokers' fire exit. Pilgrim took the door from her, holding it for Jackson so he could walk in ahead.

'We're leaving?' Jackson asked him, his voice so quiet Pilgrim had to lean closer to hear.

'We are,' he said.

'We c–could go to Elysian Fields.' Jackson wasn't looking at Pilgrim but was distractedly gazing around the Unit's hallway. Pilgrim figured he'd moved on from talk about Roman gods to Greek mythology until he spoke again. 'It's much bigger. I huh–h . . .' He hummed a little. '. . . *hear* the East Coast is beautiful. South Carolina, especially.'

Pilgrim stopped dead and stared at the back of Jackson's hairless head. The man continued up the corridor alone, seemingly unmindful of the fungus and moss, the mould and the rot – he had a dream-like quality about him, as if he weren't occupying the same spaces as the rest of them.

You're remembering something.

A pulse of pain dug into the back of his head. He raked his fingers into his hair back there, brushing over the soft, tender spot behind his ear. As soon as his fingertips made contact, the pain trenched deeper, burrowing to a grounded agony that had his teeth grinding and his breath hissing between them. His legs buckled and, with nothing to catch himself on, he dropped to his knees.

'*It's the East, isn't it?*' Lacey calls.

Another cleaver of pain hacked into Pilgrim's brain and he groaned, saliva stringing from his bottom lip. The Unit's hallway shuddered left, leaving a blurred, ghostly impression of itself in his vision. Corners realigned, sharpened. Lines solidified and, halfway down the corridor, from the middle shower stall, Lacey walks out.

Her head pans right to left as she takes in the Unit, checks out the high ceiling, and then continues over to him. She doesn't smile, not unhappy to see him but not pleased, either. She walks towards him, all solemnity and grave, striding steps. Behind her, a large black bear trundles out of the shower to follow.

Jackson makes no reaction to the girl or the beast appearing. They are far too big to have fitted inside the cubicle, and yet here they are. The bear's fur ripples, its muscles bunch. Its claws click on the floor.

Lacey unslings her rifle from her shoulder and holds it loosely, aimed at the floor at Pilgrim's knees. She approaches no further as the bear passes by on her left. Its burly head swings to her then swings back to Pilgrim, and its eyes aren't the amber-brown of a bear's but those of a human. They regard him with something close to pity. It walks the last few yards in its steady, ponderous way.

Pilgrim straightens as best he can as pain swells in his head.

'*How many times has east been a part of all this?*' Lacey asks him. '*How many times has it all pointed that way? Eastern wings on hospitals. Me to my sister. You to Ruby and her Inn. This place Jackson calls Elysian Fields. Each new day starts there, so, too, should new beginnings.*'

Pilgrim doesn't understand what she's talking about, but he can do nothing as the bear comes right up to him, its dark, wet nose inches from his face.

On his knees, Pilgrim's and the bear's eyes are level. Its hot, meaty breath snorts in his face.

'Go home, Mama Bear,' Pilgrim whispers.

The bear opens its maw wide, displaying the pink flesh of its mouth and all its sharp teeth for him. Its big head tips sideways and the bear stretches out its neck and fits both jaws delicately around Pilgrim's face.

He doesn't move, feels the tips of incisors press into his temples, his cheeks, the bones of his skull. Strong jaws close and the pressure on his head grows tighter and tighter, painfully, horrendously tight. He hears a crunch and something shifts in the back of his head, a dangerous shifting that is awful and satisfying at once. It hurts – of course it hurts – but pain is always the price.

CHAPTER 8

Ghosts

Pilgrim, who is Sol who is Hoyt who is Christopher who *is* Pilgrim, dreams of a letter. He has read it many times. The creases where the paper folds are thinning and close to tearing. Passages of it have sunken into him, weighted with meaning, settling on sea floors in billowing clouds of sand. They have been waiting to be refound.

But at this moment, sitting on this wooden porch, this is the first time he has read it.

Do you remember where I wrote this? We are in a thrift store – you, me, Albus – and a mama bear paid us a visit. She stared in at us for so long I thought she would come inside and eat us. Do you remember?

He smooths a thumb over the writing and the paper crinkles in the early morning quiet. He reads with care right down to the final paragraph.

There is an Inn on the East Coast. It will welcome you when you're ready. Not now, of course. Not yet. You won't need it yet. But if you are ever lost and don't know which way to turn, it will be there, waiting. Albus and I will be waiting.

After reading Ruby's name at the bottom, he folds the letter and slips it back inside its envelope. A creak of wood alerts him to another presence, and he turns to find Albus. The man raises a hand in greeting and Pilgrim nods his welcome, quickly finishing sliding Ruby's letter into his jacket pocket.

It's cold, despite their hats and gloves and scarves. They have stopped to rest in a gift shop at the base of a flat-topped mountain, a tourist attraction that had regularly brought visitors from hundreds of miles around. The store boasts a rustic wraparound porch, decked out with seats and benches for customers to perch on and rest. Once-colourful woven blankets, now faded and moth-eaten at their edges, drape the railings. It is a good place to sit and stare out at the slowly brightening sky as dawn gathers itself on the horizon. You can see for miles, the land like the sea, undulating in waves.

Albus brushes off the seat next to Pilgrim and sits down. He pulls the collar of his jacket up and blows warmth into his cupped hands.

They sit quietly for a time and when Albus reaches into his pocket and pulls out a notebook the sound of rustling paper and pencil scratches are the only things to be heard.

Pilgrim accepts the notebook when Albus offers it.

I know she told you about our uncle's Inn in her letter (which she asked you not to read btw). we'll hopefully be heading there at some point. you should come with us.

'I thought your sister has things to do,' Pilgrim says, passing the notebook back. 'Which doesn't include settling down in some out-the-way Inn on the coast.'

Albus writes some more. Shows him. **she does. we do. but we can't do this for ever. it's getting more and more dangerous. they've found us twice in the past two months.**

'You think Jonah will let her stop?' Pilgrim asks him, curious.

'I'd assume he has his own thoughts on the matter.'

Albus's shoulder lifts in an uncertain shrug. A sigh mists from his mouth.

'How old is he exactly?' Pilgrim asks. 'Jonah.'

Albus points at himself, points at Pilgrim, and holds his hands apart by about a foot. He hooks a thumb over his shoulder at the gift shop where Ruby sleeps and holds his arms as far-spread as he can reach.

'What's that? Hundreds?'

Albus nods and scribbles some more.

'You're literally saying *hundreds* of years?'

I believe there's something in the stories behind people like Joan of Arc and Socrates. I read somewhere Socrates would hear a voice, that it came to him whenever he was about to make a disastrous decision. that it would talk him out of it.

'So you're saying you think Jonah is an angel of God.' Pilgrim doesn't attempt to mask his amusement, and Albus smiles.

His hair falls forward as he bends to his notebook. He writes for a long time and Pilgrim returns his gaze to the scenery. The jutting mountain is a prehistoric relic, its sides ribbed and bone-like, like a leviathan dredged up from the earth, born into an unrecognisable world where, one day, it will shudder to life, boulders tumbling from its flat-topped summit, its rock-hewn limbs sturdy with purpose, and trundle off into the distance, an awesome sight to anyone left alive to behold it.

Albus passes him the notebook.

I don't believe in God or angels or the Devil. I believe in *our* gods, ones that are private to us, internal. I think our brains are undiscovered terrain. I mean, look at me. I see colours in different ways to you and Ruby, and if I can see them differently, then everyone has the ability to see them like that – my brain is the same as yours, my eyes are made of the same cells, yet they have found

ways to access different neurons, open up pathways that haven't been opened for the longest time. we shut ourselves off. close our eyes and block our ears. we lock ourselves away, maybe in fear. I don't know. but Jonah, my sister, *you* – you have all found ways to tear down those walls.

'Lots of people found ways,' Pilgrim tells him. 'And then they killed themselves.'

I think the voices have always been here, right from when we were scratching around in the dirt and starting the first fires. there is so much evidence of them, in art, in music, in what we once called mental illness, in children's imaginative play. they've been here the whole time.

'So why did they do what they did? Why now?'

like with Socrates, I think they came to avert disaster.

'What're you guys talking about?'

Ruby is standing with a sleeping bag wrapped around her shoulders, watching them from the store's doorway. Her hair is mussed, her eyes sleepy.

Voice emerges to whisper-sing a strange little lullaby.

Sleepyhead, sleepyhead, what did you dream?
Of periwinkle skies and fish in the streams?
Of flowers to smell and plants to bed?
Time to wake up now, my sweet sleepyhead.

Ruby gets a bemused look on her face as she wanders over to them. 'I dreamed of skies, but they weren't periwinkle blue. You guys didn't answer me.'

'We were talking about voices,' Pilgrim says.

'Ahh.' She sits down on the seat beside Albus and tucks up her legs. She folds the sleeping bag tighter around her. 'Has he mentioned Joan of Arc yet? He has a real boner for her.'

Albus sends her an offended frown and Ruby smiles. 'I think we need to find you a girlfriend, bro.'

He makes a *pfffft* sound, which makes her laugh.

Pilgrim looks away from their affectionate bickering, his thoughts too sombre to enjoy it. 'Albus said he thinks they came to avert some sort of disaster.'

'Makes it sound like *War of the Worlds*. It wasn't an alien invasion.'

'No?'

'Well, maybe. I mean, we *do* all come from the stars. Every seed, animal, every rock and droplet of water. All made from stardust.'

'I'm not sure I'm up for a pseudo-scientific lecture so early in the morning,' Pilgrim says.

'It's not pseudo-anything. It's fact. And I have more where that came from. Don't look at me like that,' she says to Albus. 'I have a point to make here, I swear. So, when we're born, there's this belief that we're dying from day one, right? And that's true, to some extent, but it's not the *whole* truth. Many times over during our life, parts of us die and regenerate. Skin cells fall away within hours and more are made to replace them. This happens all over our bodies, inside and out. Even in our *hearts*.' Her eyes are wide when she says this and Pilgrim smiles on the inside. She has come alive, her face animated, all traces of sleep gone. 'We're literally not the same people we were ten years ago. We're not static creatures. We're like nature, constantly changing and renewing. So why can't we change again? Why can't something inside of us, something separate, recognise that we're going wrong somewhere and take action to fix it?'

It's a rhetorical question, one Pilgrim doesn't know where to begin answering, even if she expects him to.

Ruby has turned her body, so engrossed in sharing her thoughts that she has twisted in her seat to face them. 'Disease is the same as ageing, really. It's when our bodies begin to lose that

371

balance between death and rebirth. Too many things are dying and not enough are regenerating. This whole beautiful, messed-up world we live in' – she pokes a hand out of her sleeping bag to sweep it across the land, the sky, the rib-sided mountain – 'it was losing that balance, too. It was dying and not regenerating, because *we* were its disease.'

'And the voices came to wipe us out?'

'Not *wipe* us out,' Ruby says. 'We're still sitting here, aren't we?'

A fraction of them were, sure. 'Did Jonah tell you all this?'

'No, actually. But he's said enough over the years for me to cobble a few things together. The only thing he reminds me of, when I'm feeling particularly disillusioned by everything, is that what happened wasn't an end. It was a resetting.'

'A *resetting*?' Anger rose up, much like his own mountain leviathan, ridged and bony and carving a place for itself inside his chest. 'What they've done is destroy us. There's been out-right genocide since they appeared. We've spent these past three years trying to finish what the voices started.'

'We've always killed each other. Because, as usual, people are scared of what they don't understand.'

'You don't think they have a right to be scared?'

'Of course I do, but it's not helpful. There really isn't anything to fear any more. The deaths stopped after those first few weeks. It's been over three years. People have to find a way to see past it.'

'And let me guess, you're going to help them do that.' He sounded flippant. He couldn't help it.

'If I can. Otherwise, everything that happened was for nothing.'

She's so sure of herself, so steadfast. It frustrates him, but there's also a centre of calmness in her that is impossible not to admire.

He becomes aware that his hand is in his pocket, his thumb

rubbing over the carving Matilde made for him. Over and over, smoothing the pad along the featureless face of the girl standing beside the wooden version of himself.

Which makes no sense.

They haven't found Matilde yet. Their overnight stay at the gift shop happened before their trip up the mountain roads to see her. But the thought is fleeting and he continues to run his thumb over the smooth, blank face of—

Lacey.

Pilgrim frowns. Lacey?

And there she is, a distance away, her back to the flat-plateaued mountain, as if she'd popped over to take a look and is now on her way back to him. The dawn that has been gathering itself has spilled across the sky, bleeding out in a red so deep it's like someone has cut it open. Pilgrim sits up straighter. It is definitely Lacey. And she isn't alone. A second figure walks beside her. A woman, taller than the girl. Her long hair plays in the wind.

Alex, Voice says. *The woman with artist's hands, like Clancy's.*

He hasn't met Clancy yet, either.

'Do you see that?' Pilgrim asks, but when he turns to Ruby she is smirking at her brother.

Her eyebrows climb when she meets Pilgrim's eyes. 'Albus says you read my letter.'

Pilgrim throws Albus a look. 'Traitor.'

'Technically, *you're* the traitor,' Ruby tells him. 'You promised me you wouldn't.'

'I'm sorry,' he says, but it is offered absently. Lacey and Alex have covered an impossible amount of distance in the scant few seconds he'd taken his eyes off them. 'Do you not see them?' he asks again, pointing.

And again, he is ignored.

'The Norwood Cove Inn, sixteen miles south of Myrtle Beach,' Ruby says. Sitting sideways, she has rested her head against the chair back. She is watching him. 'That's the name of the place. When you need it.'

He nods, only half listening.

Myrtle Beach is on the East Coast, Voice says.

'Elysian Fields is on the East Coast,' Jackson says, not a single stutter marring his speech. He is on the porch, leaning back against the railing to Ruby's left. A stalk of grass is stuck in the corner of his mouth. His hair is thick and full; he looks exactly as he did when Pilgrim knew him at the Unit. 'It's the biggest of its kind,' Jackson says, scratching behind his ear. A clump of hair drops out and lands on his shoulder. He doesn't seem to notice. 'Much bigger than what we have in St Louis.'

'What are you talking about?' Pilgrim asks, frowning at him.

But it isn't Jackson who answers. Lacey and Alex have appeared beyond the edge of the porch, sitting in front of a burning campfire. Lacey has her legs crossed, Indian style, as relaxed as a kid at a camp-out, but Alex is sitting with her arms wrapped around her raised knees. Her clothes are stuck to her body, her shirt plastered to her skin, but she doesn't seem aware that she is soaked in blood, that it drips from her hair, her chin, that it rolls down her face.

'My sister and I were headed east,' Alex calls over to him, 'before we met you. We'd heard there were scientists out there looking to help. And now Lacey needs help. *You* made sure of that, didn't you?' Her eyes are hard and full of reproach. 'I'll have to take her out there myself and get her fixed.'

Fixed? Voice asks.

'*Where* east?' Pilgrim asks. His head hurts, as much as it ever has, the pressure in it creaking through the bones of his skull. At the corners of his eyes, lights flicker, fast as camera flashes. A metallic taste floods his mouth as if a penny sits under his tongue.

Jackson has started crooning softly, a song about someone waiting for him in South Carolina, a girl he loves best, and a letter she wrote, telling him the weather is fine. It's paradise there, in a little brown shack in South Carolina.

Voice begins to sing with him, their voices joining in harmony.

'Is it time?' Lacey asks. She's standing at the porch railing, arms folded on top and chin resting on top of them. She has brought the campfire with her, flames licking into her hair, wicked-red tongues curling under her jaw. Fire dances in her eyes. 'Are you coming, Boy Scout? I'm still waiting for you, you know.'

Her face crumbles inward, red, glowing cracks appearing like veins. The burning ash of her chin and cheeks, her nose, all disintegrate, caving in as a sandcastle caves in to the incoming tide. Pilgrim's face crumbles with it and the agony it costs to crack his jaws open and utter, 'I'm coming. Don't be afraid,' brings tears to his eyes.

Something cold touches his temple.

He slowly swivels his eyes to the right. A girl, no older than eight, stands beside his chair. She is the phantom girl all the way from Memphis, the one who'd pointed the antique firearm at him as he'd stood in the swaying shadow of the hanging cable car. She holds the same antique gun to his head. She has locked the hammer back, and it was hard work to lever that heavy mechanism, he knows, but she persevered. She reaches for his shirt pocket – he wears the black shirt he'd taken off Glen in the morgue – and plucks out the photograph. Hands it to him.

'That's me in there,' she says, tapping a finger over the distended belly of the pregnant woman.

Addison, Voice says, breaking from his duet with Jackson to share the girl's name.

Addison. Lacey's niece. Pilgrim knows her, even if she hadn't known him when she pulled that trigger and shot a hole clean through him.

'Sorry,' Addison whispers, and there is sorrow in her eyes. A chewing-away-at-her guilt. 'But I need to do it again.'

She pulls the trigger.

CHAPTER 9

The Man Who Could Read

The catastrophic pain of the bullet awoke Pilgrim in a flash. The bear's jaws were still locked around his face in a vice-like grip; except it wasn't the bear, it was Abernathy. She was kneeling in front of him, her hands cradling his head. Her lips moved but whatever she was saying was lost in the hot, pounding rush of blood in his ears. He blinked. Realised the terrible pain in his head had vanished. No ache, no discomfort at all.

He felt . . . better.

Maybe you're dying.

Like a whistling kettle lifting off the stove, the rush in his ears dissipated with Voice's words.

'Christopher? Hey. Do you hear me? Stop fucking around, all right? We need to go. *Hey.*' Abernathy shook his head a little.

'Why'd you keep calling me that?' Pilgrim's voice was dusty, his lips cracked. He wet them with his tongue.

Relief washed over Abernathy's face. She sat back on her heels, hands falling from his head. 'It's your name, isn't it?'

'Not any more. Not for a long time.'

She shrugged, off-hand. 'I guess it's my small piece of you that no one else has. Are you done bugging out on me?'

He coughed and nodded. 'East. We need to head east.'

'Is that right? Well, I'd already be gone if I wasn't waiting on you to get your ass into gear.'

She helped him to his feet, although he didn't need it. He really did feel better.

Jackson had wandered further up the hall to stand in front of the shower stall where Lacey and the bear had appeared. The mama bear was nowhere in sight.

Of course it isn't. Your scrambled-egg head made the whole thing up.

'I'm good now,' he said.

Abernathy slid him an unconvinced look. She collected Jackson, linking her arm through his, and drew him up the corridor with her. She spoke to him the entire time, a constant, calming stream of chatter. Pilgrim trailed after them.

I don't think you're ever gonna be fully unscrambled, but that's okay. You wouldn't be you without a few missing eggs.

He didn't know if Voice was trying to annoy him or not, but it wasn't working. Pilgrim felt . . . buoyant, his body as energised as he'd ever felt it, despite the countless aches and pains, scrapes and bruises. But even they felt oddly satisfying, each one a reminder he was alive.

They arrived at the day room and his spirits rose further.

Clancy had their stuff packed and ready to go, including Abernathy's food supplies; they were stacked on and around the games table. Jay was perched on the arm of the couch, hovering over Tyler, and Pilgrim was surprised to feel a rush of relief at seeing her whole and well. Her pale features were smeared with dirt and dust and her hair was a tangled mess. At first, Pilgrim thought Jay was holding Tyler's hand but he quickly realised he was helping to clean her; her hand and wrist were splattered with more dirt than the rest of her combined.

When Tyler looked up, her eyes were a little too big, her mouth a little too soft, as if she were on the verge of tears. When she saw him looking, she retrieved her hand from Jay's and lowered her gaze, as though she'd been caught playing hooky behind the bleachers.

We really put her through the wringer. Voice sounded regretful.

'I saw what happened in the morgue,' Pilgrim said to her.

Tyler nodded, a jerky up-down of her head. 'I unlocked the door,' she said. 'They wouldn't wait. They wanted out, and I tried, but . . . they wouldn't wait, so I let them out.'

Poor old Glen. Wonder if it was one of those prisoners who started the shit-storm with the explosions.

'What happened down there?' Jay asked. He'd been left holding the cloth he'd used to wipe Tyler's hand with; it was balled up tight between his hands. 'The whole parking lot shook. It was like an earthquake.'

'The generators blew,' Abernathy told him.

'Did everyone get out?' Clancy asked.

Silence answered her.

'You said there were children down there.' She directed this at Abernathy.

Abernathy briefly looked to Pilgrim, but only for a split second. 'That's right. But there are emergency evacuation routes. We all know them.'

'Me and Tyler saw a few people milling around,' Jay offered. 'A good twenty or so. Plenty more must've got out.'

But Clancy wasn't looking at either of them; her eyes were on Pilgrim. 'But not everybody would have. Tell me, did you see children down there?'

That wasn't what she was asking, though, was it? She was asking if there were any dead children down in those unlit, smoke-filled corridors, their blood drying tacky and black. Their throats blown open and heads ripped apart. Small bodies burning, their clothing and hair alight, as they lay trapped beneath the downed rubble.

Pilgrim, don't.

'Yes,' he answered. 'There were children.'

Clancy's lips pressed flat. Tears welled in her eyes.

Abernathy stared at him for a moment then turned to Clancy. 'Look, it's not anyone's fault. We were—'

'Shut up!' Clancy's hands came up and made a grasping motion, a futile wringing of the air as if she wanted to throttle, to beat, to hurt something. Hurt *anything*. Her face flushed dark with some powerful, inexplicable emotion. 'Just please, *please*, shut your mouth.'

'We're leaving,' Pilgrim said, wanting to distance them from this conversation before it could erupt into something messy and uncontainable. 'Now. Jay, Tyler, pack up the car. Abernathy, get anything else you need. We're heading east, so that's—'

A cat's pained wail sliced through his words.

Peter Bird stood a few feet inside the ward's foyer, nurses' station to his right, day room to his left. He must have entered through the Unit's main doors. He had Jenks gripped by the scruff of the neck, holding the animal away from his body as the struggling, hissing cat twisted at the end of his hand. In his other, he aimed a steel-grey gun at them. Or, more precisely, aimed it at Abernathy. From the corner of Pilgrim's eye, he saw her slowly reach for Jackson and pull the man behind her, out of the line of fire.

'Follow the raised voices and you'll find Abernathy. A lesson that's served me well over the years.' Birdy's black, amused eyes passed over them until they found Pilgrim. 'And there he is! I knew you'd be here – a stray dog sniffing his way home.'

The man was filthy – he'd crawled out of the same grubby hole the rest of them had – but he hadn't changed a bit from how Pilgrim remembered him. His hair, sporting a few streaks of grey, had receded a little, making his widow's peak more pronounced, but it was greased back like it always had been (he'd likely neatened it before walking in). His nose was hooked, bent at the bridge, and Pilgrim wondered if he was the one responsible for it.

It hasn't improved his looks.

'I shouldn't be surprised,' Birdy said. 'I knew she'd do this someday.' A sideways nod to Abernathy. 'Turn on those who've provided for her all these years. A disloyal bitch to go with the stray dog. It's very fitting.'

Abernathy gave him a hard smile. 'You had a good run, Peter. You should be glad of that. But it's over now.'

A tautness passed over Birdy's face, but it smoothed into calmness almost as soon as it showed itself. This was how he'd always been, making out like he was in control, like he was somehow immune to the baser emotions that ruled the rest of them. Pilgrim had seen plenty of men like him. Their inflated, brittle egos did little more than build them a house of glass.

A fine tremble shook the gun in Birdy's hand. Abernathy's was holstered at her side. Pilgrim wondered if she had any bullets left in it.

A bead of sweat ran down the side of Birdy's dirty face, leaving a streak through the dust. 'Nothing's over until I say it's over,' he said quietly, but the thread of fury that ran through it worried Pilgrim. It would be a mistake to upset a man like this, a man who was on the verge of losing everything.

'Everything's destroyed, Peter. Dr Lloyd is dead. Vanessa will be long gone by now. There's nothing left. It's done.'

Birdy's eyes flicked to Abernathy's right. 'So you think you can take your precious Jackson and skip off into the sunset?'

Abernathy shrugged. 'Basically, yeah.'

Voice sighed out an expletive. *Why does she have to say stuff like that?*

'Why doesn't anyone call you Birdy now?' Pilgrim asked, taking a single, slow step to the side, away from Abernathy and Jackson. 'Birdy suits you much better.'

Birdy transferred the gun to him, blinking as if he'd forgotten he was there. The dry *click* of the hammer being thumbed back stopped Pilgrim at just the one step. He would have liked to say he'd missed that sound, but he could go a whole lifetime without hearing it and it wouldn't be long enough.

'So the stray dog can talk,' Birdy said, his lip curling. 'Isn't that something? Do your little friends here know what you did yet? Do they know who you are? Because if we're talking about old names suiting us, maybe we should discuss yours.'

'Don't,' Abernathy told him.

'No,' Birdy snapped, swinging the gun back to her face. 'You don't get to say "don't" to me. You don't get to say anything any more. I'm the one who tells people what to do in here. This is *my* ward. *My* hospital.'

The tremble in the gun had become pronounced, and Pilgrim didn't think he was the only one who noticed it.

'Buh–birdy. Birdy the little strutting b–bird.' Jackson breathed a laugh and caught the sleeve of Abernathy's jacket, tugging at it to get her attention. 'Remember, you called him b–baby Bird? Because he was so puh–pathetic?' He laughed again, a huffing sound that made him cough, but it didn't stop the chuckles.

Abernathy shushed him, her eyes darting back to Birdy (the man's were burning black holes). 'No one called him that.'

'Right over th–there after he had his baby Bird tu–tantrum. He slapped you, right across the f–face.' Jackson moved out from behind Abernathy to point at the games table by the window, where Clancy stood stock-still, the bundles of their belongings heaped in front of her. The window was cracked open. A crisp morning breeze brought with it the scent of smoke, and Pilgrim was assailed by such violent déjà vu his fingers curled into his palms with it. His knuckles brushed the solid lump of the Taser in his pocket.

No, Voice said. *We're not close enough to him.*

Pilgrim didn't move. Not yet. He wouldn't make it three steps before Birdy opened fire.

'You called him a "limp-dicked asshole", be–because it was

always puh–peckers and dicks with you. But I know.' Jackson pointed at Birdy and smiled slowly, and Pilgrim saw awareness there, the intent clear in Jackson's eyes even as his broken mouth fought him. He knew exactly what he was doing. 'A big baby Birdy with a pecker as l–limp as his hair.'

Cannon-fire shook the day room. Rattled its windows. The cat hissed and jerked, breaking Birdy's grip – he was a heavy, well-fed animal. Jenks landed on Birdy's thigh and attached himself there with claws.

Birdy screeched and swung the gun. It cracked Jenks over the head.

Pilgrim went for him, Taser out, but Birdy was too far away – Pilgrim knew it and Voice knew it. He felt Voice curl down into that tight space again, the smallest of targets, as if it could save him.

Jay jumped from the sofa and Tyler reached out a hand to stop him, her fingers skimming his back as Jay charged Birdy from the right. Clancy grabbed a pack from the top of her pile and swung it by its shoulder straps, hurling it at Birdy as hard as she could.

Birdy batted the bag easily aside and swung the gun to his next target.

Four more shots blasted out in quick succession.

Each hit their mark. All were torso shots.

Gun arm extended, Abernathy advanced on Peter Bird even as the man staggered, kicked back by the punches he'd taken to chest and stomach. Jenks streaked away as she emptied the rest of her clip into him, shot after shot after shot, even when he'd tumbled to the ground. Still she fired, his body jerking and twitching under the bullets' assault.

Click click click click, the hammer clicked on empty.

Pilgrim came up behind Abernathy and rested his hand on her forearm, felt the wiry ripple of muscles as she continued to pull the trigger.

'Enough,' he murmured. 'Stop.'

The *clicks* stopped.

'No headshots,' she said, voice flat and lifeless. 'Did you see that?'

'I saw.'

She pulled her arm free from him and turned away, leaving Birdy where he'd fallen, blood steadily spreading outward towards the day room's parquet flooring. His hair lay in oily tangles and his blank eyes stared at the nurses' station. A dark stain had spread across the crotch of his pants.

'Christopher, help me.' The crushing weight of anguish in Abernathy's voice had Pilgrim by her side before he'd even realised he'd moved.

She was trying to lift Jackson, but the man was too heavy, his hands pressed over the bloody mess of his stomach and unable to help. The one shot Birdy had fired had done its job.

'*No,*' Abernathy snapped when Clancy moved to help. 'You don't give a shit about him.'

'I was just—'

'*I said no.*'

'I have him,' Pilgrim said, and Clancy backed away.

Between the two of them, they lifted Jackson as carefully as they could and placed him on the sofa where Abernathy and Jackson had sat together to watch TV. Jackson bit back his moans as he writhed in pain, but he didn't cry out, even though Pilgrim had seen gut wounds before. They were an agonising way to go.

For fifteen minutes, Jackson squirmed and breathed hard and squinted around the room as if he were seeing it for the first time. Abernathy didn't leave his side. She talked to him gently, stroked his smooth head, held his hand. Her other hand she kept pressed over the sopping wound in his stomach. The sofa cushions beneath him slowly darkened and grew saturated.

The need to leave was a crawling nest of snakes in Pilgrim's middle, and the others must have felt it, too – Jay, Clancy and Tyler left them to jog back and forth along the Unit's long corridor, loading the car as fast as they could.

Pilgrim stayed beside the sofa and Jenks curled up in the armchair opposite, impassively watching as Jackson slowly bled out. The cat sported an impressive knot on the back of his skull. Pilgrim could sympathise.

'I got it,' Jackson whispered in his gruff voice. His lips were cracked and rouged with blood, his teeth stained red with it. 'Took me . . . some time. But I g–got it.'

'What's that?' Abernathy asked. With the back of her finger, she tenderly wiped a dribble of blood from his chin.

'*Slaughterhouse-Five.*' He smiled a ghastly red smile at Pilgrim. 'You let me buh–borrow it, even though . . .' He swallowed hard and winced. 'Even though it messed up your counting.'

'I knew you'd take good care of it.'

'I put it back. Long time after, but I . . . p–put it back. You . . . you ever read it?'

'Don't think I ever did, no.'

'You should. The main guy . . . His name . . . you–you'd like it.' Jackson stopped and gasped, his face scrunching up.

'Stop talking,' Abernathy said, laying her palm on his brow.

'No. I . . .' Jackson's eyes came back to Pilgrim, his hairless face twisting in confusion. 'I called out. It was you, wasn't it, Sol? I c–called to you.'

Pilgrim nodded. 'You did. I heard you. What they did here . . .' He struggled to find words, struggled to hold Jackson's eyes. 'I left and forgot everything. It was past time I came home.'

Jackson blinked slowly, the confusion easing from his face. 'Home.' Another smile, weaker. 'That's funny.'

Pilgrim glanced at Abernathy. 'More the people than the place.'

'You . . . didn't talk to us so much.'

'It was never about the talking. Not for me.'

Jackson's eyes had closed. His breathing came heavier, as if a weight pressed down on his chest. At Jackson's gut, Pilgrim laid his hand over the back of Abernathy's; it was hot and slick with blood. He gently pulled her hand away, letting the blood seep free.

'I called out, Sol, when I was lost in the dark. When my body locked up on me and I couldn't move, couldn't get a single word past my teeth.' There were no stutters or stammers any more, only sleepy slurs gently falling to mumbles. 'Nothing was me and everything hurt. We *all* hurt, and I was scared, but you . . . I hoped you'd hear me . . .' A silence that was filled with breathing. Then: 'Sol?'

Pilgrim leaned in nearer. 'I'm here.'

'Watch . . . for a forest,' Jackson whispered, 'When you get close, watch . . . for a forest of white. White and wind.' Parted for his last word, Jackson's lips released a long, sighing breath, and then he breathed no more.

Pilgrim was still holding Abernathy's hand, but after a minute, staring at Jackson, his mouth hanging open and eyes closed as if sleeping, she pulled it roughly away, rose and left. Her boots echoed, fading down the hallway.

Pilgrim got wearily to his feet and backed away, pausing at the armchair. He let his hand travel the cat's spine, once, twice, from neck to tail. The cat's sturdy body purred.

'Good boy, Jenks,' he said.

He went to the shelving unit beside the open window, knowing he was on borrowed time. He searched quickly, not knowing if he'd be able to recognise the spine when he came to it. He needn't have worried. Each static letter greeted his eyes like an old friend, firm and steady and perfectly readable. He read title after title, a sense of wonder lifting the corner of his mouth. His eyes stopped their scanning.

Slaughterhouse-Five, Voice read with him.

Pilgrim plucked the book from its place and glanced over at Jackson as he slid the paperback into a pocket.

Now his count will always be one short.

The cat's head turned to watch him cross the day room, green eyes aloof and disinterested. Pilgrim had already taken Birdy's gun (the dead man wouldn't need it any more) and, with everything he needed, he left the Unit for the final time.

Jenks went back to licking his paw, busily cleaning the last bits of Birdy's blood from his fur.

Clancy made everyone fasten their seatbelts and then drove them out of St Louis's grounds fast enough to rattle the teeth in Pilgrim's head and test the springs in the hearse's seats. No one complained and he didn't tell her to slow down. He held on to the roof handle and braced himself as they bounced over ruts and bumps, as eager to put miles between them and the hospital as everybody else.

Eventually, Clancy eased back, the tension in her arms and shoulders easing with the speed of the vehicle, and soon the drive began to remind Pilgrim of other drives he had taken in warmer, less rainy climes.

Lacey was a constant presence to him now. She was on the periphery of every glance, at the edges of every conversation, and he waited for her to jump in, but she never did. She rode alongside him, in the driver's seat with Clancy, the sunshine bright and warm on her face and neck, sun visor stamping a block of shade from mid-nose up. They had driven like this, just the two of them, in a pickup truck with Ruby lying in the bed. Ruby had been dead by then, and she had been no one to Pilgrim, his memories of her hacked away, his mind full of ragged, self-inflicted holes. Of course, a lost part of him had known who she was, but he'd been too afraid to go looking for her, even when Voice had prodded him, even when she'd whispered his name as she lay dying in the desert dirt at the roadside, sun glaring in her eyes. She had found her way back to him and he had looked upon her as a stranger in her last moments.

('Christopher,' she whispered.)

He'd thought she'd meant her necklace when she'd uttered that name, her fingers searching for the medallion at her throat. The St Christopher pendant she wore and would touch and press to her lips whenever she sought protection for herself and for those around her.

Pilgrim had taken Ruby's body and placed it in the truck's bed and hadn't given it another thought. He'd taught Lacey how to drive; they had spoken about being ghosts, about not having a place in this world.

Ruby was dead and he was alive. How was that fair? How many times had he cheated death now?

Three, Voice said. *You've cheated it three times by my count.*

Three was a powerful number.

THE PART
FROM THE PAST

The Man Who
Wouldn't Die

CHAPTER 1

Skills

Four years ago

Outside the leaking, grey-concrete packing warehouse, the patter of raindrops provided the backdrop to Ruby's singing.

She sang most nights at Albus's request. She'd been working her way through *Les Misérables* ('I was due to play Odette in my college's production when people stopped turning up to school,' she'd explained) and was currently depressing him with a maudlin tune about castles in clouds.

She and her brother had worked their legs into their sleeping bags and were settling down as she sang the last few notes. They echoed in the cavernous distribution area, the room bare but for the three of them set up in the middle of its endless echoing space. (As draughty as it was, Pilgrim had insisted they lay their bedrolls dead in the centre, wanting a view of all sides.)

Pilgrim, who was Hoyt, and who was someone else before that, watched them go through their nightly routines, an outsider to their rituals but content enough to observe. As Ruby's voice faded, Albus's eyes lifted as if to follow invisible air currents.

'You should sing for him sometime,' Ruby said, watching Pilgrim as he watched Albus. 'He'd probably like that. Hell, *I'd* probably like that.'

No, Voice said. *No, no, no. No one needs to hear you sing.*

Albus made a soft sound to draw Pilgrim's attention and nodded, smiling, fluttering his fingers away from his lips and uttering a quiet, wordless melody. Pilgrim glimpsed the empty hole of his mouth, an alien landscape with no evidence of a tongue.

Pilgrim shook his head. 'We all have our talents. Singing isn't one of mine.'

'What *is* your talent?' Ruby asked.

He thought about it. 'Not living in the past.'

She snorted.

You are *good at that*, Voice said.

Pilgrim shrugged at both of them. 'It's useful.'

'How is it useful? No, truly, I want to know.'

He scrubbed a hand through his hair and considered not answering. He wasn't comfortable sharing his thoughts. It was difficult enough with Voice always weaselling his way in; it made Pilgrim even more private when faced with others wanting to hear them.

'I feel like I belong in this world,' he said, letting the words go with some reluctance. 'There are bits and pieces of the old one I remember: scenes from movies, books, the smell of popcorn, the powdered stuff you'd mix into milk to make it taste like strawberries. I used to like that, I think. And I remember smaller things: the scent of brewing coffee, lyrics to songs, the feel of slipping between freshly laundered sheets. But it's all so distant. It fades from me, and I'm eager to let it. It's better – *easier* – if you let that stuff go. None of it's coming back. Who I was back then isn't coming back. There's no place for him here.'

'But memories bring pleasure,' Ruby said quietly.

'Not all of them.' He changed the subject. 'What's your skill? Other than singing and letter-writing.'

'Boy' – she pretended to look at her watch – 'how much time do you have?'

Albus laughed.

'I'm a good sister, but we can't really mark that down as a *skill*. I think . . .' She paused to frown and lay back in her bed-roll, tucking her hands behind her head and staring up at the high iron-girded ceiling. 'I think I'd have to say never giving up.'

She sounds like a contestant in a beauty pageant, Voice said.

'It'd be so easy to just stop and say, fuck it all.' Pilgrim wasn't sure she was speaking to him, her words so soft, her attention on the roof far above their heads. 'To get scared and run all the way back to where I started. There's a comfort in home, about surrounding yourself with familiar things. But it's a false security. Those things don't mean anything, not really. They don't protect you and they can't keep you safe. You have to keep moving, going forward and not looking back. Looking back does no good because you're *supposed* to leave parts of yourself behind, that's the whole point, because there are new parts waiting for you somewhere up ahead. All you need to do is bring along the right people to keep you brave. People you love.' She twisted her head to smile at Albus. Her brother returned her smile.

She's pretty wise for a beauty-pageant contestant.

'I like that part,' Pilgrim said. 'About not looking back.'

She included him within the radius of her smile. 'Thought you might. You can keep that one if you like, free of charge.'

'It's pretty similar to what I said.'

'I think yours is more about running away, though. You're not moving *towards* anything, you're just doing the leaving part.' She rolled on to her side to face him, tucking her bent arm under her cheek. Her other hand began to fiddle with the pendant on the chain around her neck. 'Albus wants me to tell you about his skill.'

Albus was lying propped on his side, head cupped in his hand. He didn't fidget or drop his gaze but something told Pilgrim he was nervous. The guy tucked a loose strand of hair behind his ear and perhaps there was a slight tremor to his fingers, perhaps not. Pilgrim couldn't swear to it.

'We didn't find you by accident that day. When you were outside Walgreens in your cute purple hat.'

He'd pondered on this. It would have been so easy for them to miss each other. If they'd passed five minutes earlier or five minutes later, he'd have been inside the store or gone and he would never have seen them.

'You found me like how you found Matilde?' he asked. 'You heard Voice talking?'

'Partly. But Voice would've needed to talk fairly constantly, right up until we were nearby, for us to have pinpointed you exactly. No, it wasn't Jonah who found you. *He* did.' Her eyes went to her brother.

Albus raised a hand, modestly taking the credit.

'You said Albus doesn't hear a voice,' Pilgrim said.

'He doesn't. But he sees people like us.'

I get the feeling this is more than regular eyeball action she's talking about, Voice said.

'You know how he can't talk like you and me?' Ruby said.

Pilgrim eyed Albus, beginning to feel uneasy about all this. 'Right. He has no tongue.'

'He was born without one, yes. Anyway, Albus has synaesthesia.'

Pilgrim stared at her blankly.

'You know how some blind people can have acute hearing? Or deaf people's tactile sensitivity can be heightened? Well, I think Albus's brain rewired itself in compensation for being born with one less thing than the rest of us. So now he hears in colour.'

There was a long silence while Pilgrim processed that. 'There's no such thing as hearing in colour.'

'Sure there is. The composer Franz Liszt would tell his orchestra to play a "little bluer" or "not so rose". They thought he was fooling around before realising he was actually seeing colour in the music they played. Duke Ellington said that if one member of his band played a note on the piano and another guy played the exact same note, he saw them as different shades. Often he'd see them in textures. Both Liszt and Ellington had chromesthesia. It's a bit different for Albus. He can only see colour when people talk or sing or hum aloud. Certain people, anyway. Like me. Like you.'

Pilgrim looked at the man, who sat quietly, as he always did. A man so soundless Pilgrim sometimes forgot he was there. 'You saw this when we first met?' he asked him.

Albus nodded and looked back to his sister.

'He says your colour is black. Or, more precisely, the black fold of velvet. He often sees colours in texture, too. I'm the silky petals of a rose.'

'Red,' Pilgrim said.

Ruby smiled. The small silver disc of her necklace's pendant winked at him, reflecting the candlelight. 'It's why he likes it when I sing. He sees the notes. Sees any vocal sounds I make, but singing is the most visually splendid, apparently.'

He knew Albus was watching for his reaction and he also knew he was doing a bad job of masking the disbelief he felt. 'So every time I say anything, you see a colour?' he asked.

Albus nodded.

'Black,' Ruby said. 'Which is kind of emo, Hoyt, I have to say. Although I shouldn't be surprised.'

'You're seeing me talk, *right now*?' he asked, and Albus nodded again.

'And it's not just imagined colour to him,' Ruby said. 'It's a real visualisation. He sees it as surely as you or I see the flame of a candle or the smoke from a fire. And he can follow that light or smoke back to its source.'

'And you expect me to believe this?' Pilgrim asked.

'We found you, didn't we?' Ruby said. Her eyes slipped away from him as she listened. 'Jonah says you see glimpses of it, too. Sometimes.'

'I don't hear colour,' Pilgrim said, irritated at how Jonah joined the conversation whenever he liked.

'Not *hear* it. But you see . . . sparks of something.'

He went to argue but couldn't quite find the words. He'd thought the glow in her hand was caused by the sunlight shining through her skin, but the sun didn't do that. Nothing did that. Only light pressed directly to skin did. And what about Matilde? Hadn't he seen an ice-blue glow in Matilde's mouth as she'd spoken to him? He couldn't explain that, either, could he?

That was *strange*, Voice agreed.

But Pilgrim had just come in from the freezing cold after murdering two people. He'd likely been in shock.

'You know what I'm talking about, don't you?' Ruby said, watching him in sly contemplation, as if knowing exactly what he was thinking.

'I have no idea,' he muttered.

She chuckled. 'No need to look so cranky about it. It just means you're sensitive. Maybe you're even' – she made a pretend shocked face – 'an empath.'

Voice sniggered.

'I think we all know I'm not.'

'No, you're absolutely right. Hearing colours is pushing it. But you being empathetic towards fellow humans is *entirely* too implausible.'

Voice laughed outright.

'Do you see it in everyone?' Pilgrim asked, speaking to Albus.

Albus shook his head and pointed at Pilgrim then at his sister and swiped a flat palm through the air.

'We're a rare breed, you, Matilde and me,' Ruby said. 'Albus doesn't come across very many of us.'

'And what exactly is it he's seeing?'

'Answer a question for me first. How do you think I came to have Jonah?'

She won him in a raffle.

'Voice thinks you won him,' Pilgrim said.

Her smirk played across the shadows of her face. 'In a manner of speaking, I did. I was in the right place at the right time. Or the wrong place at the wrong time, depending on how I feel about it on any given day. Point is, Jonah was never mine. Not like everyone else's voices were born to them. A man died so that Jonah could come to me. But I had to have a place for him to come to. And not everyone has that. An ability to accommodate them. An ability to accept them. And *that* is what Albus sees in me.'

'Why you?'

Ruby left her necklace alone and leaned up on her elbow. There was something mysterious in her expression. 'We don't know.'

'But Jonah knew you could accommodate him?'

'Only because I told him about Albus's synaesthesia, and even then Jonah wasn't a hundred per cent certain.'

'But Matilde said Jonah was old. Really old.'

'She did. And he is.'

'Then how the hell has he lived to such a ripe old age if he doesn't know who can "accommodate" him?'

'He gambles. In the past he's gone to places where there are lots and lots of people.'

'You're kidding me.'

'Nope. Stadiums, concerts, malls, battlefields. Hospitals are always good — like where Matilde was — because you're guaranteed a large number of people in one place, doesn't matter what day of the week it is. You have to wait for football games and Taylor Swift concerts to roll around.'

'He gambled on someone like you being there?'

'Pretty much. And you know what there are very few of these days?'

Crowds of people, Voice said.

'So you can see why it's important we don't blab about this to anyone,' Ruby said. She settled back down, head on her arm.

They listened to the howling rain lash the concrete and drum the roof. A coldness lay at Pilgrim's back, the echoing emptiness of the warehouse unsettling him, yet the three of them sat in their circle of flickering candlelight and there was warmth here, too, there was comfort and acceptance.

'I won't tell,' Pilgrim said, and he meant it. He was good at keeping secrets.

'We know,' Ruby said.

Albus nodded.

'You said a man died,' Pilgrim said.

Ruby made a soft humming noise. 'Frank.' Her eyes glazed over as she stared into the candle's flame. 'He was a patient in the care home where I worked part-time. He and Jonah were living out their last days there. Jonah had decided he didn't want to move on, didn't want to find a new home. He loved Frank, you see, and he'd grown weary of losing the people he loved. He'd grown weary of a world so full of cruelty and hatred, too. He could see it all sliding back to a place he didn't want to be a part of any more. And who can blame him? But he couldn't help but listen to me and Frank talk, and he heard when I told Frank about my twin brother, about how Albus could see me when I sang, about the colours that were revealed to him in people's voices. And Jonah knew what that meant. He'd known others like Albus over the years. Still, me being there wasn't enough to convince him to stay.'

'What changed his mind?' Pilgrim asked.

'The voices. He felt them stirring. All of them. He knew they were coming. And, like I said, I was in the right place at the wrong time.' Ruby blinked the candlelight from her eyes, her gaze clearing as she focused on him. 'There's only one way for them to be able to rehome themselves. Like how Jonah made the leap from Frank to me. They need to be forced out.'

'Forced?'

'Two things must happen. First, someone like me must be there and, second, the place where they live must be rendered unliveable.'

Unliveable. That sounds . . . violent.

'I took my father's handgun from the safe in my parents' room, and I sat outside the bedroom of a man who'd become very dear to me as he put the gun I'd given him into his mouth and pulled the trigger.'

The wind howled. The rain lashed. Albus said nothing, but Pilgrim could feel the sympathy in him as he gazed at his sister, a deep reservoir of love for her that transcended words.

'If you were to die right now,' Pilgrim asked, 'in this empty warehouse, with only me and Albus here, would Jonah jump to me?'

Ruby shook her head, cheek pressing into her folded arm. 'That's not how it works. First, I'd have to take some pretty serious damage to the head. And second, you already have Voice. There's only room enough for one in your head, wouldn't you say?'

'So he'd die?'

'Yes. Jonah would die with me. He *will* die with me. Matilde wasn't lying about that. Once I'm gone, he'll be gone, too, and that'll leave only one like us.'

'The man Matilde spoke of?'

'Right. And then you'll really be up shit creek. People like me? You'll need to defend them from him because he'll want them very much. He'll surround himself with them if he can. He thinks this is his world now and he'll want to stay in it for ever.'

CHAPTER 2

Hoyt

Pilgrim stared at the rain pouring down from the corrugated-metal roof. It was mesmerising, watching the flood fall in curtains of water. It enclosed them on three sides. A complete washout. The noise was tremendous, a beating, hammering war party above their heads.

They had been so careful since leaving the mountains and Matilde's cabin. They had stayed away from people. They had chosen the less direct routes to travel and stuck to minor roads. They had made no mistakes. Up until now.

'*Shhh*,' Pilgrim told the man cowering beside him. It came out sharp. He didn't care.

The sandy-haired stranger sniffed, wiped his runny nose on his sleeve. His spectacles had steamed up. One lens was broken, cracked down the middle, and the sight of it made Pilgrim even angrier.

A crack in the glass, a crack in your brain, two cracks but not the same. Pilgrim sensed Voice's bubbling pleasure at his own inventiveness.

The stranger's glasses had been mended around the arm's hinge. Taped. They had been through a lot, those spectacles. The man, too, judging by all the snot and tears.

'Can you shut up?' The snivelling was grating on his nerves.

'Hoyt,' Ruby said. 'Take it easy. It's not his fault.'

It was *all* his fault. But Pilgrim had no desire to argue over it. 'We shouldn't have interfered.'

'What should we have done, then? Let them kill him?'

I'm going to say a resounding Yes *to that one.*

'Th–thank you,' the man said, teeth chattering. 'Really. They c–came out of nowhere.'

'I said be quiet,' Pilgrim told him, told Ruby, too. Their only chance of getting out of this alive was by keeping their mouths shut.

He lifted up partway to peer over the double-stacked steel barrels. Ales, beers, lagers, ciders, the alcohol they had barrelled and distributed from this warehouse were long gone. Pilgrim, Ruby, Albus and this stranger had scaled the tall gates of the brewery and dashed for the only cover available to them: an open-sided lean-to that sheltered around fifty of the brewery's empty barrels.

There were no signs of their pursuers.

Not yet. Only so many places we could've gone, though. They'll check in here eventually. I would.

Albus made a low humming noise, a reprimand for Pilgrim being so short with his sister, judging by his scowl.

Pilgrim shook his head at him, because Albus always took Ruby's side.

Albus offered the stranger their water flask and the man took it in a hand that shook so badly he had to use his other one to steady it.

'What's your name?' Ruby asked him.

'David.' Straggles of thinning hair stuck to his glasses. Pilgrim didn't know why he didn't wipe them away. Didn't know why he didn't clean his steamed-up lenses or wipe his snotty nose again.

Stop being so cranky. Jeez. No one's dead.

Not from this man's lack of trying. They should keep

moving, but *David* was slowing them down. He'd done something to his ankle and had been hobbling for the last five minutes.

He twisted it because he couldn't see where he was going. Voice snickered a laugh.

At this stage in the chase, it was either hide or be caught. And hiding under this corrugated drum kit would dampen any sounds their pursuers made when they came for them.

'We should leave him and go,' Pilgrim said. From Ruby's expression you'd think he'd suggested they slit his throat and leave him for dead. He sighed. 'We're not abandoning him. We could lead them away from here. He could stay' – he waved a vague hand at the man's injured ankle – 'and rest up.'

You sound one hundred per cent convincing.

'We're not leaving him.' And from the uncompromising look in her eye, he knew she wouldn't be budged on the matter.

You are *a little cold-blooded at times,* Voice said.

No, he was the only sane one here. He wasn't condemning the man to death, he was prioritising Ruby's, Albus's and his own safety. Voice's, too. Hanging around was putting them all in danger.

'He brought this on himself,' Pilgrim said.

'How do you know?' Ruby asked.

'Look at him.'

David had folded in on himself, legs drawn up and arms wrapped around his knees. If he possessed any fortitude, any endurance or sense of self-preservation whatsoever, Pilgrim had yet to see it. 'He didn't get caught up in all this by accident.'

Even with her hat pulled low and hiding her brows, Pilgrim knew she was frowning at him.

'Go ahead and ask him,' he said.

Albus nudged his sister and, when Ruby looked at him, he nodded to David.

She irritably shoved wet hair out of her eyes and under her

hat. 'Fine. David? What happened back there? Why were they chasing you?'

The man was shivering uncontrollably. 'I c–confessed. I t–t–told them what I did.'

She flicked Pilgrim an uncertain glance. 'Told them what?'

'I was a store m–manager. In charge of my own store and everything. Had a staff of eight w–working for me. I was *responsible*. I earned good money. I'd have made r–regional manager within a year. I looked after my family. I *did*. I *loved* them.'

Ruby was biting her lip. 'David, what did you do?'

'I told them the truth. Told them I'd tried to h–hurt my wife, my daughter. Oh my god, my beautiful daughter.' He broke down, blubbing through his words. 'I told them that I wanted to k–kill them.'

Pilgrim's hand had moved to his gun. A coldness settled in him, a still centre that belied the quickening of his heart, the pulse throbbing in his eyes translating every sound as a vibration: the raindrops cannonballing off the ground, the metal barrels shivering like dogs. He could see his companions' heartbeats pound from their chests in sonic waves.

The downpour fell harder and the tin roof above their heads shook in a crescendo of crashing cymbals. It almost drowned out Pilgrim's words.

'How old was she?'

David knew who Pilgrim meant. 'Eight months.'

All sound cut off. No cascading rain, no heartbeats, no drumming tin roof. Complete and abiding silence. The gun was out of Pilgrim's holster and pressed to David's throat before Ruby or Albus had registered he'd moved.

David didn't flinch away and he wasn't crying any more, as though his admission had drained him of emotion.

What're you doing? A gunshot will bring them straight to us!

'Hoyt.'

But Pilgrim had eyes only for David. 'Did you kill them?'

'*No.*' The man's eyes rolled to look at the gun digging into his throat. 'My wife barricaded herself and the baby in our bedroom. I couldn't get in.'

'You left them there?'

'What else could I do? I'd have . . . I'd have hurt them.' Tears flooded his eyes again. 'Are you going to pull the trigger? You should. I wouldn't blame you.'

Pilgrim increased the pressure on his throat. 'Do you still want to hurt them?'

'It's not like that any more. The voice I hear, it . . . it stopped saying that stuff. Like . . . I don't know, like it had got what it wanted already and gave up with me.'

Like a quota had been hit.

A quota of what? Voice asked.

Dead people. 'And what's it got to say to you now?'

'It says I should go back. That I'm a bad father to leave them alone in a world like this. That they need me.'

'Quite the turn-around.'

Anger entered David's eyes, and it was a welcome change to the snivelling, pitiable man he had been up to this point.

'I don't expect you to believe me. But I've stayed away from them. Why would I *do* that if I was still desperate to hurt them?'

Pilgrim had been aware of Ruby edging closer. Small movements so as not to cause alarm. She'd removed her glove and laid her bare hand on Pilgrim's wrist. She didn't pull the gun away but the warmth of her fingers injected a steadying calm. Pilgrim stopped pressing the gun quite so hard into David's throat.

Sound filtered back in. The roar of the rain, the *ping*s of droplets hitting the metal barrels, the rush of water flooding the ground.

'Why haven't you gone back, David?' And Ruby's voice was so composed, so kind, Pilgrim felt it seep in, a cooling groundwater dousing his anger. She left her hand on Pilgrim's wrist and he was in no doubt as to why. She knew he wouldn't shoot a man with her so close, with her hand on his killing arm.

'Would *you* go back?' David asked. 'After what I did? How can I expect my wife to forgive me?' More tears. As endless as the rain. 'How can I ever look her in the eye again?'

Pilgrim lowered the gun and sat back in disgust. It would only make him feel worse to kill such a wretched man.

And he did say he didn't kill them.

Sure. That, too.

Albus waved to get their attention and tapped to his ear, then pointed towards the brewery's gate.

A *clank*. Faint over the drumming rain.

Pilgrim got to his knees.

Through the fall of water he saw three of them scaling the gate. Four more waited on the other side. They had crude weapons – lead pipes and bats, something that looked like a pool cue. It wasn't their intention to put them out of their misery. Not straight away. They wanted to inflict pain, to maim, to cripple.

Pilgrim ducked down and grabbed David by his shirt front. 'You'd better make amends, David. To your wife, your daughter, to every person you've ever let down.'

Pilgrim heard a set of thuds as the three men dropped to the ground.

He looked to Albus because, in this one thing, he knew Albus would side with him over Ruby. 'Wait for me to draw their attention,' he told him. 'Then get your sister away from here.'

'What're you doing?' Ruby asked, and she looked so confused he couldn't help but feel sorry for her.

'Let's pretend what Matilde told me was true. Let's pretend I'm setting you and your brother on your paths. David, too, I guess, if he ever decides to stop crying.'

Panic overtook her confusion. 'No. You don't have to do this. We can—'

'Can what? Take them on together? All make a run for it?

You know better. Listen, you keep writing your letters, okay? They're a nice idea. But do me a favour and stop trying to help every damn person you meet. It'll get you killed one day.' He touched the side of his chest, where the opened letter she had given him was slotted inside his jacket pocket.

They're coming. Whatever you plan to do, do it already.

Voice didn't try to talk him out of it, and that was a surprise. Maybe he'd grown as fond of these twins as Pilgrim had.

Ruby grabbed his jacket and pulled him into a hug so desperate he was shocked by the strength of it. 'Who else will help them if I don't?' she breathed in his ear. 'If *we* don't.'

She backed away and took his face between her hands. He tried to memorise her, he did, but the rain was already blurring parts of her away, softening her in his mind's eye so that she was an impression of herself, a washed-out reflection in fogged-up glass.

'Tell me your real name,' she whispered.

He hesitated, because all his secrets were wrapped up in those three syllables, all the memories he'd spent a lifetime forgetting.

'Tell me,' she said.

He hadn't voiced his name in so many years it sounded lifeless as it left his mouth and lifeless when it reached his ears. In the back of his head a door cracked ajar, the monster living behind it shifting closer.

She smiled and whispered his name back to him, and it didn't sound quite so barren coming from her. One of her hands left his face to hook the necklace out from under her collar. She pressed the medallion to her lips; for luck, for superstition's sake, Pilgrim didn't know, but it reminded him of how priests would kiss their crucifixes. On the coin's embossed surface a man carried a small child on his back.

He nodded to Albus, who nodded back – he looked more like Ruby's twin in that moment than he ever had, the bridges of their noses wrinkled with the same worried crease – and he felt Ruby's remaining hand fall from his face.

'Go,' he told them. 'And don't look back.'

Pilgrim stepped through the sheet of water, the chill startling him. He heard shouts but didn't look up. He kept his head down and hunched over, putting a hitch in his stride. He limped away from the lean-to, away from the only family he had known since this world had come tumbling down. But those were dangerous thoughts and he shut them off, locking them tightly away where they couldn't hurt him.

A bullet ricocheted off the ground and he jerked to a stop and dropped to his knees, thrusting his empty hands up in the air. He plastered a look of terror on his face.

'Don't shoot! Please! I'm not with them! I'll tell you where they are!'

He kept his head meekly bowed as the three men approached. They each wore jogging shoes. Two Nikes and an Adidas.

All the better to run you down with, my dear.

The rain pelted his head, his nape, driving him into the ground.

'Where are they?'

'They went to find a way into the warehouse.' Pilgrim pointed at the brewery; he made sure they could see his hand shake. The warehouse was on the far side of the work-yard, in the opposite direction to the lean-to. 'I heard breaking glass over there.'

A high-pitched whistle sounded and Pilgrim glanced up to see one of the men wave at the remaining four waiting on the far side of the gate.

'*They're here!*' the man yelled.

They began to climb.

The same man turned to his companion on his left. 'Go check that out.' And he nodded to the lean-to that Pilgrim had appeared from.

'Let me join with you guys,' Pilgrim begged. 'Please? Come on. I can be a big help, I swear.'

'Shut your mouth.'

The guy on the left broke away and Pilgrim made a grab for him, clutching at his jacket, hanging off it, pleading. 'Come on, man. You'll let me, won't you? Don't leave me out here. Be a pal.'

'Getdafuckoffmefreak!' It came so fast it was a jumble of outraged words. He kicked out, striking Pilgrim in the hip. It hurt but he didn't let go.

'*Hey*. Don't be like that! I'm *helping*. Give me a chance!'

He got kicked harder. A third kick came from the guy who'd whistled for his friends. It stamped into his side and Pilgrim felt his ribs creak. He groaned and bent inward but he didn't loosen his grip on the jacket, and a third and fourth kick landed – his back, his kidneys. He went down, dragging the jacket-wearer with him. The guy cried out and Pilgrim wrapped himself around his legs, clamping on, babbling out requests and pleading for help.

Then they really laid into him, and not only with fists and feet. He felt the lead pipe come down across the back of his legs and he couldn't help but bellow his hurt. They took turns on him, all of them, and that was good. This is what he wanted, what *they* wanted. Someone to lash out on. A blood-letting that would sate them, would drain their restless, impotent rage, and they could go home, his blood staining their knuckles, their weapons, imbedding in the soles of their Adidas. They wouldn't need to chase anyone else down tonight.

Your neck! Voice yelled.

Groggy from pain, Pilgrim groped for his throat. A rope came down, cinching tight, trapping his hand. A yank and he was on his back, blinking in the rain. He let out a strangled rasp as they dragged him by the neck like a lassoed calf across the work-yard, and, as disoriented as he was, as blinded by rainwater and his own blood, he knew where they were taking him.

He didn't see them throw the rope up over the top of the brewery's gates. Didn't see the man who climbed the railings to jerry-rig the hangman's noose. All Pilgrim felt was the wrench and the lift, his head, his shoulders, his back rising off the ground. He heard the exertions as the men heaved, the whoops of those who stood back to watch, the hot, agitated energy in them. The shared excitement. His butt lifted, the weight on his neck and hand choking him. If there *was* air to breathe, it wasn't his, it belonged to these men, the ones who shouted, called him murderer, told him his kind was a disease that needed to be wiped out. The rain could never douse such hatred.

The backs of his heels scraped across gravel and then the ground was gone. He kicked, his feet clanging off the gates, the railings vibrating up his back. His boots scrabbled, found purchase, and the terrible pressure on his throat lessened and air trickled in. Someone kicked his feet away. His hand cracked as something snapped inside it and he let out a hoarse, wheezing cry.

Voice was talking, saying something, the back of his head buzzing with his pleading, but it couldn't beat down the rabid hammering of his heart.

. . . stop . . . fighting . . . I can . . . let me . . .

He kicked and twisted at the end of the rope until he could kick and twist no more. His body convulsed, twitching in spasms, the oxygen-starved parts of his brain sparking him into a mindless dancing jig. If he was aware of the men down there, watching and laughing, he didn't know it. If he realised he was dying, there was no abstract space for him to acknowledge the fact. And if there were any thoughts of how he could save himself, he was unable and unwilling to act on them.

They never did ask if he heard a voice or not.

In the end, it didn't really matter.

PART FOUR

The Man Who Surrendered

CHAPTER 1

Rebirths

*H*oyt died that day, and everything died with him.
Pilgrim flexed his hand on his leg, knew he was doing it, could see his fingers stretching, but his hand was someone else's, the movement mechanical, severed from him, like his past had been severed from him. He'd cut off all feeling, starving it of blood; no broken bones, no hanging, no chase, no Ruby or Albus. He flexed his hand again. There was no grinding or indication of any past damage. Almost like it had never happened.

They hanged you, Pilgrim, Voice said.

They didn't do a very good job. He was sitting right here.

You'd be dead if not for getting your hand trapped in that noose. It saved your life. And so did Voice.

Clancy turned right when Abernathy directed her to, putting them eastbound on the I-64, but only half of Pilgrim's brain registered his passengers' hushed conversation or their drops into silence when they became hyper-vigilant, keen eyes directed out the hearse's windows. None of it could pull him out of his head and away from Voice.

He slowed your heart, calmed the beats so that the trickle of oxygen allowed to you was enough. We relieved the desperate hitching in your lungs. You'd have appeared dead. Everything slowed down, no signs of life. Comatose. Still.

He didn't know how that could be possible.

You were unconscious. Helpless. You can hardly bring yourself to trust me now, and it takes a lot more to hand that kind of control over when you're awake and aware. I imagine it'd feel like drowning.

'Or surrender,' Pilgrim murmured.

Yeah. Full surrender. Like how you described it to Gunnar. Except I don't think you were ready to hear it, then. You were just saying the words, not knowing where they were coming from.

Three times, Voice had said. Three times Pilgrim had cheated death. The hanging, the shot to the upper chest (doled out by an antique revolver), and the third time . . . He touched his fingers to the softness behind his ear. A lick of nausea lapped at his stomach, as it always did, but the spot felt firmer. Less sore. It was healing. Slowly. Much more slowly than his shoulder wound had.

It was the reason you warned Abernathy never to shoot anyone in the head. It was how you lost him. Your old Voice. He abandoned you for Lacey, just as Jonah did for Ruby. Two guns and two bullets, both meant to kill but only one doing its job.

There had been a brief period of time, before Vicksburg and backyards and their shallow graves, when Pilgrim's mind was silent. As silent as it had been for most everyone before the voices came. That voice inside Pilgrim's head had been his own, a dual version of him, in delivery and intonation, and he'd believed it was himself he was speaking to, as everyone speaks to themselves in the privacy of their own thoughts. As Jay did, even though he feared it was something more. But it had never been that simple for Pilgrim. The voice he'd heard had mimicked him. It had taken time to adopt its own personality, one that, when he awoke to the churned ground of Ruby's grave, was on its way to being so close to Pilgrim's old Voice it was uncanny – the same Voice Pilgrim had lost to Lacey the very moment he'd gained the terrible injury to his head.

And wasn't that proof? Didn't that mean that both old and

new Voice had come from the same place? For how could two things be so similar, be siblings in attitude and nature, if they had not been born of the same person? If Pilgrim was not, for want of a better word, their father?

The thoughts pounded his head like crashing waves against rocks. It became too much and he asked Clancy to stop the car so he could take over driving. He needed a distraction, something to focus on, or he risked having the thoughts snap and chew on his attention, all these new bits of information arriving with the pounding waves, bringing with them a ravenous pack of piranha to feast on him. All he wanted was to sit and be still.

Settled in the passenger seat, Clancy asked to see Dr Lloyd's folder. It got passed forward from the hearse's rear compartment, where Abernathy sat alone, via Tyler in the back seat and up to Clancy. She spread the papers out on her lap.

As Pilgrim kept his eyes trained on the road, alert to movement of any kind, she began reading parts out. Much of it, she said, was psychological reports.

'This is a recent one,' Clancy said. '"I have spoken to patient #321 on numerous occasions since the procedure. She is incoherent, mumbling, and is unable to hold a level of discourse that is comprehensible by me or anyone else (see report ref. 030321 for individual's assessment prior to treatment). She shows signs of distress and confusion, has severe difficulties in concentration and is experiencing frequent episodes of anger, most often aimed towards staff. She has been in restraints for up to 16 hours per day. The only time she becomes coherent is at night, when the patient sleeps. During these periods, she is calm, although suffering a type of parasomnia in the form of sleep-talking. The words are whispered and of low volume but discernible and of the English language. They include the words *pain, slaughter, burning, sacrifice, madness, death, red* and *skies*. Repeated on a loop. These words coincide with a number of other patients' experiences, most notably patients #307 and #315 (see report refs.

070307 and 020315) in their testimony of their recurring dreams, prior to and post-treatment."'

'Red skies,' Pilgrim murmured. He could feel Jay and Tyler watching him from the back seat. He could feel Voice watching him, too. 'Everything is escalating.'

'Three hundred and thirty-two people,' Clancy said. She leafed through the papers. 'It goes up to patient #332.'

'What happened to them all?' Jay shifted to the edge of his seat and wrapped his arms around Clancy's headrest, looking over her shoulder. She passed the sheet of paper to him.

'Some got taken outside afterwards,' Abernathy said, her voice coming from the back of the hearse. In the rear-view mirror, Pilgrim saw she wasn't looking at any of them but was staring out the back window. 'Rolled out on gurneys in long black bags. We had an incinerator, too, but we could only run it at night.'

Perhaps they had dug a mass graveyard out on the west side of the hospital. The dead in their body bags would explain the flock of circling birds Pilgrim had seen on their way in. Maybe the birds the hearse had disturbed during their escape had been carrion waiting for their breakfast.

'Jesus,' Clancy whispered, and covered her mouth.

Pilgrim thought she was speaking in response to what Abernathy had said, but she'd come to a section of photographs placed in see-through sleeves. He only glanced over for a second, but he recognised the dull-eyed stares, the drooling mouths, the burnt and shiny skin. There were other pictures, too, of patients he hadn't seen; scalps with the thick, black sutures of spiders' legs sewing skulls back up after they'd been split open; excruciatingly thin patients who had their heads wrapped with reams of what appeared to be gaffer tape, their eyes and ears covered so they were rendered blind and deaf.

They really were monsters.

Pilgrim hadn't shared what he'd seen in Recovery with the others, and Abernathy hadn't been forthcoming with the details, either. 'Does it mention other hospitals?' Pilgrim asked, wanting to divert Clancy's attention away from the horror. 'Anywhere else that might be doing similar things?'

Clancy didn't react; she was transfixed by the photos. He said her name and she jumped. A sheen of shock glazed her eyes, and when Jay reached over the seat to take the photographs from her, she let him take them without comment.

'Can you see if they mention any other hospitals?' Pilgrim repeated, saying it slow and even so she could latch on to his words.

She brushed shaky fingers across one cheek, wiping away a tear that had escaped. She nodded. 'Yes. Of course.'

He'd returned his attention to the road when she dug back into the notes, a soft rustle of papers coming from her side of the car. She went quiet for a while as she read, and the others in the back were quiet, too, only the occasional slick of a photograph being turned coming from the back seat. The sombre silence suited the vehicle. The hearse's upholstery was made from equal parts leather and anguish.

'Here's something,' Clancy finally said. 'It's a . . . radio transcript, I think. Between two call-signs.'

'What are the call-signs?' Pilgrim asked.

'W9SLH and W4EF.'

'What do those mean?' Jay asked. He passed the photographs forward and Clancy accepted them and quickly tucked them under the folder where they couldn't be seen.

'Can you say them again?' Tyler spoke from behind Pilgrim's head. She had sat forward in her seat, too, copying Jay.

Clancy reread them.

'Tommy's wondering if the SLH stands for St Louis Hospital.'

'That makes sense.' Clancy scanned the paper. 'What about EF?'

Elysian Fields? Voice suggested.

It fit, Pilgrim couldn't deny it.

A second later, Tyler asked, 'What's Elysian Fields?'

Pilgrim silently cursed. Both he and Voice needed to start remembering that he could be overheard now.

'Something Jackson told me,' he said, not ready to share but not seeing how he could avoid it. 'He said it was out on the East Coast.' He didn't mention the South Carolina part. He remembered that Abernathy had told him there was a larger facility out east, too. Everything seemed to fit.

'The East Coast is a big area,' Clancy said.

So was South Carolina. But maybe the radio transcript could narrow it down. He nodded to her lap. 'What else does it say?'

She went back to the notes, didn't look up from the pages in her lap for long minutes. 'Seems they're checking in with each other. Asking about test results. Seems W4EF are conducting experiments, too? Something to do with the electro-conductivity of . . . bone and brain tissue. They . . .' She paused to read some more. 'They keep referring to "FM". Asking for news about "FM".'

'The bandwidth?' Jay asked, still hanging off the back of her seat.

'No. It's always "him" or "he".'

Voice and Pilgrim said it at the same time. 'Flitting Man.'

The rhythmic swipe and thump of the windshield wipers was the only sound to break up the heavy silence. They were on a near-empty stretch of highway, very few abandoned trucks or cars to navigate around; Pilgrim seized the opportunity to lean into the steering wheel and look up at the sky. It was overcast grey, full of rain and dreariness, but the scattering of birds wasn't difficult to pick out. Maybe only ten or so, they'd been keeping pace with them since they had left the hospital.

What are they doing?

'How can so many people know about that guy without him actually, you know, *being around*?' Jay asked.

'He *is* around,' Tyler said, and the soft certainty of her voice sent chills down Pilgrim's spine. 'I think he's always been around.'

She was right. The Flitting Man had been here all along, just like Matilde had said. Biding his time, waiting on the sidelines, for seven long years, until the timing was right. If he'd turned up at the start, immediately following the masses of deaths, he'd have been fighting against a rising tide of panic and confusion, terror and grief. If he'd waited a year, so many had already dug down into their holes, boarding themselves away and attempting to go it alone, to ride out the worst of the storm. Three years and those with voices would have still been too afraid to emerge, because, especially in those early years, they'd have been met by gangs of people like the one that had brutally beaten and hanged Pilgrim from the brewery gates, who wanted nothing more than to exact revenge on those they believed responsible for all their loss. No, the Flitting Man had waited until the time was ripe. For the fear to marinate and become something bitter and resentful, to catch the despair as it turned to unrest, stirring it into a rebellious fervour that *wanted* to strike back because there was nothing left to lose and everything to gain.

Pilgrim didn't speak much after that, his mind a swirling tempest lifting pieces of junk from the roadside and kicking it around his head. Clancy, Jay and Tyler made up for his silence; they talked about what Clancy had said, what it could mean, acting like old friends. Old, annoying friends who didn't know how to be in each other's company without an incessant stream of talking.

Talking helps. You should try it sometime.

But Pilgrim wasn't the only one who was quiet during the drive. Abernathy hadn't spoken more than a handful of words since she'd climbed into the hearse. The polished wood and plinth where the coffins had once been displayed had long ago been ripped out. So, too, had the hidden compartment below where the undertakers would store an extra body (for when they didn't have time to swing by the funeral home between services and morgue pick-ups). Abernathy had shuffled to sit near the rear window, just her and the supplies, as silent and still as one of those long-ago corpses.

After a while Pilgrim stopped the vehicle and told Jay it was his turn to drive. Jay readily swapped places with him and Pilgrim stretched his arms and shoulders as he made his way along the side of the hearse. He opened the back up and climbed in.

Abernathy sat with her arms crossed and her temple resting against the side window. She didn't turn her eyes away from the advertising billboard rising tall on the other side of the freeway. It was a mundane sign, but Pilgrim took pleasure in reading it. *Twin Rivers Camping. Kayaking. Fishing. Canoeing. Cabin Rentals. FUN FOR ALL THE FAMILY.*

'What do you want?'

He didn't want anything, so he didn't answer as he settled down on the opposite side of the hearse to her. Jay had asked for Pilgrim's copy of *Something Wicked This Way Comes* to read, but he had another book and he pulled it from his pocket, running his eyes over the back cover.

Well, look at that.

A soft laugh escaped Pilgrim.

Abernathy's head twisted enough so she could look at him. 'What?'

'What Jackson said about the main character's name. He was right.' Pilgrim offered her the book and, after a long stare, Abernathy took it.

'"Billy Pilgrim,"' she read. She shook her head. Tossed the book on the floor between them and went back to staring out the window. 'Stupid.'

'Jackson read every single word of that book, stupid or not.'

She said nothing.

'Turned every page. Lived inside it.'

'I thought you couldn't read,' she said to the window.

'I couldn't. I can now.'

'Well, congratulations. I'm still not fucking reading it.'

Pilgrim became aware of the lull in the others' conversation. Their spaced murmurs a blatant pretence to cover their eavesdropping.

It was Pilgrim's turn to look out the window. They were passing flooded fields, the grasses darkly green and lush, swimming in water so black and bottomless it could have been ink. What innumerable creatures lived in there, thriving in their untouched worlds? A flourishing eco-system, teeming with life, while Pilgrim's world lay broken and bare, seemingly incapable of doing anything but cause more pain, more misery.

Abernathy turned on him as if he'd said something inciting. 'Reading it won't change a damn thing.'

'It won't,' he agreed. 'But you'll be going where he went, looking where he looked, smiling when he smiled. You'll be in all the same places.'

She fell silent after that, and Pilgrim did, too. The book remained untouched on the floor.

The gentle rocking of the hearse encouraged him to rest his head against the window, his posture unintentionally mirroring Abernathy's. He didn't mean to close his eyes, didn't mean to relax his shoulders and chest, his body curving inward, his breaths evening out, the swells of the road and the drone of his friends' voices lulling him. He didn't mean to sleep.

He dreams of flying.

He is the eyes of a bird. He is its wings. He is its beak and its humming tongue as it calls out. He is trapped in the bird and the bird is trapped by the flow of the wind. Except it isn't the wind, though it feels the same. Invisible. Powerful. Consuming. It crosses the earth in channels, tunnelling through the air in transparent contrails, buffeting the bird's wings. It leads south and the bird banks south. It curves north and the bird wheels a half-circle and wings north.

The bird senses it and, because the bird senses it, Pilgrim senses it, too.

It meets a larger, powerful contrail heading east and its blood sings in its fast-pumping body. It's like a drug and it can ignore it no more than Pilgrim can. They flap their wings and blink into the morning sun.

More birds join them; it has never flown with those not of its kind before. More cawing, more strident birdcalls, so loud the fragile curve of its tiny skull vibrates and its bones, as well as its blood, hum and sing along, and it is a good feeling. A *right* feeling.

It's also right to fly, to keep flying, to not stop flying. It must fly because the singing, humming, *good* feeling in its body is outside of its body, too. The air is singing and its wings are caressed by it.

Blink and blink and blink, the sun is behind them now. The day is darkening. But it is warm and the bird is with its brethren.

Ahead is a forest, but not a forest it has seen before. There are no green leaves, no brown bark, there is only white upon white upon white. A forest of white trunks topped with white flower petals, long and thin, and they move. They spin, round and round, and they can't stop, it can't stop flying, Pilgrim can't stop flying, and it doesn't *want* to stop, and neither do the birds flying beside it, in front of it, behind it, all the birds flying towards the white forest to join the thousands of birds already there, banking in circles, big circles and little circles, following the powerful, singing, humming static in the sky, in the air, in the earth, in their beaks and blood and bones, and they fly into the huge spinning petals, the *death*-petals, as they cut down their sisters and brothers, slicing them out of the skies, and bursts of blood paint the air red and it *drip-drip-drips* off the once-white blades, because that's what they are, they're spinning blades, not petals, and there are bodies on the ground, so many small, feathery bodies, smashed and broken, their wings – wings that have flown so hard and so far to bring them here – are bent and split. Feathers mist the air and it looks like it's snowing, all around snowing, but the snow is black, brown, a darkness of feathers falling to carpet the grass until the forest is nothing but white trees with their spinning death-blades and a for ever field of dead birds.

So many dead.

So many dead.

So many dead.

Slaughter and death and the sky is full of red death, red skies, and Pilgrim and the bird fly together, because that's all they can do. They fly and fly and fly and the thud of the turning blade hits their bodies and it's over so quick they're dying and falling, feathery and falling, dying, like all the other birds, looking up at the red sky because it's red with their blood. It's red, so red, and the bird, it – *they* – the bird and Pilgrim are dead, too.

A wind farm, Voice whispered.

Pilgrim opened his eyes. His heart beat in secret; no one knew how it thundered and shook inside of him. On the other side of the car, Abernathy didn't look up from her reading.

A forest of white and wind. That's what Jackson had said. Watch for a forest.

Pilgrim craned his neck and looked up at the sky. It was still raining, but not heavily. He saw no birds. He shifted on to his knees and leaned over to Abernathy's side of the hearse. Looked out her window, too.

'What're you doing?' she asked, disgruntled at being disturbed.

'There were birds. Following us.'

'Why would birds be following us?'

Why indeed?

Tyler had twisted in her seat. 'What's the matter?' she asked.

The dream had been unsettling, but it was just a dream. And

birds were just birds, even if they did appear to be shadowing them.

Abernathy was still looking at him.

He settled down next to her and searched the sky out the back window. And there they were: an untidy formation of around ten birds. He pointed to them. 'Can you see what kind those are?'

Abernathy lowered the paperback and frowned into the distance. She seemed to be having some trouble focusing on them.

She needs glasses, Voice said.

Tyler hooked her arm over the back seat and clambered into the rear with them. Pilgrim moved a backpack out of her way and she crawled awkwardly over to stare out the rear window.

Eventually, she shook her head. 'There doesn't seem to be one type. It's a mix.'

'I thought birds migrated with their own,' Pilgrim said.

'I think jackdaws and rooks migrate together, but they're from the same family.' She noticed the look Abernathy gave her. 'What? I liked watching birds when I was a child.'

'Of course you did, little rabbit.'

'So you'd class that behaviour as strange?' Pilgrim asked.

'I'd say so.' Tyler went back to watching them. 'What do you think they're doing?'

'Dr Dolittle here thinks they're following us.'

Tyler raised her eyebrows at him. 'Why would they be following us?'

'*Exactly*,' Abernathy said.

'Hey, guys,' Jay called. 'Fuel's getting pretty low.'

'Find somewhere safe to pull over,' Pilgrim told him. 'Tyler needs to give me a lesson before we go any further.'

'I do?' Tyler asked, surprised. 'What kind of a lesson?'

'One that might save my life,' he said.

CHAPTER 2

Surrender

J ay drove them on to a huge forecourt with a long, narrow, roof-covered refuelling station that, when each of its ten or so gas pumps were in use, would have resembled the starting gates of a dystopian *Death Race 2000*-type truck contest. The forecourt was also somewhere those same eighteen-wheelers came to die. The wrecked and rusted carcasses of over twenty sat abandoned across the lot, in all states of disrepair. Three had been dumped at pump numbers 5, 8 and 10.

At its far end the covered roof of the pumping stations met the service station store and, neighbouring it, a family-themed restaurant. Jay parked the hearse outside the restaurant and, while he and Clancy went to investigate the premises, Abernathy hefted the full can of fuel out of the rear. It had been the trickiest item on their list for Abernathy to procure; she had disappeared the night before they went into the west wing and arrived back with it strapped to a dolly. Her clothes had been dishevelled, her hair mussed. When Pilgrim had opened his mouth to ask, she'd stopped him dead with a look and reminded him that he wouldn't like the answer. He'd shut his mouth again.

As he and Tyler wandered across the forecourt towards an empty semi-container, he felt Abernathy's curious eyes on his back. She wasn't the only one who could have secrets.

Both ends of the container had been opened to the elements and Pilgrim dragged out two packing crates for them to sit on. When they were both settled, Tyler looked at him silently. She had pulled on the oversized rain slicker with the too-long sleeves. Her hair was frizzy from the rain but she sat primly, knees together, the cuffs of her jacket laid one over the other on her lap.

'When we met, you told me you thought I'd been resisting Voice.'

'Tommy said that, but yes.'

'I need for her to teach me how to stop,' Pilgrim said.

A slight pinch between Tyler's eyebrows was the only indication of her puzzlement.

'I know he'll be able to hear other voices if I let him. I don't want to resist any more.'

It was as though Voice were holding his breath, his attentiveness knife-sharp. There was a deep awareness there that what Pilgrim was saying was bigger than the simple components of its syllables and sounds.

Tyler nodded slowly. 'Tommy says she can hear him more clearly. He's stronger. Less quiet.'

'That's good. Tell me what else I need to do.'

'It's not really something that can be taught,' she said, a tentativeness to her words as though she were feeling her way. 'It's something you do when you're ready to trust them.' She bit her lip, eyes leaving him to roam the container. There wasn't much to see: leaves, dirt, twigs, empty beer and soda cans, decayed chip packets, a candy bar whose bleached packaging made the brand unrecognisable. When she finally spoke, her words were considered, chosen for him. 'It's been almost eight years since Tommy came. I've heard her every day. I was terrified at first, like everyone was. I thought it meant I would hurt myself. Hurt someone I cared about. But she . . . Tommy never really did that. She told me terrible things, sure: about the world, about those I considered my friends. She got mean about me having one hand, about how I smile wrong, how my hair is ugly, that I'm too nice to the wrong people and not nice enough to others. But all those things were *true*. I couldn't argue because *everything* she said to me was stuff I had to accept about myself. She never could dig out the right thing to prod me with.' Now that Tyler was looking at him, her focus stayed on him and didn't falter. 'We're always fighting ourselves, aren't we? All the time, we fight – our insecurities, our selfishness, our worries, our fears. It can be so exhausting. But I made a decision to accept myself for who and what I am, the bad along with the good. I can't speak for anybody else, but I believe that's what saved me. Maybe it's what'll save us all.'

'Even the worst of us?'

She paused to consider. 'I don't know the answer to that. All I'm saying is, Tommy and I understand each other. I trust her, and she trusts me. And that's everything.'

That's us screwed, then.

Tyler smiled with her eyes. 'You're not screwed. Tommy and her kind watched us for a long time from the stars before coming. They lost as many as we did, remember, but it was all to give us a new start.'

It was strangely similar to what Ruby had said, except she had called it a resetting.

And Ruby wasn't delusional.

A delay while Tommy passed that on, and Tyler smiled outright, unoffended. 'It's not so easy to see the big picture, I know.'

'Many would say we're in a far worse place.'

Tyler's smile faded. 'I know,' she said. 'We have a lot of work to do – difficult work – but at least we're on our way now.'

Pilgrim went into his pocket for Glen's flip lighter and his fold-up knife. Prising the blade out, he thumbed the lighter to life and passed the sharp edge back and forth over the hot flame.

Tyler watched him. 'What're you doing?'

'Trusting,' he said.

Pilgrim, I don't think you should be doing anything rash.

'We don't have the luxury of time. Not where we're going. And I'm feeling pretty good.'

You feeling "pretty good" isn't making me any more confident.

'I trust you,' he said, because he hoped saying it out loud would make it true.

No, you don't. You hate me.

Pilgrim paused what he was doing. 'I don't hate you,' he said quietly. 'Maybe I resent having you here sometimes, but I don't hate you.'

He flicked the lighter closed and put it away. Pushed his sleeve up and bared the inside of his elbow.

'I really don't understand what's happening.' Tyler was openly distressed, and he suspected the only thing keeping her in her seat was the fear he might try to stab her if she attempted to leave.

'It's okay,' he told her. 'You will.'

Pilgrim cut downwards, making sure to go deep, inhaling a quick breath to keep his hand steady. Blood immediately flowed, a red so rich and dark it could have been wine. It spilled from his arm, hitting the container's floor with a soft but rapid *tink-tink-tink*.

Pilgrim closed his eyes and began to count his heartbeats, the numbers flowing with the pumping of his blood as if they, too, were spilling from him.

He heard Tyler move and opened his eyes to find her reaching for him.

'No,' he said, sharp and commanding.

She stopped dead and stared. Then sank back on to her packing crate.

Stop this, Voice begged. *You're bleeding really badly.*

'No,' Pilgrim said again. '*You* stop this.'

Pilgrim leaned his head back and closed his eyes again. Breathed. The roof of the semi-container felt closer. Closer than it should be. It brushed his hair and he tried to ignore it, tried to stop hearing the too-fast *tink-tink-tink*s of his leaking blood, but the roof wouldn't stop pressing down, compressing him into the ground, flattening him to it, steel-hard and unforgiving, front and back. Any light filtering through his clenched eyelids disappeared, bit by bit, and a loose, shifting weight was piled on top of him. Heavy and pungent, it covered his feet, his thighs, his hips and stomach, chest and face. Pile after pile thrown on top, burying him alive. He couldn't move, couldn't speak, he was frozen as soil packed itself into his lungs, his throat, a pressure that squeezed out every ounce of oxygen and pushed panic into his cells. Life bled from him in a silent, open-mouthed scream. He wanted to struggle, thrash, but the earth held him tight in its embrace. He was helpless. Alone. Dying.

Not alone. It's time to breathe.

Every muscle tensed. His fingers ached in their clawed fists. His eyes were squeezed shut so tightly nails stabbed into his temples. His heart accelerated, beating so fast it quivered.

Pilgrim, you have to let go.

But he couldn't. If he did, he'd die.

I won't let you. Trust me. Let me do this.

The voice was one he'd heard for what felt like a lifetime. A voice that had been friend and foe, a confidante, an annoyance, but it was his, and Voice was not scared and Pilgrim *did* trust him. He had to. What other choice did he have? Voice would always be with him, one way or another.

Don't be afraid, Voice whispered.

A *click*. An unlocking. Pilgrim's chest cracked wide, a direct line running through to feed life into him: air, light, blooming space. His lungs were fully open but they sipped in small, calm swallows. His heart expanded, thumped once, twice, kicked into a calmer rhythm and then kicked into an even slower one, the beats halving, halving again. Pilgrim eyelids fluttered and he saw that the container roof was nowhere near his head. He was surrounded by space. He looked down at his arm and there was blood pooled between his feet, but now the flow slowed, slowed, the *tink-tink-tink*s losing their tempo, and then they missed count altogether and stopped.

'Oh my God,' Tyler whispered.

Pilgrim reached into his other pocket, bringing out the first-aid kit he'd grabbed before leaving the hearse. Tyler took it from him and opened it, exclaiming all over again as she cleaned his arm off and blood didn't well up from the deep laceration, didn't trickle free. And still his heart beat its sluggish beat. She bandaged the wound, shaking her head, face blank with disbelief.

For as long as he's needed me, Voice said, and Pilgrim didn't understand what he meant until Tyler spoke.

'How long have you heard him for exactly?' Her ministrations paused as her eyes lifted to his, Tommy no doubt relaying that Voice had already answered her question.

Pilgrim smiled. 'A while. He's a fast learner.'

CHAPTER 3

Allies

The late afternoon sun cast cross-hatched shadows through the bridge's towering metalwork frame, stamping dark slashes on the hearse's hood and dashboard, creeping inside. In the passenger seat, the shadows cut Pilgrim's body into sections. The bridge's suspension cables and supports formed an M, its two distinct curves arching over the interstate, the belly of the road suspended fifty yards above the sedately running river below. It was the perfect place to set up a roadblock.

Vehicles had been piled lengthways across both eastbound and westbound lanes, but directly in front of them, in the centre lane, concrete highway blocks had been angled to form a small throughway, wide enough for a single vehicle to pass. God knew how they'd been positioned; they must have weighed 800lbs a piece. Abernathy had no choice but to slow the car and pull to a stop.

'Oh, this doesn't feel like a trap at all,' she said. 'Nope, not one bit.'

'Voice?' Pilgrim asked.

From the back seat, Tyler beat him to it. 'No one we can hear.'

She didn't even give me a chance, he complained.

'Okay. Stay here. All of you.' Pilgrim said that last part to Abernathy.

She feigned surprise. 'I wasn't planning on budging.'

'Good. You can read your book while you wait.'

Her mouth partway opened. She closed it again and flipped him the bird.

Pilgrim pulled out Birdy's gun as he climbed from the passenger seat, made sure anyone who was looking could see it, too. He started the walk to the blockade and a flurry of shadows swirled over him, skimming the road. He looked up. The birds were up there, swooping and turning, but always coming back to start their gliding banks again, keeping him and the car at their centre.

I'm sure there's some ill omen about birds following you, Voice murmured.

Pilgrim glanced over his shoulder. The sun glared off the windshield, preventing anyone from seeing inside, but he knew they were all following his every move. He carried on to the barricade, approaching cautiously, but all his care was for nothing. No one was waiting to ambush them. The blockade had been a strategic spot at some point in the past, but not for a long while.

He waved Abernathy forward and the hearse rolled towards him. She didn't rush herself.

What in the world made that woman pick a hearse?

'Maybe she thinks it suits her sunny disposition.'

Voice sighed at his attempt at humour. *At least it might discourage a few people from messing with us. It is kind of spooky.*

Abernathy rolled to a stop beside him. 'How much to cross, fella?' she asked, squinting an eye at him through the open window.

'For you?' Pilgrim said. 'Everything you've got.'

She smirked and hooked a thumb towards the back seat. 'How about a surly-mouthed, past-her-prime Yankee? You can have her even if you won't let us cross.'

From behind the driver's seat, Clancy quite seriously mimed strangling Abernathy.

Voice laughed.

Pilgrim shook his head and ducked down to speak to everyone. 'This is as good a place as any to have a conversation,' he said.

'What sort of conversation?' Jay asked, sounding equal parts interested and suspicious.

'About if we part ways here or not.'

Pilgrim stepped back as Abernathy pushed open her door and a minute later he had all four of them lined up and facing him.

Everything led east for him now. He could feel it beat in his blood as though he stood before a huge wind turbine, taller than the tallest redwood, its blades sweeping far over his head, the great gusts of displaced air sounding out the direction to him. *EAST. EAST. EAST.* And he heard Ruby's words, written to him in her letter, as if she were speaking them aloud: '*Those moments when you see a colour that dances brightly, or a number that sings in perfect pitch – heed them. They mean something to you, if to no one else. And that makes them important. Don't be afraid to trust your instincts.*'

'I'm set on this path,' he said. 'I'm stuck fast to it and there's no getting off, even if I wanted to. It's leading me to places I'm not sure I'll be coming back from. This Elysian Fields, for one.'

'Is it like the hospital we came from?' Clancy asked.

Pilgrim shook his head. 'It's bigger.'

'How much bigger?' she asked.

One wind turbine became a dozen wind turbines, and they became fifty, a hundred, a *forest* of wind turbines stretching as far as the eye could see, all their blades turning above the feathered carpet of crushed and bloodied birds at each of their bases.

'Big enough,' Pilgrim replied.

Jay spoke up. 'What about Lacey? She's still out there.'

Pilgrim hadn't mentioned to anyone that Lacey visited him a lot now. She didn't speak any more; she was a silent passenger, riding along with them. Sometimes he'd glance in the rear-view mirror and see her sitting between Tyler and Jay. Sometimes she'd be in the back, leaning against the side window beside Abernathy while the woman read. Occasionally, she stood at the roadsides as the hearse drove past, her head swivelling to follow their progress. She would flit in and out, never staying for long.

'I'm not forgetting her,' Pilgrim said, not looking at the girl who stood three feet behind Jay, her rifle butt resting on the ground, gun leaning against her hip. 'There's an Inn, too. Sixteen miles south of Myrtle Beach. We'll need to make a stop there.'

'That's a very precise location,' Abernathy said.

'There's someone there I hope can help us.' Matilde and Ruby may be gone, but there was every chance Albus was still around. It was worth checking. Pilgrim had the feeling he'd need as many allies as he could get in the days to come. He needed to understand more about the secrets Jonah had imparted to Ruby. More about what Ruby had been doing in her years of wandering with her brother. Pilgrim couldn't imagine she'd have left her twin unprepared for the Flitting Man and his plans.

'Everything's changing,' Tyler said, quieter than the others, the kind of quiet that caught your attention and grasped it tight. 'I know you feel it. It's impossible not to. The Flitting Man, us, what we found in that hospital. It's like a big wheel is winding us tighter and tighter, and soon it'll be wound so tight it'll either snap and unravel, or else explode, spitting pieces of us out. I'm not sure which it'll be.'

'I'm staying,' Jay said, and he seemed to draw himself up when Pilgrim looked at him. 'I'll never find my cousin. I've known that from the start. But me and Manny were never like you. The way you talk about Lacey . . . You try to pretend like it's not there, but I can see how much you love her. She's not just someone you miss because you're scared of being on your own. That's how I miss Manny. Sometimes I try to imagine his face but all I can see are parts: his eyes when he got mad; the way he chewed on his moustache. But I can't hear his laugh any more – that's already gone. He was never the kind of family to me like you and Lacey are to each other. I stared at her so much in that photo, man, it's like she's *real* to me. As real as Tyler standing right here. And I want to help find her – I always wanted that. I want to shake her hand and say hi. I want to ask her if she likes Ray Bradbury and Stephen King. I can't leave until we find her. I *won't*.'

Lacey wasn't standing behind Jay any more but Pilgrim wasn't looking for her; he was looking at Jay.

Tell him he can come, Voice said.

Pilgrim nodded and said, 'Okay.'

Jay's smile was so wide it dimpled his cheeks. Pilgrim didn't think it was a smile he'd soon forget.

He told the rest they should stretch their legs, have some time to think. Once he got back in the car, he wouldn't be stopping again. They had a lot of miles to cover and he didn't want to waste any more time.

Jay and Tyler wandered off together, stopping at the edge of the bridge to look down at the water below. Abernathy went only as far as the rear of the hearse, where she searched through one of the packs, her arm sunk elbow-deep inside its compartment.

Clancy came to stand beside him, staring out at the bridge as the sun set, those shadows cast from the suspension cables creeping further, stretching into long, slinking arms.

'Someone I met once warned me all this would happen,' Pilgrim said. 'She was very old, had been around a long, long time. She asked me what the Devil looked like. Do you know what she told me?'

He had Clancy's attention as soon as he started talking, her eyes on his lips, watching as each word formed. He felt the power of them as he spoke, weaving some ancient spell, a pattern of sounds and trickery, a slick web that caught her in its grasp. 'What?' she asked.

'She said he looks exactly like us. He didn't have a name back then. He wasn't called the Flitting Man, but she knew he was coming. She told me to remember that there will always be someone who grasps on to what isn't theirs and refuses to let go. That they'd need to be forced to. I understand that everyone's searching for something,' he said, meeting her eyes. 'But I'll never understand the ease with which people fall into believing one way is better or more right than another. When we were in that hospital someone set that place to burn – they left a spiral calling card for all to see – and you know not everyone got out of there alive. Way I see it, no matter what side you're on, you're all still killing each other.'

A faint scowl dented her brow. 'You say "you" and "you're" as if you don't include yourself in any of this.'

'If I could leave you all to fight it out in the dirt, and not come out until the dust had settled, I would.'

'Then why don't you?' she asked. There was no spite in her question, only curiosity.

He felt the weight of the photograph in his pocket, the picture of nine-year-old Lacey smirking out at him. He could see her older, sitting behind a home-made-lemonade stand in the ass-end of nowhere and giving him that same amused smirk. He thought of Ruby and Albus, of them laughing together, of the attentive tilt to Ruby's head as she wrote her letters. She had left a letter in every place they'd visited, a part of herself for someone else to find so that they might feel less alone. But she had never looked back, the same as Pilgrim never had. Now it seemed he could do nothing *but* look back: at the person he'd been, at the people he'd lost. And it didn't hurt to remember them, not like it once had. He *longed* to be with them, to be with Lacey. He ached for Ruby, for what had been done to her, and wished that soon he might see Albus again and tell him that he'd been with her at the end. That she hadn't been alone.

His gaze drifted to his companions. Jay was laughing at

something Tyler had said and her head was tilted up to him, smiling as he laughed. Abernathy had brought out a lighter and was lighting up a cigarette. Pilgrim didn't know where she'd got them from, but she'd always had a knack for getting the things she wanted. He watched the cigarette's tip glow as she drew on it and her eyes closed in pleasure, head tipping back to exhale a long, smoky plume. She saw him watching, smiled a bit and started over to him.

Why didn't he leave them to fight it out in the dirt?

'Because I started to care,' he answered.

From the corner of his eye, he thought he caught a glimpse of a smile from Clancy. Her hand found its way to his arm and gave it a brief, warm squeeze. Surprisingly, he felt no great urge to pull it away from her.

Abernathy reached them and he accepted the lit cigarette she offered. He inhaled a deep, hazy lungful, holding the smoke in for a slow count of three. And that felt warm, too, right in the centre of his chest.

CHAPTER 4

East

They pulled over for bathroom breaks and to stretch their legs and when it became too dark to drive safely, but that was it. Still, it took nearly three days to travel six hundred miles. They had to reroute, slow or backtrack a number of times. People had learned plenty of ways to make a traveller's life difficult. Hidden trenches across roads; steel cabling (particularly hard to spot) stretching from street lamp to street lamp; blockades made up of vehicles or items dragged out of stores and homes. Mounds of desiccated bodies eight feet tall blocked off main streets at both ends, the corpses forming rickety-boned pyres decorated with hanging streamers of paper-skin. Their rot had once covered the cities in rancid hazes, the smell of decomposition so potent it would bury its way into your pores, the stench following you around for weeks. But old bodies didn't smell bad. They smelled of your grandfather's wardrobe. Of musty fabric infused with ageing pinewood. Of dust. Of life that had slipped away. It was almost nostalgic.

It wasn't always *things* that blocked their way or slowed them down. In downtown Sevierville, a child had sat on the sidewalk, waving at them to stop. Jay had been driving and, being the soft touch that he is, he'd automatically slowed the hearse before Clancy spotted that the kid wasn't a kid but a man missing his legs from the knees down. Movement had caught Pilgrim's eye, darting along rooftops, and Abernathy had called out a warning as gunshots rent the air. Clanging thuds hit the hearse and knocked four holes into the front fender before Jay reversed the car so quickly the tyres shrieked like four shrill toddlers demanding to go home. Tyler had covered her ears with bent arms. They lost a side mirror and half their tyre treads.

It would have taken twice as long to travel those six hundred miles if Pilgrim had been alone. Turned out Clancy was by far the best map reader, so Pilgrim, Abernathy and Jay alternated driving duties while she plotted their route. They took turns sleeping in the rear of the hearse, staking claim on the space where corpses had once rested. At one point, Jay and Abernathy were laying back there, both stretched out on their backs, their heads buried in their books. Pilgrim had watched them for a while, ingraining it into his memory like snapping a photograph. It was an image he didn't want to forget.

There was a simple pleasure in driving, in watching the scenery roll by, feeling the wheels turn and the road swell and dip beneath you. The overall atmosphere between everyone was friendly, for the most part. It was only Abernathy and Clancy who clashed, and whether that was down to the close confines of the car and the length of time they'd spent in each other's company, or the dwindling miles between them and the unknown dangers ahead (or something that had spilled open and soured back in St Louis), tensions between the two began to run high.

I'm not sure which would ease the most tension: if Abernathy throttled Clancy, or if Jay dry-humped Tyler's leg and got it out of his system.

Jay was driving, Clancy riding shotgun. Pilgrim and Abernathy were in the back, and Tyler was trying to sleep in the rear, though the raised voices would be making that difficult.

'*Of course* you were,' Abernathy was saying, tone biting with sarcasm. 'How could I have not guessed that? You've got the exact right ratio of patronising helpfulness and know-it-all superiority that ninety-five per cent of all teachers have. Wait, let me try and guess what ages you taught.' She rubbed at her temples as if massaging the answer out. 'Fifteen to sixteens. Am I right?'

Clancy didn't turn around but kept her head bowed over the map. 'No. You're wrong – as you so often are. Eleven to twelves.'

'Oh, well. Kids are kids, right? They're all stupid until they hit eighteen, and even then it's hit and miss.'

'It's hit and miss when some get to their late twenties, too,' Clancy said, and Pilgrim winced at the pinpoint accuracy of her barb.

'I bet you taught some really fucking boring subject, too,' Abernathy said, not finished with her. 'Like Geography. Or Social Sciences.'

'I taught English. My turn to take a stab at something.' Pilgrim thought one of the reasons Abernathy was getting so mean was because Clancy refused to look at the woman when she spoke to her. 'You didn't finish school, did you?'

Abernathy stared at the back of Clancy's head, her mouth a flat line.

'You dropped out and probably got to be a familiar face to the local police force. How am I so doing so far?'

'Guys, can we not do this?' Jay asked, sounding tired. 'This really isn't conducive to a relaxed driving environment.' They had entered the Great Smoky Mountains an hour earlier, the winding road climbing as it followed sheer rock walls and metal safety barriers, the hearse's wings only ever a few scant inches away from screeching contact. The route needed concentration.

Abernathy slow-applauded him. '"Conducive". *Great* word choice there, Sanjay. I'm sure Teach here will give you extra brownie points for that one.'

Clancy finally turned in her seat, but it was only to show Abernathy the self-satisfied smile she wore. 'I'm right, aren't I? High school dropout. Extensive criminal record.'

'Fuck you.'

'*You* started this, Abernathy. You can dish it out, but you can't take it?'

Pilgrim's eyes flicked down to Abernathy's lap. Her hands were balled into fists on her thighs.

You're going to have to break this up, Voice told him.

It wasn't his place to mediate. They were both adults.

They're not acting like it.

Pilgrim was sure they would see the pointlessness of their argument eventually; there was no students left to teach and no high schools to drop out of any more. What had happened in their pasts held little to no relevance here.

You give them too much credit. If they weren't arguing about this, they'd find something else to argue about.

'Why are you even here?' Abernathy asked Clancy. 'You just *decided* to come along for the ride with a bunch of people you hardly know? At least me and Christopher have history. You're—'

'I,' Clancy corrected. 'You meant to say, "Christopher and *I*".'

Abernathy punched the back of Jay's chair – through pure frustration, Pilgrim was sure – but it was hard and unexpected, and the hearse swerved.

Jay stomped on the brakes and the car's back end fish-tailed as it rocked to a stop.

Pilgrim, Voice said, and he sounded distracted. *There's something's not right here . . .*

There was no need to worry about being rear-ended – there was no other traffic on the two-lane route besides them – but Pilgrim did a quick three-sixty anyway. They were at higher elevation here, sandwiched between sheer, wet rockface to their left and a view that dropped off to their right, a verdant sea of

National Park trees spreading out for tens of miles, blanketed in mist. They were in more danger of being ambushed by a moose or a bear than by other humans.

Pilgrim, I think I—

'Would you guys *shut up?*' Jay had twisted in his seat so he could glare at both Clancy and Abernathy. 'I've *had* it with you two. You've been at each other's throats all day. Can't you give it a rest?'

Unimpressed by his outburst, Abernathy said, 'No need to get your garters in a bind.'

Voice's cry was so unexpected a jagged seam of glass ground into the back of Pilgrim's skull. It was a broken, wretched cry and Pilgrim cried out with him; he had never heard such a sound from him before. It sent a panicked, prickly heat bursting through him and he fumbled for the door release, needing to get out.

His knees hit blacktop and he sucked in a breath. Hanging from the handle, he dragged at the collar of his shirt, needing to feel cool air on his skin.

When he raised his head, Lacey was waiting for him.

She was too far away to see her features clearly, but he knew it was her. She stood at the next bend in the road, the road curving out of sight.

Pilgrim, Voice rasped. *I heard myself. It sounded just like me. I was calling out and I was so loud.*

Lacey didn't come any closer, only gazed back at him. She slowly unslung her rifle from her shoulder.

Voice was still talking. *It came out of nowhere. A massive blast. It was like being pummelled in the head.*

She flipped the rifle around and, when Pilgrim saw what she was doing, he staggered to his feet and away from the door.

Voice raised his voice when Pilgrim started to run. *It came from her, Pilgrim! I can hear it echoing back to where she is!*

His friends shouted after him, but Pilgrim didn't stop, didn't turn around or waste his breath.

The barrel of the rifle slid into Lacey's mouth. She had to stretch for the trigger. It was an awkward reach, but she could manage it. Her thumb hooked into the trigger guard.

'*No!*' Pilgrim shouted, frantic. He ran faster. He heard someone chasing after him, but they couldn't catch him. No one could.

The gunshot ricocheted off rocks and tree trunks and hard-packed ground. The blast blew out the back of Lacey's head and the girl dropped to the road.

His gasping breaths stripped the skin from his throat, his blood thundered, his heart became a battering ram. He ran so fast the world fell away from him, colours distorting and bleeding into the wind. The road and trees became formless and untouchable. He reached the bend in the road in maybe twenty seconds, stood on asphalt and soil, but no blood, no bits of brain or bone. There was no whiff of discharged gunpowder. And no Lacey.

He turned on the spot, lungs pumping as he struggled to regain control. Miniature waterfalls splashed down the rockface to his left. He went to the safety barrier and leaned over its edge. A fall of maybe a hundred feet, the covering canopy of trees blocking any view of the ground.

She's not here, Pilgrim, but I . . . A rising wonder broke through Voice's words, brightening them as the sun brightened and flickered through tree trunks as you drove past. *I think I know where she is.*

Slaps of feet pounded up behind him and Jay almost ran into the barrier. Not far behind came Abernathy, her gun drawn.

Jay panted, gulping at the air. 'You're like . . . a cheetah.'

Abernathy sucked in her own quick breaths before saying in a panting rush, 'What the hell did you see?' Her eyes darted, her whole body alert.

He turned from them, concentrating on Voice. 'Where?' Pilgrim demanded.

South-east, Voice said immediately. *It came from the south-east.*

'How far?'

I don't knooow! he whined. *I'm not Tommy. I'm still learning.*

The hearse approached, driving down to meet them. Clancy was at the wheel and Tyler gazed through the windshield from the passenger seat, eyes large as she watched Pilgrim stride towards them. The car was still moving when he yanked open her door.

'Did Tommy hear it, too?'

There was a pause as Tyler's eyes shifted to his left. After a moment, she shook her head. 'She didn't hear anything out of the ordinary. But she knows Voice heard something.'

It was a burst of sound, Voice rattled out, the same adrenaline coursing through him as it was Pilgrim. *Like turning a stereo on full blast, but it was too garbled to work out what he was saying. I could tell he was shouting, though. He was . . . I think he was afraid for her.*

Pilgrim said it out loud for Tyler and the others' benefit.

It was like hearing myself, Pilgrim. Trapped in a storm and yelling as hard as I could.

There was only one other thing on this entire planet that sounded like Voice. The door to his own Voice's locked-in world, a world that had centred exclusively on Pilgrim, had been slowly cracking open ever since they'd heard '*Burning*', '*Slaughter*' and '*Death*' together back in Vicksburg, but now that door was being beaten down. These revelations came saddled with feelings of amazement, yes, but they also came with a healthy dollop of paranoia.

Voice had fallen into silence and Pilgrim knew he was listening to something he couldn't hear. Two separate sides of Voice existed now: a spouse who Pilgrim knew intimately, but also an adulterer who was sneaking off to meet some stranger at a seedy, backwater motel.

Tyler smiled slowly, as if she were watching him unwrap a

birthday present. 'They're talking freely to each other. I hear her speaking to him.'

Abernathy hadn't put her gun away and, going by the scowl she wore, she wasn't in a mind to. She turned to Jay. 'You realise we're the only normal ones here, right?'

'I thought "normal" usually applied to the majority?' he said. 'They outnumber us three to two.'

Her scowl deepened. 'Shut up,' she told him.

Pilgrim left Tyler and headed around the hood, brushing by them, 'Stop talking and get in the car,' he growled. 'I'm driving.'

Voice guided them south-east in a direct line to the coast. Checking the map, Clancy said they would hit somewhere between Myrtle Beach and Charleston if they headed straight through.

Pilgrim couldn't stop himself asking one last time. 'You're sure about this?'

Of course I'm not sure, Voice snapped. *But I heard it.* There was a hesitation, but it was so fleeting Pilgrim could have imagined it. *I can find her.*

Pilgrim's foot lay heavy on the gas pedal. He braked late into corners and accelerated hard out of them, pushing the hearse up to seventy on straights. From the corner of his eye, he saw Clancy glance repeatedly at the speedo.

'We're going to eat through the last of our fuel,' she said, concerned.

He knew, but he didn't ease off the gas. Though he felt closer to finding Lacey than he ever had, she hadn't 'spoken' to him since they'd been in the Unit. Rationally, he knew that had more to do with his mental state than her physical one, but it felt like an ill omen all the same. He didn't know if watching the phantom image of her blow her brains out meant anything, but he'd grown accustomed to trusting his instincts and his instincts were a gun between his shoulder-blades urging him to go faster, to press the gas harder, telling him that speed was more important than fuel.

He paid little attention to Voice, who held a muted one-sided conversation in the back of his head with Tommy. It could be a distraction if Pilgrim let it (he didn't let it). Tyler and the others asked questions, but when Pilgrim answered in monosyllabic grunts, they gave up and talked between themselves instead. He left Tyler to explain the intricacies of how hearing other voices worked. She'd do a far better job of it than him.

The needle on the fuel gauge tipped into red. He didn't know how far the hearse's reserve tank would take them but Pilgrim pushed the vehicle even harder, knowing it was foolish but doing it anyway. He felt possessed, his control hanging by a thread so frayed all it would take was a single tug to snap it.

He didn't know how long he'd been driving when someone laid their hand on his shoulder. He stiffened. He expected it to be Clancy's, maybe even Tyler's, but it was Abernathy who squeezed him.

'You need to calm down,' she said.

'I can't.' And it came out taut, seeded with desperation, and that served only to harden his stomach and clench his hands on the wheel.

Voice was silent and Pilgrim felt an expanding in the back of his head, an inflating like a balloon. Not uncomfortable but elastic and growing. He noticed Tyler straighten in her seat and lean forward, her seatbelt stretching out before locking her in place.

Abernathy had shifted closer, her mouth near to his ear, breath ticklish. 'Would you die for this girl, Christopher?' she asked.

He already had, in his way. 'Yes,' he said.

'Good, because you'll end up dead in a car wreck before you get anywhere near her if you don't calm the fuck down.'

A rustle of a map. Clancy's arm appeared from the back seat and she pointed. 'Here. Keep left.'

The road skirted a large lake, following its long northern bank. The skeletons of boats bobbed in a gentle line, tethered to a submerged jetty, only the mooring posts visible. On the far end of the lake a glass-fronted restaurant or hotel looked out over the water.

'They're hearing something,' Tyler whispered.

Tommy is helping me, Voice told Pilgrim. *She says we're getting closer.*

'How close?' Pilgrim asked.

She can't hear past a city block or so, but this is much further. Twenty miles, maybe? It's hard to pinpoint. But we're going the right way.

Twenty miles was nothing if Pilgrim put his foot down.

He stamped the gas pedal.

Nothing happened.

He stamped it again.

No spurt of speed. No power. Nothing.

Tyler had unbuckled her seatbelt and was leaning against the dashboard, her face close to the windshield. She looked over at him. 'Let's *go.*'

They had come around the head of the lake and were chugging their way uphill past the window-fronted restaurant. *Lakeview Fine Dining,* the sign said.

'No, no, no,' Pilgrim muttered. '*No.*' He slammed his palm on the steering wheel.

The hearse's engine didn't cough or splutter, it didn't jerk them in their seats or blast out a greasy cloud of smoke, it simply cut out. Silence filled the vehicle as the last of their momentum rolled them to the brow of the hill, slowing, slowing as the hearse hit the road's gentle summit, nose tipping over the crest, weight carrying them over. They coasted down the other side, picking up speed. Pilgrim shifted to neutral. They rolled another three hundred yards.

Pilgrim didn't say a word as he set the parking brake and got out. He went to the rear of the hearse and popped open the hatch, grabbing two large bottles of water, two wrapped packages of food, a flashlight, his first-aid kit, two spare hoodies, their extra map, and stuffed everything into one of the packs. It had started to rain, a fine, gentle shower, a good ten degrees warmer than cold. He pulled on the long, waxed raincoat he'd taken from the fishing and tackle store in St Louis and, by the time he'd slung the pack over his shoulder and was checking the steel-grey handgun he'd picked off Birdy's body (its magazine was one round short, which left him with eleven), the others had joined him.

'You're going on foot?' Jay asked.

'No, he's going to flap his arms and fly.' Abernathy reached past Pilgrim and started stuffing her own gear into a second pack. He said nothing as he followed her movements, an odd feeling of gratitude stirring inside him.

'What?' she asked, noticing him watching her.

'Nothing,' he said.

Clancy and Tyler stood together as Abernathy slipped on her jacket and Jay squatted to tighten and retie the laces on his boots.

The older woman was as still as a statue, her face pale. 'I'm not sure I'll be able to keep up with you,' she said.

'The Inn I told you about,' Pilgrim said to her, as he finished checking the gun and tucked it behind his belt. 'Sixteen miles south of Myrtle Beach. On the coast. It's called the Norwood Cove. Head there and we'll meet you. If there's a man called Albus there, tell him Hoyt sent you.'

'I'll go with her,' Tyler said.

'No. I need you. Voice needs Tommy. He can't do this by himself. Jay will go.'

Jay stopped double-knotting his shoes and shot up. 'What? Hey, no. I'm coming with you.'

'It'll be safer for Clancy if you go with her,' Pilgrim told him.

Jay glanced over at Clancy, guilt lowering his head, same as it did his voice. 'But why me? Can't you send Abernathy?'

'I don't trust many, Jay, but I trust you. I know you'll get her there.'

'But . . . I thought we would find Lacey together. That's what I said to you back on the bridge. It's why I came. I want to help.'

The way he said it made Pilgrim reach for Jay's shoulder and grip it. 'I know. But right now you'll help most by doing this for me. Keep hold of her book, okay? And, here, take the photo.' He pulled it out of his shirt and offered it to him. 'You can give them back in a couple of days when I see you.'

Not looking at him, Jay accepted the photo and stepped back out of Pilgrim's reach.

'Listen,' Tyler said, looking uneasy. 'I'm not going to be able to keep up with you any better than Clancy. I can't run.'

'You will. I'll help you.' He looked to Abernathy. 'Ready?'

She nodded, settling her pack on her shoulders. 'All set.'

'The Norwood Cove Inn,' Pilgrim told Jay. 'Sixteen miles south of Myrtle Beach. Say it back to me.'

'I—'

'Say it, Jay.'

Abernathy handed Tyler her rain slicker and, lost in a daze, Tyler slipped the jacket on. Clancy stepped in front of her to thread the zipper.

Like helping her kid get ready for school, Voice said.

As if the words were being dragged from him, Jay said, 'The Norwood Cove Inn. Sixteen miles . . .' he faltered.

'South,' Pilgrim said.

'South. Of Myrtle Beach.'

'Good. We'll see you both there.' Pilgrim looked at Clancy. She'd finished fastening Tyler's slicker and was lifting the woman's hood up for her. She didn't look at him when she nodded. 'See you there.'

Tyler stared at the older woman, at a loss, and Clancy pulled her into a hug. She rubbed the younger woman's back before letting her go, and Jay moved in to hug Tyler, too. She kissed his cheek, held on to his hand until Pilgrim pulled her away and broke their clasp. He towed her after him up the road, not looking back.

You should *look back. This time, you should look.*

He was holding the crook of Tyler's arm, marching them up the two-lane highway – Tyler had to take two quick steps for each of his long strides. As they came to a curve in the lane, Pilgrim felt his pace slow, his boots grow heavy, and before they walked out of sight, he halted. Abernathy walked right past them and kept on going.

Clancy and Jay were standing side by side. Jay cupped his hands around his mouth and Pilgrim heard the thin thread of his shout, dampened by the rain.

'*Good luck!*'

Tyler lifted her hand in a wave and Jay waved back.

For some reason, Pilgrim found himself staring at Clancy. She hadn't retrieved her jacket from the car. She stood motionless, the rain soaking her through. As they'd walked to St Louis Hospital she'd asked if any of them would get a name-check at the end of all this, and he'd somehow failed to reassure her. But she wasn't nameless to him and he wouldn't forget her. He didn't want to be that person any more.

Pilgrim raised his hand to her, their eyes meeting across the distance.

After a moment, she raised hers in return.

He couldn't be sure, but he thought she smiled.

CHAPTER 5

Lucky Rabbit Paw

It was full dark, the moon faded out, veiled by wispy, diaphanous clouds. They had been cutting through fields to save time; it was quicker, but the land was boggy and uneven.

For the fifth time, Pilgrim heard a soft gasp behind him, followed by a thump, and he turned to find Tyler on the ground. He went to her and helped her up, hands scooped under her armpits as if she were a child. His shoulder, which had begun to feel completely whole again, complained at the extra weight, slight though it was.

From the knees down, his pants were caked with mud. His shirt sleeves were soaked through to the shoulder, despite him wearing a slicker. Tyler looked as though she'd spent the evening wrestling pigs. He supported her with a hand under her arm as they continued their trudge through the thigh-high grass.

No one had spoken for a while; no one had the breath or the desire to speak.

'We should take a break,' Abernathy said, mist puffing from her mouth. 'It's too dark to walk straight.'

She's right. Someone's going to turn an ankle out here. Then we'll be screwed.

The thought of stopping made every muscle in Pilgrim's body stiffen in resistance. He had to consciously loosen his grip on Tyler's arm when he heard her sharp intake of breath.

'Let's head back to the road.' Abernathy didn't wait for his agreement but veered right, slogging her way through the field.

Pilgrim didn't move. Tyler murmured his name and, looking down at her exhausted, dirty face, he sighed. He turned and followed after Abernathy.

A mile later, they found an old mobile trailer driven off the road; it canted at an angle, its tyres missing. Pilgrim had to kick a path through the weeds and undergrowth to get to the door. It didn't smell great inside – the walls were spongy with damp and the carpeting had rotted away in mangy patches – but it had walls and a roof and the leaking was minimal.

'Come on, little rabbit, let's get you out of this.' A surprisingly considerate Abernathy helped Tyler out of her sodden raincoat and hung it to dry over a cupboard door. She stared for a moment at the smaller woman's hand, mud having caked up her wrist from where she'd fallen, and then she cleaned the dirt off, spending longer on the task than Pilgrim expected her to. He passed Abernathy the spare hoodie he'd brought along and she tucked the woman's arms inside it and fastened the zipper. She didn't once crack wise about Tyler's missing hand.

It wasn't cold, but Tyler's teeth chattered. Abernathy pulled the hoodie's hood up over her hair and rubbed Tyler's arms to warm her. She met Pilgrim's eyes over her head. He read the grimness of her look to mean *She's not going to hold up much longer*, and he shrugged uncomfortably, rolling his sore shoulder. He'd push them as hard as needed.

They ate and drank in small sips. It wasn't long before the aches bedded in for the night: his feet, his knees, his back and shoulders – all his joints throbbed abominably. His chest started to make an odd clicking noise when he breathed too deeply. It tickled him into rattling coughs.

Tyler had curled herself up on the floor next to them, her sleeve-covered hand tucked under her cheek. Pilgrim and

Abernathy sat across from each other, their backs pressed to cabinets, feet flat on the floor and knees bent to fit into what was once the trailer's compact kitchenette.

Voice came back from wherever he went when he withdrew to listen ahead.

Everything's gone quiet. But it's late. They're probably resting.

'The closer we get, the better you'll be able to hear where they are?' Pilgrim noticed how Abernathy's gaze sharpened on him.

That's what Tommy says. She hears another voice now. Not our Voice. I can't hear it at all. But she says it sounds angry.

'Angry about what?'

She doesn't know. She can't hear what it's saying yet. It's still too far for her.

'What about Lacey? You hear her Voice?'

I sense him more than hear him, Voice said. *But I know it's Voice whispering in all the static; it's like listening to an old recording of myself.*

'They'll need to be quiet soon,' Tyler murmured.

Her eyes were a dull shine in the dark. He'd thought she was sleeping.

'They'll hear us coming if Voice and Tommy talk too loudly,' she said.

He hadn't thought of that. 'How soon?'

'We wouldn't want to risk anything. Maybe two miles at most. Tommy hears this other voice because it's strong. Stronger than her. But it'll hear her, too, eventually.'

'"Stronger than her",' Abernathy said, listening to them. 'What does that mean?'

'It means it must have been here longer. Could have even been one of the pioneers to this planet.'

Voice snorted gently and murmured, *Aliens.* He began to sing softly, something about being in a tin can far above the moon and the earth being blue. The melody was familiar.

'Is it Flitting Man strong?' Pilgrim asked, trying to tune out the singing.

Tyler was silent for a moment. 'No. Not anywhere near as strong as that.'

Voice stopped singing. *How'd she know?*

The dull shine of Tyler's eyes disappeared when she closed her eyes. It didn't take long for her breathing to deepen and even out. The rain drummed soft fingers on the roof as Pilgrim waited for the infinitesimal slump in her shoulders to indicate she was sleeping for real this time.

Abernathy was a shadowy shape in the dimness. She'd also pulled her hood up. He couldn't tell who she was looking at, but her head was angled in Tyler's direction.

'"Pioneers to our planet"?' Abernathy said, a dark mockery in her hushed voice. 'Seriously? I'm starting to think I should have done myself a favour and got myself blown to smithereens back at the hospital.'

'You'll have plenty more opportunities. There's every chance we could die tomorrow.'

A soft, breathy laugh. 'Boy, I'm so lucky to have such a ray of sunshine in my life.' He heard her draw in a breath and release it on a long, sobering sigh. 'Do you have any idea what we'll be walking into?'

'No. That's why we have guns.'

'Guns can't save us from everything, Christopher.'

'They've saved me a time or two.'

They're also responsible for your broken head and your bum shoulder.

He decided to not pass that on.

Abernathy was silent for a time. The clouds cleared outside, moonlight slipping through the grimy Perspex windows. The gloom inside the trailer lifted a shade or two.

'I should have stopped what they were doing,' she said quietly, almost as if speaking to herself. 'I knew it was wrong. I knew what I was doing was wrong, but I kept doing it anyway.'

She was playing with her fingers, tugging at each one, doing an inventory, then starting over again. He couldn't help but count them with her.

'You had your reasons,' he said.

'Maybe. But I didn't think about them too closely. I never do.' Her finger-tugging stopped and he got the feeling she was looking directly at him from inside her hood. 'You know, when I was younger, I used to think I might be dead – and I don't mean in a melodramatic way, like one of those prissy queen teens who got upset when no one paid them enough attention, or, God forbid, the boy they liked didn't ask them to prom. No, I felt like a real dead person, walking around like everyone else but not feeling a thing: not happiness or sadness, not fear or exhilaration or love. Only this numbed emptiness. So, I got it in my head I needed to check myself to see. I picked the easiest way I could think of. If I cut myself and I bled, that must mean I was alive, right? And I did feel it, Christopher. The pain as I sliced open my skin and watched what was inside me suddenly spill to the outside, it was the most thrilling thing I'd ever felt. Even when everything else was numb, the pain was always real and it made me feel real, too, like I was a part of the world just like everyone else was. For the longest time I tried so hard to understand the emotions that ruled over the rest of you, because all I seemed to get were these weak facsimiles of them. But honestly? From where I'm sitting now? I think I got the better end of the deal.'

The darkness between them breathed, a slumbering rise and fall, as if the black bear from the Unit had followed them out here and settled down between them. He could feel the warmth of Abernathy's leg close to his. It was very real and very alive, despite what she'd said. She bumped her knee against his and left her leg resting against him.

Her hands disappeared inside her hood as she rubbed at her

face. 'I find things to latch on to, and they help keep me grounded. Jackson did that for me. Even Birdy, to an extent. All those years, I did what I did, and I slept like a kitten every night. Don't think that I didn't. But sometimes . . .' Her hands fell, dropping to her lap, and her voice weakened, got lost somewhere in the back of her mouth. 'Sometimes I wonder what would happen if all the things I've done rose out of the ground and came for me. I think they would bury the world. And when they did, I don't think I'd care much. A facsimile of regret, that's what I'd feel.'

Her leg rested heavier on his now, as if she'd given up on holding it upright.

'People like us need others,' Pilgrim said into the breathing silence. 'We don't think we do, but we need to be told when we're stepping too far off the path, when we're wading into the wildness that grows at the sides. But they need us, too. Because we do what they can't.'

'Yeah, I think you're right about that. That last bit, anyway.'

A *snick* sounded in the quiet. The trailer may have been lit by nothing but weak moonlight but it was enough to see the faint shine of her switchblade.

'Abernathy . . .' he began, and she must have felt his leg tense because she clamped his ankle in a forestalling grip.

'Stop.'

Before he could do or say anything, she grabbed Tyler by her hoodie and dragged the gasping woman on to her back, pinning her to the floor. Tyler screamed, but Abernathy struck her so hard across the face she was stunned into silence.

Abernathy fisted a handful of the woman's hair and yanked her throat bare. Pressed the point of the blade to her skin.

'It was you, wasn't it, little rabbit?' She leaned low to breathe her words into Tyler's face. 'Sneaking around down there in the dark, setting your fires. It's plain as mud to me now. I told you not to forget your homework, and you didn't.'

Pilgrim was on his knees, his hand buried in the back of Abernathy's sweater, but that's as far as he got. He didn't try to pull her off.

'All those damned maps I drew showed you exactly where to go, didn't they?' Abernathy must have either tightened her grip on Tyler's hair or pressed harder with the blade because Tyler winced. 'How many died? Trapped by the fires, crushed under the ceilings? How many did you kill?'

Tyler's face may have been creased in pain, but she didn't recoil from the accusations. 'You're the only killer here, Abernathy,' she whispered, and she didn't sound angry or scared. She was stating a fact. 'You've been killing us for years.'

'Oh, it must be nice to feel so *righteous*. How did you do it, hm? Was it that cache of fuel in the generator room? Did I make it *easy* for you, little rabbit, giving you *so much* fucking information? You know what you did was for nothing, though, right?' Abernathy's voice was hardening, her anger a serrated, cutting edge. 'You realise that, don't you? We were already stopping everything they were doing. There was no need to blow everything up.'

'It's not just about stopping them,' Tyler said, eyes squinting with pain. She shifted her head back a little to ease the pressure at her throat. 'It's about them understanding that they can't do those things to us. Not any more. Not ever again. He's here now and he's not going away. None of us are.'

Pilgrim sat back on his heels, staring at the young woman pinned to the floor, at her oversized hoodie and thin arms. There was absolutely nothing threatening about her, and that's what had made her camouflage so perfect. He'd watched Jay clean her hand with a cloth, but he should have looked closer. It hadn't been dirt he'd been wiping away, it had been paint. Brown spray paint. Pilgrim had been right – Abernathy hadn't spray-painted that crop-circle-sized spiral on the concourse floor, the biggest calling card of them all.

'Were you alone?' he asked Tyler.

Her eyes turned to him, except they weren't her eyes, were they? They were Tommy's eyes. They were the Flitting Man's. 'I'm never alone,' she told him, her whisper sending a shiver crawling up his back, a chill that had nothing to do with the dampness of his clothes or the *plip-plip-plip* of water dripping in the corner. 'And neither are you. You should know that by now.'

'What about Jay?' he asked. 'He helped clean you up. I saw him. You've been spending a lot of time together.'

Her demeanour cracked; a slight wobble of her lip. 'He had nothing to do with it, I swear. He doesn't know what I did.'

Pilgrim wasn't sure what alerted him; maybe it was a subtle tensing in her muscles or a creak in the rotting floorboards, but he caught Abernathy's wrist as her hand jerked. The blade's point cut into Tyler's neck. Both women hissed, one through anger at being interrupted and the other through pain. But it was only a nick.

'What're you *doing*?' Abernathy demanded, yanking her arm out of his grip.

'I need her.'

'*I* don't need her for shit! She's *dangerous*, Christopher. People are dead because of her. Jackson's dead. She's a fucking terrorist.'

We still need her, Voice said, and he sounded both pained at the admission and apologetic. *I can't do this by myself.*

'I said I need her,' Pilgrim repeated.

'To find your precious Lacey?'

There was real animosity in Abernathy's words, but Pilgrim didn't take it personally. She had lost someone who had meant everything to her. Jackson had been her touchstone in that regimented, artificial world, her one anchor point, and he might still be here if not for what Tyler had done.

'Check her for weapons,' Pilgrim said. 'We'll take turns watching her tonight.'

Abernathy stared at him for an uncomfortably long time then shook her head in disgust. But she did as he asked and started patting Tyler down. She wasn't gentle about it.

'I don't have any weapons.' Tyler yelped when Abernathy shoved her on to her front to check her back pockets. 'I'm not – *ow!* I'm not a terrorist. We're on the same side.'

'Be quiet,' Pilgrim told her. 'Go to sleep. You'll need all your strength for tomorrow.'

Abernathy had come prepared with more zip ties and, for the second time, Tyler got fastened to the belt-loop of her pants.

'You know that Billy Pilgrim character in Jackson's book?' Abernathy asked, grunting in effort as she tightened a second zip tie around Tyler's wrist (she wasn't taking any chances). She had secured the woman to a rear belt-loop this time, twisting Tyler's arm awkwardly behind her in order to reach. Pilgrim didn't interfere. Tyler was lucky Abernathy hadn't slit her throat.

'Yes,' he said. He'd been the one who pointed the character out to her.

'He's a complete and utter idiot.'

In the back of his head, Voice made a soft snorting sound.

Pilgrim waited, but nothing else was forthcoming. 'That's it?' he asked.

'Yes. I wanted to share with you that the name you'd picked out for yourself suited you better than you realised.'

'Well. Thank you.'

'You're welcome. You're on first watch.'

She backed off, leaving Tyler trussed up on her stomach, and settled down at the far end of the kitchenette, as far away from them as she could get. He watched her lean her hooded head back against the sink unit and fold her arms, tucking her hands into her armpits.

She did a good impression of sleeping, even if she didn't get any.

★ ★ ★

459

It was harder to start once you'd stopped. In the few short hours they'd rested, every muscle had seized and every ligament stiffened, and Pilgrim knew Abernathy and Tyler were hurting just as much as him; in the gloom of pre-dawn he saw the shadows of it clench across their faces, recognised it in their limping gaits. Neither woman complained, though.

Voice had been readjusting their direction when needed and, as the sun broke free, they came upon a small town the signs all identified as Norwich. They stayed on the outskirts. Pilgrim felt conspicuous as they jogged through silent, uninhabited suburbia, long lines of identikit homes and their overgrown front yards, rusted family vehicles abandoned crooked on sidewalks and in the middle of streets. A sedan had careened into the front of one house, its rear end poking lewdly out, the whole building slumping around it like a squatting dog readying to poop it back out.

As they left Norwich behind, Tyler began to slow them down. Her face and throat were shiny with sweat. The outer corner of her eye was bruised where Abernathy had hit her. Her hand had been cut free to enable her to move more easily, but Abernathy hadn't been happy about it. She trailed after the woman, leaving no more than six yards between them. She hadn't taken her eyes off Tyler once.

'We're getting close,' Tyler gasped out. 'Tommy says she'll have to go dark soon.'

'Go dark'. *We're in the alien military now.* It was meant as a joke, but Voice couldn't mask his nerves. *We're behind them,* he told Pilgrim. *West of their position. They're heading directly east.*

'They're on the move?'

Yes. Walking speed.

Pilgrim passed the information on to Abernathy.

'We're actually trusting what the Unabomber says now?' she asked.

I trust her enough for this, Voice said.

'Yes,' Pilgrim replied.

She shrugged. 'Fine. It's your funeral.'

Stick to the more northern routes going east. We don't want to stumble on them by accident.

They fell into an easy run. Pilgrim and Abernathy carried the packs but, even still, Tyler struggled. He began to wonder if they should stow her away somewhere and collect her later. Voice didn't say anything, but Pilgrim felt his vague disapproval, either at his use of baggage terminology or because she had helped get them this far and Pilgrim probably shouldn't overlook that.

The road they were on was more dirt track than blacktopped highway and their boots kicked up dust, turning the air hazy. It tickled their noses and coated their tongues. Cornfields rustled on either side, their tall stalks hemming them in, funnelling them down the track. The smell of rotting corn was everywhere and the chittering of what sounded like a thousand insects itched in his ears.

Pilgrim, I hear a buzzing, too, but it's not insects. It's Lacey. They've stopped walking.

Hearing her name galvanised Pilgrim. He grabbed Tyler's arm and drew her into a faster jog with him. She lasted maybe a dozen yards before she stumbled and pulled him short.

'I can't . . . Please . . . I can't run any more.'

Pilgrim took her hand and squeezed. 'You can. We're almost there.'

He encouraged a few more steps from her, but Tyler's legs gave way and she dropped to her knees. Her head hung low, her gasps hitched at her shoulders. 'I'm sorry,' she panted.

'Can we do this by ourselves?' he asked Voice.

Maybe? But I wouldn't like to swear to it.

'Maybe' wasn't good enough.

'What's going on?' Abernathy was marching back to them. She breathed in great swelling breaths, a grimace on her face, irritation as well as pain narrowing her eyes.

Pilgrim shrugged off his pack. 'Give me your backpack,' he said.

He pulled his jacket out and slipped it on, a blanket of heat closing around him. It would be one less thing for Abernathy to carry, though, and, strangely, he felt better for wearing it, as if it provided an extra layer of protection.

Abernathy shot glances at him as he stuffed her bag inside his, jamming it in and fastening it closed before handing it back to her. Her mouth was tight, but she wordlessly shouldered the double-loaded pack while he cajoled Tyler back to her feet. Her legs were those of a newly born deer. She could barely hold herself upright. He turned his back to her and bent his knees.

'Get on,' he told her. When she didn't move, he looked back at her. 'It's this or I sling you over my shoulder. Your choice.'

Her hand gripped him and, when he felt her press close, he crouched down even further. She climbed awkwardly on. As she wound her arms around his neck, he hiked her higher. He could feel the rabbit-thump of her heart pressed between his shoulder-blades. She wasn't heavy – she was a slight woman – but she weighed more than his pack and his creaking back let him know it.

Abernathy watched them without comment, though her expression didn't hide the fact she thought he was being a fool to even bother.

'Go,' he told her.

She went.

CHAPTER 6

Cornfield

Stop.

Voice's whisper was so quiet Pilgrim didn't hear him at first – his hoarse breathing, the pounding of his and Abernathy's feet, the clamour of his heart, all combined to drown him out.

A disconcerting prodding sensation tapped the spot behind his ear and he chugged to a slow jog, and then to a walk.

Listen, Voice said, and it was the tiniest breath of sound.

Pilgrim gave a low whistle and Abernathy, half a dozen paces in the lead, looked back. Her face was flushed. She dripped sweat.

Pilgrim stepped off the dirt-tracked road and on to the grass. He let Tyler slide off his back, and the relief at her weight leaving him was glorious; the claws of pain in his neck and shoulder, the spikes of agony in his lower back, withdrew a little, became tolerable.

Pilgrim struggled to contain his heaving breaths. Unable to speak, he pressed a finger to his lips, warning the others to remain silent.

There wasn't much of a breeze and it did nothing to ventilate him in his jacket. Sweat drenched him. His heart thundered in his chest, rattling him as much as the cornstalks rattled beside them. His tread was muted as he walked over grass to the swaying stalks, their bases shrouded with green-leafed weeds. The corn formed a continuous barricade, stretching as far as the eye could see. The stench of decay and mouldering dust grew stronger, planting a dry catch in the back of his throat.

Then he heard it.

Talking.

He glanced at Abernathy and could tell from the attentive look on her face that she heard it, too. Someone was in the field, maybe no more than a hundred yards away. And Lacey was with them.

The crawling trickles of sweat became unbearable, as did the exhausted twitching of his thigh muscles and the hot tightness at the back of his neck. None of it would leave him be, not until he moved, not until he entered the corn and made his way to her.

'What's happening?' he murmured to Voice.

He got no response.

'It sounds like a man,' Abernathy whispered.

A lone hawk had marked the field, wings spread wide as it glided in graceful looping circles in the cloudless sky.

His eyes fell to the dead cornstalks threaded together by the verdant growth of morning glory. Their husks were as dried and brittle as autumn leaves. They would surely crack and crunch as soon as they entered. 'We can't move through this without making noise,' he whispered back to her.

'I'll skirt around,' Abernathy said. 'Come from the other side. Flank them.'

He didn't like splitting up, but what she said made sense. 'Start counting as soon as you go,' he told her. 'When you hit three hundred, no matter where you are, head in. But tread softly. The element of surprise might be all we have.'

Abernathy nodded and slipped off her pack, placing it quietly next to Tyler. She paused, appearing as if she might say something else, but stopped herself with a tiny shake of her head. 'Just try not to shoot me by accident, okay?' she said to him. She sent Tyler a look. It wasn't a pleasant one. 'Touch my bag, little rabbit, and I'll cut your last hand off.'

Pilgrim watched her go, moving fast and low. He started his count.

'I'd be more worried about her shooting you,' Tyler said in a hushed voice.

'I don't suppose Tommy has broken her silence?' he asked her.

He got a headshake in reply. 'It wouldn't be safe. We're too close.'

A hook had embedded in the muscle of his heart and it was reeling him in, dragging him to the centre of that cornfield where Lacey waited. He wanted to trample into the vegetation and barrel blindly towards her, but he *had* to be cautious. A hundred things could go wrong if he were to—

'*I've been here for two whole decades!*'

The shout lifted high and clear, carrying easily across the field. In a nearby thicket of trees, a nest of birds burst into flight, startled by the noise. (In his head, Pilgrim continued to count: 98, 99, 100.) And he felt a clutch, a shivering tug in his stomach, because the voice that had shouted brought with it the same niggling familiarity as when you opened a brand new book to read, only to quietly suspect you might have already read it a while back.

(110, 111, 112.)

And he sees Lacey in those pages, kneeling amidst the threshed words, her lank hair hanging to hide the pain she suffers, a pain he sees in the droop of her neck and the defeated slump of her shoulders. She has shrunk in on herself, her fingers loosely curled on her thighs because she has no energy left to clench them and fight. This version of her is so heart-wrenching he longs to call out to her, to tell her he's found her, not to give up. He's come so far but he's here now. She doesn't need to wait for him any more. She doesn't need to be afraid.

(140, 141, 142.)

Tyler gasped, her hand fluttering to her head, and at the same moment Voice broke his silence, his shout sharp and fearful. .

Go, Pilgrim, go! Defend her!

CHAPTER 7

Abernathy

As Abernathy hit the count of fifty, she came to a narrow pathway cutting right and into the corn. It would have been wide enough for her, Christopher *and* Tyler to walk three abreast if they'd needed to.

She was perilously close to overheating, her head a pressure cooker about to blow its top. In another time and place, she'd have stripped down to her underwear and boots and given Christopher an eyeful. As it was, she pulled off her top layer, walking blindly for a couple of paces while fabric covered her face. It left her in a sweat-drenched white T-shirt. She worried its whiteness would make her too visible but there wasn't much she could do about that.

She realised she'd lost count and muttered, 'Shit,' under her breath. She started back up at 100. Good enough.

'*I've been here for two whole decades!*'

She halted mid-step, her gun gripped hard in her hand. But the shout had orientated her; it came from her right, at two o'clock.

'Well, I've been here for getting on three,' she whispered. 'What's my prize?'

She unclicked the gun's safety and began searching for a gap in the corn, counting under her breath as she did. There was a spot where the stalks were tramped down as though someone had recently cut through them.

She eased her way in, wincing slightly when the soles of her boots squeaked. She considered taking them off, but she had drawn the line with removing her sweater. What if she needed to run? She didn't want to be a lame duck. No, her boots stayed on. She almost cursed a second time when she realised she'd forgotten to count again. She wasn't good with numbers like Christopher was; she was good with words and getting people to do what she wanted. Fuck numbers. She stopped counting altogether.

She placed her feet with care, the gun's grips sweaty in her palm. Following the path of bent and crushed stalks, she went as far as she deemed safe and then slipped left along a planted row, moving deeper into the field. Stinking vegetation brushed her face. She heard a second voice, possibly a woman's, from somewhere up ahead. At least two people waited for them in this goddamn field.

Unsure what made her do it, she lifted her eyes to the perfectly blue sky. Inbound and flying in the same V formation that had trailed the hearse from St Louis, a company of birds winged its way towards the centre of the cornfield. Swift and aimed, they arrowed in from where she'd left Christopher with Tyler. Her heart, not yet calmed from all the running, clenched painfully at the sight.

She eased quickly forward and caught a glimpse of movement, shadowy and indistinct, passing through the stalks six rows ahead. A man. He halted before someone. A child? No, not a child; she was on her knees. A teenager?

Was this Lacey? It had to be. Christopher had shown her the photograph of the girl and her family, had explained in his own way who she was to him. Abernathy had a decent idea of what she'd look like now.

The teen was kneeling on a mat of flattened stalks in a

cropped circle. The man stood over her, not much older than Lacey. Skeletally thin, a ragged mess of reddish-brown hair and facial fluff that he should have been embarrassed about. A flare of sunlight glinted as he lifted a glass bottle over Lacey's head, upending it. Liquid glugged as its contents spilled over her, soaking her hair and darkening her shirt.

What the hell was he doing?

Abernathy sidestepped around a cornstalk and lost sight of them. A second glimmer of light caught her eye. Not sunlight, but a hot, sinuous flick. A breeze rustled through the stalks, a humid breath hitting her hot, sweaty face, bringing with it the scent of spilled alcohol and the distinct odour of sulphur dioxide.

Matches.

Dread crawled through Abernathy's stomach. Alcohol and fire were a *bad* combination.

'Stop! *No!*' A woman. Older. Not Lacey.

The scream that followed *was* Lacey's, though – had to be – and Abernathy didn't think about Christopher counting to three hundred any more, didn't care about the noise she'd make or the element of surprise; she pushed forward, hands snatching at the stalks, shoving them aside, the crunch of dead corn under her boots lost in the commotion. A fire blazed in the cropped clearing, peeking between the stalks, nothing tiny or match-like about it, and with it came the crackle and pop of burning corn.

A sudden flurry of activity burst into the cleared space and the field became a crunching, slapping, gasping scene for a series of uncountable seconds as Abernathy dodged around cornstalks as fast as she could, knowing she was too far away, knowing speed wouldn't help anyone now. Two people were waiting at the edge of the clearing, and Abernathy almost stumbled in surprise; they had been so still, so quiet. Their backs were turned and they seemed to shimmer before her, an invisible fire raging beneath the earth, a heat-haze rising from the soil to blur her vision. She heard Christopher speak and, trying to quieten her heavy breaths, she craned her neck to look. He stood over a heap at his feet. It was covered by his jacket. Tendrils of smoke rose from under it.

Good God, the crazy fuckers did it. They set her alight.

Abernathy felt a stab deep in her gut because she knew what Lacey meant to Christopher; despite all his non-words, she had watched him at night, when he believed everyone was sleeping, remove that photograph from his pocket and long minutes pass by as he gazed at it.

But they had arrived too late. All their running, all their efforts to get here, and it hadn't been enough.

Christopher was speaking. To whom, Abernathy couldn't see. She risked advancing a few steps nearer. Two rows away now, and one of the figures in front of her – a man – raised an arm and pointed at Christopher. Except it wasn't a finger he was pointing, it was a gun.

Panic cramped through her and she jerked her own gun up, the barrel catching on a cornstalk, knocking her aim off and nearly jolting it from her grip.

A gunshot rent the air – not from her; her gun pulled heavy and useless in her hand – and it was like taking the hit square to her chest. Her eyes darted to Christopher, to the blood, to the agonised groping of his wound, and she saw Jackson all over again, the sopping mess of his shirt, how hot his blood was on her hands, how he writhed in pain but couldn't escape it, no matter where he moved. But there was no blood on Christopher. He stood uninjured and whole.

She angrily blinked the tears from her eyes.

'What the fuck!' the gunman blurted, turning on the woman at his side. She had a hand clamped to his gun-arm, holding it down. This stranger had saved Christopher's life.

Enraged, the gunman snatched his arm from her grip and Abernathy knew he was going to shoot the woman at point-blank range for interfering.

Abernathy was calm again, all panic doused by a numbness that deadened her. She strode forward, all furtiveness gone, levelled the gun at his head and squeezed the trigger, dropping the muzzle at the last second (*Don't shoot anyone in the head*, Christopher had told her), and the bullet blew through the back of the man's neck. She was swinging the gun on the woman even as her dead friend face-planted the floor.

She pressed the muzzle to her cheek. 'Don't even think about it, sister,' she warned softly.

The woman wasn't thinking about anything. She was breathing too quickly, close to hyperventilating.

It smelled like a family barbecue gone terribly wrong in the clearing – burnt corn and strong alcohol, and just a hint of ammonia from the dead man's emptied bladder. Abernathy looked over at Christopher and met his eyes.

The first man she'd seen, the one who'd poured alcohol over Lacey's head, didn't spare her, or his fallen companion, a glance. 'You have *no idea* what he's capable of,' he said.

Abernathy had missed who they were talking about.

The guy's reddish beard-fluff, growing in patches on chin and cheeks, was even worse close up. He was young, but there was an arrogance in how he held himself, in how he stared Christopher down with his flat, dead eyes. There was something wrong with them – when they looked at you they weren't seeing you at all.

'I'm one of the few who can help you,' he was saying. 'There'll be no one left by the time he—'

Christopher made a harsh sound in the back of his throat. 'Always with the talking. Will there ever be any peace?'

The gun Abernathy held to the woman's face shifted as she broke her silence.

'You have to help him.'

Abernathy shoved the muzzle harder to her cheek to dissuade her from opening her mouth again. It didn't work.

'Please,' she whispered, and Abernathy heard the tremble in her voice – could feel it shake through the woman's body, too hot and too close to hers. 'It's not his fault.'

'There's only one way to help him now,' Christopher said, and the frank, uncompromising look in his eye was something Abernathy had missed. He had always been the first thing she sought when returning to the Unit, gravitating towards him like you would an old, favourite armchair. He was more a part of the furniture than anything or anyone else in that place, and he saw more than all the blinking red eyes of the security cameras put together. Even when he'd been at his most lost, at his most uncommunicative, he'd always been a reassuring presence for her. Someone she could lower her guard with. Someone she could trust. She'd forgotten what it felt like to be able to rely on someone like that, to have someone who'd never once asked anything of her.

'Close your eyes,' Christopher said, and for a second Abernathy thought he was talking to her.

The woman's eyelids fluttered and fell, lashes coming to rest on her cheek, close enough to almost touch the muzzle of Abernathy's gun.

The young man opened his mouth – set on arguing more, or pleading his case, no doubt – but he never got the chance. A double-punch of bullets struck his thin chest, his face alive with disbelief as he staggered back, and it was shocking, not for its noise or the abruptness, but for its cold-bloodedness. He wasn't armed. He hadn't attacked. And Christopher had shot him, anyway.

The guy dropped on to his butt. He blinked, his eyes two black sinkholes, and all that disbelief swirled down into their dark, endless depths. Nothing waited down there – no distant galaxies, no angels with wings or rabbits with timepieces. He slumped slowly into it, settling on his side, knees drawing up to his ruined chest as if he were getting comfy for a long-needed nap.

Christopher didn't give him another glance. He bent and snatched the jacket off the body at his feet. Abernathy almost jerked her eyes away, not wanting to see the burnt husk of the girl.

Lacey lay motionless. Her chest didn't move. Her hair was singed short, but her face was remarkably unburnt. In fact, all Abernathy could see were swollen, half-lidded eyes, a split lip, some bruises.

Abernathy nudged her captive closer, their feet creaking, cornstalks popping. She gripped the woman's arm above the elbow and pressed her gun into her ribs, but Abernathy didn't take her eyes from Christopher as he went to his knees beside the girl.

'Lacey.'

He slid his arms under her, gathering her to his chest, and Abernathy didn't think she'd ever witnessed such tenderness from him. Hadn't thought him capable.

She knew she should check the woman for weapons, do something other than stare, but she couldn't. Christopher had started to rock a little, an imperceptible sway. He stroked a hand over the girl's head, thumb gently running across her brow. An ache filled Abernathy's throat, one she couldn't swallow away, no matter how many times she tried.

He said Lacey's name again, soft as a prayer, and Abernathy did avert her eyes then, the picture of him kneeling there with the dead girl cradled in his arms too much, even for her. Too many people had been burnt, slaughtered, were gone for ever. Each of them had to find a way to make peace with that. She couldn't do it for him.

A rasping gasp. A dry croak, as creaky as the corn under Abernathy's feet.

When she looked again Lacey's eyes were open. She was staring up at Christopher, her swollen lips moving, slowly and painfully, sounding out a name. His name. *Pilgrim*. And his shoulders slumped but, at the same time, Abernathy noticed how his arms tightened, wanting to hug the girl but not quite able to bring himself to do it because she was too precious, too fragile, a bird with a broken wing, one that needed to be handled with care.

He smiled, a small curve of his lips, and that was something new to her, too. He didn't smile much. She wished he'd do it more often.

'I still like how my name fits your mouth,' he said, the words for the girl alone, and Abernathy felt like a voyeur, intruding on their moment, but she didn't stop watching as Lacey lifted a hand to his face, tracing his cheek with fingertips, not quite believing he was there. And then she was reaching for him, her arms groping awkwardly to hook around his shoulders, pulling him close so she could bury her face against him as sobs wracked her, cracking on her ragged breaths. She sounded broken. Exhausted.

Finally, Abernathy turned away, giving them their privacy.

She checked her captive over, uncaring how heavy-handed she was being, pleased when she elicited a wince or a gasp from her. She dragged a hemp pack off the woman's back and threw it aside for now, then patted down her pockets, felt through the seat of her pants, even crouched and checked the tops of her boots. She grabbed the back of the woman's neck and forced her to her knees. She hadn't noticed the open book lying face down on the ground until now, some of its pages loose and fluttering, but she felt no immediate need to check it. It was just a book.

She leaned in to whisper in the woman's ear. 'You move, I blow your spine out your throat like I did your buddy.'

The woman shuddered against her. Abernathy didn't think she'd be having any trouble from her.

Keeping a wary eye on her all the same, Abernathy went to the downed gunman and picked up his gun, tucking it into her belt. Next, she went to the young bearded guy and squatted next to him, taking a moment to study him. His eyes were open, their sinkhole pupils fully dilated. She found herself staring into them, drawn in by a darkness that reached so far down she was sure she was looking at the exact place where he ended and something else began. Bugs crawled over her skin. She didn't know what made her do it, but she cupped a hand over his eyes, closing them, absurdly relieved to have them hidden from view.

When she looked up, the kneeling woman was staring at her.

'What the fuck are you looking at?'

A jerky headshake and the woman went back to staring at the corn.

Abernathy stood and crossed to her, her shadow falling over her. 'You have others with you?'

The woman gave a quiet 'Yes.'

'Near enough to give us trouble?'

She jerked her chin back the way Abernathy had come. 'They're that way. Maybe twenty minutes or so walking.'

'What's your name?'

'Sunny.'

'What's his name?' Abernathy pointed to the dead guy whose eyes she'd closed.

Sunny glanced up to see where she was pointing. 'Posy.'

'He in charge?'

'Kind of.'

Abernathy frowned at her. She must have looked fierce because the woman's eyes skittered away again.

'The thing inside him was in charge,' Sunny murmured.

'What thing?'

'The voice he heard. *It* was in charge. Not him.'

Abernathy pondered that for a moment and didn't like where it led her. She turned in the general direction Christopher had come from and shouted, 'Little rabbit! Are you still over there or did you take off?'

A second later, faint and uncertain, Tyler called back, '*I'm still here.*'

'Then get your can over here! And bring the packs!'

Lacey's sobs had dried up, thankfully.

'Abernathy. Grab Posy's shoes.' Christopher was hunkered down by the girl's feet, and it was the first time Abernathy had noticed Lacey was shoeless. The bottoms of her socks were torn and bloodstained.

'I don't want his shoes.' Lacey's voice was husky and low, but mostly it was stubborn.

The shoes weren't in the best condition – the soles were crumbling and worn thin – but they were a sight better than nothing. Abernathy didn't look at the dead guy's face as she pulled them off.

A series of crunching stomps marked Tyler's arrival, and Abernathy followed her with her eyes as she entered the clearing. The little rabbit stopped dead at the carnage in front of her. She met Abernathy's gaze and, if Abernathy didn't know any better, she'd say she was bothered by the sight. Tyler didn't hold her eyes for long, though; she zeroed in on the teenager beside Pilgrim.

'We found you,' she breathed, and the amazement in her tone annoyed Abernathy more than it should have. What seemed like genuine happiness tugged a smile from Tyler but, of course, Abernathy knew she was a snake and didn't trust a single thing the lying bitch's mouth said or did.

'You're Lacey,' Tyler said, and Abernathy rolled her eyes. Who the fuck did she think she was?

Lacey shot a glance at Christopher, who was busy peeling the socks from her feet, her expression two parts curious and one part suspicious. 'Yeah, that's me. Who're you?'

'Tyler.'

Lacey's eyes flicked to Abernathy, but Abernathy stared back without saying anything.

'And that's Abernathy,' Tyler said, and Abernathy sent her a scathing *shut-your-mouth* look. She didn't need her to make any introductions on her behalf.

'It's okay,' Christopher said quietly. 'They're friends.' That almost made Abernathy splutter a laugh because what a crock. Tyler was the *furthest* thing anyone needed for a friend on this side of the earth or any other.

Lacey gave him an odd look. 'Since when do you have friends?' She spoke as if she knew him better than anyone. And maybe she did.

Something unpleasant wormed its way into Abernathy's belly and, realising she was still holding Posy's crusty boots, she carried them over and dumped them next to the girl's feet. Lacey leaned back on her hands and cocked her chin up at her. Her expression was now all parts suspicious and no parts curious.

Christopher didn't glance up as he reached for the boots. And don't think Abernathy didn't notice that not one word of gratitude had left Lacey's mouth, either. No 'thank you' for trekking countless miles to her rescue. No whoop-de-doo for saving her ass from getting burned alive.

Christopher held his hand out to Tyler and she carried their pack over to him. No 'thank you' from him, either, as he took it from her and rummaged inside. Tyler waited for him to pull out the first-aid kit and went in after him, bringing out a bottle of water. She clamped it under her right arm and unscrewed the top before offering it to Lacey. The girl accepted it eagerly, fumbling it in her rush and almost dropping it.

'*Watch it*,' Abernathy snapped. 'We don't have much left.'

Lacey squinted up at her as she tipped her head back and drank. Abernathy eyed her in return. She wasn't sure what she'd been expecting from her. Not so much attitude, for one.

Lacey hissed in pain as Christopher cleaned her feet and began to bandage them. But as she looked at him, her grimace dissipated to be replaced by something sad but also full of wonder.

'You were dead,' she whispered, the water bottle now resting forgotten in her lap.

Christopher grunted. 'You should be dead, too.'

Lacey touched a hand to her chest, near the hollow of her throat. 'My lungs wouldn't work.'

Christopher raised an eyebrow. Nodded. 'Voice can do that.'

Lacey shook her head and her eyes got kind of squinty. Abernathy wondered if she'd start crying again. She hoped to God not.

'I wanted to scream,' Lacey said. 'Wanted to yell. But I couldn't. I couldn't breathe.'

'You'd have inhaled fire into your lungs if you had,' Christopher said.

Lacey's eyes slipped away from him and fell on the dead guy. 'The voice he heard, it took control of him. Moved his limbs. Spoke from his mouth. There was nothing of Posy left.'

'He had a weak mind,' Christopher said absently, focusing on his work.

'You knew him?' Abernathy asked, too harshly, judging by the sharp look Lacey gave her.

'We crossed paths once.' And that was all she got from him. No explanation. No nothing.

'That's it? You just happened to cross paths with him and now, *voilà*, here he is. There's nothing else you want to add?'

Christopher looked at her with his steady eyes and she wanted to scratch them from his head because he made her feel like she was being unreasonable to ask.

'If we went over every single thing that's happened to us during the past seven years, there'd be no time for anything else.' He turned back to Lacey. 'How did you get here?'

A trembling sheet of water seemed to fall over her face, her composure wavering, her mouth and chin quivering. 'Alex is gone, Pilgrim,' she whispered, voice thick. Her throat rippled as she swallowed.

Christopher had finished bandaging Lacey's feet and was lacing on the first of Posy's boots, but now his hands stilled. 'How?' was all he asked.

'The voice inside him.' Lacey lifted her chin to Posy, a small, tired motion, as though it were all she was capable of. 'It's been hunting us for days. We were trapped. Alex . . . she saved me and Addison. She gave us time to run.'

Christopher finished lacing the first boot and moved on to the next, carefully slipping it on. 'Where's Addison?'

Addison. Abernathy knew that one. She was Lacey's niece. The baby bump in the photo. The rugrat would be a good seven or eight years old now.

'She escaped, but I think I can maybe find her.' Lacey reached down to grab his hand, forcing his attention to her. 'Pilgrim, *so* much has happened since Vicksburg. Voice has started to hear other voices now and he says—' She stopped, catching the knowing glance he and Tyler shared. 'You already know?'

'We do,' Tyler said. 'I should tell you that Tommy hears everything your voice is saying. It's how we found you. She says your voice and Pilgrim's sound remarkably alike.'

'You hear a new one?' Lacey breathed, eyes bright with surprise. A soft smile came to her lips.

Abernathy was beginning to get lost in all this. 'What do you even mean by "a new one"?' she asked.

Christopher motioned to the dead bodies around them. 'No headshots.'

'Yeah, I didn't forget.' She almost had but wasn't about to admit it.

'I said no headshots because they can cause a voice to jump.'

Abernathy held a hand up. 'Wait, wait, wait. Let's just rewind that back for a second.'

'They can jump,' Christopher repeated. 'I took a serious injury to the head not too long back and I lost the voice I heard. It left me.'

'And it came to me,' Lacey finished. 'He's mine now. Right here.' She touched a finger to her temple. 'I never heard anything before Voice came. I've only heard him for maybe six weeks.' Her eyes unlatched from Abernathy's face and her head cocked. 'He says six and a half.'

'It's similar to what they were doing at St Louis,' Christopher explained. 'Damage the brain enough, and the voice leaves. What they don't understand is that the damage will either kill you or the voice will come back anyway. Like mine has. Like Jackson's did.'

Abernathy wasn't sure she was following. She looked back and forth between Christopher and Lacey. 'No. They *cured* Jackson. I saw it. I spent years with him. He didn't hear anything.'

'He may have been repressing it, but he heard.' Tyler was guarded. Or maybe it was apologetic – Abernathy always had difficulty telling the subtle differences with such things. And, honestly, she didn't care which it was because Tyler could be telling her the sky was blue and she wouldn't believe it.

'I can't imagine how difficult it must have been for him,' Tyler said. 'To hide it from those he was closest to. It'd be enough to drive a person insane. But Tommy heard it, even if it was mostly broken. Everything they were doing there was based on a lie. It's not possible to cure anybody or make the voices go away.'

'It's true,' Christopher said. 'I'd have never heard him calling out to me if he didn't have one. It's the only thing capable of relaying such a message, of projecting so far. His did it differently to Lacey's, but it's essentially the same way we found her. Jackson still heard his voice, Abernathy, whether you knew about it or not.'

'Not–Posy was doing experiments, too.'

They all turned to stare at the kneeling woman. She hadn't made a peep in so long Abernathy had almost forgotten she was there. Sunny was all lean bones and thin muscle, but there was something soft about her. Maybe it was the way she spoke, her syllables pouring out, easy and smooth like treacle from a spoon. Her hair was knotted on top of her head and she had a pleasant enough face if you disregarded the exhaustion and unhappiness dragging at it.

'Not to cure anything like you're talking about,' Sunny said. 'But he wanted to understand how they could move from person to person. He knew it had something to do with' – she gestured at her head, a weary wave of her hand – 'causing some sort of damage. His journal, the notes he collected . . .' Her eyes shifted to the upended book on the ground. It had lost more of its pages. Loose sheaves had skipped across the flattened corn to catch in the browning leaves on the cornstalks. 'It was all so he could learn. He'd do such . . . such awful things to people,' she whispered.

'What things?' Abernathy asked.

Sunny's lips thinned. Maybe she didn't want to spill the beans because she'd played a hand in all those awful things. Abernathy neither knew nor cared, she just wanted the details.

'You want I should beat it out of you?' she said, taking a step nearer to her.

The softness in Sunny's voice was a different kind now; it was tinged with defeat. She could have been reciting from a hymn sheet, her eyes downcast, trained to a safe spot on the ground.

'I watched him push a spike into a man's eye socket while he kicked and screamed. He used a hammer to smash a person's skull. He would shoot them point-blank: in the mouth, the face, the temple. It's all there.' She nodded to the fallen book. 'Everything he did, he recorded. But none of it ever worked and he couldn't understand why. So he came for Lacey because he knew her voice wasn't hers, the same as Posy should never have had his. He was willing to burn her alive to find his answers. Knowledge is power, that's what he believed. He'd gain his wisdom through Lacey, through Red, and that would make him equal in the eyes of the Flitting Man.'

'He's equal to no one now,' Christopher said, getting to his feet. He seemed taller somehow as he walked over to the kneeling woman. 'Posy was looking for a woman called Red?'

Sunny craned her neck to squint up at him, the sun glaring from overhead. 'The one with no teeth? They're all looking for her. We'd never have picked up Lacey's trail if not for Red.'

Christopher was looking at the kneeling woman with such intensity Abernathy edged closer to him, wanting to somehow telepathically pick up on what he was thinking. Her world felt crushingly silent, soundtracked only by the whispering heads of rotted corn rubbing up against each other, the calls of bird cries, the squeak of stalks under their shifting boots. Everything was quiet. She heard no whispers or secret conversations in her head like the rest of them.

'What does Lacey have to do with Red?' Christopher asked.

'She got spotted wearing her necklace,' Sunny said, flicking Lacey a glance. 'A St Christopher. They mistook her for Red.'

'Lacey is younger,' he said, frowning.

'We all look older than we are,' Sunny said with a shrug. 'This world, it ages us.'

Amen to that, sister, Abernathy thought. Lacey's bloodied and bruised face, singed hair, tattered clothes, could have placed her anywhere between ages sixteen and twenty-three.

'You still have her necklace?' Christopher asked Lacey.

She shook her head. 'I gave it to Alex. For safe-keeping.'

That seemed to sadden him. 'They'll never find Red,' he told the kneeling woman. 'It's impossible.'

'They'll keep trying,' Sunny said, and that seemed to sadden her, too. 'He wants her and, from what I hear, the Flitting Man gets what he wants. That's all I've been hearing over the past few weeks. They'll go to the coast next – if others haven't already – to the Inn she talked about in her letter.'

Alarm bells went off in Abernathy's brain, and Tyler's head came up.

'What letter?' Christopher was so still Abernathy wouldn't have been surprised if his lungs and heart had stopped mid-beat. The cornstalks at his back swayed, a soft *shh-shhh-shh* passing through them as they breathed in his stead.

'Posy showed me a letter she'd written. It spoke of an Inn. It's a real place, he told me.'

Christopher was on the dead guy, shoving his hands inside his pockets, searching, coming out empty, and then Abernathy heard the crinkle. Christopher pulled out a creased, folded piece of paper. He tore it open and scanned the text. Stopped. Reread.

'What's it say?' Tyler asked.

'"*Along with Ruby's brother they explored this newly broken land . . . And eventually found an Inn by the sea to call their home.*"'

'Is that it?' Abernathy said. 'It doesn't say anything about the location. It's probably not even the same one.'

'Red spoke about it,' Sunny said. 'Posy said she was made to talk. That the Flitting Man was real good at making people talk.'

'She saw him?' Tyler asked, too quickly. 'The Flitting Man spoke to her?'

Sunny nodded tiredly. 'I was never convinced he was real. It all sounded like campfire stories to me. But I'm not so much of a doubter these days.'

'Posy told me the same,' Lacey said. She hadn't moved from where she sat. Abernathy doubted she'd be able to get up even if she wanted to. 'Not about the Inn, but about how the Flitting Man came to see her. That he scared Red so much she escaped and ran.' Her eyes found Christopher. 'Ran straight to us.'

'So they *do* have an idea where her Inn is, then?' Abernathy asked, trying to keep up.

'Some of them do, yeah,' Sunny said.

'The same Inn you sent Jay and Clancy to,' Tyler added, her worried eyes also on Christopher.

But he didn't appear to be listening. He was staring up at the sky, at the handful of wheeling birds, watching them go round and round and round above their heads.

CHAPTER 8

Horizons

The weather was warm and the rain promised to stay away. They didn't want to be closed in by four walls and Pilgrim wanted to see the sky, so they slept under the stars. The four women, wrapped in jackets and hoodies, the grass their cushions, fell asleep one by one.

After some discussion, Sunny had come with them, which seemed to annoy Abernathy but please Lacey. Tyler and Pilgrim had stayed neutral on the subject: Tyler, for her own reasons, and Pilgrim because Sunny seemed almost as exhausted and beaten down as Lacey, and he wasn't in the mood to send someone away only to have them return later to cause more problems. He erred on the side of caution, of course, and remained watchful of her, as did Abernathy. She had confiscated all the woman's belongings, including her belt. Sunny hadn't argued.

Pilgrim had slept for a time but had repeatedly awoken, lifting on to his elbow to check that Lacey was curled on her side where he'd left her. She hadn't moved, her face peaceful in repose. The other times, he'd woke up because his sleep had been so dark and so endless he was afraid he'd never find his way back. It was like being buried alive.

The final time his eyes flicked open, he got up and wandered a short distance away from the women to sit, his back to them.

He and Abernathy had bullied the others up a final incline before they had collapsed, and it now afforded him a view of the rolling highway and the swathes of trees, burnished in russets and browns as dawn prepared to break. The sky in the east was a deep, burning red. Its colour discomfited him and he wasn't sure why.

It's like the skies in everyone's dreams, Voice said.

Footsteps approached and Voice delicately withdrew, leaving him and Lacey alone.

She settled herself next to him, close enough that her shoulder brushed his. He studied her profile: the slope of her nose, the delicate shell of her ear, staying away from the bruises and cuts that marked her face. She had changed in the few short weeks they had been apart.

'You've changed, you know,' she said, mirroring his thoughts. 'Not in a bad way,' she added, glancing at him. 'But you're different.'

'So are you. Not in a bad way,' he added.

She smiled. 'How am I different?'

'Like the world took a bite out of you and is still chewing on it.'

She rubbed her nose with her sleeve. 'Yeah. Wonder when it'll spit me back out again.'

'You're a bony thing. Probably won't be long.'

'Hey,' she complained, bumping her shoulder into his.

He stilled at the feel of her. It was nothing like the phantom touch of the Lacey who had haunted his journey here. This Lacey was warm and solid and real. He wanted to reach out and check that *all* of her was: tug gently on her hair, feel the flutter of her eyelids under his covering palm, press his fingers to the delicate skin at the inside of her wrist to feel her pulse. But he didn't do any of those things. Instead he looked away, his gaze lingering on the angry sky, its burning red lightening a little as the sun crept nearer the horizon.

'Your eyes are different,' she said, even though he hadn't asked. 'You talk with them more.'

He frowned, not sure what that meant.

She shrugged, and her smirk, the one he'd been waiting to see, played at the corners of her mouth. 'You're more like the rest of us now.'

'And that's a good thing?'

'I never said it was "good". I said, "not in a bad way".' He felt her pause, her breath held for a moment. 'Pilgrim?'

When she said it, he smiled, just a little.

'I missed you,' she said, and he knew those words were hard for her to get out, because missing people was always hard. He knew that now. 'I really thought you were gone this time. Gone for real and never coming back. Like my grams. Like Alex.'

He stared out at the world, because it was easier to do that than to look at her, to look at the grief filling up her eyes. It was beautiful out there – nothing moved but the gentle sway of the trees and the rows upon rows of corn, a stitched blanket laid over the land. From here, nothing looked blighted or rotted. Nothing gave away the fact that, if you studied it closer, things were dying.

'I saw you,' he said, feeling the weight of her sitting beside him, the soft swells of her side as she breathed. 'So many times I saw you. Everywhere I went, you came with me. I couldn't lose you even if I tried.' He turned his head. Found her staring at him, a single tear tracking its way down her cheek. 'I buried my heart a long time ago, along with everyone I knew. Buried it good and deep so no one could find it, not even me. And I didn't go looking for it. I didn't think on it. Not once. Then you came along, with your lemonade and your rifle and all your questions, and you started digging and you wouldn't quit till you'd dug it up. And now I'm stuck with it again.'

Another tear fell, even as her mouth smiled. 'You're not gonna try and bury it again, are you?'

He pretended to give it some serious consideration and she bumped her shoulder into him again.

'You know,' she said, 'for someone with the conversation skills of a rock, you're pretty good at it sometimes.'

And he couldn't help himself – he reached over and thumbed her tear away. She knocked his hand aside and wiped her face dry herself. He smiled.

She took a deep breath, her cheeks puffing out as she exhaled. Drawing her knees up, she rested her chin on them. 'Life sure is crazy fucked up,' she said.

'Hm,' he agreed. 'It's why we need Boy Scout rules.'

She breathed a soft laugh. 'Yeah, and I went and broke the first one. Lost my shoes, didn't I?' She wiggled her feet a bit. Posy's boots were at least three sizes too large for her.

'Don't tell anyone, but so did I.'

She looked at him, eyes widening. 'No way.'

He nodded. 'We're both wearing dead men's shoes.'

'It's true, he is,' a voice said from behind them.

Tyler shuffled towards them, her raincoat wrapped around her like a blanket. Her hair was mussed and her jaw cracked wide on a yawn. She didn't attempt to cover it. She stopped when they both stared at her, saying nothing. 'I'm sorry. Am I intruding?'

Lacey shook her head; Pilgrim remained quiet. There were things he needed to discuss with Tyler that he didn't think he should voice in front of Lacey and her voice. Thoughts were not theirs alone any more and information could spread so easily now. He had to be mindful of that.

'I need to speak with you both,' Tyler said, settling herself on Pilgrim's other side, neatly folding the overlap of her jacket over her thighs and smoothing it flat. 'Abernathy, too, but I'm not sure she's ready to listen. She's very angry with me.'

'She has a right to be.' He felt Lacey's eyes on him, but now wasn't the time for explanations.

'I know.' Tyler's back was very straight and she met his eyes with a forthrightness that impressed him, despite his better judgement. 'I want to say how truly sorry I am,' she said. 'And that I was wrong not to trust you. He told me . . . he told me that it would be hard, doing the things we needed to do. But what he failed to say was how difficult it would be to betray those I'd come to care about, to respect.'

Pilgrim watched her and waited.

'Shut off your doubts, he told me. Push away the weakness of conscience because it has no place in this.' Tyler's gaze faltered from him and her head turned, eyes moving to those still sleeping. 'Abernathy would have a similar stance, I would think, if it came to something she cared about. Still,' she said, her gaze making its way back to him, 'I was unsure I would be able to follow through on it. Walking by all those people in that hospital, hearing the hum of life, seeing what they had built for themselves – it all seemed so civilised. Right up until Tommy described to me what she could hear. Not coming from those poor people locked inside the refrigerated lockers. No, not them. She told me about the gibbering voices of those who'd already been experimented on. You saw them in their hospital beds, I know you did. Broken and lost and turned to madness in the attempts to burn away their voices. And any hesitation or uncertainty I felt vanished.' There was a sheen to her eyes, but they weren't tears. It was something more than tears. 'I under-stand the enormity of what I did, the damage I caused, but three hundred and thirty-two patients, Pilgrim. That's how many of us passed through that place.' Her voice had grown dusty and dry. 'Three hundred and thirty-two.'

Pilgrim didn't reply. None of this could be fixed by explanations or excuses. It couldn't even be fixed by numbers, no matter how she tallied them up.

'I also came over here to talk to you about the red skies,' Tyler said into his silence, and Pilgrim felt Lacey stiffen beside him.

He nodded for Tyler to go on. 'I'm listening.'

'He said that, as soon as we saw them, it would be time. That we'd be ready. We would need to defend those like us and stop anyone who was hurting them. I hadn't planned on meeting you or Jay or Clancy. I thought I'd need to do what I had to by myself. But when Tommy and I heard you in that van, and when you came over to me after the crash, I knew' – her voice grew quieter – 'I knew you would be useful to me.'

They each had uses for the other, it seemed. 'You spoke to him,' Pilgrim said. 'He told you these things.'

'Yes,' she said, in her careful, considered way.

'Face to face?'

Tyler nodded, the movement slight. 'For the longest time, I thought it was pure chance that I found him. I had been travelling with a woman for a while. She was older, but she was kind to me. She said she wanted to look after me, but really it was she who needed caring for. She was . . . unwell. Her skin and eyes had yellowed. She bled from the mouth. Sometimes she could barely talk for shaking.' Tyler glanced at them, seemingly embarrassed by the details of her story. 'I stayed with her until she didn't need me to look after her any more, and two days later he was there, sitting high in a maple tree, the largest I think I've ever seen. It had this grotesquely bent trunk at the bottom, like a flexing bicep.' She demonstrated, bending her arm at the elbow, showing off her guns like a muscle man. 'It was so unnatural, as if the whole tree were trying to point me in the wrong direction. I don't even know what made me look up. He didn't have any rope on him – nothing like that – but I got the feeling he'd been thinking about jumping before I came along. Maybe with the hope he'd crack his head open or break his neck. I don't know. I talked him down, branch by branch. He never revealed to me who he really was and I couldn't have known. This was before all the stories, before his name began to drift around like so much smoke. And even if I had known, I wouldn't have believed.'

'Why?' Lacey whispered.

Tyler smiled, a confused smile, as if still unsure of what she'd seen. 'Because he isn't what you'd expect. He insisted on carrying my bag while we walked, and we talked for a long time. About everything. He made everything sound so simple. As if he could look at what had happened through the clearest of lenses and see it for what it was, while the rest of us were still stumbling around, trying to wipe the filth from our eyes. He was so bright and he spoke so beautifully; his voice was like music, and I hadn't heard such hopeful music for so long.'

Pilgrim wanted to throw what she said on to a burning pyre because he knew her truths could be untruths and her explanations were manipulation, but all he saw was a woman who had desperately wanted to believe in something. In *anything*. Achingly so.

'And so I waited to see them. The red skies in my dreams. And when I did, Tommy and I listened, like he told us to. We went where we heard more voices and ended up in Memphis, and all the while those skies waited for us when I slept. So when I heard you talking about them, about what you'd heard and that you were searching for where those terrible words were coming from – I knew what I had to do. And I remembered what he'd asked of me.' She stopped as if she'd hit a ditch in the road and was unable to cross without encouragement.

'What?' Pilgrim asked.

'He asked,' she said, and looked deep into his eyes, 'if I would be brave enough to help him when the time came. To help change things. He asked if I wanted things to be better.'

'And you think what he's offering is better?'

For the first time, she seemed upset with him. 'You've *seen* what they've done to us, what they're doing. How can it possibly be any worse? It can never be *worse*.' She was close to tears. 'You've both seen the red skies now,' she said, her voice low. 'I know you have. Which means others have seen them, too. And more will, until this is finished.'

'Finished?' Lacey said.

Tyler passed her palm over her lap, although there were no creases to smooth. Her expression was grave.

'*Who* is he, Tyler?' Pilgrim asked.

'He's everyw—'

'*Who* is he?' he cut in, sharper than he'd intended. 'If you want to gain my trust again, this is how you do it. With the truth.'

She bowed her head, and it reminded him of how he'd seen her sitting on that kerb (alone, but not alone. Waiting. Listening), her gaze on his boots as he'd walked towards her.

It's going to be hard for her to lie to us now that I can hear most everything Tommy says, Voice said.

And whether or not Tommy passed on what Voice had said, Tyler came to a decision. She lifted her head, looked him square in the eyes and said, 'I think it's why he picked me, because we're alike, him and I. Who would suspect a one-handed woman who weighs barely more than a sack of dog food? *You* didn't,' she told him.

'He only has one hand?' Lacey asked, confused.

Tyler smiled at her. 'No, he has both his hands, but he probably weighs less than me. Although, he'll have grown a bit since I last saw him.'

Pilgrim stared at her, the spit drying in his mouth, the realisation a sapling, its baby green shoots curling free from the soil in search of the light.

'He's a child,' he murmured.

Tyler lifted her brow as if to say, *Clever man*. 'And who's more innocent than a child?' she asked.

She's never seen The Omen, Voice said, his humour a hastily-constructed shield against the unease Pilgrim was feeling.

'He's not innocent,' Pilgrim said.

'He'd barely be thirteen,' she said, although what her point was Pilgrim didn't know. She was the one who'd called them pioneers to their planet; she knew he was far from being an innocent thirteen-year-old boy.

There was something else she had said. Something that scratched at the back of his head like all those buried memories had when wanting to claw their way out. Something about his voice sounding like music . . .

'Did he speak with an accent?' Pilgrim asked, watching her.

She was watching him, too. 'He did.'

'He wasn't from around here.'

She shook her head. No. No, he wasn't.

'Hari,' Pilgrim whispered.

CHAPTER 9

The Norwood Cove Inn

Albus sat kneeling in the tall grass of the back lawn, five freshly dug graves before him. He looked at the mounds of earth and wondered if the theory of liquid displacement held true for soil, too. Was the amount piled on the graves equal to the amount of space each body occupied? The two on the right were smaller than the two on the left, which seemed to imply it was.

He could hear the gentle ebb and swell of the ocean but didn't look out across the sands. The evening view was always beautiful this time of year, and he didn't want to gaze upon anything so perfect when his heart hurt so much. Instead, he dropped his eyes to his half-hands, resting dirty palms up on his thighs. He tilted them to look at the shiny scarring where his fingers had been cut away. Healed but still ugly. They were useless, hateful lumps. He hadn't even been able to hold a shovel to help dig.

Whenever he and Ruby had visited their uncle's Inn, they would sit on the back porch, blankets over their laps, and rock in their matching rocking chairs as she sang the sea shanties their uncle had taught them. And he would watch the deep red strands of her voice lift into the briny air, trailing endless comet tails across the dusk sky. He had always felt safe here. No one could ever reach them to hurt them. Nothing could break into this world they had built, safe by the ocean, the grasses and the beach their fortifications.

'They didn't die quickly,' Bruno said.

The big man had been sitting a few feet from Albus this whole time, as silent as him. As twilight had fallen, the darkness had cloaked Bruno, rendering him almost invisible. If he sat there until full dark, he would disappear entirely. The thought sent a shiver through Albus and he pulled his attention away from his hands to look at his friend.

'Whoever did this, they either wanted them to suffer' – Bruno's voice broke and he had to wait a moment before he could continue – 'or they wanted information.'

Albus shook his head. What information? None of them had any information to give. The only person who did was Albus and, before today, only two people in the whole world knew about his ability to see colour in those special like his sister. Two people who knew about him and this Inn. And both those people were gone.

'Gwen wants to stay,' Bruno said, and it was the tilled brown earth of his voice that captured Albus's gaze, the colour he spoke as unique to Bruno as Ruby's had been to her. 'She thinks whoever did this will come back. She wants to kill them.'

Albus shook his head, adamant this time. No, it wasn't safe here. Not for any of them. If they *had* been looking for Albus, they would surely return, exactly like Gwen wanted, and more of his friends would die. He couldn't let that happen.

'We need to leave,' Bruno said. 'Amber and Jasper are missing. We need to find them. But she won't listen to me.'

Albus caught his meaning, loud and clear. He got to his feet, holding back a groan of pain; he'd put his body through a lot these last few days. They all had.

'I'll watch you in,' Bruno said, and picked up the axe. It had indented the grass beside him, a tool they'd used solely to chop wood a week ago but was now carried as a weapon.

Albus limped his way inside, feeling more like a geriatric than a man of twenty-three. He knew he would find them sitting on the wide central staircase leading up to the first floor because he could see golden, honeyed ribbons drift out to greet him as he entered the brightly lit back reception. As for Addison, the newest member of their group, he could sense her like he'd sensed his twin; as a second sun, a warmth that bloomed on his face. Whether he stood in the shade with his eyes closed or in the dead of night, Addison was there, reaching out to him, because Addison carried his sister's St Christopher necklace and, with it, she carried Ruby.

As he came into the front foyer, there they sat, exactly where he expected them to be, perched on the bottom step and talking earnestly to each other. Hari glanced up as he walked by and his dark eyes were, as always, unreadable and doe-soft. Far too serious for a boy his age. Addison seemed equally as sombre.

Not stopping, he nodded to them (Addison offered a small smile in return and Hari inclined his head), then Albus continued through to the parlour.

At the front picture window Gwen sat in the gathering gloom. She held a rifle across her knees and a sidearm holstered at her hip. She didn't look up at his approach but kept her eyes trained on the front lawns and the driveway.

He pushed a chair up beside her, having some trouble when it caught on the lip of an antique brocaded rug, eventually setting it where he wanted and sitting down.

'Bruno sent you.' It wasn't a question and she didn't bother to look at him.

Albus made a soft affirmative noise.

'He wants us to leave and forget about what's been done to our friends.'

That wasn't true at all. Bruno had more reason to want vengeance than any of them.

'I can't do that, Albus. I can't sit by while all the people we love are taken away from us. I can't. I *won't.*'

Albus slipped his notebook from his pocket, opened it and wrote two words. It took some time – he couldn't scribe as fast as he used to.

Gwen took the notebook from him and read. She closed her eyes. 'I know. I know Amber and Jasper are out there. I don't know what you want me to do about that.'

He tapped the page of his notebook where he'd written their names, and then tapped his chest.

Gwen looked at him, and her gaze was so penetrating he wanted to look away. He didn't, of course. He met her eyes and tapped his chest again.

'You can find them.'

He nodded. *Yes, maybe,* he wanted to say. *But only if we leave here, and leave soon. Before they get too far.* He pointed out the window. Out there. That was where they had to go.

He pulled the notebook out of her hands and wrote five more words.

this isn't home any more.

Footsteps clomped quietly across the parlour and they turned to find Hari and Addison standing behind them.

'I think I know where Amber will go.' The inflections of Hari's accent, rising and falling with each word, were like loops of honey stringing from a ladle to Albus. He had always enjoyed listening to him.

Albus shared a look with Gwen, then nodded for the boy to go on.

'You are not going to like it.'

'Talk,' Gwen said.

'The birds. I think she would follow them.'

'What?' Gwen's voice was a blunt cudgel of white that made Albus blink.

Hari made a come-hither gesture, beckoning them to follow

as he turned and made his way out to the front porch, having to unbolt the large main door to do it. They lined up at the white railing and he pointed.

The sky was indigo blue and cloudless, the full moon strong and bright. In the distance, a hazy mist made up of many dark particles dipped and swooped, and it took Albus a moment to identify them as birds. They banked in formation, winging north, and then abruptly veered east, the edges breaking into wisps as trailing birds were delayed in their change of direction. It formed a solid mass again as they flowed south.

'When she became scared,' Hari said, gazing at the distant horizon, 'I would tell her stories about how rats, blind and lost, would find their way out of the dark by feeling for fresh air. I would tell her how birds could fly home by sensing the magnetic pull of the earth in their blood. Wild animals have much better instincts than you or me.'

'What're you getting at, Hari?' Gwen asked, impatient for him to get to the point.

'Whenever I am uncertain, I look to nature, to its animals. There is meaning in their behaviour, in the patterns they hold to. I told her she should become an animal, too.'

His arm shifted right and he pointed further north. There, a second swarm of birds performed the same sweeping turns, the two groups, although a distance apart, moving in eerie synchronisation.

Gwen watched along with them now, her words absent-minded, the birds' display a hypnotic dance and she caught in its spell. 'Why would she head for them?'

'Because it is where I would go. An animal's instincts are to survive.'

'That out there isn't normal animal behaviour,' Gwen said.

'No. But they know something we do not.'

Albus had remained quiet while they talked, but now he couldn't help but hum a quiet sound of unease. The birds' murmurations weren't something that offered him comfort; theirs was a beautiful but sinister dance. It was an aberration.

And yet, he knew he and his friends couldn't wait for much longer. They had to leave, they had to find Amber and Jasper, and if that meant heading for these birds until Albus could pick up Amber and Jasper's trail, then that was better than staying.

'Something's happening,' Addison murmured, staring off into the distance. 'What's over there?' she asked, looking up at Albus from her place at the railing.

Albus shook his head. That way lay farmland: long stretches of green that had once yielded rows of tobacco, soybeans and peanuts; fields of fluff-ball-white for cotton-picking; the rolling golden-yellow of naturalised wheat and corn. There were other farms, too (more the cattle variety and one large-acre wind farm), and a sprawling-acre nature reserve, but little more than that.

'Bruno will get his way, then,' Gwen said, her head tilted to the darkening sky. 'We'll leave tomorrow. But if anyone turns up here to finish what they started . . .' She turned her eyes on Albus and they brimmed with a grimness that made him worry for her. 'If *one* stranger steps foot on this land between now and then, I'll blow their goddamn head off.'

Hari bobbed his head and a flash of something brightened his eyes for an instant. Maybe satisfaction that Gwen was so keen to exact revenge on those who had so brutally torn their family apart, or maybe it was relief that they were leaving this place before something else terrible befell them; it was there and gone too quickly for Albus to tell.

Hari stepped out of the conversation, eyes lowered as he walked past Albus to head back inside.

Albus felt a touch on the back of his hand. Cool fingers stroked him. He looked down at Addison and she smiled up at him. A reassuring smile from an eight-year-old, and what did that say about the grimness in *his* eyes? He didn't shift his hand away from her like he would for most others. When they had first met, Addison hadn't gazed upon his disfigured hands in disgust or pity. There were no expectations with her, no measures to meet. She looked at you and accepted what she saw. And that was a humbling thing.

Albus smiled back at her, even though a moment ago smiling had been the furthest thing from his thoughts.

'It'll be okay,' she whispered.

Her touch disappeared and she trailed after Hari (who had waited for her by the doorway).

'Come,' the boy murmured, reaching to take her hand, and as they moved to enter, the wind chimes hanging beside the door pushed into a gentle sway.

The tubes set to tinkling and it was a peaceful, delicate sound, but Albus frowned as a swift chill shivered through his bones, raising gooseflesh on his arms and neck, as if – as the saying goes – someone had walked across his grave.

Acknowledgements

Let's see how brief I can keep these this time around (because Book 4's are going to be bloody massive). Thank you to Camilla Bolton for always being there when I need her and for just being an all-round excellent literary agent and top, top person who always knows how to make me laugh. Big gratitude to the team at Darley Anderson Literary Agency for their unfailing dedication and ongoing efforts to bring Pilgrim and Lacey to a wider audience. As ever, thanks to the hardworking Headline lot – Mari Evans, Frankie Edwards, Caitlin Raynor and Jo Liddiard – for being such enthusiastic and passionate advocates for these books. And a special mention to Sara Adams for her superlative editorial skills.

I'm thankful to Richard Plowman of the Wates Group for giving me an extensive guided tour around Dudley Guest Hospital (which also – for any movie fans out there – makes an appearance in the film *The Girl With All the Gifts*). At the time of visiting, the building had stood derelict for seven years, which was perfect for *Survivor*'s timeline. It quickly became the blueprint for many of my descriptions of the fictional St Louis Hospital.

Lastly, I'm also hugely fortunate to have a wonderful core of people supporting me: Cath Hancox, Gilly McAllister, Tom Bissell, Andrew and Sonya Todd, my mom, Veronica, and both the Watkins and Foster clans. Thank you for being my family.

Resources Page

This book is a work of fiction, but suicidal thoughts and auditory hallucinations are very, very real. I spent a lot of time researching and reading in these areas, so if you'd like more information, or need help and support for yourself or a loved one, please take a look at the following websites.

Mentalhealth.org.uk
Papyrus.org.uk
Rethink.org
Mind.org.uk
Samaritans.org (their helpline is free and available 24/7 on 116 123)